WELCOME TO
OSAN AIR FORCE BASE

Within the mammoth U.S. base, racial tensions were at the boiling point, with the base commander determined to look the other way, and the military police going out of their way not to do their job.

Outside the base, a village devoted to providing airmen with all the sex and drink they could pay for seethed with every kind of vice and crime.

It was here that Mike Hunter's best friend, Paul Crandell, had fallen drunk into a ditch and drowned. Except that Paul Crandell never drank.

And it was here that Mike Hunter vowed to find the truth—in a one-man war against all that was rotten in Osan and all the odds against him. . . .

THOMAS C. UTTS is a twenty-year veteran of the U.S. Air Force and retired as a captain in 1981. Also a Marine for two years, Utts has traveled to such countries as Thailand, Germany, and Korea. He currently is on the staff of San Diego State University. *Korea Blue* is his first novel.

KOREA BLUE

Thomas C. Utts

A SIGNET BOOK

SIGNET
Published by the Penguin Group
Penguin Books USA Inc., 375 Hudson Street,
New York, New York 10014, U.S.A.
Penguin Books Ltd, 27 Wrights Lane,
London W8 5TZ, England
Penguin Books Australia Ltd, Ringwood,
Victoria, Australia
Penguin Books Canada Ltd, 2801 John Street,
Markham, Ontario, Canada L3R 1B4
Penguin Books (N.Z.) Ltd, 182-190 Wairau Road,
Auckland 10, New Zealand

Penguin Books Ltd, Registered Offices:
Harmondsworth, Middlesex, England

First published by Signet, an imprint of New American Library,
a division of Penguin Books USA Inc.

First Printing, June, 1991
10 9 8 7 6 5 4 3 2 1

PUBLISHER'S NOTE
This is a work of fiction. Names, characters, places, and incidents either are
the product of the author's imagination or are used fictitiously, and any resemblance to actual persons, living or dead, events, or locales is entirely coinci-
dental.

For William Warner Utts—brother Bill. Unlike his older brother, Bill wanted nothing to do with the military or exotic adventure in foreign lands. However, as a result of bad timing and bad luck, he was inexorably sucked into the war in Vietnam. There, while serving as a combat infantryman with the Americal Division in the Central Highlands in the Republic of South Vietnam, he died as a result of enemy action on March 19, 1969.

Chapter 1

October 1969

The aircraft lurched, rocked by a violent explosion. The control stick ripped from his hands as he tossed about in the cockpit. The big F-105 fighter bomber began a sickening roll, out of control. Red emergency lights lit up the warning panels. Intense pain shot through his body. No longer a flying machine, the sleek two-seat jet was now a flaming coffin. Cold air roared through the smashed canopy. The stench of burning rubber and plastic stung his nose, and he felt heat through his boots as fire hungrily consumed the aircraft's innards.

Punch out!

The thought screamed in his mind as he struggled to reach the ejection handle. But the message from his brain could not get through his damaged body to his hands. He had to get out—but he could not do it himself.

Paul.

Captain Paul Crandell was his "bear," the weapons-systems officer who flew in the rear of the aircraft. If Paul wasn't hurt, he could eject them both with the dual controls.

Come on, Paul . . . But wait, Paul couldn't save him. Paul was dead. Not from the devastating anti-aircraft fire over the Ho Chi Minh Trail, but from drowning in Korea, thousands of miles from the war.

Captain Mike Hunter's body jerked involuntarily. His eyes snapped open, wide with anxiety. The battered cockpit, the flames, the dreadful sense of imminent death slipped away. He was stretched out on a hard hospital bed in a sterile room. Clammy, panicky sweat had soaked through his T-shirt and pajama bottoms into the twisted sheets.

He sat up, took a deep breath, and tried to shake the dazed feeling. It was the nightmare again, he realized as he stretched to work the kinks out of his lean, six-foot-one-inch body. He was in his room at Big Willie, the Air Force nickname for Wilfred Hall Medical Center at Lackland Air Force Base in San Antonio, Texas—a long way from either Vietnam or Korea.

He was waiting for the paperwork which would make his release from the place official. After a last workout earlier he realized he was getting one of his headaches, the ones that did their best to imitate both a vice and a jackhammer. He had returned to his room, popped a couple of super pain pills the doctors prescribed, and laid down. The pills worked, but they also made him groggy. Once asleep he dived into his favorite private nightmare. Luckily, it hadn't gone as far this time. The last time the North Vietnamese had marched him halfway to Hanoi before he woke.

Thinking back on this latest version, he remembered calling out for Paul Crandell, then realizing his friend was dead. That was a new twist.

He sat up, swung his feet around, and slid off the bed. He felt right—a lot more right than when he'd checked into this place. The body, and the lightning reflexes that went with it, were not something he could take credit for; they had been a gift that came with the genes. He did ten quick bends, touching the floor between his feet with his knuckles rather than fingertips to toes, just to prove he could go that extra couple of inches, and straightened up.

Dark brown hair in a short military brush cut capped the most striking feature of his face: intense blue-green eyes that could always arrest the attention of others. His nose was a bit too large, but then it complemented the wide mouth. The only real imperfection in the face were the scars on the left side of his head near his hairline. But they were fading, helped by his Texas tan. All in all, it was a face with features a bit too bold to be considered handsome in a conventional sense, but a face that looked good—considering what it had been through.

Kathy Wright entered the room. Even with her long blond hair pinned up to conform with military regulations and the starched hospital whites doing their best to conceal the outrageous figure underneath, there was no way to disguise the dazzling effect she worked on the average male libido.

Kathy, a first lieutenant and a physical therapist for the hospital, stood for a moment looking at Hunter, objectively evaluating the results of the hospital's work. When he had arrived he was a mess. Shrapnel from a Soviet-built SAM had ripped him from waist to head on his left side. Hospital surgeons were able to patch everything back together. After their work healed, Lieutenant Wright's had begun. Their long hours together had started as a professional relationship, but soon turned personal.

Keeping her voice flat, she said, "Administration called, your release papers are on the way." Despite her attempt, she couldn't hide the angry frustration she felt. Knowing it, she added, "So you can take off on Mission Inane."

Her resentment had been building since Hunter told her that he had orders for Osan Air Base in the Republic of Korea. She immediately knew he had engineered the assignment, and she had not taken it well.

"Thanks," he said. He tried a smile. "Are we on for . . ."

"Of course." She made it sound as if he was doubting that the sun came up in the morning. "It's the least I can do . . . or is it the most?"

"Kathy, please don't . . ." She shook off the words, turned, and left the room.

After she was gone Hunter experienced the emptiness left by her departure. He wondered if she was right. He had questions too. But the time for questions was past. He stood up and walked across the room, glancing out the window at the flat Texas landscape. The view made no impression; he had been looking at it for nearly six months while recovering from the damage suffered when he was shot down.

He stripped off his clothes and entered the shower. Draping his washcloth over the shower head to contain the water, he adjusted it to a temperature that suited him. The refreshing water improved his mood. He felt good, ready to hit the road.

He knew he owed Kathy. Once his wounds had healed, rehabilitation under her close supervision had begun. Easy at first, then increasing in intensity as he regained his strength. His progress surprised everybody. But he was not content. On his own he sought out the base martial arts instructor and added a private program to polish his skills in tae kwon do, the Korean form of karate he had first undertaken while stationed in that country.

Medical science and hard work triumphed. Just a few days over six months from the day he was shot down, Hunter was ready to return to active duty. Not flying, of course, there was a complication. The surgeons were not able to get all the metal splinters from the SAM. Those left were not suppose to bother him— much. The doctors thought the occasional blinding headaches, loss of balance, and off-again, on-again difficulties focusing his eyes were most likely temporary—like the bad dreams.

He would be behind a desk—the Air Force could always find room for another paper shuffler. So back to duty, "and whenever you get a headache, take two pills and lie down." When, and if, his lingering problems cleared up, he could see about getting back to the cockpit.

Wonderful, wonderful.

Finishing the shower, he dried off, returned to his room, and dressed in a pair of civilian slacks that had been tailored in Thailand and a shirt bought at a Taiwan shirt factory. He was thinking how his world had been irrevocably changed by a debt to a friend he owed his life—and by those pictures.

It had begun with a telephone call two months before. A major who had been in his squadron in Thailand was passing through and called to say hello. After the "hi, how're you doing?" remarks, he said, "Suppose you heard about Paul Crandell?"

"No. I wrote to him. I expected him to answer, but—"

"He won't be answering, he's dead."

"What?" His first thought was that it couldn't be right, Paul survived the ejection without a scratch. Crandell had been his bear, the guy in the backseat who operated the special weapon systems in their F-105 Wild Weasel when the SAM tagged them. The missile had exploded slightly forward of the front cockpit. The aircraft was totaled. So was Hunter—nearly.

Paul had been the lucky one. He wasn't hurt and was able to trigger the ejection system and get them both out. On the ground he directed the rescue operation to their position in the dense rain forest. Hunter knew that if it hadn't been for Paul he would have been a prisoner in the Hanoi Hilton or, more likely, dead.

"Was he shot down?" Hunter asked.

"That's the sad part. It wasn't the fuckin' war. It was an accident. In Korea."

"Korea?"

"Yeah, at Osan."

"What was he doing at Osan?"

"You remember he was going to marry a Korean gal?"

"Yes." Hunter remembered all too well.

"Well, after you were evacuated, Crandell started acting strange. Later, I heard the letters he was getting from that sweet honey had him all screwed up. Anyway, his flying was really off, then he asked for leave."

"Leave?" Hunter was surprised. Combat crew members didn't normally get leave in the middle of a war.

"His flying was so bad the boss figured a quick trip to Korea might do him some good. Then, a few days after he left, we got official notification from Osan saying that he'd died in an accident."

"Accident? What kind of accident?"

"We didn't get many details, just that he drowned."

"Drowned? How can anyone drown at Osan?"

"Christ, Mike, I don't know. That's what they said."

Paul's death hit Hunter hard. He had been more than just another buddy. Though they were totally different, they had become close friends.

The depression he felt over the news of his friend's death became more acute a week later, after a long delayed letter from Paul arrived. It had been sent to the hospital at Clark Air Base in the Philippines, where Hunter had spent several weeks after being evacuated and patched together so he was well enough to travel back to the world. Then it had gone back to his old squadron. After a couple of other stops it finally reached him, months after being mailed.

Hunter ripped open the envelope and read the words written by his dead friend. After he got past Paul's concern for his recovery, he came to the lines that said, "I'm in Korea. After you left, Soon Ja's letters started sounding funny and getting further apart. I talked the boss into letting me take leave to come here and see what is happening. I'm still not sure what is going on, but things are really in a mess. Somehow Soon Ja has become involved with some people who are real trouble. I saw her today when I arrived, but she was very frightened and won't tell me much. She did say enough so that I am considering going to see the base commander to make a complaint. Anyway, as soon as everything is settled I'll write again. Get well soon."

Hunter checked with the Air Force Personnel Center and learned the letter had been mailed the day before Paul Crandell died. The more Hunter considered the ominous tone of Paul's letter, the less he felt inclined to accept the idea that his death was an accident. He tried to get more information from the Air Force, but learned little beyond what he already knew. First he wrote to their former squadron commander in Thailand, Lieutenant Colonel Robert "Black Bart" Bartly, now on a fat-cat tour in Naples, Italy.

A return letter from Bartly arrived in a few days. He said that after Hunter was wounded Crandell was paired up with a new pilot, but in a very short time it became apparent that his mind was not on his flying. Bartly had called him in for a talk—Hunter remembered those talks, the boss's why're-you-fucking-up chats.

He said Crandell reluctantly told him about the problem with his fiancée and asked if he could take a short leave to go to Korea and see if he could straighten things out. Bart had said yes. Crandell left, and a few days later Bartly was notified of Crandell's death. "They didn't tell us much, just that he'd been found drowned," Bartly wrote. "They said it was an accident. I didn't like it much, but with running the squadron and fighting the war, there wasn't much I could do. I wrote to his parents, told them that he'd been a good officer and a good pilot. Told them that I was sorry. God, I hate writing those letters."

Hunter's second letter was to the base commander at Osan. In the first draft he explained about his letter from Crandell, mentioned that he was having problems with his fiancée. He added that Crandell was considering a visit to the base commander, and asked if the visit had taken place. Thinking it over, he decided not to let on what he already knew. He threw that one away and wrote a second version, a straightforward request for as much information as possible about his friend's death. He wanted to see if the Osan commander would mention whether Crandell had come to talk to him.

The answer had the look of a letter written by someone else for the commander's signature. It was long on officialese, with statements about how everything was done according to Air Force regulations, but short on any additional facts. There was no mention of a visit by Crandell.

Shortly after the letter, Hunter passed his last medical evaluation. The doctors decided that, pending a few more tests, he could be released from the hospital. Faced with finding a desk job, the idea of trying to get assigned to Korea occurred to him. It took a few lengthy telephone calls to a sympathetic assignment officer, but he finally wangled orders for the flight-safety job at Osan.

So, at age twenty-nine, Captain Michael C. Hunter was a seven-year veteran of the Air Force who had flown 169 combat missions in the air war over North Vietnam. For those missions he had a pile of medals including two silver stars, a Purple Heart, and a pair of clipped wings. In addition, he had a bottle full of pain pills and PCS (Permanent Change of Station) orders for Osan—headquarters for all U.S. Air Force activities in Korea, and one of his all-time favorite places.

Once more around the park, driver.

Chapter 2

Mike Hunter and the war in Vietnam came of age at the same time. Born and raised in the American heartland, Kansas City, he grew up during America's golden age of innocence—the eighteen-year period between victory in World War II and the assassination of John F. Kennedy. In 1958 he went straight from high school to a hometown university. He enjoyed the college atmosphere and soon discovered that he could come up with a respectable grade-point average by not skipping classes and by taking copious notes.

With the legend of America fostered by Hollywood and all those World War II films as a part of his youth, it seemed to be a natural choice that upon graduation in 1962, with the conflict in Vietnam looming larger, Hunter volunteered for military service. To stand up against his country's declared enemies was, at that time, looked upon as both honorable and patriotic. Especially since with his degree he could be an officer. In the early days of this new war few Americans questioned the rightness of defending mom, apple pie, and the American way against the monolithic communist conspiracy.

Hunter chose the Air Force. The three months of officer training was a blur of classes, marching, and not very intensive physical training. He emerged with gold bars and, due to his lightning reflexes, orders for flight training at Williams Air Force Base in Arizona.

Early on he decided if he was going to fly, he wanted to be a fighter pilot. This goal was shared by many of the young officers in the flight-training program. Knowing this, the Air Force required those who would end up flying fighters to graduate in the top ten percent. To make the cut Hunter applied himself as he had never done in his university days. And even then, if the standards had not been dropped some due to the anticipated need, he probably would not have been able to swim upstream through the river of bureaucratic bullshit that constituted a large part of the program.

By keeping a tight rein on his unorthodox sense of humor, he made the cut for a fighter assignment. And for his first pick of aircraft. For Hunter there was only one choice. He had observed that technology had taken much of the glamour out of flying. A modern military aircraft was a complex piece of machinery that was supervised rather than flown. No aircraft in the current inventory could be operated, maintained, and flown by one man. It took a legion of support and maintenance people to get any airplane from point A to point B. Teamwork was all-important. This was especially true with bomber and cargo aircraft. It was less true with fighters. Although they required numerous technicians, once they left the ground there was only one seat in the cockpit and one engine to get the pilot where he was going.

However, in the early sixties even this was changing. The Air Force's newest fighter, the F-4 Phantom, had two engines, and worse, two seats. Hunter's selection was the slightly older F-105. A behemoth of an aircraft, at the time it rolled off the Republic Aviation assembly line the F-105 was the biggest single-scat, single engine fighter bomber ever built: over sixty-four feet long with a thirty-four-foot wingspan, it could carry more than seven tons of bombs. Originally christened the Thunderchief, the F-105 over the years became known to its pilots as the Thud.

As the United States became more deeply involved in the conflict in Southeast Asia, a decision was made in 1965 to start bombing North Vietnam. Because of its rugged construction, high speed at low altitude, and those big bomb loads, the Thud was well suited for the daily pounding of ground targets in North Vietnam, conducted in what became the most heavily defended, most concentrated antiaircraft environment in the history of aerial warfare.

In early 1966, after two years of flying Thuds in a stateside unit, Hunter received PCS orders for the Pacific Air Force. With high anticipation he flew across the wide ocean to Kadena Air Base, on the island of Okinawa. One of the Japanese home islands, Okinawa had been the site of the last major Pacific battle in WWII, and had been a U.S. protectorate since the end of that war despite a growing clamor among its residents to return to Japanese rule. Nicknamed "The Gateway to the Pacific," the sprawling installation had originally been built and used by the Japanese in World War II. Stretching across the center of the island, the air base was one of the largest and busiest in the Pacific.

The base was home for the 18th Tactical Fighter Wing with its three squadrons of Thuds and one squadron of photoreconnaissance jets. The wing had a long record of service in the Pacific, including combat in World War II and Korea, and it was adding Vietnam to its battle streamers. Pilots and aircraft from the 18th, operating from forward bases in Thailand, were flying missions in the new air war against North Vietnam. These bases in Thailand were one of the many open secrets of the war. Temporary duty (TDY) in Thailand was the norm for 18th pilots and an assortment of operations and support people.

Hunter spent his first months training with men who had already flown in the first strikes in the war. He also discovered there was more to a Pacific assignment than just Vietnam. Training missions included flights to Taiwan, Japan, and Korea.

For Hunter it was the calm before the storm.

In his fifth month with the wing, Lieutenant Colonel Ishill, his squadron commander, called him in. "Mike, you've done real well since you joined us. You catch on quick and you're a good pilot. I think you're ready. What do you think?"

Hunter knew what he meant. "I'm ready."

"That's good, because Korat has asked for five more pilots, and I'm putting your name on the list."

"Thanks, boss, I—"

Ishill, a careful man who went to great lengths to look after the men assigned to him, interrupted. "Make it back in one piece. Then you can thank me."

"Ken chana." Hunter used the Korean phrase for "no sweat." It was one of the bits of that language he'd picked up during several TDYs to that country.

Ishill shook his head dolefully. "I never should have let you spend all that time in Korea."

Korat was a Royal Thai air force base which had been transformed into a major forward operating location for U.S. Air Force units. Located in the middle of a large plain in the center of the country, Korat was hot and dusty in the dry season and hot and muddy when it rained.

During the next year and a half Hunter bounced back and forth between Thailand and Okinawa until he had emerged a certified hero, having flown one hundred combat missions over North Vietnam during the course of which he dumped tons of bombs on targets which never seemed to quite get destroyed and, even more unusual for a Thud driver, shooting down one North Vietnamese MiG-17. The MiG earned him his first silver star.

He returned to Kadena Air Force Base just in time to take part in one of the more bizarre episodes of geopolitical politics and military madness. In the middle of one war the United States got blind-sided by an old adversary, the North Koreans. Their capture of the U.S.S. *Pueblo*, a Navy electronic reconnaissance ship on an intelligence mission off their coastline, caused a jarring note of discord into the reassuring rhetoric being fed to an already jittery American public.

The U.S.'s first reaction was to rush all the assets not directly involved in the war to South Korean bases—including Mike Hunter and all of the 18th aircraft and equipment which could be spared. This was followed in succeeding months by a large buildup of military forces to show the dogmatic brothers in the North that the United States was not going to be kicked around.

The buildup failed to impress the North Koreans, who never did give back the ship, but the dollars that poured in to support it supercharged the already steaming South Korean economy.

Hunter stayed at Osan for five months before being called back to Kadena to help train new pilots for the hot war in the south. During the last months of his tour at Kadena he was faced with the prospect of returning to the States to be a flight-training officer. That prospect seemed too anticlimactic after having lived on the outer edge for so long, so he volunteered for a second combat tour.

The Air Force, experiencing a pilot crunch, was more than happy to oblige him. In Wild Weasels, the two-seated trainer version of the F-105 with new electronics and armaments designed specifically to hunt and kill SAM missiles.

On the sixty-ninth mission of that second tour he lost the day to a North Vietnamese missile crew. And if it hadn't been for Paul Crandell, he knew he would also have lost his life, or worse, become a POW in the Hanoi Hilton.

Now, on his last night in Texas, Hunter looked across the table at Kathy. She seemed more beautiful than usual. A flickering candle gave off a soft glow that highlighted her perfect features. She looked up from a half-finished plate of pasta and caught him watching. She smiled at first, but her face turned despondent. Nervously she reached for her glass of wine—her third.

Their romance had blossomed during the long hours of physical therapy. Kathy's beauty and brains had earned her a bevy of admirers among the young officers at Lackland, who were not pilots and who resented the attention she gave the flyboy. But the two enjoyed each other's company and soon discovered they were good together in bed. At first he thought she might be the right woman for his life. He wanted her to be.

Then Crandell's letter arrived and Hunter's world changed. He hadn't meant for it to happen, hadn't wanted it, it just did. When he began his efforts to get an assignment to Korea he realized he wasn't in love with her. He felt guilty about that.

She had arranged to get off early today. When his release papers finally arrived, they left the hospital together and drove to her apartment. At first it went well enough: they spent two hours in bed. Later they came to the restaurant. It was a special place for them, for Kathy had brought him here the first time he was allowed to leave the hospital.

During dinner she brought up his leaving again. "This is such a pathetic situation. There is nothing you can do for Paul Crandell. He's dead."

It was a variation on the theme, but he recognized the melody. At first she had tried reason: "I just don't understand why you are going back there. You don't have to. You've done your part. Twice. You could get an assignment right here at Randolph." Randolph Air Force Base was a pilot-training base on the other side of San Antonio, a logical career choice for a combat veteran fighter pilot.

Later the argument changed: "Oh, Mike, why don't you quit lying to me . . . and to yourself. It's more than just that friend of yours. It's partly that macho fighter pilot code. But it's also an excuse for you to go back. You are one of those men who go crazy about Asia—what do they call it? Oh yes, yellow fever. That's it, isn't it?"

"Look, Paul saved my life." He hoped she did not notice he had not denied the accusation. "I owe him. He . . ."

By now it was an old argument. Although he didn't admit it to her, she wasn't the only one who had doubts about his plan. Still he felt compelled to press on. He knew that time was against him. The big summer rotation period was over. Many people who had been at Osan in early May, when Paul died, would likely be gone. Still, he felt he had to go. He owed Paul that much for saving his life. But he knew that no matter how well he explained his reasons, Kathy would not be satisfied.

When they returned to her apartment, her eyes were red with tears. As soon as they were inside, she rushed into the bedroom, slamming the door behind her. Hunter located his favorite FM station on the radio, one of the new, self-styled underground stations that played music to take drugs by. He set the volume low, then went to the kitchen, found her jug of burgundy, and poured a glass. Maybe Kathy was right. Maybe he was playing games, creating an excuse to go back, inventing a reason so he would not have to face up to the fact that he was a Far East freak.

What's to worry? You're not doing so bad with Kathy, his inner voice sneered, *just a few tears when she should be going for your balls.* It was the voice from deep inside his head, the underside of his mind, there to let him know that while he might be shucking the rest of the world, he was not fooling himself.

The voice reminded him that he had known all along that this evening was going to be a disaster. Experience had taught him that when two people have loved, but when one of them doesn't love anymore, the end is always difficult. There was a sense of loss for something that should have been, but never quite was.

His glass was almost empty when Kathy reappeared. She had changed into a short white robe. The tears were gone and she was calm, almost remote. Even if he had not smelled it, he would have understood. In her right hand he saw a half-smoked joint. When Hunter had left the country in '66, marijuana was something associated only with the exotic life-styles of musicians and hippies. Now it had become an integral part of the counterculture movement. And since San Antonio was a major distribution point for Mexican dope, grass was easily obtained around the military bases.

Kathy glided across the room and held it out to him. He took it and carefully sucked in a medium hit of the harsh smoke. He did it slowly to keep from coughing, no easy feat for a nonsmoker. He had developed a nodding acquaintance with the evil weed in Thailand, where some of the best in the world was grown. Kathy's dope tasted like Mexican commercial, not nearly as potent as its Southeast Asian cousin, but with enough hitting power to bang the drum slowly.

After exhaling, he looked at Kathy who was standing, half turned, several feet away. "How're you feeling?"

"Oh, are you still here?" she said with feigned surprise. He knew it was an act. She wasn't that stoned.

"Yes, still here."

"So, Michael is leaving in the morning. Going back to Asia. Too bad. So sad. But don't worry about Kathy. I still have my little friend here." She held up the joint, now just a roach. "And Scott will still be here. And Marc and Chris and all the others. They don't have your special devotion to friendship. They're not fighter pilots—not heroes like big, bad Mike Hunter. But they'll still be here so little Kathy won't be lonely."

She gave him a wide, forced smile as she began untying her robe.

"Kathy, please, I'm sorry. I didn't want—"

"Oh, skip the bullshit, Hunter." She opened the robe and let it fall from her shoulders. She wore nothing underneath. Her long, trim athletic body was lovely. "Now, come make love to me in that way that all you fighter pilots are so proud of." She turned and walked toward the bedroom in naked majesty. "Come on, hero."

Chapter 3

Hunter had intended to spend two weeks' leave visiting his family and friends in Kansas City, but after ten days he was climbing the walls. Making excuses, he left and flew commercial to San Francisco. From there he took a taxi to Travis Air Force Base. The northern California base, located about forty miles east in the rolling California hills, was the departure point for the majority of military people going to Pacific assignments.

The airman on duty at the crowded Military Airlift Command terminal wasn't happy to see him. ''You're early, Captain. Your flight isn't for four days.'' Gentle persuasion and a twenty-four-hour wait produced a duty-space-available seat on a civilian contract flight.

It was his second crossing with MAC. This one was a World Airlines 707, the usual stripped-down military charter flight: no movies, no booze, and old stews. The passenger load included all ranks and branches of the U.S. military plus Department of Defense civilians and a sprinkling of foreigners, mostly Vietnamese, Thais, and Cambodians. The rest of the passengers were military dependents, wives, and children traveling with or going over to join husbands and fathers in Japan, Okinawa, or the Philippines.

He was seated in a row with a large woman and her four squirming, noisy, unhappy children. Only two of them got sick—the two next to him.

The flight took off at nine that evening and went to Anchorage, Alaska. It arrived just after midnight for a scheduled one-hour refueling stop which, due to a maintenance problem, stretched into more than three hours. When that was finally fixed, the bird got off for the nine-hour flight to Japan.

To pass the time Hunter tried to read, but troubling questions kept intruding. Was Kathy right? Was Paul just an excuse to go back? That was possible, assuming he needed an excuse. Still there was Paul's letter. ''. . . Things are really in a mess. Somehow Soon Ja has become involved with some people who are real trouble.'' Paul Crandell had been a deliberate man, not given to exaggeration. When he looked into the mess his fiancée had gotten herself into with some people who were ''real trouble,'' he turned up dead. That was not an excuse, that was a reality.

Those thoughts led him even deeper into himself. Why was he leaving? Why had his relationship with a bright, attractive woman like Kathy ended like all the others? In the beginning he had wanted her so much. After surgery, laying there, hardly able to get up and go to the bathroom by himself, the beast inside roared each time she came into his room with her cheery smile and those high, Playboy-perfect breasts. Somehow her closeness made the long, intense hours of pain and struggle more bearable. When his attention got past her breasts, he found she had many qualities he thought he was attracted to. Still, when the heady lust of romance and the courtship ritual ended, there was not enough to take its place.

What did he want in a woman? What did it take to hold his interest? To make him love? He liked women, but he realized since college he'd drifted through several relationships without finding whatever it was he thought he was looking for. And, unlike in past years, that was worrying him.

Maybe you're just a romance junkie, his voice offered, *which is another way of saying you're an immature ass.*

Was that it? And if so, why was it bothering him now? And how much of that was caused by Crandell's photographs?

After flying eight and a half hours and crossing the international date line, the airliner arrived in the skies over central Japan just after noon on the same day they had left California. Hunter watched out the window as the 707 dipped its right wing and went into a turn. Below, barely discernible through the morning mist, was Yokota Air Base.

Hunter and the passengers destined for tours in that country and Korea left the flight there. The majority were to continue south, since Vietnam was still number one. Looking at the young and old warriors staying on the flight he wondered how much longer the war would continue. And how would it end? He quickly put those thoughts out of his mind. The question did not seem to have the same clear answer it once had.

"Captain, you ain't supposed to be here yet." The airman at the Yokota passenger section was even less thrilled at his early arrival than the one at Travis.

"I don't like to make waves," Hunter said pleasantly, "but I think there's a reality that has to be faced: I'm here."

The young man thought about that for a moment, then pulled out a clipboard. "This is the duty space-A list for tomorrow's Korea bird. I'll sign you up. I can't promise." He shrugged noncommitally—that gesture common to bureaucrats large and small around the world. "Show time is oh-five-hundred."

Hunter thanked the airman and went to collect his bags. The terminal was swarming with military people and families waiting for flights. The lucky ones had orders. Others on leave were playing the space-A lottery, hoping for free transportation back and forth between the States and their duty locations. One of those "bennies" of military service everyone talked about but which seldom come easy. He decided there was no way he was going to spend the rest of the day and the night in this zoo. He checked his large bag in a locker, and with his carry-along he went outside.

It was a typical Yokota day: smoggy gray overcast and a light drizzle. He stood for a moment looking across the parking lot and beyond the fence at the real Japan. On this side it was calm, a few vehicles moving back and forth on the base streets; on just the other side of the wire it was quite different. A main Japanese roadway was packed with four narrow lanes of bumper-to-bumper traffic. Each year as Japan increased its industrial productivity and economic power, this "island USA," which had once dominated the area, seemed to shrink.

A base taxi swung up and discharged a young sailor, his Filipina wife, their three children, all under five, and a mountain of bags. Hunter got in and asked the driver to take him to the billeting office.

The long flight and the squirming, discontented children sitting next to him had made sleep nearly impossible, and triggered one of those headaches. He longed for a quiet room and some rest. But the billeting clerk, a slender, stone-faced Japanese civilian employee, wasn't happy to see him either.

"Oh, very sorry, sir. Too many people stay now, no rooms."

Hunter had played this game before over the years, with this same clerk, who never seemed to recognize him. He supposed all GIs looked alike to the man. "There are no vacancies? Every bed is full?"

"Ohhh, no have empty room. If you share with another officer, then I think I have."

"I'm not shy."

The clerk didn't smile. He never did. "How long you stay?"

"I'll be leaving for Korea in the morning."

"Oh, you go Korea? Okay. I put you with another officer who go Korea too."

"Die jo bee." Hunter's Japanese for "That's just dandy" earned a grudging nod from the man.

Hunter carried his suitcases across the street to an older two-story BOQ. Naturally his room was on the second floor at the far end. Unlocking the door, he found himself looking at a younger, somewhat overweight individual wearing only a pair of extra-large white boxer shorts. Thick, dark hair covered almost every visible part of the man's body except the top of his head, which was mostly skin. Two suitcases and numerous boxes and packages were spread over all the available surfaces in the cramped room.

The man turned, looked at Hunter standing in the doorway with his bag, and frowned. "Oh shit, I suppose I have a roommate."

Hunter wasn't sure whether to apologize for the inconvenience or throw his bag at the guy.

"No sweat," the man added, now grinning and extending his hand. "My name's Ron Shaw. Anyway, I'm leaving in the morning."

"Korea, right?" Hunter asked, shaking hands.

Shaw looked bewildered. "I didn't know it showed."

"The billeting clerk told me," Hunter explained. "I'm going the same way. Osan, PCS."

"No shit," Shaw said as he pulled on a whale-sized T-shirt. "You married?"

"No. Why?"

"It's better that way. You can enjoy it with a clear conscience."

"I've been there before," Hunter said.

"Then you know: it's the best-kept secret in the Air Force."

Hunter laughed. "It used to be, before the *Pueblo*. Now I'm not so sure."

"You were there before the *Pueblo?*" A reverent tone came into Shaw's voice.

"Yeah, pulled my first TDY there from Kadena three years ago." He saw a gleam light up Shaw's eyes while at the same time his mouth took on a smirk. Hunter knew the look—the male ego in a sexual feeding frenzy. Guilty pleasures. He smiled, it was a clear case of yellow fever.

He saw Shaw's khaki shirt draped over a chair, with first lieutenant's bars on the collar but no wings. "What kind of work do you do?" Hunter asked.

"Run the vill mostly," Shaw said, grinning, then remembering himself. "Officially, I'm an information officer."

Air Force Information, sometimes called Public Affairs, was a combination of in-house journalism and public relations. A more correct name would have been "propaganda," but the Nazis had made that word socially unacceptable. The few civilian news media people Hunter knew usually referred to it as the "office of misinformation." However, Hunter figured Shaw was a good person to get to know. In order to keep the civilian media at arm's length, an IO had to be well informed about what was happening on his base.

Looking at the names of the stores on the pile of packages and boxes, he could tell that Shaw had been making the rounds of camera and stereo stores in the area. Because of the raging black market in Korea and the limited availability of products through the base exchange outlets there, Japan was a popular shopping trip for Korea-based GIs.

Shaw went over to a pile of clothes, selected a shirt and a pair of slacks, and began getting dressed. "I gotta go get some of this stuff wrapped and mailed. MAC gets kinda pissed when you show up with more than two bags."

Hunter helped Shaw carry some of the boxes down to a taxi and then returned to the room. He popped two pain pills, took a long shower, and lay down on the bed that was now empty. Shaw was a funny guy. Obviously crazy about Korea. It was like that with most new guys. When they heard they were going to Korea, their first reaction was "This is some kind of joke." But sooner in most cases, and later for a few, the place got to you. It was later for Crandell.

Chapter 4

That evening the two men went to the Yokota officers' club for dinner. They both had the prime rib special with wine for $3.95. During the meal, Hunter asked Shaw how things were going at Osan.

"You know how it is. Take five thousand men, separate them from their families, automobiles, monthly bills—everything that gives the average guy stability—then you put them on a small, confined base where the main forms of recreation are drinking and fucking, and well, there's gonna be some problems."

"Yeah, I know," Hunter said, laughing, "but what I meant was, other than the usual run-of-the-mill stuff."

"To tell you the truth, lately it sucks."

"How so?"

"When I first arrived seven months ago, it was a nice down-and-dirty, anything-goes place. But lately, damn, it's turned to shit. There's a racial confrontation brewing. Lots of drugs. All the crap that's been happening in Vietnam is spilling over into Korea." Shaw took a large swallow of his bourbon and seven. "Then there's the brass we got. Talk about having your head up your ass—how some of those limp-dick yo-yos made it to positions of authority is beyond me."

Thinking of Paul's letter, Hunter asked, "What about your base commander?"

"That sonofabitch, he's a golfer and the number one ass-kisser for the commanding general. And the general, he's more worthless than a wet fart. He never talks to anyone but colonels, and he's such a chickenshit motherfucker the colonels are afraid to tell him anything he doesn't want to hear.''

"If things are that bad," Hunter said thoughtfully, "then it'd be easy for something to slip through the crack.''

"Crack. Shit, we got holes so big the slicky-boys are driving five-ton trucks through them.''

Hunter grinned, he hadn't heard the expression "slicky-boy," GI slang for a thief, since he'd left Korea. Koreans had a penchant for adding an e-sound to many English words, so steak became steakee, and make was often pronounced makee.

After dinner they went to the bar. Shaw went through a couple of more bourbon and sevens, then asked, "You wanna go out and run 'em a little?''

"You mean women?''

"Sure.''

"Here?" Hunter knew the GI occupation of Japan was long since past. "Surely, you can't mean the Fusa strip?''

Fusa was the Japanese city next to Yokota. The strip was a section of bars and clubs that had once been the GI village. That had changed in the mid-sixties. Most of the bars now had changed their names from English to Japanese, and few Yokota GIs went there anymore. There were still young, beautiful hostesses, but it was all a facade. Now most customers were Japanese businessmen, and GIs new to Japan quickly discovered they had been priced out of the market.

"Fusa's not so bad," Shaw said defensively.

"Sorry, Ron, but I don't think I'm up to Fusa.''

Shaw spent one more drink trying to talk Hunter into accompanying him, then finally gave up. As they got up to leave, Shaw said, "I know I shouldn't, but I just can't go to bed alone when there's a vill out there. Not without at least trying.''

Hunter smiled: the enthusiasm of youth. As he walked from the Yokota Club back to the BOQ, Hunter was somewhat surprised at himself for turning down Shaw's invitation. It wasn't just Fusa; in times past he would have led the charge to town for a few brews and a round of touch and giggle with the bar toots. And it wasn't the headache either. The more he thought about it, the more he realized that he knew what it wasn't, he just didn't know what it was.

Back in his room, he took two more pills and got into bed with his book. After a while he drifted off to sleep and was off dreaming again. The dreams had started in the hospital, sometime after he realized he was going to make a full recovery. Before being shot down, his dreams were fairly ordinary half-remembered bits and fragments. In the hospital he started having vivid nightmares about flying combat.

One dream was about shooting down the North Vietnamese MiG. In life it had been one of the high points of his career. The dream was different. It started out like the real thing, during his first combat tour when he was flying a single-seat Thud. He was coming off a bombing run on the Doumer Bridge when the MiG flashed past. Hunter kicked in the afterburner and roared off after it. The difference was that in the dream when he pressed the trigger switch, nothing happened. He was overwhelmed with a sense of terrible frustration. Followed immediately by a dreadful realization— if he didn't get the MiG, it would get him. The dream went on and on like that, screaming endlessly around the skies over Hanoi. The MiG was oblivious to his presence while he kept pressing the trigger switch on a gun that would not fire. Finally he'd wake up, shaken and anxious.

His main dream, however, was about being shot down. It started like the real thing, with the SAM exploding. He was always in pain and helpless as his big aircraft tumbled from the sky toward a frightening fate. Sometimes he crashed in flames, which always awakened him. Sometimes he ejected, to float endlessly in pain, seeing Charlie waiting on the ground. Other times he would drop to the ground, wounded and in pain, and terrified as the enemy closed in. Sometimes they came to kill. On other occasions he would be captured and marched through an endless jungle toward the living hell of prison. Most often he was alone.

But the dream this night was different. It started in the cockpit. He was on a combat mission, but he was alone, trying to catch up with the other U.S. fighters ahead of him and not able to remember where he was supposed to be going. Then, without realizing how it happened, he was walking in the street of a large Asian city, unsure what city or even what country it was. At one point there were temples, like Korat City or Bangkok. Other times it seemed more like Korea, yet why he felt this he wasn't sure.

He was on a main street with shops and buildings crowded close together, walking in a crowd of dark-haired Asians. Something about the people was unfriendly, ominous. In front of him in the crowd he caught sight of someone he thought he knew. He wasn't sure why the person was known to him, but he started following the familiar figure, trying to get closer, trying to identify the person. Despite his best efforts, he just could not catch up. At the same time he never entirely lost sight of the person. As he tried to get closer, he kept trying to figure out who it was. It seemed to go on for hours. Then a door opened. Light flooded in from the other side. The door closed.

He woke, sweating and nervous. It took several moments before he remembered that he was in a BOQ room in Japan. The door had been opened by the lieutenant with whom he was sharing the room; he had come back from chasing girls. Hunter lay there thinking about the dream. He had the impression this was not the first time he had dreamed this dream, just the first time he remembered it when he was awake. Who was he chasing? And why?

He recalled a conversation about dreams he had had with a shrink at Big Willie. The doc asked how Hunter interpreted his dreams. He explained that he didn't believe dreams were an omen from some higher power, or something to be interpreted as a sign of good or bad luck. He more or less subscribed to the theory that it was the mind's way of cleansing itself, a catharsis. He said, "I figure it's the brain's way of sweeping out the dusty corners to get ready for a new day of rational thought."

The shrink seemed to feel that was probably as good a frame of reference as any. "We know nightmares are common for people who've recently experienced combat," the shrink said, adding that with time the dreams usually became less frequent, less frightening.

Wonderful, wonderful.

A few minutes before five, Hunter and Shaw walked into the Yokota passenger terminal. Outside it was damp and cool, wisps of fog giving the dark streets an unreal, ghostly quality. Inside, the terminal was in a turmoil. The daily flight that shuttled around U.S. air bases in Korea was due to leave shortly. In addition, there was a C-141 military cargo plane due in from the Philippines. It would be taking on cargo and some passengers before heading to Norton Air Base in San Bernardino, California.

More than a hundred people were milling about. Some had been there all night, others were just straggling in. Active-duty airmen, soldiers, marines, and sailors, as well as family groups, all loaded down with suitcases, bags, and boxes. Then there were the terminal rats, military retirees, mostly former enlisted men living overseas on meager pensions. They seem to haunt MAC terminals, looking for flights to some place that would give meaning to their lives. Retirees were at the bottom of the list of those who had space-available privileges, and they often had to spend days, weeks sometimes, before they got a seat.

Hunter checked in. As a duty-space-A passenger he was assigned a seat immediately. When all the passengers with reservations and the duty-space-As were processed, all but five of the forty-two seats on the flight were filled. Then they started calling leave-status space-As, which included Ron Shaw. An Air Force sergeant got the first seat, followed by three Army types. As each name was called, Shaw became increasingly agitated. "I gotta get back today," he moaned. "I'm already a day late. My boss will hang my ass if I don't make it."

The next name was a DoD civilian employee. He was a no-show. Shaw moaned, "Come on, God, let me be next."

The clerk said, "Lieutenant Colonel Robert Erpelding."

"Please don't be here," Shaw whispered desperately. To no avail. The colonel stepped up to the counter. "Oh, fuck me to tears," Shaw moaned, slumping. However, the Army officer had his wife with him and needed two seats. There was only one, and he was passed over. Shaw's name was next.

"Here, here," he shouted, rushing frantically for the counter, just narrowly avoiding trampling two small children in his path.

Once they had boarding passes and checked their bags, they went to the terminal cafeteria. Since the alarm clock woke them, Shaw had been nursing a big head, a result of his night out. After getting cups of steaming coffee they found a place to sit. At the next table two terminal rats, men in their mid-fifties, were making ketchup soup—survival rations for retirees who were out of money—free ketchup mixed with sugar in hot water.

"What time did you get back last night?" Hunter asked Shaw.

"Oh, ah, three-ish."

"That late? You must have done well."

"I, ah, did okay," Shaw mumbled.

"Okay?"

"Yeah, not bad . . . for Fusa."

Hunter was beginning to enjoy himself. "Not bad, huh. Exactly how not bad?"

"Well, ah, I spent, ah, thirty-seven bucks on drinks, and, ah, I got kissed."

"Kissed, huh," Hunter said, nodding. "Open mouth?"

"Oh yeah."

Trying to keep a straight face, he said, "Hey, that's not bad. For Fusa." Then he started chortling.

Shaw looked indignant. "Wait 'til we get to Korea, you'll be laughing outta the other side of your ass, fella."

A few minutes later a voice announced the immediate boarding of their flight. A big grin lit up Shaw's face. "Next stop, Disneyland for dirty old men." He paused, grinning. "And the rides are so much more fun."

Chapter 5

MAC's Korea shuttle, a 727 civilian contract flight, hauled cargo and passengers on a round-robin flight beginning and ending at Yokota, with stops at the air bases at Taegu, Kwang Ju, Kunsan, and Osan. Although the flying time from Japan to Korea was just over an hour, with the stops it was after noon when the flight turned onto the final approach to land at Osan.

As the bird swooped down toward the base, Hunter looked out the window, remembering the many times he had been sitting in the cockpit of a Thud, rushing toward this same long expanse of concrete. He noticed a number of dump trucks, earth movers, and other pieces of construction equipment toiling in the dust at the end of the strip. The runway and taxi ramp were being enlarged. Osan just kept getting bigger and busier every year.

As the wheels of the 727 thumbed down, he felt a surge of elation. He'd really made it. Until now, deep in his mind, he had experienced a nagging doubt that somehow, something would prevent this moment. After landing, they waited nearly ten minutes for the aerial port representative to board and give them the greeting routine.

A young two-striper finally arrived. In a monotone he said, "Welcome to Osan Air Base in the Republic of Korea. The time is twelve-twenty. The temperature is seventy-one degrees. Please gather all your hand-carried luggage and proceed to the terminal for in-processing. No smoking until you're in the terminal. Thank you."

There was the usual fumbling and crowding as everyone jumped up at the same time to leave. Hunter and Shaw walked through the aircraft and down the back ramp behind two young Army troops. Obviously newcomers to Korea, they were wide-eyed with wonder. The sun was shining and Hunter was pleased to discover that it was sunny and warm, a perfect day. October was his favorite month in Korea. The country's climate was quite similar to that in the midwestern United States: hot, humid summers and cold, snowy winters. But great springs and autumns.

"Damn, it's good to be back," Shaw said, grinning. "Japan's a nice place to visit, but I wouldn't want to live there. Not at Fusa prices."

Hunter started to answer, but his attention was caught by a hauntingly familiar sound, one he hadn't heard in months: the deep-throated roar of J-75 jet engines, the engines in F-105s, being revved up to full military power prior to a take-off roll. He stepped out of the slow-moving line of people, paused, and looked in the direction of the end of the long Osan runway. From where he was standing he couldn't see that far. Still, from the sound he was sure there were two of them.

As they increased power, all other sounds on the flight line were diminished. Then came the familiar whomp as the pilots lit their afterburners. The roar seemed to double. Hunter could almost feel the huge fighter vibrating under him. He sensed the pilots popping their brakes, felt the birds surge forward, gathering speed as they rushed down the runway. Now the thunderous blast blotted out all other sounds.

Then he could see them. Two fat, cigar-shaped fuselages in their war-ugly camouflage paint jobs hurtling down the runway. They flashed past where he stood watching. With almost half the runway used up, they were still hugging the ground. The heavy Thud had a notoriously long take-off roll and needed a lot of speed to get into the air. He continued to watch. They were more than three quarters of the way down the concrete ribbon before they started to fly. The sound of the engines diminished some as they lifted off. Slowly at first, then faster, higher. In seconds they disappeared into the blue and white Korean sky.

Familiar flight-line sounds returned: vehicles moving back and forth, footsteps of the last of the passengers passing Hunter and Shaw going to the arrival area. Still looking at the sky, Hunter promised himself, "Soon. Soon you'll be back."

"I guess you miss it." He hadn't noticed Shaw waiting for him.

"Yeah," Hunter answered softly as they moved to catch up with the other passengers, "I miss it."

The arrival area in the Osan terminal was part of a large, new beige-colored metal building that had replaced the little, old, dilapidated wooden building Hunter remembered. Inside, arrivals were processed by several Air Force security policemen and one Korean government customs officer. In the old days they were lucky if anyone showed up to give them a ride in from the aircraft parking spot.

Noticing that each bag was being opened and thoroughly inspected by the SPs, Hunter figured there was a crackdown on black-market activity in progress. His bag, which contained only uniforms and some civilian clothes, passed through quickly. When they opened Shaw's two large suitcases, Hunter expected to hear bells, like those signaling a jackpot in a Las Vegas casino. In addition to a bunch of new camera equipment, one of his suitcases was full of women's cosmetics. Hunter remembered that cosmetics could not be purchased in Korean BXs by GIs without official dependents in-country—and that didn't include Korean girlfriends.

But the customs cops just dug around the boxes, jars, and tubes, then passed Shaw's bags through. Seeing Hunter's surprise, Shaw said, "These days they're more interested in dope than face cream."

Almost to himself Hunter said, "The times they are a-changing."

After clearing customs they went into the main terminal. Just as at Travis and Yokota, throngs of people were waiting for flights. It was somewhat overwhelming to realize that there were more people in this building right now than Hunter had seen on the entire base during his first TDY here three years earlier.

Shortly after his arrival at Kadena, Hunter's squadron commander had called him in. "Mike, you're going TDY next week."

"Thailand already?" He was excited, anticipating the call to combat.

"Naw, not Thailand. You're still too green. This trip's to Korea."

"Huh? Korea?" He wasn't sure he'd heard correctly. "Hey, boss, that was the last war. This one's in the other direction."

"No shit, Dick Tracy. Except that we got about fifty thousand Army grunts guarding the DMZ in Korea to make sure that one doesn't get started again. They've gotta train. We've been tasked to provide air support for an exercise. We're sending eight aircraft, crews, and support people. It'll last a couple of weeks."

"Well, at least I'll be getting some stick time and—"

"Not exactly. We also have to provide one pilot to work with the Osan Operations weenies. You're the only guy I can cut loose right now."

"Aw, come on, boss, I don't want to go to Korea, I want—"

"I know, I know. Look, Mike, you'll get to the war soon enough. This is only for two weeks, so take it while you have the chance. Besides, Korea is the best-kept secret in the Air Force."

That was the first time he had heard that line. Best-kept secret in the Air Force? What was he talking about? Whatever it was, it certainly was a secret to Hunter. He remembered old newsreels from that war. A harsh, rugged land of mountains, snow, mud, and ragged refugees. The ravages of war. That didn't sound like much of a secret. And worse, he was not going to fly, he'd be a ground pounder.

The support element flew to Osan on a C-47 Goony Bird, the military version of the ancient DC-3. Hunter felt as if he'd taken a step backward to a time only dimly remembered from old films. The group included an element commander, a major from wing headquarters, and fifteen operations and maintenance NCOs.

Once the aircraft was off the ground and lumbering slowly northward, he realized that something peculiar was going on. Instead of the exasperation he was feeling, the faces of the other men in the airplane reflected great expectation. They obviously knew the secret. He wanted to ask, but pride kept him from displaying ignorance in front of enlisted men.

After their arrival, when the eight Thuds were down and safely buttoned up for the night, he and the major headed for the BOQ. The older officer said, "Change clothes and I'll meet you at the O Club for a big orange."

That was the start of three hours of serious drinking during the course of which he heard a lot about the Korean War. The major had participated as a lieutenant flying an F-86 Saber jet.

After several hours of war stories, Hunter finally said, "Yeah, I've seen all that in the movies. But I also noticed that everyone in those films couldn't wait to get the hell out of Korea and beat it to Japan. So what makes this place the best-kept secret in the Air Force?"

"Ah, my son," said the major, his expression reeking of condescension, "partly because everyone's impression about Korea comes from those old movies. But things have changed." He pointed away from the direction of the flight line. "Over the hill and beyond the gate is Chicol Village. *That* is the best-kept secret in the Air Force."

Hunter already knew that outside most U.S. bases overseas there were towns or cities where the primary business was bars and girls. GIs had a stock expression for such places, the village—or more often just the vill. When he first arrived at Kadena he'd plunged into the dimly lit clubs of neighboring Koza City with great anticipation. To his dismay, he discovered that the Okinawans, long used to massive numbers of U.S.

troops, had refined the system to a fine art. It consisted of a very expensive kiss and a promise—which was seldom a contract one could depend on. On the occasions when thee promise was honored, there was often a decided lack of enthusiasm. He was left feeling considerably underwhelmed.

"So there's a vill, big deal."

Placing his hand on the younger man's shoulder, the major sighed and said, "My heart is filled with both envy and sympathy for you. Envy because you are so innocent, because you are about to experience Chicol Vill for the first time. And sympathy because you are so fucking dumb." He sighed loudly. "Damn, it's like being cherry all over again." ~~woly dued~~

They left the club, marshaled a base taxi, and headed for the gate. Hunter was still wondering if he was the butt of some twisted joke. It just could not be that special.

After that night he understood.

His knees weak, he just managed to get to work before ten. He told the major, "I'm sorry I doubted you, but who could know?"

"No shit, dummy."

It took a long time before he fully understood what made this county so unique. Part of it was economic. Everything was cheap. And there was no hustle. In the mid-sixties the Korean economy was just staggering to its feet. Many of the people were still pitifully poor, and they jumped at any opportunity to improve their lives. But it was more than just that. It was the Koreans themselves. They possessed an intensity and a spirit which were just beginning to be recognized as a hallmark of their national character.

"That's why they're called the Irish of the Orient," the major said.

Hunter realized later that the Koreans were in the process of transforming their battered nation into a major third world power. It was a phenomenon which would be felt around the globe, particularly in the United States. On his first TDY to Korea, the thing that stood out most was that in the entire fifteen days, the base BOQ maid never once had to make his bed.

When he returned to Kadena, his squadron commander asked, "So, how did you like Korea?"

Hunter hesitated a moment, then said it was okay.

"Just okay?"

"Well, you know, if you have to send somebody TDY to Osan again, I'd be willing to go. In fact, how about next week, or tomorrow, or . . ."

His commander walked away, smiling. In the months before Hunter went to Thailand, he managed to worm his way on two more TDYs to Korea.

Shaw dumped his bags near the entrance of the waiting area in the main room of the terminal. "Hang loose, Mike," he said, "I'll call the office and get someone to pick us up."

Chapter 6

The man who came to get them was a staff sergeant assigned to Shaw's office. He was a tall blond, about the same age as Hunter, with a friendly grin. When he saw the wings and medals on Hunter's chest, he couldn't disguise his surprised curiosity. As he helped load the bags in back, Hunter saw him taking several more long looks. Then, as he drove away from the terminal, he asked, "Excuse me, Captain. Are you Michael C. Hunter?"

Suspecting they might have served together at a previous base, he said, "Do we know each other, Sergeant?"

"No, sir. I mean, you don't know me, but I know who you are." Hunter didn't know what to say. "I read about you, sir. In *Airman* magazine."

Hunter nodded. A few months before, the official magazine of the Air Force had done a feature article on the combat role of the Thud. It included a side story recounting experiences of several F-105 pilots, including Hunter's.

"Sergeant Ziegler is a fighter pilot buff," Shaw said. "He's the office expert on the war. Always on my ass 'cause I don't usually hang around with the fighter jocks."

"Sir, I'd like to do a story on you for the base newspaper."

Feeling a little embarrassed, Hunter said, "Ah, well, let me think about it first, okay?"

"Don't worry, Zig." Shaw grinned. "I'll get him to do it." Hunter was saved by their timely arrival at the billeting office. As they pulled to a stop, he was happy to see that it was still in the same building. Shaw said, "Come on, I'll get you a good room. The OIC is a buddy of mine."

They went in and walked up to the desk. The desk clerk, a Korean, was filling out a form. Shaw started talking, "Is Lieutenant Williams here?" The Korean didn't look up. "Ah, I got a new officer here and I want to see he gets a room"—finally the Korean glanced up—"so I'd like to see Lieutenant Wil—"

The Korean jumped up, smiling, and came to the counter. "Captain Hunter, you come back."

The look on Shaw's face was a mixture of surprise and awe. "Hi, Mr. Lee, still stealing blankets?"

The Korean laughed, and as they shook hands he said, "You come alone this time, no have you friend, Captain Bo-gas!"

Hunter was surprised, for he hadn't realized they knew about that deception. After a few minutes of conversation, Hunter got the room he asked for, without help from the lieutenant, in the BOQ building with Shaw. As Lee handed him his key, he said, "No roommate, okay? Because you always need private room."

"Ah, yeah, thanks." As they left, Shaw was looking at him as if he was the inspector general. Embarrassed, Hunter said, "Well, I told you I was here before."

Shaw nodded. "Fuck me to tears, I guess!"

After completing his hundred missions in Thailand, Hunter had returned to Okinawa. He was assigned to training newly arriving pilots, using his experience and knowledge to prepare them so they too might survive the brutal crucible that lay ahead. In late 1967, the White House ordered a Christmas bombing halt of North Vietnam. Optimism ran high that the end was in sight.

It seemed to the Americans who had been there that Hanoi's leaders would seize the opportunity to stop the daily pounding to which they were being subjected. Hunter experienced a feeling of pride in a job well done, and his personal life had also taken a turn for the better. He was involved in a heated romance with a local Japanese-American nurse who worked at the base hospital.

Then, in late January of the new year, from the far left of left field, Uncle Sam got sucker-punched. By, of all people, the North Koreans. They attacked and seized the USS *Pueblo*. Their timing was perfect. U.S. attention was riveted on Southeast Asia in hopes of getting a cease-fire. The only American combat aircraft in South Korea were four Thuds from a Japan-based unit sitting on alert and armed with nuclear bombs set to atomize China if the big one began.

Other U.S. aircraft stationed in Japan were useless. Concessions to that government vetoed offensive missions. The next nearest usable aircraft belonged to the 18th. At the time Okinawa was still a U.S. protectorate, and Japan had no say about U.S. operations from there.

The whistle blew at noon and Kadena went on alert status. The surprise of the attack and the lack of verified information created mass confusion in the command communications channels stretching between bases in the western Pacific and Washington. On the East Coast it was the middle of the night, and no one wanted to wake the president.

Hunter and other pilots in the wing spent the afternoon and evening waiting in vain for the launch order while watching darkness close in.

The next day Hunter flew the fourth Thud to thunder into the dark Okinawa sky on that cool, early morning of January 24, 1968. That flight from Kadena touched down in the gray light of dawn on the cold, snow-patched Osan runway less than an hour later.

The Korean base had been a dormant housekeeping operation for years, stripped of all its flying assets for the war to the south. Suddenly it found itself at the center of a major crisis, and the situation quickly became chaotic.

Washington and PACAF had not bothered to consult the folks at Osan on the sudden dispatch of combat aircraft and crews with support people and equipment following close behind.

The base command post radioed frantically to the arriving flight of Thuds. "Why are they sending all you people here?"

"You're asking us?" replied the flight leader.

Confusion reigned for the next days and weeks as facilities at Osan were stretched to the limit and beyond. For a while it seemed as if there might really be a shooting war on two fronts. Soon it was clear, however, that the United States military buildup in Korea was only a show of force.

Hunter spent the rest of that winter and most of the spring at Osan. After the first flush of excitement the TDY turned into long, boring hours on alert waiting for battle orders everyone knew were not going to come. He was there when the war in Vietnam, which had seemed to be ending, exploded anew in the disastrous Tet Offensive. He experienced a keen sense of personal disappointment, which was slowly but inevitably followed by questions about that war—questions he'd never considered before.

The laid-back, country-club atmosphere that characterized Osan during Hunter's first TDY had vaporized into near panic. The attention of the United States was abruptly forced back to Korea, and the fate of the *Pueblo* sailors, now North Korean POWs, occupied a large part of the national consciousness.

The resulting buildup of U.S. forces thrust Osan into the cold, cruel world of the real Air Force. As the primary combat force, the 18th pilots and their machines were on constant alert. The nearest North Korean airfields were less than a hundred miles away. U.S. aircraft were kept fueled and armed so that they could be airborne within ten minutes. This meant the pilots had to sleep in alert quarters or in nearby BOQs, but definitely not in Chicol Village, which was off-limits to air crews.

In the first few weeks Hunter attempted to keep his morale up with nightly phone calls on the military telephone system to his nurse back on Okinawa. Then she started working nights and it became increasingly difficult to reach her.

In his second month a newly arrived pilot, a friend of his, had the explanation. "She just got engaged. A doctor on the night shift." The doctor was a twice-divorced urologist who was rumored to be on the promotion list for bird colonel. Hunter's friend consoled him by saying, "Just thought you ought to know."

"Well, sure, thanks . . . I guess." No promises, no commitments, a way of life which he was discovering had built-in hazards.

As the buildup continued, men and equipment poured in from other Pacific locations, then from bases all over the world. Soon Osan's limited resources were bulging at the seams. In a once empty field a tent city seemed to spring up overnight, like a patch of giant military-green mushrooms, to house new arrivals. As one of the first newcomers Hunter had a private room in a small BOQ building just across the street from the officers' club. One day he returned from the flight line to discover that his single bunk had been converted into a double-decker. He suspected that he was about to get a roomie.

That definitely did not fit in with his current needs. He went to see the overworked Korean billeting clerk. "Look, an old friend of mine is coming up tomorrow. Would it be all right if we shared the room I'm in?"

"Oh, good, can do easy." Mister Lee, the Korean clerk, was sick of pampered pilots whining about being doubled up. Hunter gave him a set of orders he'd manufactured with the help of a typewriter and a copy machine, and checked in his old buddy, Captain Robert E. Bogus. The cost of his room went from two to four dollars per day, but from then on he and the commanding general were the only people at Osan with private quarters.

His need for privacy was necessitated by a new circumstance. The defection of the nurse had been a surprise, but he discovered that only his ego was hurt. That was soon remedied by the realization that being a young, single officer with a private room on Osan constituted the ingredients for success in his campaign to win the affections of Miss Yee Chong Ah, the cutest of the gaggle of new waitresses hired by the officers' club. She was Hunter's first real *yobo*.

Yobo, the Korean word for darling or sweetheart, was a permanent part of GI slang. Once an American started a sexual relationship with a Korean woman on a regular basis she was his *yobo.* Forming such a relationship was not referred to as going steady or living together, it was called *yoboing.*

He and Miss Yee were *yobos* until mid-May, when his boss announced, "Mike, you're going back to Kadena."

"Hey, why me? I'm happy here."

"Maybe that's why," the lieutenant colonel said with a leer. Then he added, "Hell, I didn't make the decision. It came from the head shed at Kadena. They're getting a lot of new people, and we need some experienced heads back there to check them out for combat."

That night he told Miss Yee that he was leaving in three days. She cried, they commiserated about the unfairness of life, the U.S. Air Force, and chickenshit colonels. Then to show how much she cared for him, she let him make love to her in the way he'd wanted to try for a long time, but which she said nice girls didn't do.

Later, in that soft time of relaxed exuberance and total expenditure, while playing with the hair on his chest, she said, *"Yobo,* there is another officer man who likes me very much."

"Oh."

"He is civil engineer loo-tenant. He stay Osan one month."

"Umm."

"He say he want to marry me."

"What did you say?"

"I tell him wait. I think I talk to you first."

Hunter looked at her and felt that familiar twinge. Jealousy? Of course. But more than that. Regret. He really liked this sweet and very attractive young woman who had always been good to him. He liked her a lot.

But . . . "Chong, I really like you, but I'm not ready to get married. I—"

She nodded. *"Ada sumnida."* I understand.

They were both silent for a long time. Finally he said, "What are you going to do?"

"I tell loo-tenant we marry."

"Um, then, I guess I won't see . . ."

She didn't move. "You stay three more days?"

"Yes."

"Okay. I tell him after you leave." She came into his arms, their faces just inches apart. "You are first American man I know. You always nice guy for me. I care about you. We have to say good-bye."

He nodded. "That's fair."

When he returned to Okinawa, Paul Crandell was one of the new people. He was a navigator/systems operator assigned to the 18th's fourth squadron, which flew the new two-seat photoreconnaissance version of the F-4 Phantom. Since Hunter was working with new Thud pilots, he didn't have an opportunity to get to know the new F-4 backseater. Then, as soon as Crandell was checked out in the Phantom, he was tapped as a replacement GIB, guy-in-the-backseat, for the birds at Osan.

Hunter spent the rest of the year working with new pilots destined for the meat-grinder air war still going on in Southeast Asia. Twice he wangled trips back to Korea to see Miss Yee, but the long distance made it difficult to maintain the level of passion in the relationship that had once been there.

By the beginning of 1969, Osan was settling in to its new role as a major part of the Pacific Air Force. The base had gone from a sleepy, housekeeping operation to an installation bristling with new people, improved facilities, and the constant roar of aircraft takeoffs and landings. Chicol Village was doing its part. The older clubs expanded their operations as fast as they could build. New clubs seemed to open every few days. And the number of young women in the village constituted a mini-population explosion.

Back at Kadena during this period, Hunter first heard about Paul Crandell's *yobo*. Pilot gossip described her as young and breathtakingly beautiful. But it was emphasized that despite her youth and beauty, she was "one of them." Asian. This negative connotation was evident in a conversation Hunter overheard in the squadron lounge between two pilots who'd just come from Osan.

"Did you hear what that crazy bastard Crandell wants to do?"

"I heard he's gonna marry his Korean toot."

"Yeah. She's really fine, but that's not a smart move career-wise."

"You know Crandell, he's strange. He never comes to the club, doesn't drink, what can you expect?"

"Yeah, I know what you mean." They nodded in agreement.

Hunter knew too. While many enlisted men and a number of nonflying officers married Asian women, such an action was considered inappropriate for a young, career-oriented, rated officer. Strangely enough, while it was an accepted part of the code for pilots to attempt to seduce a fellow officer's wife, they were not supposed to get serious with "those women." A little fooling around on TDY was all right, as long as it wasn't public, but one had to uphold the proper moral standards of the rated officer corps.

Hunter knew that his own penchant for oriental women was considered somewhat of a blemish on an otherwise good record. But he chose to ignore those senior officers who felt moved to counsel him on proper image.

So, although he hardly knew Paul Crandell, he had a lot of sympathy for the guy.

After going with Hunter to his room, Shaw said, "I gotta go over to the office and stroke my boss so the evil bastard won't roast my nuts for getting back late. How about we get together at the club at four-thirty for happy hour?"

Hunter agreed. Shaw left to take care of damage control.

Chapter 7

The BOQ was one of the newer buildings on the base. The spacious room was opulent compared to the one Hunter had occupied in the *Pueblo* days. There was a large new single bed with an innerspring mattress rather than an old steel-frame bunk and the traditional GI fartsack, a thin lumpy mattress. There was also a large wooden bureau-style double locker, a desk, an overstuffed chair, and, most surprisingly of all, a refrigerator. This certainly wasn't the Korea Hunter remembered, but he decided he liked it.

Shaw's room was just down the hall, next to a central day room with couches, a new television, and a soft-drink machine. Next to that was the central latrine area with sinks and showers shared by all. Even that was better than the old days—here the commode stalls had doors.

After he got his bags unpacked, he stripped off his uniform, wrapped a towel around his waist, and headed for the showers. After four sweaty takeoffs and landings, Hunter felt a bit ripe. Returning to his room, he finished unpacking and then put on a clean uniform: the lightweight, tan, short-sleeved shirt and trouser summer uniform authorized to be worn until the end of October. After that everyone had to switch to winter blues. He'd read in the *Air Force Times* that this was the last year for the comfortable tan uniform. Next year the Air Force was changing the summer uniform to a light blue shirt and dark blue trousers—more in keeping with the Air Force blue image.

Since happy hour was still two hours away, he decided to get a head start on in-processing, the agonizing business of checking into a new base. He left the BOQ building and walked to the headquarters building.

Despite a lot of new buildings, the headquarters was still a relic from the middle fifties. It was actually a complex of more than fifty old Quonset huts interconnected by dark, musty halls and plywood floors that creaked and undulated underfoot. Offices in the building were heated in winter by heavy, old cast-iron barrel stoves that burned kerosene from five-gallon GI cans. The place is a goddamn firetrap, he thought. Still, it made him feel more like he was really back in Korea than the new buildings he'd been in so far.

A bored-looking master sergeant at the personnel office explained that Osan now had a centralized in-processing which was held only on Monday mornings. He said nothing could be accomplished until then. It was only Wednesday. Hunter had a feeling it was going to be a long weekend. Almost as an afterthought the sergeant added that Hunter could not leave the base until after he finished in-processing. That was because it included a security police briefing that explained the Status-of-Force (SOFA) agreement between the U.S. and Korea. This was necessary so that newcomers would be able to stay out of trouble off base. After the briefing everyone would be given a SOFA card. "You see, sir, without a SOFA card, you can't leave the base. That's the rule." He was smirking now, as if to say, "Fuck you very much, Captain."

Hunter smiled pleasantly. "No problem, Sarge." And it wasn't. In his wallet, among other bits of trivia collected over the years, were two old SOFA cards.

He left the office and walked through the dim, musty halls until he found the finance office. The young one-stripe airman there was a lot more agreeable than the older NCO. He took Hunter's pay record, helped him fill out several forms, and said he would get it into the system right away. He added that it would be several weeks before Hunter started receiving his regular pay-checks and asked if he need a special payment to stay solvent.

Hunter declined. The Lackland finance office had paid him through the end of the month. There was also the money that had accumulated during his six months in the hospital, most of which had just piled up in the bank. Even in Thailand he had saved quite a bit of his income, which had included flight pay, combat pay, and overseas pay. At the moment he had more money to his name than at any time in his life. It was a comfortable feeling.

His last visit was to the Osan dispensary, where he checked in with the flight surgeon's office. They took his medical records, asked him how he was feeling— he said fine—then they made an appointment for a full examination and said to let them know if he had any problems. The medical technician added, "Meanwhile, you're still grounded."

Wonderful, wonderful.

The dispensary was just across the street from the base chapel, which was right next to the officers' club. Those two buildings had been new when he first visited Osan and had not changed that much on the outside. He had always wondered what prompted the decision to put the chapel right next to the club. Maybe long ago some chaplain had figured he would pick up a few extra parishioners—drunks who staggered through the wrong door.

U.S. military clubs, both for officers and NCOs, are GI versions of private clubs in the civilian world, but a lot cheaper. For a nominal monthly fee, members get to dine and drink at reduced prices, as well as enjoy special entertainment. Stateside clubs were usually just okay, but overseas clubs often formed the hub of base social life. This was especially true in places like Korea, where most people were not accompanied by their families.

On his first Korea visit, the O Club had seemed much too large for the needs of the small officer population. Now it appeared hardly adequate. His first stop was the cashier's cage. He presented a copy of his assignment orders and told the Korean girl working there that he wanted to join.

She was counting money and took his orders without looking at him. She said, "Dues are five dollars a month and . . ." She noticed the name on the orders and looked up, *"Igoo,* you come back."

"Hi, Suzie." Choe Yong Su, nicknamed Suzie, was a college graduate who had been hired by the club during the *Pueblo* boom. She had been a pal of Hunter's former *yobo.*

"Hunter-*san.*" Adding -*san* after the name was another custom borrowed from the Japanese and used by better-educated Koreans to show respect. "Really good to see you again. You come PCS?"

"One more year."

"That is good." She smiled brightly, then asked, "You remember Miss Yee?"

"Of course. How is she?"

"Very good. Married now, living in States. She has one baby boy."

"That's nice."

"What about you, you have wife?"

"No, still single."

"I think still playboy too," she said in a teasing voice as she filled out the necessary forms and punched out a plastic membership card.

"How about you, Suzie, you married?"

"Oh, nobody like me. Maybe I'm too ugly girl."

"Sure," he said, taking his card. He personally knew of two majors and one lieutenant colonel who had broken up marriages only to discover that Suzie wasn't interested.

They talked for a few moments more, then said good-bye. He went into the bar area. It was a large room with a square bar built on two levels. On one side were low captain's chairs, on the other regular bar stools. Hunter preferred the swivel captain's chairs.

Almost immediately he was recognized and greeted warmly by both the head bartender and the number one cocktail waitress. Both had worked for the club since the late fifties. The bartender, Mr. Yim, was a burly, balding man in his fifties who spoke little but did his job expertly.

Jeanne, the waitress, was a tall, luscious, sexy woman of unknown age with a face and figure that could send the blood pressure of both young lieutenants and senior colonels soaring. Hunter had heard that over the years she had parlayed her earnings and other financial advantages—such as brokering jobs for other Koreans, gray- and black-market opportunities, and the gratefulness of a few well-chosen personal relationships—into a killing in Chicol Village real estate and that she was one of the richest women in the town. That wasn't difficult to understand when one realized that a job on an American base which included good tips provided a gross income higher than that of a general in the Korean Army. Some of those who knew about her wondered why she continued to work, but Hunter understood that the power of her position was at least as important as the money it provided.

Though not quite four-thirty, the place was already doing a brisk business. During a lull, Jeanne stopped by to chat. After the standard, nice-to-see-you, how-long-you-stay questions, Hunter asked, "Did you know Captain Paul Crandell? He was a friend of mine. He died in an accident here in June."

To say that time stood still for a heartbeat would have been an exaggeration. In fact, there was no overt change in Jeanne's face, but just as surely, he knew that the name meant something to her.

"Captain Crandell . . . ah, yes. I did not know him. He did not come to the club much. I hear about his, ah, accident."

"We were friends, we flew together in Vietnam."

"I see. I am sorry."

"He was going to marry a Korean girl. Do you know her?"

"No," she said slowly. "Many GIs marry Korean girls. I do not pay attention, not my business."

It was a standard answer, yet he had the feeling she knew more than she was telling him. Still, they had always been friendly and he couldn't understand why she would hide anything.

"Jeanne, I'm looking for that girl. I'd like to talk to

her about my friend's death. Even if you don't know her, you have many friends in the village. You must know someone who can find out something about her. I'd really appreciate your help.''

There was a long pause. "I-I will try." Then she moved away, and he had the impression that she was deliberately keeping busy so she wouldn't have to talk to him.

And maybe Mr. Yim is a North Korean spook, the voice in his head taunted. *Talk about jumping to conclusions, Captain Paranoid. You're leaping at the absurd.*

His thoughts were interrupted by a loud voice. "I see you still remember how to find the bar."

He swiveled around to see Shaw grinning at him. "Actually, I was on my way to the chapel and got lost," Hunter answered, smiling.

Shaw dropped into the next chair, and it groaned slightly under his weight. *"Ken chang."* No sweat. "We got gods here too. Johnnie Walker. Jim Beam. The god of St. Louis, Budweiser. Now personally," he said as he signaled the bartender, "I prefer the Canadian gods.''

Without being told, Yim poured a CC and seven and set it in front of Shaw. He was obviously well known in this watering hole. "Sorry I'm late. I had to make a quick trip to the vill. Dropped off the goodies for my *yobo* and got a kitchen pass. You shoulda seen her. When I unloaded all those cosmetics her eyes damn near turned American.''

During the next hour of talking and drinking Shaw related endless tales about how screwed-up things were—in his office, with his boss, and especially with the command section. At one point a black lieutenant entered the room and started past them, heading for a table where three other young black officers were sitting.

Shaw called out, "Hey, Hawkins, what's happening?''

The lieutenant, who hadn't noticed Shaw, looked startled. "Oh, Ron, hi.''

"Didn't you get my message?" Shaw said, "I called your office twice this afternoon. I was hoping we could get together tomorrow for some handball. After a week in Tokyo, I need the exercise."

"I didn't get the message," Hawkins said quickly. "Look, ah, I'll call you tomorrow, okay?" He walked over to the table where his friends were.

"What was that all about?" Hunter asked.

"Beats me, Mike. We both got here about the same time and used to be pretty tight. When my boss started ragging me about being overweight, Hawkins got me playing handball to lose a few pounds. Then, just when I was beginning to enjoy it, he gets involved with his black brothers. Now it's like he's afraid to be seen talking to a honky."

Shaw sighed and took a large swallow from his glass. "I tell you, this racial shit is getting to be a real pain in the ass."

Sometime later Hunter noticed two more young black officers joining the group. Several had their hair in the new, puffed-out Afro style, and on a couple it far exceeded the length considered acceptable by Air Force standards. Increasingly the noise level from their corner got louder. They seemed to be purposely creating a display, as if daring anyone in the room to challenge their right to be obnoxious. Hunter had seen similar displays before, but never in an officers' club.

He wondered how long such conduct would be tolerated. Interestingly enough, when the challenge came, it was from a black lieutenant colonel. The older officer was drinking with a group of other white senior officers. He walked over, said something to the group and there was a quiet but sharp exchange of words. When it was over, although the noise level went down some, the lieutenant colonel looked as if he had gotten the worst of it.

Shaw said, "They probably told the colonel he was an Oreo."

"What do you mean?" Hunter asked.

"You know, the cookie. Black on the outside, white on the inside."

A few minutes later the two went into the dining room. Hunter ordered the Mexican special. When it arrived the waitress announced that the club was temporarily out of hot sauce. Some things never change, Hunter decided. Despite the big buildup in the country, Korea always seemed to be dead last as far as the supply system was concerned. Shaw, in deference to his expanding waistline, had a large salad. From the quantity of blue cheese dressing he heaped on, Hunter figured it was a lost cause.

After dinner Shaw was planning a big night in the vill to reacquaint his new friend with the magic land. Hunter declined, however, with a tinge of regret. A headache which had started small was building fast, and he knew if he did not get his pills and some rest, he would be in trouble.

Shaw said he understood. "Of course, an old war wound. You flyboys have to take it easy. I, on the other hand, as a member of the lowly, unrated officer class, will go, alone and unarmed, and attempt to satisfy the natives."

"All of them?"

"Duty is duty."

Hunter reached over, put his hand on Shaw's shoulder, and gave it a friendly squeeze. "You're a real buddy, buddy."

In a magnanimous tone Shaw acknowledged, "I know, I know."

Back in his room, Hunter realized he shouldn't have consumed so much beer. Since his release from the hospital he'd learned that one of the quickest ways to do himself in was with alcohol. The doctors said the headaches were part of the healing process, his body's way of letting him know it was time to ease up.

He undressed and got into bed. Yeah, that's what it was, just temporary, not that he was getting older, that he might actually be developing a sense of maturity. Ugh! What a horrible thought. If the fighter pilots' union found out that he actually had been in the BOQ, contentedly snuggled under the covers before 10 P.M.

two nights in a row, well . . . it was just too terrifying to contemplate. He might end up flying C-141s—long-haul truck drivers in the air.

Suppressing the urge to giggle, he switched on the clock radio thoughtfully supplied by the BOQ. It was tuned to AFKN, the Armed Forces Korea Network station. They were playing jazz. He liked that.

Kathy's image came to mind. Sweet, beautiful Kathy. Kind Kathy. He missed her.

Sure, you do.

Now come on, I really do, he answered himself. After all, she was everything an Air Force officer could want in a wife. In addition to beauty and brains she had a job which would be a career asset to any upwardly mobile officer, enhancing his opportunity for advancement to the higher levels of the command bureaucracy.

Absolutely.

So what was he doing in Korea?

The photographs—Crandell's photographs—were suddenly in his mind, washing away Kathy's image.

Stop it, Captain Jerkoff.

He tossed back the covers, rolled out of bed, and went to the bathroom. Returning to bed, he picked up his book, a reissue of Raymond Chandler's *Farewell, My Lovely.* He'd first read it when he was a teenager. After all, he assured himself, a good book is almost as much fun as going to the vill.

Sure it is.

Chapter 8

The morning of Hunter's second day at Osan was spent putting his life back together. He started with a call to the base transportation section and learned that two shipments of his personal belongings had arrived. A small one from Texas and a larger shipment with all the things left behind in Thailand.

"When can I get them delivered?"

"How about an hour?" the transportation NCO answered. That was a surprise. The bureaucracy of the blue machine seldom responded with such alacrity.

Even more astonishing, it arrived before the hour was up. The box from Texas was mostly clothing and books. The larger shipment from Thailand was more fun. He didn't know what to expect—it had been packed by others after his evacuation and held in storage. He didn't remember half of what he'd left behind.

He was delighted to find that his stereo system, his color TV, and his camera equipment were in perfect condition. There were more books, boxes of reel-to-reel tapes, albums of photographs he had taken in pilot training, paintings and art objects purchased throughout Asia, Thai-made brass, and other souvenirs he'd forgotten about. He found more clothing, including his flight suits and his special flying boots.

Hunter spent the next hour putting away his things. He was almost finished when he got hung up leafing through his photo albums. He had one for each of the bases at which he'd been stationed, including Kadena and one each for his tours at Korat. The last album was only half full.

* * *

"Mike, you sure you want to do this?"

"Well, it's too wet to plow."

The squadron commander, Lieutenant Colonel Smokey Johnson, looked at him sharply. "What the hell does—"

"Sorry, boss, Iowa humor." Johnson had been given command of the squadron at Kadena after the former commander was killed on a routine training mission. He had safely ejected out of the Thud he was flying after the engine exploded—but his parachute failed to open and he fell into the ocean and drowned.

"Damn, Mike, you can go back to the world," Johnson said. "You've earned the right."

"Yeah, I know, but the job's not done."

"No one can finish the war by himself, Mike. You do your part; if you make it, you go home."

"Smokey, I'm not the first to volunteer for a second tour."

"No, you're not. But if you live through it, you'll be one of the few who've done that." Hunter didn't say anything. Finally, Johnson said, "Okay, Mike, you got it. Hell, with your luck you'll probably shoot down four more MiGs and end up being the first ace in this war." He grinned as he stuck out his hand. "I think you're crazy, but good luck."

While Hunter, Johnson, and a lot of other Kadena people had been in Korea, the real war in Vietnam was going badly for the United States. The first months of 1969 were dog days for U.S. pilots. Looking for a cease-fire, the White House restricted combat strikes to targets below the 19th parallel in the southern third of North Vietnam while continuing to strike at the Ho Chi Minh Trail in Laos and Cambodia.

At the end of his two-and-a-half-year tour at Kadena, Hunter had found himself facing options. He'd completed his original five-year commitment to the Air Force. He could request release from active duty and go back to being a civilian. If he wanted to stay in, he could be assigned to a Stateside base to train new pilots. At the last moment he decided he didn't like either choice. There was no way he was ready to go back to either the civilian world or the straight-laced bureaucracy and rigid formality that was so much a part of the Stateside Air Training Command. So he volunteered for a second combat tour.

The Air Force was quite willing to accommodate him—in Wild Weasels, SAM hunters. Theirs was one of the most dangerous flying missions in the war. At first Hunter was unhappy with the assignment. Not because of the danger, but, like a lot of fighter pilots, especially Thud drivers, Hunter thought he wanted nothing to do with aircraft with more than one seat.

Wild Weasels were Thuds, but they were a bastardized version. The F-105F, the two-seat model originally designed as a trainer, had been modified. The Air Force jammed the back cockpit full of newly developed electronics to be operated by a weapons-system operator. Their primary weapon was the new 390-pound, Mach Two, Shrike missile. It had a seven-to-ten mile range and homed on SAM radar emissions.

Lieutenant Colonel Smokey Johnson, Hunter's new squadron commander, explained to a group of incoming pilots, "Since the president ended the bombing of North Vietnam, most of our missions are against SAMs that have been set up to protect the Ho Chi Minh Trail." He ended his in-briefing by adding, "What makes Weasel missions a tad more exciting than flying normal strike aircraft is that to find and kill the SAMs, we gotta fly around in their area while they're trying to kill us. Our success depends on your being smarter and quicker."

Within a week after he started flying Weasels, Hunter had to admit that this job was at least as exciting as flying strike aircraft. On his fifth mission, he was in a flight of four fighters hunting SAM sites in the southern part of North Vietnam where the Ho Chi Minh Trail began. Enemy gunners got off two missiles before the Thuds located their position. The first missile went off behind Hunter's aircraft, causing it to rock and shudder. Although he couldn't see the damage, he could feel it in the flight controls. He determined that his aircraft was flyable, and while the other three F-105s were turning the control van and launchers into a smoky hole, he limped on back to Korat.

Later in the officers' club he was unwinding with a group of pilots when their squadron maintenance officer came by.

"Hey, Hunter, nice going. My boys found a double break in the fuselage frame of your bird. Plus the flight controls and hydraulics are all fucked up." He reached in his pocket. Pulling his hand out, he tossed a dozen pieces of jagged metal on the table. "Here's some souvenirs. Some of the SAM we picked out of the shitpot that's left of your vertical fin and rudder."

Hunter looked up at the man. The relationship between pilots and maintenance officers, though friendly, was often adversarial—pilots broke airplanes, maintenance officers had to get them fixed. Smiling thinly, he looked down at the small, dull, fire-blackened fragments for several moments, then he reached over and shoved them back. "That's okay, you keep 'em. I'm done playing with 'em."

In truth, he didn't feel nearly as indifferent as he pretended. It was the pilot's way of facing danger, refusing to acknowledge it. He realized later he didn't have his emotions under quite as tight a rein as he thought. A few minutes after the maintenance officer left, a Phantom driver from Ubon Air Base came over to their table. He had been flying strike earlier.

"Where the hell were you Weasel guys today?" challenged the young California beach-boy-type lieutenant.

One of the oldest Weasel pilots, a grizzled, grayhaired major who had been passed over for promotion so many times that if it hadn't been for his ability to fly combat he would have long since been retired, smiled, and setting up one of the groups' favorite gags, said, "Hey, everybody, say hello to the loo-tenant."

In unison the Weasel pilots chanted, "Hello, *asshole!*"

The lieutenant, obviously a new guy, looked shocked, then baffled, and finally walked away shaking his head sadly.

So many faces of people and places gone by. And too many clear-eyed, clean-faced, smiling young men in flight suits who were now in a living hell in North Vietnam. Or dead.

He put the photo album away.

At the bottom of the last box, wrapped in an old flight suit, was a smaller cardboard carton sealed with nylon tape. He opened it and discovered his guns: the big Browning 9mm and the smaller .25-caliber Beretta. Each had been cleaned, oiled, and wrapped in an old T-shirt. He also found a note: "Mike, I packed this stuff for you. Not supposed to include the guns, but like you always say, if they can't take a joke, screw them. Sure hope you are around to open this soon." It was signed with Paul's familiar, neatly written signature.

He rewrapped the weapons in the T-shirt and put them into a small travel bag. That went into the bottom drawer of the bureau, which he secured with a combination padlock. His friend's smiling face flashed into his mind. Thanks, Paul, he thought, I'm going to do my best to find out what happened to you.

During Hunter's first two months in Weasels, WSOs had been in short supply, so he didn't have a regular bear and flew with whoever was available. In late February, Kadena shipped over five new WSOs, including Paul Crandell, who'd been retrained from the Phantom to the Thud. None of the new men had flown combat before. Crandell was assigned to Hunter for his checkout ride.

"Glad to meet you," Hunter said. "I saw you around back at Kadena, but I don't think we ever met."

"No, I don't think so," Crandell said. "But I've heard a lot about you." Hunter looked surprised. Crandell grinned. "The Hunter, the coolest man in the cockpit and the biggest playboy in the Far East."

Slightly taken back, Hunter looked at Crandell for a moment, then said, "It's possible my reputation exceeds me."

In the first mission briefing, as with most new guys, Crandell did not join in the undercurrent of jokes and mock dramatics the veterans used to belie their tension and fear. He was quiet, intent on absorbing all the details. When it ended, the crews headed for the equipment room to suit up.

First came the G-suit, a girdlelike device that went around the waist and legs. It automatically inflated and tightened whenever the aircraft pulled excessive g-forces. This kept blood from rushing to the lower parts of the pilot's body and causing him to black out.

Then came the survival vest, a canvas affair with many pockets filled with goodies to help a downed pilot stay alive on the ground. Such things as a radio, maps, compass, knife, first-aid supplies, water purification tablets, and rations. There was also a gold coin and a blood chit—a promise of payment by the U.S. government. These last two were to help a downed flyer buy his way out if he could find a sympathetic or greedy local.

Next was their personal weapon. Crandell carried the Air Force standard-issue .38-caliber Combat Masterpiece, a sturdy six-shot revolver. Hunter preferred something more substantial. His weapon was a Browning Hi-Power, a big brute of a 9mm automatic with a thirteen-shot clip. He also had something extra that he had come up with in the early zeal of his first tour. He wore special Wellington zip-up boots which had been made at his direction by a Thai boot maker. What made them different was that on the side of the right boot he'd instructed the Thai to fashion a clamshell pocket. The pocket was for a small five-shot Beretta automatic. While Hunter had never used either of the weapons except on the practice range, he always carried both.

Last was the parachute backpack. Once they had it all on, they picked up their flying helmets and oxygen masks and, with the other crew members, headed for the flight-line van to ride to their airplanes. Fully suited, Crandell, a slender man about five-eight, almost disappeared beneath his equipment.

Their first mission was a milk run. They checked out a SAM site in northern Laos that had been hit the day before. Hunter had participated in the original attack, and apparently they had done the job right the first time. There were no radar emissions and nothing visible other than the burnt-out control van and launch vehicles. On the way back they went hunting for a new site that had fired on a flight the day before. They flew over the area, but couldn't detect any activity. If they were down in the thick forest below, they were keeping their heads down.

Throughout the flight Crandell displayed a sure knowledge of the Thud and its equipment. He knew his job and accomplished it well. Hunter was impressed.

The next day was different. The target was a particularly nasty stretch of the trail where two birds had been damaged by SAMs which had apparently been moved in during the previous week. They were part of a four-ship flight assigned to take out the new site. Hunter and Crandell flew the third fighter in a four-ship fire-suppression mission in advance of the main strike force of Phantoms. Their call sign was Ripper.

They took off at fourteen hundred, joined up with tankers south of the DMZ, refueled, and headed east. As usual, the radio channels were cluttered with chatter, and it took a practiced ear to separate the information for their flight from the dozens of other conversations and voices. Ripper Lead called out the altitude and heading settings to bring the flight in medium low, under where flak would normally be, a little west of the target. About two miles out they climbed to a higher altitude to set up, then rolled to the right in a steep, g-pulling turn.

The flight leader selected an element attack, One and Two, Three and Four. Lead and Hunter were flying Weasels with Shrikes and CBU-24s, cluster-bomb units that spewed thousand of steel balls designed to kill SAM crews. Two and Four were flying single-seat Thuds armed with napalm and five-hundred-pound bombs.

The attack began with Hunter and Crandell's aircraft four thousand feet behind Ripper Lead and Two. Nasty puffs of flak began exploding around them, accompanied by angry streams of tracers. Hunter lost sight of Ripper Lead in a cloud of bursting shells. To avoid the mess they broke right.

Suddenly the radio crackled. Two shouted, "Lead's bought it. I'm hit too. We lost our fire-control system." There was a moment of silence, then, "We're heading home."

Hunter, second in command, radioed, "Roger, Two." Two clicked his mike button twice, radio shorthand for affirmative.

The sky over the target had turned into a black mushroom cloud of flak. On their first pass to acquire the SAM site a bevy of gunfire opened up. He spotted fire from 37mm and 57mm guns. Just as they were pulling up, his wing man spotted the muzzle blasts from a nasty radar-controlled 85mm anti-aircraft battery, the gun which had taken out Ripper Lead.

It was some of the most intense ground fire Hunter could remember along the trail. He would have been scared, but there just wasn't time as he piloted the Thud down through the sudden storm of metal and death.

Crandell broke in: a SAM site was on them. In minimum time it tracked and fired at them. Before they could break, the lethal dark telephone pole spouting flames rose out of the smoke and passed just to their left. They watched as it streaked past without exploding. The gunner had miscalculated their altitude; if not, Hunter knew, they would've been in deep *kimchee*.

Even worse for the dink missile crew, Crandell had a lock-on. The two Thuds came screaming around and down, barreling in. Crandell identified the SAM position, and Hunter located the large 85mm gun battery that had nailed Ripper Lead. He crooned into the mike, "Ready or not, here we come."

The two aircraft screamed through the exploding sky. In a frantic effort to give the ground gunners as difficult a target as possible, Hunter moved the control stick from side to side and mashed on the control pedals. This caused the big Thud to pitch and roll as it roared past the exploding guns.

Inside the busy cockpit Crandell acquired the SAM site with his sophisticated detection-and-positioning systems. Hunter set up and launched a Shrike. Then, just to add insult to injury, their wing man dumped canisters of napalm. The target, receding behind them, exploded in a boiling blister of flame and smoke.

"Right on," called out Four.

"They're crispy critters now," Hunter said.

They turned hard right, going after the big gun battery. Through the smoke and fire Hunter caught a glimpse of its belching barrels. Hunter smiled grimly, pulling a tight turn and pressing on after the gun battery. The strike force was in the area now, and the battle raged on all sides of them. He had the Thud right down on the deck, screaming along just above the treetops. At that level they were an almost impossible target for the gunners on the ground.

Locating the big gun battery, Hunter lined the F-105's electronic gun sight on the belching barrels and thumbed the switch. The Vulcan cannon hissed a three-second burst, and the patch of real estate in front of them erupted in hundreds of tiny volcanos. Four unloaded his remaining five-hundred-pounders, adding to the general destruction.

Flashing past the burning gun battery, Hunter hit the afterburner and hauled back on the control stick. The Thud thundered upward as he and Crandell were pressed back into their seats by a five-G pull.

One pass and haul ass.

But they weren't quite quick enough. He felt the Thud lurch slightly: a hit. As they rose up out of the smoke and flak he quickly scanned the emergency panels and checked the operations of the controls. All seemed well. Then Four came over the radio.

"Hey, Hunter, you been hit."

Maneuvering in, the wing man took a closer look. He said there was a jagged hole in their fuselage.

Hunter detected a little drag, but otherwise the bird was flying fine.

"Let's *cutta chogie,*" he said, using the Korean expression for "get the hell out of here." He knew they had destroyed or damaged two SAM sites, one big gun, and a couple of smaller ones. As they raced toward the Red River and the waiting tankers, he said, "I think we earned our pay today."

After landing, Crandell discovered automatic-weapons fire had put hundreds of holes along the left side of their fuselage in addition to the big hole from the 85mm gun, which had just missed several important hydraulic lines.

An overweight, morose tech sergeant, one of the ground mechanics, stood studying the damage. In a despairing voice he said, "Ga'damn, that's a lot of work. Why din you just jump out and leave this sick fucker in the jungle?"

"Golly, Sarge, I don't know," Hunter answered accommodatingly. "I guess I just didn't think of it. *C-H-I Dooie,*" GI slang for the Thai phrase for "Sorry about that."

A blue Chevy van, the air crew taxi, pulled up and stopped. The three men climbed aboard. As they headed back to operations Hunter noticed Crandell looking solemn. "So, Paul, how do you like Weasels so far?"

Crandell blinked, then slowly dug up a smile. "Ah, not so bad. Only ninety-eight missions to go."

Hunter grinned back. He had a good feeling about his new colleague. Crandell was going to be okay.

Hunter let the memories go. Life goes on. The mental journey through the back streets of his life had started that tight feeling in his head. Just to be on the safe side he popped two pills, then left to meet Shaw at the club for lunch. When he arrived, his friend was already there, and he had news.

Chapter 9

"I got to thinking about your friend Crandell this morning," Shaw said, "so I did some checking. I found out who was assigned as the summary court officer to handle the paperwork on his death." Whenever someone died, the procedure was to appoint an officer to take care of the details a death generates: paperwork, settling debts, disposition of personal possessions, and shipping the body to the next of kin. "I asked him to meet us for lunch. I figured you'd want to talk to him."

"Good thinking, Ron." A few minutes later a slender, light brown-complected lieutenant entered the dining room. Shaw waved and he came over. Shaw introduced him as Fred Reyes, a supply officer.

After Hunter explained his interest, Reyes said, "I never met him. I got the assignment after the accident. It wasn't that difficult. He was on leave. We didn't have his records or anything. I took care of the necessary paperwork, cleaned out his room in the transient BOQ, sent some messages and so on. I also notified his parents and made arrangements to have his body sent to his hometown for burial. That's about it."

"How did he die?" Hunter asked. "Exactly."

"Water in his lungs. He drowned."

"How could that have happened?"

"Apparently he got loaded in one of the clubs in the vill. It was late when he started back to the base, and raining. I guess he got lost or disoriented in the back alleys, then he slipped or fell into the creek. Normally he would have been okay, but it had been coming down regular for about three days and the water was running pretty deep. I guess he just couldn't get out. Very unfortunate.''

"Any witnesses?''

"Some Koreans found the body. No one saw him go in.''

"In that case, who figured out the story you just told me?''

"Huh? Well, the doctor . . . and the security police.''

"It all seems to fit,'' Hunter said. Reyes started nodding. "Except for one thing.''

"What's that?''

"Crandell didn't drink. Not at all. Never. Wouldn't touch the stuff.''

"I don't know. He'd sure been drinking when he went into the water.''

"How do you know that?''

"The doctor's report. At least that's what the security police said.''

"I'd like to talk to that doctor.''

Reyes thought a moment, then said, "I think he rotated last month. Back to the States somewhere.'' As he spoke, the waitress came by and took their orders.

After she left, Hunter said, "What about his fiancée?''

It was a shot in the dark, but it worked. Reyes looked surprised, then uncomfortable. "Ah, nothing official on that.''

"Okay.'' Reyes started to relax, then Hunter said, "Now tell me the unofficial part.''

"Well, ah, I did find some personal stuff about a Korean girl. Some letters and pictures. But they weren't married. There wasn't any paperwork that I could find. So, you know how that goes around here. I thought she might come forward after his death, but she didn't. The security police figured maybe she was shacked up with someone else when he got back.''

Hunter tried to keep his face straight. Obviously it didn't work because Reyes quickly added, "It happens, you know. I always thought that was the reason he went out and got drunk."

The waitress arrived and served salads. Shaw asked why there were no tomatoes. The waitress shrugged and said, "Tomatoes *oop so.*" All gone. "Temporary shortage."

Hunter took a bite of salad, chewed and swallowed, then said, "I suppose you sent the letters and pictures back to his parents with his other things?"

For the second time Reyes looked ill at ease. "Ah, actually no. I was going to, but I didn't know if his parents knew about her. I figured, considering everything, it might just cause hard feelings . . . ah, so I didn't."

Hunter smiled thinly. "That's reasonable. What did you do with them?"

"They're back in my office, in my alibi file."

"May I have them?"

"Huh? Well, I don't know, ah . . ."

Hunter's face got hard. Something about this man irritated him. "Paul Crandell was my friend. He saved my life after we were shot down—in the war." He emphasized the last three words, making sure Reyes got the message: while Korea might be an inconvenience, it was a country club compared to what was going on farther south.

"I intend to find that girl. I want to talk to her because I'm not satisfied with what I've heard so far about the way my friend died. The pictures could be a big help locating her, unless you have some personal reason for holding onto them."

Reyes flushed. "No big deal. I just thought I ought to keep them for the file, but I can make copies. You can have them."

Hunter relaxed and smiled pleasantly. "Thank you. So, let's eat. Then we can go get them."

The waitress served their lunch. Reyes got a club sandwich, which was lacking bacon. The waitress explained, "So sorry, bacon *oop so.*" Shaw had the fried chicken, which came with all the parts. Hunter stuck with a grease burger and fries, but discovered sweet gherkins had been substituted for dill pickles, which were also *oop so*.

As they ate, Shaw said, "Mike, do you really think you can find the girl?"

"Chicol Village isn't all that big," Hunter said, "and I know a lot about Miss Kim already. She didn't work in a club, but her friend did. Paul told me that they used to go there sometimes with her friend and the friend's *yobo*. Someone working there should know her."

"Yeah, but the way the girls move around . . ."

"I also know that one of the lawyers down there was working on their marriage paperwork. There aren't that many paper doctors, and they keep records. I think I can run her down one way or another."

After he finished eating, Reyes seemed to want to say something. "Look, I hope you don't think I screwed things up. I was just trying to do my job and—"

Hunter decided to be nice. "No, I don't think that. I think you did just what anyone would have done, given the same circumstances. I just happen to have information you didn't."

"Well, it really bugs me. You're not the first one to ask about Crandell."

That got Hunter's attention. "Really. Who else?"

"Well, ah . . . the OSI."

The OSI was the Office of Special Investigation, the Air Force's super cops. That they were asking questions about Paul opened a whole new world of possibilities, only a few of which could even remotely be considered positively.

Reyes said, "A guy named Troxler called me just a couple of days ago. He said he was checking over some old accidents. He asked me about your friend's death."

"What did he want to know?"

"Just about the same questions you asked. How'd he die? What'd I do? Like that."

"Did he ask about Crandell's fiancée?"

"No, I didn't even think about it then."

After they had finished lunch, Shaw went back to

his office. Hunter and Reyes walked to the base supply complex. Reyes had a partitioned-off corner in the back of one of the large old warehouse buildings. At his desk, he dug into a drawer and came up with a file folder marked "CRANDELL." He flipped through the papers, found a small envelope, removed it, and shook out two wallet-size photos. "Here they are."

And then Hunter had them—those pictures whose image had become as permanent a part of him as his own name. These were smaller versions of the photographs Crandell had kept in the gold frame on his desk in their trailer at Korat. As Hunter studied the photographs he became aware of Reyes also staring at them.

"She is really beautiful," Reyes said. "I never met one like her in the vill. I looked, but, ah . . ." He stopped, reacting to the harsh look that came over Hunter's face. "I mean, I looked for one as good-looking as her, but . . ."

The dislike Hunter felt earlier returned, and now he knew the reason. He also knew why Reyes had kept the photographs. He understood—but he didn't like it.

Reyes quickly went back into his folder and came up with two letters in opened envelopes that were addressed to Crandell at Korat. They had been mailed in the village. Keeping a tight rein on his emotions, Hunter waited while Reyes made copies of everything for his files. Accepting the originals, Hunter thanked Reyes for his help, then left.

Chapter 10

Once outside the supply building he took a deep breath and willed himself to relax. His inner voice mocked, *Isn't righteous indignation fun? After all, Crandell's girl is your private property, right?*

He opened the folder and looked at the photographs again. Time and memory hadn't been wrong. If anything, she was even more beautiful than he had remembered.

At Korat many combat crew members had lived in two-man relocatable trailers, one more wonder of modern warfare. Two weeks after Crandell arrived, Hunter's trailer mate was shot up and medevaced back to the States. Since they were flying together on a regular basis, he told Crandell, "If you don't believe in jinxes, why don't you move in with me?"

"Anything to get out of the TDY quarters. The other day they stuck a visiting information officer from Pacific Air Force headquarters in Hawaii in with me. Boy, was he full of it."

Hunter had developed a protective attitude toward his younger, by two years, new bear. This serious, gentle, well-mannered son of a moderately wealthy Virginia family did not seem cut from the same cloth as the average hard-drinking, fast-living fighter jock. He didn't use alcohol in any form, and he liked to read weighty tomes on history and philosophy rather than the trashy mysteries that Hunter preferred. And, the greatest sin of all, he often made fond remarks about his time spent flying multiengine cargo aircraft for

MAC. They seemed to complement each other: Hunter the gung-ho fighter jock, Crandell providing restraint.

Even after the younger officer proved he could cut it in combat with the best of them, he was never accepted as a member of the squadron in-group. Instead of spending his evenings in the club lapping up all the booze in sight and cursing the demons of death, he was back in the trailer working on correspondence courses which he hoped would get him into a master's degree program back in the world after he finished his hundred missions. If he wasn't studying, he was usually writing letters, some to parents and friends, but most to Korea.

He didn't talk about her much—not at first. When he moved in he put up a gold picture frame with two eight-by-ten photographs of her. In the first, a full-length shot, she was standing in front of a historic Korean building. The picture showed off her long, shapely legs and her slender, elfin figure. The second was a close-up, an informal portrait back lit by the sun, capturing the golden highlights in the long, dark hair that flowed around her shoulders and down her back. Extraordinarily beautiful, she had large, expressive eyes that sparkled with fun and fire yet still conveyed vulnerability. Added to that were her fashion-model high cheekbones and a dazzling smile that showed off perfect white teeth.

Hunter often found himself staring at the photographs. He was captivated by her special combination of innocence and sensuality. He began trying to analyze what it was that made her face stick so firmly in mind. She was beautiful, sure, but it was more complicated than that. He had known more than a few Korean women, and, as with any ethnic group, their faces fell into certain categories or types. As he probed his memory, however, he realized he had never personally known another woman, Asian or Western, quite as striking as this one. Her cosmopolitan beauty could not be automatically typed—she could be Japanese, Chinese, or even an Asian-Western mix. The only faces that seemed even close were a few high-fashion models and a couple of movie stars.

One day, coming out of the shower, Crandell caught him looking. At first Hunter tried to act innocent, not admitting the stunning effect the pictures had on him. After all, even he knew it was churlish to be caught drooling over a friend's fiancée. But he couldn't help commenting.

"That's one *manee epuda* woman." Crandell looked puzzled. "That's Korean for 'very pretty girl,' which in her case is a gross understatement."

"Thank you." Crandell looked embarrassed. "She really is beautiful, isn't she? Sometimes I feel guilty."

"Guilt. You're way beyond simple guilt," Hunter kidded him. "With a woman like that you're into wickedness." Crandell actually blushed. Realizing he might be going a bit overboard, Hunter pretended interest in the art of his friend's photography. "Where did the pictures come from?"

"I took the close-up at Osan. The other's Seoul, a historic palace. We went there once when we visited her sister."

"Her family knows you're going to get married?"

"Her sister and mother do. She hasn't told her father yet. He's old-fashioned. Many Koreans look down on marriages between their women and American military men."

Hunter nodded. "A lot of Korean parents aren't all that different from those back in the good ol' U.S. of A."

"I know. Most Americans think Asians just can't wait to marry their daughters off to GIs. But it's not true. A lot of them aren't any happier than American parents about mixed marriages. It's a stigma there too."

"Just goes to prove that cultural snobbery isn't an exclusively American trait," Hunter said. "What's her name?"

"Kim Soon Ja."

"No nickname?" Most of the girls used Americanized nicknames because often the GIs were too lazy to learn to pronounce the more difficult Korean names.

"No, right in the beginning she said if I wanted to know her, I would have to learn how to say her name correctly."

"My, my, a girl with spirit."

"Very much so," Crandell said with pride. Then he added, "She wasn't part of the Osan crowd. I mean, she didn't work in a bar or anything." As he said it, he looked guilty, "Not that I mean anything bad about the girls that do . . ."

"Don't get caught on the horns of that dilemma," Hunter said, grinning.

"What I mean is, I love her. I loved her the minute I saw her, and even if she had been one of . . ." he paused, ". . . one of the Osan girls, I don't think it would have made any difference."

"It makes a difference to a lot of people. That's a simple fact of life. I don't put down the Osan girls, or for that matter any of the girls who show up at U.S. bases in Asia. Having enjoyed their company more than a few times, I figure I sure as hell would be the world's biggest hypocrite if I looked down on them for being there."

Crandell laughed, "Most people aren't quite so egalitarian."

"Many GIs—and when I use the term I include officers—are redneck bigots."

"Damn, Hunter, you *are* different."

"True. But I figure if they can't take a joke, fuck 'em!"

Several weeks later, Hunter learned more about her. It was a late night after a particularly hairy mission. They took several bad hits over the trail and discovered their fuel system was shot to hell and pissing all over Southeast Asia. Hunter radioed for an emergency tanker rendezvous and was able to coax the leaky Thud to the meeting place. Then, just as they jockeyed into position for a hookup, the engine flamed out.

Without power the massive F-105 immediately started to live up to its nickname. They lost three thousand feet in the next few seconds. Keeping a tight rein on his apprehension and ignoring the blaze of emergency lights, he went through the emergency procedures, by the book. Once. Nothing. *No sweaty-da. Do it again.* Twice. Nothing. *Come on, you ground-lovin' hog.* Thrice. The huge engine coughed, burped, then roared to life. *Thank you, Lord. Thank you.* Hunter slammed the Thud into position for the hookup with the tanker, which had followed them down.

Hanging on the KC-135 tanker's boom, Hunter and Crandell monitored the fuel-control gauges as they sucked up JP-4. After several minutes Crandell radioed, "Mike, I think we've got trouble."

The Thud fuel tanks were shot so full of holes that they were unable to maintain fuel pressure. The only way to keep the turbine cranking was to hang on and let the flying gas tank drag them back to Thailand, all the while pumping fuel directly to the big engine.

Maintaining the connection with the big four-engine tanker took all of Hunter's concentration and flying skill during the long flight to Korat. Just before they crossed into Thailand they were caught in sudden turbulence. Hunter watched in dismay as the boom nozzle jerked out of the receptacle located just forward of his cockpit. The sudden disconnection caused jet fuel to shower over the Thud cockpit, filling it with noxious fumes.

Fighting nausea, Hunter zapped through the restart procedures again. He and Crandell were only seconds away from punching out when he got it going again and was able to plug in once more to the tanker, who had again followed them down.

After the wounded bird was finally on the ground, all the tension and terror of the agonizing flight surfaced. Even the normally icy-calm Hunter was unnerved. He dealt with it by going straight to the officers' club and spending the next three hours getting crazy drunk. Then he decided he needed the comfort of a sweet thing in town—and he didn't feel like waiting for the bus. So he took the blue station wagon the base commander had conveniently parked in his reserved spot in front of the club.

Hunter was lucky. The security policemen who chased him down after he tried to crash the main gate were accompanied by their new boss. The first lieutenant, a new man just in, was still in awe of fighter pilots. He had been in the club earlier and had heard the story of Hunter's flight. The lieutenant had his men relieve Hunter of the keys and take him to his trailer.

Crandell received his drunken companion from the arms of the SPs and hauled him inside. He maneuvered his big friend, still in his grimy, sweat-crusted flight suit, to the shower, turned it on, and pushed him in.

After a long while Hunter emerged, still drunk but somewhat cleaner and wide awake. Crandell, in a somber mood, was lying on his bed, balancing the picture frame on his chest. He looked up and said, "You okay?"

Hunter took a deep breath and exhaled slowly. "Yeah, I guess. How about you?"

"I've been thinking about dying," the younger man said slowly. "I've been thinking how much I would regret it if I never saw Soon Ja again."

"Damn, don't talk like that."

"I love her so much."

"You're lucky, you've got somebody you really care about."

"That's what scares me. I would feel better if I didn't love her so much. If I didn't have to worry about leaving her."

"Hey, don't sweat it. As long as the Hunter is doing the flying, we'll make it."

Crandell grinned. "You know, Mike, I really believe that—well, most of the time." The smile faded and he looked serious again. Hunter realized he needed to talk.

"Did I tell you how I met her?" Hunter shook his head. "My crew chief at Osan, a young sergeant, had a *yobo* in the vill. I'd only been in Korea for a month, and I was so damn naive. I was one of those people who thought there was something immoral about American men who got involved with Asian women."

"You're not the only one like that. There are a lot of ex-wives who would agree with you."

Despite knowing he shouldn't encourage his friend, Crandell grinned. "Anyway, we had a Sunday downday coming up. My crew chief—Mac Farlin, a short, stocky kid from Nebraska—figured I was spending too much time on the base so he invited me down to his hooch for a barbecue party. I didn't want to go. I was afraid of eating Korean food, which I thought was awful."

Hunter grinned. Most Americans, including himself, were that way the first time they encountered *kimchee*.

"But I couldn't think of a way to refuse without looking like a snob, so I agreed. Hell, it was on a Sunday afternoon. I didn't think anything too wicked could happen to me."

"What a hero."

Crandell continued. He agreed to meet Farlin at the main gate at noon. Just to make sure no one got the wrong idea why he was in the village, he wore his uniform. It was an early November day, cool with low clouds. Farlin was waiting for him. They walked down the main street and turned off by the alley that went past the Playboy Club. It was Crandell's first time beyond the shops on the main drag, and he was fascinated by the place but still somewhat hesitant due to its wicked reputation.

As they walked back into the vill, shops and clubs gave way to a residential area. Here were rows of single-story buildings behind six-foot concrete walls. Many of the walls were toped with broken glass set into the concrete. After several twists and turns they stopped before a metal gate in one of the walls.

"Home sweet *hooche*," Farlin said, grinning. He pushed the gate open and shouted, "Hey, *yobo*, we're here."

Crandell followed him in. He found out later this was a typical Korean residence. Just inside was a small concrete courtyard with a water pump at one side. Two children who were playing with a dog stopped to look at them and giggled. Farlin waved at them, saying, "Mama-san's little *kimchee* burners."

The single-story, *L*-shaped building was made of concrete and had a tile roof. A narrow, roofed wooden porch raised several inches off the ground skirted the front of the structure. The place was divided into five one-room apartments, called *hooches*, GI slang derived from *uchi*, the Japanese word for house. The doors to the rooms were made of wood strips covered with heavy paper.

The family that managed the building lived on the small leg. Their unit included a large family room and a small cooking room. The wife was the hooch mama-san. The other rooms along the larger leg were rented to girls. Mama-san also provided them with other services if they wanted—cooking, laundry, loans—all at exorbitant prices.

In front of the door at the far end of the building, Crandell saw a small tin barbecue grill set up. A Korean girl stepped out of the open doorway from behind a plastic mat that acted like a screen door. Crandell could see she was around twenty, attractive, with medium-length dark hair. She was wearing a pair of red wool pants and an American long-sleeve athletic shirt that was too large for her. On the front it said, "CENTRAL HIGH, OMAHA."

"Hi, *yobo*," she said, smiling shyly. "This your friend?"

"Well, he's my pilot." Farlin grinned. "I let him fly my airplane. Cap'n Crandell, this is Miss Yee, my, ah, girl. Yee, this is Cap'n Crandell."

"*Anya hasha meeka*, Captain," she said, stepping out.

"Hello, nice to meet you, Miss Yee." Slightly embarrassed, he told Farlin, "I guess I shouldn't have worn a uniform."

"Aw, hell, Cap'n, we all understand. Officers are strange."

As Farlin spoke, Crandell noticed there was another

person standing inside the room. Miss Yee turned and said something in a quick burst of Korean. Another girl hesitantly stepped out.

Crandell was astonished. She was young, not really a girl but certainly not a woman yet. Outside of pictures he had never seen anyone so beautiful.

Miss Yee spoke: "Captain, this is my friend, Miss Kim."

"Oh." For a moment he could not get any words to come out. Then he realized he was staring. "I mean . . . *anya hasha meeka.*"

Her face was turned down, shyly, and when she looked at him, her eyes tilted up, wide and bright. Softly she said, "Hello, sir."

"No, please," he said quickly, "call me Paul."

"Hel-lo, Paul." The Korean's difficulty with certain letter combinations made it sound like "Prall." He loved it.

"She don't speak English so good yet, Cap'n," Farlin said, grinning. "She's a good girl, from Seoul. Ain't used to hanging around with nasty GIs. Hey, *yobo,* get us a couple of beers."

"None for me," Crandell said quickly. "I don't drink beer."

"Oh. Well, I got a little Jim Beam if—"

"Actually, I don't drink alcohol."

Farlin thought about that for a moment, then asked, "You a Mormon or something?"

"No, no. It's just a personal thing."

"Really? Well, how about a Coke?"

"Yes, please, that would be fine."

Farlin pulled two floor pillows from just inside the door and motioned for Crandell to join him in sitting down. When the drinks came, it was Miss Kim who brought them. A beer, a Coke, and two glasses on a small tin tray. She sat down on her knees and served with careful grace. First she opened the Coke, then offered a glass to Crandell. After he took it, she took the bottle in both hands and slowly poured Coke into his glass.

As she repeated the service with the beer, Farlin

said, "Two hands is the Korean way of showing respect."

"Thank you very much, Miss Kim," Crandell said. That seemed to embarrass her and she darted quickly back into the room to join her friend. Crandell took a drink, then said, "Mac, you say she is from Seoul. You mean she isn't . . . ah . . ."

"A business girl?" Crandell was familiar with the term *business girl,* the defanged term for bar girls. He had thought it strange until he found out that they had a union of sorts. The Korean government recognized the Business Women's Association, and the group had officers who officially represented the women who worked in bars and other aspects of the profession.

Farlin went on, "Kimmie there, she and Yee used to go to high school together in Seoul. Yee dropped out and worked in Seoul for a while. But a young girl without a good education can't make much money, so she came down here about a year ago and started working in the Playboy Club. We met maybe six months ago. She's real good to me."

"That's nice, but . . ."

"Yeah, I know. You really want ta know about Miss Kim. Well, she even went to college for a year, but she's been having some family problems. Her parents ain't poor or nothing, but they ain't rich either. Seems they been trying to marry her off to some older guy who is crazy about her. He's a lawyer or something. His family has big bucks. But she don't want to. Says he's too old an' she's too young to get married. So she's hiding out down here till she can figure out how to get out of it."

The two women had come out and were putting chicken on the grill. As Farlin talked, Crandell couldn't take his eyes off Miss Kim. She was aware of it, and from time to time she glanced at him, then quickly looked away.

He said, "She certainly is attractive."

"That's one way of putting it, Cap'n," Farlin said, grinning widely. "A'course, I usually just say she's fucking beautiful."

Farlin laughed at Crandell's shocked look. "Just playing, Cap'n. Yeah, she's good-looking, but she won't have nothing to do with GIs. I tried to introduce her to some friends of mine, good guys—a couple were even single—but she wasn't interested."

"That was it," Crandell told Hunter. "I was in love with her from that first time we met. She stayed on with Mac and Yee. I started going down to his hooch every time I wasn't on alert. We didn't do anything at first. Walked around the village—you know Paradise Lake?"

Hunter nodded. It was a man-made reservoir that had been turned into a run-down recreation area in the rice fields east of Chicol Village. "We used to walk over there a lot. Climb the hill and just talk. She didn't speak English well, not at first. But she'd studied it in school, and pretty soon we could communicate without any problem."

"Sounds nice," Hunter said. "Sweet, but still nice."

"Then a couple months later, somehow her mother found out where she was staying. I came down that evening after I got off and there was Mama crying and carrying on."

Hunter understood. Koreans didn't hide their emotions.

"Mama was sure that Kim was living a life of sin. She was trying hard to get her to go back to Seoul. Then something happened that really surprised me. Kim had always seemed so shy, so fragile, but I saw her stand up to her mother, eyeball to eyeball, spitting Korean and sounding like they were going to start throwing punches at any moment."

Hunter smiled. The Korean language was like that: very harsh sounds. When you saw two Koreans greeting each other on the street you would swear they were about to kill each other. Later, you'd find out they were just making small talk.

"I didn't understand them, but after a while Kim told me to go back to the base and come back the next day. I didn't want to go, but she said not to worry, that she wasn't going to leave. I hardly slept that night. Since I wasn't scheduled to fly the next day, I got away at noon and went to see her.''

''Was she there?''

''Oh yes. At first she acted as if nothing had happened. Finally she told me. She said that since her mother had accused her of having done something, she told her that she had—that we had. She said that I was her *yobo* and that we were going to find a place and live together.''

Hunter nodded. ''Ah, so.''

''Yeah. I was surprised; shocked actually. I suddenly realized that was exactly what I'd been wanting, but I hadn't been able to admit it, even to myself. Before I could say anything, she told me that I wasn't obligated, that if I didn't want to, she could always return to Seoul and marry the old man.''

''Let me guess which one you picked,'' Hunter said with a big grin. ''The old man, right?''

''Not hardly.''

They both laughed. Turning serious again, Crandell said, ''You know the saying about a day being the first day of the rest of your life?''

Hunter nodded.

''That was mine.''

Chapter 11

Hunter was walking. Without making a conscious decision he found himself heading in the direction of the Green Monster. The two-story building was so named because of the sickly shade of dull green paint covering the exterior. Located near the flight line, the building was the operations center for flying units. The offices there included the flight safety office.

Inside he discovered that the flight safety office, which had been on the first floor before, was now on the second. Nothing was so constant in the military as the shuffling of furniture and office space to give the appearance of managerial improvement.

He found the new location and entered. Battered gray metal desks and five-drawer filing cabinets bulging with official-looking papers were crammed into the small room. There were four officers in flight suits and two sergeants in green fatigues. Only a couple of them looked up as he entered. The others continued reading magazines, paperback books, and copies of *The Pacific Stars and Stripes*, the daily newspaper published in Japan for all U.S. military people in Asia.

He said, "Hi, I'm Mike Hunter. I'm the new guy."

A captain sat at the closest desk. A Korean-made nameplate, polished wood with brass inlaid letters, identified him as Jake Watney. Looking at Hunter, he said, "Hey, everybody, say hello to the new captain."

In unison the men in the room called out, "Hello, asshole."

Hunter smiled. "Cute. Working here is going to be fun."

A lieutenant colonel at a back desk stood up, walked

over, and stuck out his hand. As they shook, he said, "Sorry about that, but we're pretty relaxed around here."

"No problem. It's an old joke."

"Yeah. I understand you been here before. I'm Ed Colvin, what passes for a boss in this zoo. I don't—"

Suddenly one officer who was on the telephone, a captain, slammed down the phone's receiver and screamed, "Fucking worthless fucking telephone!"

Colvin turned to the captain. "Hey, Matt, take it easy."

"I been trying to get through to Kimpo operations for two goddamn hours." Kimpo was the U.S. air base outside of Seoul, which shared the runway with the Seoul airport. "It's easier to call Hawaii than it is to get through to Seoul."

"Matt, you know the phone system over here hasn't been improved since Truman relieved MacArthur," Colvin advised.

"That's it," the captain said loudly. "I don't care if the F-4s coming into Kimpo take out a Korean passenger jet, I'm not screwing with these phones anymore."

Shaking his head, Colvin turned back to Hunter. "That's Matt Zhalan, he's only been here a few weeks. He still hasn't adjusted."

"I remember," Hunter said. "I suppose you still can't call off-base."

"No. There's no interface with the Korean system. I guess they figure that cuts down on *yobo* calls." Shaking his head, Colvin said, "I don't understand why you were assigned here. We only have three officer slots—you make our fifth assigned."

Watney, the captain who had initiated the greeting, called out, "Hey, Ed, he can take my place. I wanna go back to the world."

Colvin responded, "Yeah sure, tell that to your *yobo*."

Watney looked shocked, *"Yobo?* What's a *yobo?* Besides, now that I got her a job on base I can get away clean."

"You call putting her to work at the enlisted dining hall getting away clean?" asked Zhalan.

"Better than the massage parlor," Watney answered.

Ignoring them, Colvin said, "Look, Hunter, things are sort of slow right now. This is Wednesday, and I know you gotta get squared away and all that. Take the next couple of days off to get that done, and come in Monday."

Hunter said, "I've got central in-processing Monday."

"Okay, make it Tuesday, or—"

Hunter held up his hand. "Sounds fair to me." He was not sure what he was going to do with the time, but after a glance around he decided not to protest. It was apparent that his absence wouldn't seriously affect the office's productive capability. As he left, he noticed one sergeant carefully folding a safety-warning notice into a paper airplane.

After leaving the building, Hunter set off walking. People at Osan did a lot of walking. The base was not a huge, sprawling place like Kadena or Clark in the Philippines. Most of the facilities were within a few blocks of each other. Because of the denseness, narrow streets, and limited parking space, command policy prohibited ownership of private vehicles without special permission. A large taxi fleet operated by the base exchange and a contract Korean bus service was available, but most of the time, people found it was just as convenient, and usually as quick, to walk. Also, he rationalized, it was healthier.

As he went along the street parallel to the flight line, he saw the BX massage parlor and smiled. He had discovered the place on his first trip here and had spent more than a few hours in there letting the magic fingers do the walking. The girls who worked in the place were well trained and, unlike places off-base, all they offered were straight massages.

Which was not always the case, according to a story he'd once heard. He wasn't sure it was true, but because it was a good story he liked to believe it. According to the tale, sometime back in the dark ages of the early post-Korean War era, when someone went to the massage parlor and asked for "the works," he got it. Until one day when a young, energetic chaplain new to the base, after a long hard day of saving souls, decided to get a massage. Unknowingly, the sweet thing who took him, thinking he was just another GI, gave him *the works*. The story didn't say whether his wrath rose before or after she touched certain parts of his body, but in short order the place was closed. For a long time. When it reopened, the new staff made sure they didn't rub anyone the wrong way.

Hunter continued down the street, enjoying memories of times gone by. Past the bowling alley and the building where Korean concessionaires offered local products. Looking at the things displayed in the window, he could see that they still offered handmade boots for twelve dollars; oil paintings, originals or copies of famous artworks, for ten to twenty dollars; and instant antique wood chests. Brass still seemed popular—bowls, candlesticks, lamps and so forth—which legend claimed were made from U.S. Army artillery shell casings. The brass vied for space with carved stone chess sets and tailor-made clothing.

Two men came out of the shop wearing lavishly embroidered nylon jackets. One had a multicolored dragon, the other carried the slogan: "When I die, send me to Heaven. Because after a year in Korea, I've served my time in Hell." Considering what went on in the village, Hunter felt that line was somewhat hypocritical.

The next building was the main base exchange store. More and more, he reflected, BXs were beginning to look like K-Marts back in the world. Next was the exchange cafeteria, a grease-burger and fried-chicken joint for those who got tired of the clubs. As he continued walking he became aware of a vehicle moving slowly along the street just behind him. He turned to see if it was someone he knew, and saw it was a security police jeep with two Air Force cops inside. As soon as he looked in their direction, the jeep increased its speed and went past him. It continued until it came to an empty parking spot about twenty yards down the street, where it pulled in and parked.

When Hunter was only a few steps from where it had stopped, the man on the passenger's side got out and stood beside the vehicle, not really seeming to look at him, just scrutinizing the people on the sidewalk. He was big-chested with broad shoulders and long arms. He was wearing all the usual cop accessories: black leather belt, holstered gun, and badge. He had eight stripes on the sleeve of his fatigue uniform— a chief master sergeant, the top rank in the enlisted heap. He was also a black man—not a deep, shiny black, but more of rich mocha. His face was strong, solid, stoic, giving nothing away.

The one who stayed in the jeep was also a large cop, white with light-colored hair showing beneath his white police hat. He had senior master sergeant stripes on his arm, one rank below his partner. Two high-powered NCOs. Neither seemed to pay overt attention to Hunter, but he experienced the unsettling feeling that he was the object of their interest.

Hey, Captain Paranoid, his inner voice protested, *those pills are turning you into a raving loon. What the hell would they want with you?*

Yet even after he passed the two men and turned the corner by the base library, he couldn't shake the feeling of having been under observation.

Chapter 12

After the nonencounter with the two security police NCOs, Hunter walked on, up the hill on the street that eventually led to the main gate. He went past the large recreation-services building, Ping-Pong and pool tables and another snack bar with more hot dogs, hamburgers, and Cokes—white American soul food.

The next building was the headquarters. It was not really a single building, but a complex of more than fifty interconnected Korean War-vintage Quonset huts. This complex, one of the oldest structures on the base, housed most of the administrative offices including the information office, where Ron Shaw worked, and the office of the base commander, the man Crandell had said he was going to see after he finished writing his letter to Hunter.

He entered the building and walked down the long, dark hall. The old plywood floor undulated beneath his feet, spongy after years of rot. The place was a firetrap, and he was amazed it had not burned down long before. After a couple of wrong turns in the maze of dark, dank corridors he finally located the office he was seeking. Entering, he found himself in a different world. Walls paneled with imitation wood, a thick carpet, and new wood desks rather than the standard gray metal ones—and this was only the outer office, occupied by a portly senior sergeant and a thirtyish Korean secretary. The woman was dressed in a manner calculated to downplay the fact that she was quite attractive.

After entering, Hunter stood for more than a minute waiting for either of the two to acknowledge his presence. Neither looked up. The master sergeant continued to shuffle through a pile of papers in front of him and the secretary typed. He decided, from the secretary's attitude of unconcern, that it was a good bet either the sergeant or the commander was screwing her.

By the time the NCO got around to noticing him, Hunter was annoyed. In a tone of voice that said he really did not like to be bothered with unimportant things, the sergeant said, "Kin I help you, Cap'n?"

Another good ol' southern boy. The military was full of them. "Yes, you can. I'd like to see the base commander."

"Well, Cap'n, what's it about?"

"It's personal, and confidential, Sergeant."

"Ah, the colonel is pretty busy. If you can gimme some idea what—"

At that point Hunter had exhausted his quota of suffering petty bureaucrats. "Look, Sergeant, I know this is Osan, and I know that a lot of people around here think they aren't in the real Air Force, but if I wanted to discuss what I have to say with you, I would have said so. But I don't." He paused for a moment to let his words sink in. He didn't want to overload the NCO's obviously limited brain circuits. "Now, I would appreciate it if you'd hoist your backside out of that chair and tell the commander that there is a captain out here who wants to talk to him."

Hunter didn't play officer often, but when he did the hard look on his face and the whip crack in his voice was calculated to get the point across.

Ah yes, the old make-friends-and-influence-people routine, his voice sassed.

The sergeant jumped to his feet as if bit by something nasty. The secretary paused in her typing long enough to sneak a look at Hunter. Then, not used to having his gatekeeper function challenged, he started to protest, "Look, Cap'n, I'm only trying to do my job. No reason for you to get—"

"In that case," Hunter interrupted, "stop trying and just do it, Sergeant."

The NCO looked as if he didn't know whether to bellow angrily or break down and cry. After thinking it over, he turned and went through the door to the inner office. Hunter caught the secretary looking at him again. He flashed her a knowing leer which sent her eyes scurrying back to her typewriter.

After several minutes the sergeant returned, face all composed, voice coldly impersonal. He said Colonel Davies would see him. Hunter walked past him into the inner office. He had the feeling the sergeant would probably end the day at the NCO club crying in his beer and telling his fellow sergeants what shits officers were.

The base commander's office was even nicer than the outer office: more dark wood paneling, even thicker carpeting, and executive furniture. The man behind the desk, Colonel Al Davies, according to his brass and wood nameplate, certainly looked the part. Slim, blond, sparkling blue eyes in a ruggedly handsome face, and a nice tan that looked like the product of long hours on the base golf course. He could easily have been the winner in a Steve Canyon look-alike contest. Then Hunter remembered something Ron Shaw had said earlier: "Davies reminds me of what they used to say about an old-time politician from Nebraska—he's got a personality like the Platt River: a mile wide and one inch deep."

Davies stood up, displaying a sincere smile that for some reason Hunter didn't believe for a second. He extended his hand. "Captain, I don't think I have seen you around before."

Shaking the outstretched hand, Hunter said he had just arrived. He half expected the colonel to say something about the encounter with the sergeant, since he was sure from the amount of time the NCO had been in there he had told in vivid detail what had happened in the outer office. Davies, however, didn't mention it. Yet something about the man gave Hunter the feeling that after he left, the colonel would tell the sergeant how he really chewed the smart aleck captain's ass.

"What can I do for you, Captain, ah . . ." The colonel, seeming not to recall the name, blinked and looked down at the visitor's nameplate on Hunter's uniform.

"Hunter," he supplied. "A friend of mine was in an accident here a few months ago. I heard about it secondhand and I'd like to know more about it."

"I'm the big daddy rabbit around here," Davies said, getting a little more candlepower out of his smile. "I'll help you if I can. What was his name?"

"Paul Crandell."

"Ah, yes." He paused, seemed to be remembering. "In fact, didn't you write to me about that?" Apparently he didn't forget everything.

"Yes."

"I don't know what I can add to that letter. I remember the incident," he said slowly. "I—"

"It wasn't an incident, Colonel," Hunter cut in. "It was the death of a United States Air Force officer who also happened to be a combat crew member."

"Yes, of course, that's what I meant." Davies quickly turned his face into the perfect picture of sympathy, but for a fraction of a second Hunter was sure he had seen something else. Surprise, or maybe dismay. At least he thought he'd seen it, but the man was quick.

Cranking up his compassion, Davies said, "Every death at this base is important to me, Captain Hunter. But your friend wasn't actually assigned here. He was on leave, which was rather unusual in itself."

He seemed to imply that in some way it lessened his responsibility. Hunter wasn't about to buy that. "It's all the same Air Force, Colonel."

"Yes, of course it is. And we did all we could, but really I'm afraid there wasn't much we could do. The first we knew was when his body was discovered. Apparently he was down in the village drinking. He had too much. On his way back he somehow fell or slipped into a small stream that runs through the village. There were no witnesses. A Korean found him and reported it. We recovered the body and tried to find out what happened, but . . .'' He shrugged and waited for Hunter to say something.

Hunter let him wait. There was something strange going on here. They were the same words. Almost. He wondered if someone had typed up a script and passed out copies for everyone to memorize. Finally, Davies added, ''That's all there was to it. Just an accident.''

''He didn't come in to talk to you prior to that?''

This time Davies let the surprise show. ''What? Why, no. Why do you ask?''

''Nothing,'' Hunter said evenly. ''I just wondered if he had paid a courtesy call.''

''No, no.''

''There is one thing that bothers me, Colonel.''

''What's that?''

''Crandell didn't drink,'' Davies blinked. ''Not ever.''

The colonel shrugged. ''Who knows? Maybe it was that girl. That sort of problem could make a man, even a man who didn't drink, do something—''

Hunter leaned forward quickly. ''Girl? You mean his fiancée? I thought no one knew anything about her.''

The colonel blinked again. He looked as if he had swallowed one of his golf balls. After a moment he said, ''Well, there was a story about a girl. I think I heard it from my security police. Some gossip they picked up. I heard he planned to marry a woman from the village, but apparently when he got back she was gone with someone else . . . something like that. You know how those girls in the village are.''

''Yes, Colonel, I know about those village girls,'' Hunter said, his voice heavy with sarcasm, ''unlike those who work here on the base, who are all untouched by American hands.''

Davies' expression got a bit bleaker. ''I didn't mean to stereotype, it's just that, well—''

Hunter smiled affably, then said, ''That doesn't change the fact that Paul Crandell did not drink.''

By now Davies had his composure back. The re-

mark didn't faze him. He was a professional bureaucrat who had learned early in his career to play it as it
lay, without giving away too many strokes—a primary
ingredient for success as a senior officer. "Who
knows? People do unusual things in times of stress.
That's really all I can tell you. I'm sure there's nothing
to indicate that Captain Crandell's death was anything
other than an unfortunate accident."

He had his sincere look turned up to full power.
Trust me, his face begged. I hear you, Hunter thought
as he looked into those crisp blue eyes, but I don't
believe a fucking word. Standing, he said, "Thank
you for your time, sir."

As he went out, he kept his face impassive, but inside he was seething. Outside in the hall he paused
and took a deep breath. Calm down, he told himself.
After all, there was always the chance that Davies actually believed the odious crap he was passing out. Or
wanted to believe it.

The conversation had only made Hunter feel more
strongly than ever that there was more to Paul's death
than the pat story everyone was telling. All the way
from San Antonio to Osan he'd had to contend with
the idea that he was on a fool's quest, a victim of an
overly active imagination. But now there were just too
many people who reacted strangely when Crandell's
name was mentioned. Something wasn't right.

But what? And why? Maybe Crandell had been assaulted and robbed by a Korean, and the officials didn't
want to deal with the bad press which might result. Or
possibly he had been killed by a GI in a fight. It was
known to happen. If it was something like that, it was
possible that everyone decided to take the easy way
out and call it an accident.

Or did it go deeper? Chicol Village could be a pretty
bizarre place. Strange things had happened down there
over the years—although they were usually isolated incidents. For the most part the vill was safer than the
average city in the States. It had its faults, but it wore
most of those faults with an air of proud dishonesty.
The town had been created to sell pleasure, to anes-

thetize the Americans stationed there from a year of pathetic drabness in a country which, immediately after their war, had little to offer but its spirit and its women.

It was a way of accommodating the large foreign garrison needed to ward off their more dogmatic brothers to the north. And to make some sorely needed hard cash. Over the years this arrangement had succeeded beyond the wildest expectations of those who had created it back in Korea's stone age, the postwar era of the mid-fifties. Now, through the investment of the money earned by its women, and years of hard work, the country was on the verge of an economic boom.

A side benefit that cemented the country firmly to the United States was that American soldiers found Korean woman to be not only exotic but irresistible. They had married them in large numbers and brought them home. And while some marriages ended in divorce, the women stayed in the United States, became citizens, and were responsible for sponsoring the second wave of Korean immigrants: mothers, fathers, brothers, and sisters.

Still, Chicol Village continued with few pretenses and little illusion. Like it or hate it, the village existed and thrived. The clubs got bigger, people prospered, but the main commodity was the same. It had been doing business in that way too long to be contrite or hypocritical. Now Hunter sensed a new element. Someone was using the village, taking advantage of the delicate balance of a system built on understandings about sex and money to achieve malevolent ends. And he didn't like it. The vill deserved better, people who loved it or hated it for its own delightful wickedness—not those who came to use and abuse it for their own evil intents.

CHAPTER 13

Leaving the headquarters building with his mind in a whirl over the meeting with Davies, Hunter started to cross the street and stepped off the curb—into the path of a large blue Air Force van. The driver, a base Korean, honked his horn and gave Hunter a dirty look. The American smiled a sheepish apology which the driver spurned with a disdainful expression as he drove off.

Back in his room, Hunter wished he had a dog so he could give the sucker a kick. As a consolation prize he got a beer from the small refrigerator and set to work hooking up his stereo system. He got the amp and speakers going first. AFKN was playing vintage Elvis, "Don't Be Cruel." Words to live by.

As he continued working on the rest of the components he remembered his last mission. It had been a blistering hot day in mid-April when Korat received a frag order directing a maximum effort against a target the pilots unaffectionately called Thud Buster Alley. The heavily defended complex of bridges with underground storage and maintenance facilities was tucked into a mountain valley on the Laotian–Vietnamese border and formed a major link in the Ho Chi Minh Trail. It had been on the list of restricted targets for several months because of the horrific number of U.S. aircraft which had been damaged or destroyed during previous raids.

Hunter and Crandell heard about the mission shortly after touching down at Korat after an unsuccessful morning hunting SAMs along the trail in Cambodia. Hunter had big plans for the rest of that day. It was to be the end of a long quest. The object of the campaign was a club waitress who had been a former Miss Thailand runner-up. She had worked at the club for more than two years, since she was barely nineteen, and was considered by most of the American officers to be the most beautiful waitress working at any officers' club in Southeast Asia. They had nicknamed her Peanuts, because, according to most, she was so eatable.

The evening was, for Hunter, the end of a long courtship—by GI–Thai standards. About a month earlier he had learned that Peanuts' current *teelock,* the Thai equivalent to *yobo,* would soon be rotating back to the States. The man, a married major in supply, had told Peanuts he was in the process of divorcing his wife so he could take her back to the States with him. He was lying and Hunter knew it.

Thereafter, Hunter spent hours at the club cultivating the beautiful girl—being a friend, without making any moves. As the truth that the lying major was lying slowly dawned on Peanuts, Hunter was there to provide a strong shoulder to cry on. Finally, just the day before, after a long, loud, tearful quarrel with the black-hearted major, she had packed her belongings and moved from his trailer back to the dorm shared by the single waitresses.

At breakfast that morning, before the mission, she accepted Hunter's invitation to go to Korat City that evening for dinner and dancing. As Hunter was jubilantly finishing his steak and eggs, she came back to the table he shared with Crandell. She looked him squarely in the eye and challenged, "You sure you really not married man?"

He reassured her he was indeed single, and turned to Crandell, trusted by all the waitresses because he was a straight arrow, for confirmation. After she grudgingly accepted his friend's reassurances, the two left for the mission briefing.

By the time they got to the briefing room two other pilots who had been at the next table had spread the word: "Hunter's got a date with Peanuts this evening!" As they took their seats, a major they'd often flown with stood up and said, "Hey, guys, everybody say congratulations to Hunter."

"Congratulations, asshole!" sang out the assembled group. The shameless grin on his face, however, seemed to take a lot of fun out of it for his compatriots.

Now that mission, Hunter's 168th, was history. As they climbed from their aircraft, he was in a hurry to complete the post-flight debriefing. He planned to go jogging and then to head to the pool and lie in the sun. It was his way of preparing for what he anticipated was to a most memorable evening.

Wonderful, wonderful.

He climbed out of the cockpit and hit the concrete and was met by the accusing eyes of the enlisted crew chief, a young, under-motivated sergeant from a hot little town southwest of Fort Worth named Glen Rose. Looking at the unexpended missiles and rocket pods, the young man whined, "You didn't fire nothin'."

"Not a single round." Hunter was in too good a mood to let a maintenance grunt rattle him. "We couldn't find the bad guys."

"You could of leastways dumped this shit into the side of a mountain so I wouldn't of had ta bust my ass downloading it."

"C-H-I Dooie," said Crandell, filling out the maintenance forms. They finished the paperwork, noting problems for the maintenance crews, just as the blue pickup truck driven by Lieutenant Colonel Bartly drove up and screeched to a stop.

Wearing a shit-eating grin, Black Bart called out, "Come on, you two, you don't want to be late for the briefing."

"Briefing?" Hunter howled in an anguished voice. "We're not on the schedule for another mission today." He turned to Crandell, imploring, "We're going to the pool. We already did our duty for God, motherhood, and the American way, right?"

"You weren't on the schedule," said Bart, still grinning. "But it's been changed. Now you are."

"Aw come on, Dad, let the other kids do it. We

already had our fun for today." Hunter's voice had taken on a whining tone. "Besides, I got a date, I got to rest, and—"

"I know, I know," Bart answered patronizingly. "I heard about your date. Shit, everyone heard; even the great mission shakers in the White House War Room. And you know what, Hunter? They sent you a present. Everything in-country is going against Thud Buster Alley."

"No-o-o thanks," Hunter said, backing away from the pickup. "I can't make that party. I already been. I had two birds shot full of holes hitting that ball breaker in sixty-seven."

Looking annoyed, Bart said, "Whenever you're ready."

Dragging his feet, Hunter followed Crandell into the pickup. As the vehicle pulled away, their crew chief called out, "Don't feel so bad, guys. At least I don't have to download this pig."

"You're very unfucking welcome," muttered Hunter.

A wheezing air conditioner was doing little to cut the heat, humidity, or sweat in the crowded room when they arrived. The briefing officer didn't have much to cheer the flyers. He opened with some hazy, unclear recon photos saying, "We know they've been building up the defenses since the last time you went in. You can expect the heaviest antiair and SAM concentrations this side of the Red River."

A ripple of tension rolled around the room. Most of the men had been up against this target before. "You'll be getting a lot of help," the briefer continued. "Tahkli will be putting up all their Thuds as part of the joint strike force. There will be Phantoms from Udorn and Ubon flying both strike and MiG-Cap. Tankers from U-Tapo and from Kadena will be on three sides of you to keep anyone from running out of fuel. B-52s from Guam will go through and soften up the area just prior to the strike."

One fighter pilot called out, "You mean the monkey killers are gonna get that close to SAMs." The disparaging term was the fighter pilots' unkind reference to B-52 crews and their habit of raining down tons of bombs on sections of the dense jungle from the safety of high altitudes.

"Very high, one pass," the briefer answered. "Mission planners estimate that the strike will take out twenty to fifty percent of the defensive weapons."

"Is that the same guy who estimated that the war would be over by last Christmas?" called out another pilot.

The briefer's face got tighter as he plowed forward with specific mission details. After the B-52s, the Wild Weasels were next into the target area, to find and hopefully kill remaining SAM and assorted weaponry.

Hunter and Crandell led the first four-ship flight. Their wing man was a single-seat Thud with iron bombs and CBUs. Three and four were in the same configuration. "Oh, by the way," the briefer grinned at Hunter as he spoke, "your flight has been assigned a special call sign for this mission. It's Peanuts."

A collective hoot echoed throughout the room. Hunter could think of only one appropriate response. He stood, turned his back, and pretended to drop his pants, an action not possible in a flight suit. After the noise level in the room decreased, the briefer got back to business. He indicated a green patch on the northern end of the target. "There are an estimated three to five active SAM sites here, in addition to the usual antiair stuff."

"Beautiful," moaned Hunter, "just fucking beautiful." Crandell shushed him.

When the briefing ended, they started back to the flight line, but at Hunter's urging, stopped by the snack bar. He got a ham and cheese sandwich, which was cold, and a beer, which was warm. Their wing man, a new lieutenant who had only half a dozen missions under his belt, asked, "How can he eat that shit before a big one like this?"

"He's got security," Crandell said, working on a cup of black coffee. "He knows only the good die young.'' The look the lieutenant gave Crandell suggested that Hunter wasn't the only one who was crazy.

On the flight line, the crew chief handed over the aircraft forms. Only two of the six maintenance problems they had noted had been fixed. Shrugging, the crew chief said, "We didn't have much time. With all this shit, maintenance control is only sending specialists out on safety-of-flight write-ups."

"Beautiful," Hunter sighed, "just . . . ah, to hell with it. We got a ragged engine, spongy hydraulics, bum communications, and a half-dozen blown circuit breakers, but as long as this pig can crawl into the air, tally-fucking-ho!''

"*C-H-I Dooie,*'' grunted the crew chief.

Crossing into North Vietnam, they flew through a mild rain front, but as they neared the target the weather cleared. While refueling on the outer edge of the target area, they listened to the voices of the B-52s crews who were doing their best to blow the bottom out of Thud Buster Alley. As the last of the big bombers cleared the area, their flight came sweeping in at mountaintop-hugging altitude.

The complex was deep in a narrow valley surrounded by high, jagged green cliffs. The only way to get at the bridges was to fly down into the valley, which ran from southwest to northeast, search for the camouflaged structures, and slam them, while at the same time fighting to get the aircraft's nose up high enough to clear the jagged peaks at the other end of the valley.

To discourage behavior of this sort, the bad nasties put SAM sites in the dense jungle at each end of the valley floor and lined the mountain slopes with antiaircraft guns. North Vietnamese gunners knew where the attackers would come from and where they would have to go. In numerous past strikes that knowledge had proved to be deadly for many American pilots.

Seeing the ground fire blossom and burst around them as they neared the valley, Hunter knew the B-52 bombs had done little effective damage. There was a lot of dust and some smoke, but it appeared that the heavily fortified guns of Thud Buster Alley had once again withstood the best SAC had to offer.

Just minutes ahead of the strike force, it was now time for them to go to work. He dropped the nose of the Thud and pushed the throttle forward to full military power, reserving afterburner for the getaway. Jinking and rolling, they roared into the smoky, churning abyss. Though they were not really able to avoid the intense fire, the manuevers at least made the gunners' work more difficult.

Hunter depended on speed and agility, at first staying down low on the deck to make the SAMs useless, and he hoped to outrun the radar-controlled 85mm guns. According to intelligence, those guns had recently been modified so that flak patterns automatically adjusted to a target's speed, altitude, and heading.

In the backseat, Crandell operated his computerized electronic systems in his usual quiet, intense manner. Moments after starting the attack he said, "Tracking two active sites."

He announced headings and locked on the fire-control systems just as a close explosion buffeted their aircraft. Hunter fought for control and they continued undamaged. He lined up on the first site, flipping switches which set the missiles for launch, and told the wing man to take his best shot at the second site.

A moment later the fire-control computer signaled lock-on and Hunter cut a Shrike loose. The Thud shuddered slightly as the missile streaked straight and true into the green jungle. Seconds later there was an eruption of fire and flying earth, followed by a chain reaction of secondary explosions.

"Bingo!" crooned Hunter. He lit the afterburner and the big aircraft leaped upward, out of the valley.

Peanuts Two dumped bombs and CBUs on the second site. Behind them, Three and Four went after a gun concentration they spotted along the left slope.

"We got two," Crandell said.

"Fan-fucking-tastic!"

They continued through the maelstrom of arching tracers and angry puffballs of exploding fire and steel.

Twice their Thud was rocked by nearby explosions. Crandell identified a large gun position. Hunter nosed in and sprayed the site with Vulcan cannon fire. Then, just for good measure, and to lighten the load, he dumped the three five-hundred-pounders from their belly rack. As the iron bombs let go, Hunter hauled back on the stick and slammed in the afterburner.

Behind them Three and Four unloaded everything they had left into the same general area. As the Thuds thundered skyward, Crandell yelled, "We got the bastards for sure."

Hunter was too busy getting them out of there to answer. They heard the radio voices of the strike force as the main attack commenced. The highest peak at the end of the valley approached rapidly. Their aircraft was in a steep climb, clawing for altitude. Then Crandell yelled, "SAM launch!"

The best way to avoid a SAM was to head for the deck—posthaste. But they couldn't do that, they had to clear the peak first. "Come on, baby," Hunter implored, "just a few more seconds over the top and—"

A violent explosion burst left and forward of their Thud. A millisecond later Hunter's world exploded and he blacked out.

Reality rippled back moments later. But he was in another world. A world filled with the roar of wind, the stench of things burning, and intense pain. Part of his cockpit had been blown away and he was being whipped about by air rushing in. Smoke billowed up from somewhere down by his feet.

The Thud continued its forward motion far enough to get on the other side of the mountain peak, but it was now in a slow roll at a sick, contorted angle. Hunter tried to reach for the controls, but discovered his hands would not respond. Then he noticed the blood on his left arm, which magnified the pain he was feeling—searing, throbbing through his body.

Dimly he heard a voice in his headset. "Mayday! Mayday! Peanuts One! Mayday! We're going to eject. Fix on this position!"

"Roger, Lead. This is Three. Got you."

Ejection. Hunter's mind reeled: even for men in perfect shape ejecting from a Thud had proved to be a dangerous proposition. If you were not in the correct position you could be killed, or worse, seriously fucked up. *Stop that.* It was no time for jokes. Hunter exercised a tremendous force of will, forcing his unwilling, pain-racked body to assume the proper position; back straight, legs against the seat, arms tucked in . . .

He felt a tremendous jolt, as if he had fallen from a very high place and crashed to a stop. Then he was falling again. It was all very confusing, tumbling about as unconsciousness enveloped him.

When awareness returned, he was plummeting through the sky. He rolled his head back, saw a large white canopy of silk above. The sight of the parachute brought it all back, along with the pain. He looked down. The green jungle was rising up at him. His head throbbed. His left side burned. He couldn't feel his legs.

You're in deep kimchee, *Mike ol' buddy,* his voice consoled.

He tried to reach the chute risers, but his arms were too heavy. The green jungle was getting close now. He was able to get his right arm up in time to protect his face as he plunged into the thick treetops. He crashed through the triple-layered forest canopy, branches tearing at him as he went down. The blackness threatened to take him back. He fought it. The heavy foliage caught at the chute canopy and slowed his fall.

Still, when he hit the ground, a knee-jarring jolt wrenched through his body. He fell forward, his head slammed into the ground, and he passed out.

Chapter 14

The world returned slowly. He felt the cool, moist earth against his face. A high-pitched scream filled his head. And he hurt. Bad. At first he tried to reject the sensations, to go back into the darkness where there was no pain. But the world insisted on being acknowledged.

A memory played back in his head. The explosion. Ejection. Parachuting into the jungle. He was amazed to be alive. Many uninjured pilots who had ejected from Thuds had not survived the experience. Yet here he was, ripped fore and aft, but alive and on the ground.

Yeah, on the ground. In Charlie's backyard. That was bad. Very bad. Fucking terrible to be exact.

Do something, he commanded himself. Sure, but what? And how?

Try moving, Captain Shitbrain, his voice suggested.

Easy to say. His whole left side seemed to be nonfunctional. Nonfunctional. That had a nice military sound to it. Much better than all fucked up.

He discovered that by concentrating, he could move his right arm. Then his head. He was still in his parachute harness. He looked up. Oh, shit! His parachute was caught in the trees. Like a huge white finger pointing directly at him. It would take the zipperheads about five seconds to find him if they were anywhere nearby.

Enduring a ripple of pain, he moved his right hand ever so slowly. After what seemed like an eternity, he managed to fumble open the quick disconnects, releasing himself from the chute harness. He rolled away, onto his back. Damn, that hurt. Every movement caused spasms of intense pain.

Rescue.

Even amid his torment and confusion that thought raced through his mind. The most important element in a successful rescue was a radio. He had two, one in his survival vest and one in his chute pack. The chute radio was automatically activated on bailout, sending out a transponder signal for the rescue force to follow. And to the dinks who had captured U.S. radios.

He should shut it off, but considering his condition there was no way he could get to it. So forget it. Hope the good guys get here first. Speaking of the good guys, where the hell were they? He concentrated on getting the second radio out of his vest. It took a lot of trying, but finally he dug it out and switched it on.

"Whoop! Whoop! Whoop!"

The automatic channel was going strong. He searched the sky for planes. Nothing. Had they copied Crandell's Mayday? Hell, they must have. Still, where were they? And where was Crandell? He ought to be nearby. Assuming he'd survived the bailout. What if he had—no, no, don't even think it. He had to be around somewhere. He switched over to the voice channel.

". . . we got a good fix on your bailout position," he heard a voice say. "Stay cool. The rescue force should be in the area in approximately nineteen minutes."

All right.

Another voice, Crandell's, said, "Roger. I'm okay, but I don't know what happened to my frontseater. The SAM went off in his face. I haven't been able to make contact since I got on the ground."

Good ol' Paul, hanging in there.

"Understand. Sit tight. Rescue will be there shortly. Over."

"Roger, over." Then, "Mike, do you hear me? Damn it, turn on your radio."

"It's on."

"Mike, is that you?"

"I don't see John Wayne around anywhere, so I guess it's me."

"Thank God. I thought you were . . . ah, are you okay?"

"Not exactly. I'm . . . wounded." What a trivial, impersonal little word. A word that did not begin to illustrate the agonizing intensity of the pain which racked his body.

"Hold on. Rescue got a good fix on our position and they're on the way, over."

"That's nice. over."

"Maybe I can find you. Can you tell me anything that would help pinpoint your location?"

"I'm not sure. I think I'm about three hundred meters below the mountaintop. My chute's hung up in a tall tree. You should be able to see it if you get close."

"Okay, that helps. I think you're above me. I'm going to start moving. Keep your radio on, keep talking."

"Sure, buddy." As long as he was talking, he wasn't dying.

"Keep your eyes open for Charlie, he'll be looking for us."

"That's a cheery thought." As Hunter spoke, he was assaulted by another wave of pain. When it passed, he put the radio handset down and struggled to reach his gun. He was glad the big Browning was on his right side, for his left arm was still numb and unresponsive. After an agonizing effort he was able to unfasten the holster and remove the big handgun.

Then he was confronted by a problem he hadn't anticipated. One reason he had chosen the big 9mm weapon was because it had a thirteen-round clip rather than the six in the pistols the Air Force passed out. But it was an automatic. To chamber the first round the slide had to be jacked back. He always did that with two hands, one to hold the weapon and one to push the slide back. Now he didn't have two hands.

He tried pushing the gun against his left hand, but gave up when he discovered that he could not exert enough force with the dead fingers. He tried using his teeth, but he couldn't bite down on the metal hard enough to hold it. Finally he jammed the gun between his knees and after several tries got the slide back enough to chamber the first round. However, the pain and exertion sent his head spinning and he passed out. He slumped forward, hunched over so that his body covered the gun in his right hand.

The next thing he was aware of was a voice.

Paul?

Then he realized the voice, a loud whisper, was not speaking English. Unfortunately, the words sounded like Vietnamese. A jolt of fear shot through him. He tried to hug the ground. Maybe they wouldn't see him.

He felt a sharp object prodding his back. His first reaction was panic. "No. Please, God, no!"

A hand gripped his shoulder and tugged. Then Hunter got mad. He was cold and hurting, but also overwhelmed by a fierce rage, fed by his long-held conviction that death was preferable to capture by this enemy who observed none of the conventions of civilized nations toward prisoners of war.

The hand pulled, rolling him onto his back. He stared up into the mysterious face of Asia. Black eyes behind narrow lids looked back into his. The eyes moved down, until they saw the gun in his hand. That was the last thing in this world they saw.

The Browning roared three times. The green-uniformed Vietnamese jerked up and back, spinning, and fell. It was then that Hunter saw the other two. They were standing about ten feet away. Raising their rifles. Aiming at him.

Then a rapid succession of loud cracks.

He expected to feel the pain, sense the bullets tear into him. Instead the two Vietnamese soldiers lurched and fell to the ground. The loud whine in his head intensified. He could not comprehend what had happened. Was this some sort of twisted game?

"Mike, are you all right?"

Paul Crandell stepped out from behind a large tree

in back of the Vietnamese. His .38 was in his hand. In spite of the pain, Hunter smiled.

After Crandell checked the three downed Viets to make sure they were out of the game permanently, he hurried to Hunter.

"Hey, guy, you don't look so good."

"Easy for you to say." The words came out in a weak croak. Nodding to the dead Vietnamese, he said, "How'd you manage that?"

Crandell grinned, looking mature and confident. "Survival school. I paid attention."

Hunter wanted to say, "That's nice," but passed out instead.

When he regained consciousness the first thing he noticed was a roaring sound and wind whipping the trees around him. Then he realized he was being jostled around. Crandell was next to him, struggling to put something under his arms and cinch it tight about his chest.

"What are—" he started to say. Before he could get the words out he was jerked up off the ground, through the tall trees, into the sky. He rolled his head back and looked up. It took several moments before he realized the large black shape looming above him was a hovering Jolly Green Giant rescue helicopter. As he hung on the end of a steel cable and watched, it seemed to get nearer and nearer.

Off to his left he heard the angry buzz of an aircraft engine and the hammering of machine guns. A propeller-driven A1E Sandy was diving into the jungle, guns blazing, to discourage any Vietnamese troops in the area.

He looked up again. Now he could see the large open hatch in the side of the chopper as it got closer. Two sets of arms reached out and dragged him into the hovering machine. They were the arms of two young enlisted men in sweat-stained flight suits, members of the elite Air Force para-rescue corps. Unlike the pilots, these men were more representative of the young men, kids really, who were doing most of the dirty jobs and most of the dying in this war.

They got him into the chopper and down on the floor. One man quickly removed the rescue harness, went back to the open hatch, and dropped it out. The other began applying first aid, putting dressings on his wounds.

The pain hit again, and he couldn't stop moaning as the young man worked on him. Hunter saw him fill a hypodermic needle from a medicine vial. As the young airman flicked the needle into his arm, he said, "This'll make you feel better."

He was right. Hunter also discovered he could talk. "Crandell, is he okay?"

"Your bear?" Hunter nodded. "He's fine. He's coming up now."

"That's nice."

"You're lucky he was there," the young man said. Hunter tried to ask why, but the stuff in the hypo was working too well. The para-rescue man answered the unasked question. "If he hadn't got to you and guided us in, I don't think we would've found you."

Hunter tried to say, "That's nice" again, but the effort was too much. He lay quietly, his head whirling as the world slowly faded. He saw Crandell being pulled in, watched them talking, saw Crandell look at him with concern as the engines of the helicopter roared with increased power as the pilot put it into a steep climb.

Suddenly his body jerked convulsively. The para-rescue man at his side looked down with alarm and leaned closer as three words escaped from Hunter's lips just before he passed out.

The young man looked up at Crandell, surprise on his face. "I don't believe it."

"What's wrong?" Crandell asked.

"I think he's hungry."

"What?" Crandell asked, bewildered.

"He said, 'Peanuts. Oh, shit.' "

The chopper bay filled with Crandell's laughter, and the two youngsters looked at him as if he had gone mad.

Chapter 15

He showered, put on clean jeans and a short-sleeved shirt. It was time, he decided, to go to the vill. He considered calling Ron Shaw, but it was only a little after two and more than likely his friend would have difficulty getting away. Besides, this was something he felt he had to do alone, reacquainting himself with Chicol Village—a pilgrimage of sorts.

Taxi traffic on Osan's main street was heavy, but all the cabs were occupied. It was the time of day when Korean wives of Osan GIs made their runs between base shops and their black-market drops in the vill. Seeing the parade of gray taxis scurrying back and forth carrying the women and their bulging brown-paper shopping bags was reassuring.

A slight breeze kept the pleasant afternoon from being too warm. Leaves on the trees were a mixture of green, red, and golden brown. He decided to walk to the gate. The base, which was laid out roughly in the shape of a *T*, was situated on the side of a prominent hill. At the bottom of the hill was the street that formed the top of the *T*. This was the street with the base shops and recreation facilities which Hunter had passed earlier. Across from the shops were the runways and aircraft operations and maintenance facilities.

The street he was on now was the vertical leg of the *T*; it went up and over the hill to the main gate. On both sides of this street were many of the administrative offices and facilities such as the medical clinic, church, the officers' clubs, and the BOQs, including Hunter's, which was about a mile from the main gate.

Just beyond were more offices, NCO barracks, and the NCO club. It was a very compact base.

As he neared the top of the hill, he saw the Korean Army compound, home for a ROK antiaircraft unit with its silent guns pointing north. He continued walking over the hill and to the gate on the other side. Just inside the gate was a large blacktop area which served as a combination parking lot and bus stop. Beside the parking lot and next to the base fence were the security police headquarters and a checkpoint manned by both American and Korean security people.

Everyone entering or leaving the base had to show some sort of identification. For the Americans this was a quick flash of their military ID and SOFA cards. Koreans were subjected to a lot more hassle. According to rules dictated by their government, civilians were not allowed on any military base without a special pass. Bases with U.S. forces, however, had special rules. GIs were allowed to bring guests—most of whom were female—onto the base by signing for them at a temporary pass office run by a steely-eyed Korean woman who was a member of the Korean National Police. From early morning until just before midnight, this office was one of the busiest at Osan. After that all guests were supposed to be off base. Most of the Americans took their temporary or permanent *yobos* to the base for an American movie, bowling, or dinner and drinking at one of the clubs. Some guests ended up spending at least part of the evening in the barracks, especially those who had to come with senior NCOs and officers who had private rooms.

Hunter passed through the gate, showing his military ID card and one of his old SOFA cards to a bored young security cop who gave them only a perfunctory glance. Immediately beyond the gate was the town, officially Son Tan, although most knew it only as Chicol Village. The main street of the vill continued on down the hill, where it intersected the MSR, or Miliary Supply Route, an ancient two-lane, blacktop highway that ran from Seoul to the southern port city of Pusan.

Both sides of the main drag from the gate to the MSR were crowded with clubs, small hotels, souvenir shops, tailors, shoemakers, dressmakers, coffee shops, restaurants, and other commercial outlets. There had been a lot of building going on right after the *Pueblo* buildup, but most of that seemed to be finished. Few of the brick buildings were higher than two stories, and though none were older than twenty years, most looked as if they wouldn't survive a strong wind. The area nearest the gate was the high-rent district. Here the most prosperous shops clustered, making a pile of money catering to those Americans who left the base only long enough to buy bargains before darting back inside the confines of "Little America."

Among the largest shops in this section was Lee's Brass and Souvenirs. When Hunter had made his first trip to Korea, Lee Chun Wah had owned a small, shabby shop near the bottom of the hill. But Lee had the magic touch. He combined a likable personality with ambition and an aggressiveness that would have made a shark blush. He always sold his brass lamps and carved stone chess sets cheaper than the competition, and like most of the Koreans in the vill, Lee had several profitable sidelines. The first was changing GI MPC (Military Payment Script) that GIs were given instead of dollars, for *won,* Korean money. Most money changers offered only a few more *won* than the official rate, about three hundred to a dollar. Lee's rate was a few *won* higher than that.

His most profitable sideline, however, was the black market. For his GI friends, and friends of friends, who wanted to sell their Nikon cameras or Sony TVs, preferably straight off the BX shelf and still in the original box, unopened, Lee again offered a price a bit higher than other black marketeers.

Thus, through the time-honored mercantile tradition of low prices and high volume did Lee make so much money that he could move up the hill and open the biggest shop of its kind in town and make even more money. Hunter and Lee had met two years before. On his second TDY to Korea, he had a short relationship with a cashier at the base bank who was the niece of Lee's wife. Following the basic rule of keeping as much business as possible in the family, she took him to Lee's shop the first time they went off base. After she married a young sergeant and went to the States, Hunter and Lee remained friends and occasional drinking companions whenever he was at Osan.

Just beyond the gate, Hunter dodged a couple of ragged youngsters begging for coins and crossed the street to Lee's shop. Lee's wife, a round, moon-faced woman, was helping a customer. She did not seem surprised to see him. She was that way, eternal and unshakable, providing stability for Lee's frenzied ambition.

"Captain, how are you? When you come back Osan?"

"Two days ago."

"Cho sumneda," that is good, "my husband will be happy to see you again. You number one customer."

Although Hunter had not bought any brass since his first couple of trips, Lee's wife had never forgotten his big spending spree. On one of his pre-*Pueblo* TDYs to Korea, his commander's wife had tasked him, none too gently, to buy three thousand dollars worth of Korean brass. It was for the Kadena gift shop run by the Officers' Wives Club, of which she was vice president. Despite the woman's influence with her husband he would not have done it, except he knew profits earned by the shop helped support a variety of cultural and family activities at Kadena. He had given the entire three grand to Lee, who not only gave him a good deal on the brass, but worked out the details of getting it back to Okinawa. He had an arrangement with some Air Force cargo handlers who had their own sideline, making sure that excess cargo space on military aircraft did not go to waste.

"Is Lee around?"

"No, he go Seoul. Maybe come back tonight, I think."

He was hoping Lee could help him locate the man

who had processed Crandell's marriage paperwork, and through him, the elusive Miss Kim. These quasi-lawyers charged as much as the traffic would bear to unstick the red-tape obstructions put up by both governments to thwart the course of true love. Hunter thought Lee would be able to find the right man quicker than he could on his own.

"When will he be back?"

"Maybe eight."

He thanked her. Lee was probably up in Seoul doing business with his brother, a middle-ranking member of the Korean CIA, the government intelligence service which had been patterned and named after that of the United States. In an unguarded moment during a long session with Johnnie Walker Red, Lee had let it slip that his brother had a lot to do with his family's success. Most of the black-market items Lee got in Chicol went straight to his brother in Seoul, who sold them to stores there. Koreans were big on family ties, especially when it eliminated the chance of being bothered by the law.

On the street he decided his next stop should be the club where the best friend of Crandell's Miss Kim had worked. He knew he would not find her friend. In Thailand, Crandell had gotten a letter from Kim telling him that her friend had married her crew chief *yobo* and was going to the States. Still, there must be someone working there who knew her.

The place was the Playboy Club. There seemed to be a bit of magic in that name. Every Asian city that catered to GIs had at least one Playboy Club, although they seldom bore any resemblance to the real thing. This one was a medium-sized club typical of the village. Unlike GI villages in many other countries, Chicol didn't have dozens of small clubs. Instead there were about fifteen to twenty large establishments, including those in Papa Joe's Alley that catered to blacks.

Each of the large establishments had anywhere from a few hundred to a thousand girls "associated" with that club. That didn't mean they were paid to work there, for the Koreans had a unique system. For a girl without family or regular employment to stay in a GI village, she was required to be associated with a club, a sponsorship of sorts. She received no salary, but when she went out to meet a GI, she did it at that club. There was no set schedule, but it was understood that if she was not *yoboing,* she was to show up at that club to attract customers.

One of the things that made Korea such a sentimental favorite among GIs in Asia was that the system involved a minimum of hustle. The clubs didn't sell buy-me drinks, such as Vietnam's famous Saigon Tea or Japan's Ladies Drinks, those high-priced dabs of cola or tea where the cost was split between the club and the girls. Clubs in Korea sold only real drinks. In addition, the clubs did not cut into the girls' earnings. There was no bar-fine system such as in the Philippines, where you paid the club in order to take a girl out, so that the girl's livelihood depended upon a tip later. In Korea the girls made their own arrangements and kept all the proceeds from those arrangements.

The Playboy Club was off the main drag, down a narrow street beyond a Chinese restaurant he had frequented in the past, which served a superb chicken fried in a hot, spicy sauce. As he approached the Playboy Club he noticed that, like most of the clubs and businesses he had seen so far, it had grown since the last time he had been there. The one-story building had gained a second floor and an open-air rooftop lounge. Some glass and chrome around the entrance was also new. Inside, the main room had changed. The old iron tables and chairs with red plastic covers were familiar, but the long bar had been extended around one corner of the room.

He had never cared for this club. It was favored by younger GIs who liked heavy-metal music and funny-smelling cigarettes. Now, in the early afternoon, there were only a few customers, half a dozen girls and one duty mama-san. His arrival created only a mild stir of interest. Apparently they could tell he was not a serious spender. He walked to an empty section of the bar, near where the girls were gathered talking in Korean, and waited. After about a minute the girl behind the bar detached herself from the group and came over.

"You want drink?"

"OB." OB was the more popular of the two Korean brands of beer. While the label clearly stated that OB stood for Oriental Brewery, most GIs maintained it really meant "old *benjo* ditch."

The waitress nodded, opened an ice cooler, took out a bottle, returned, and placed it in front of him along with a tall paper cup. The paper cup was required by U.S. health regulations. When he first had come to Korea he thought it was a fine idea, until one late evening when he was stumbling around behind a club and saw an old woman squatted down next to the water pump washing a stack of paper cups with cold well water.

As she poured the beer into the cup, the waitress asked, "You Green Bean?" The expression, slang peculiar to Korea, meant a newcomer.

"I just got back."

"Stay Korea before?"

"During the *Pueblo* time."

"Oh, long time ago." Two and a half years really didn't seem that long ago to Hunter. "I only stay this place couple months," she said.

It might have been true, but then again it might have not. He had discovered long ago that "Only stay two months" was the standard answer to "How long has a nice girl like you been doing this sort of thing?"

"You have *yobo?*" she asked.

Maybe this was going to be easy. "Yes, before. I'm trying to find her again. She had a friend who worked at this club, and she came here sometimes."

"What she name?"

"Kim."

The girl laughed. "Many Miss Kims."

"Yeah, but this Miss Kim is about twenty years old, tall, very slender, and her first name is Soon Ja."

"Kim Soon Ja." Her eyeballs almost clicked into place when she said the name. She looked down at the bar, wiping a wet spot, then she slowly said, "I don't know. I think maybe she no stay now. Maybe go away.''

"Maybe go away," he repeated slowly. It wasn't going to be easy after all. "Would you ask mama-san to come over here?''

The girl moved down the bar, glancing back at him several times. When she got to the group she spoke to the others in Korean. Whatever she said, it caused everyone there to stop talking and turn to stare at him. He got that feeling again. The look on their faces was the same look everyone got each time he mentioned Crandell's name.

Trying not to show what he was thinking, he took a drink of his beer. OB was a bit thin for taste buds accustomed to American beers. Still, when he was off base in Korea, he always drank OB. A nod, he felt, to cross-culturalization.

It takes more than sampling the beer and the women to get to know another country, Captain Kimchee Breath, his inner voice said scornfully.

While he was dealing with that internal conflict, the older Korean woman moved away from the group and walked slowly over to where he stood. She was wearing a traditional Korean dress with a short, boat-shaped blouse and a full-length skirt that almost touched the floor. She was somewhere between thirty and fifty, with a substantial figure and a wide, flat face that let you know it knew the score but that if you wanted to know, you were going to have to find out for yourself.

"May I help you?" Her words came out easily, hardly any accent: she was comfortable with the language.

"I recognize you from before." Hunter said, trying to look boyishly innocent. "You've been here a long time." He'd never seen her before.

"Ah, yes, I work here long time."

"I'm looking for a girl I used to know. Actually, I didn't go with her, my friend did. I was hoping to see her."

"Did she work this place?''

"No, she didn't work at any club. But her best friend worked here and she used to come here a lot."

The woman's face remained polite but impassive. "So many girls, it would be hard to—"

"Her name was Miss Kim, Kim Soon Ja."

"Many Miss Kim Soon Ja."

"That's true, mama-san," he said, still smiling as he reached into his shirt pocket and pulled out the close-up picture of the girl he had obtained from Fred Reyes. He put it on the bar in front of her. "But there is only one Miss Kim Soon Ja that looks like this."

That knocked a chip out of her stone face. "Ummm. Yes, I think she used to come here."

"No shit, mama-san." His frustration was rising.

She reacted strongly to his words. "Why you talk bad?" She had apparently decided the best defense was to take offense at his language. "All time GIs talk bad, all time makee trouble—"

"Enough." Hunter banged the bar with his hand. It made a loud sound. And it hurt like hell. He knew he was losing his cool, but he was beyond caring. Putting as much menace into his words as he could muster, he demanded, "Tell me where she is."

The woman shrank back, "She go. I not know where. Why. . ?"

He picked up the picture, pushed past her, and went over to the younger girls, who were watching wide-eyed. Slapping the picture down for them to see, he reached into his pocket, pulled out his money clip, detached a twenty dollar MPC note, and placed it next to the picture. That got their attention. The money was about a month's pay for the average Korean and more than a couple of good nights' earnings for most of the bar girls.

"That's for anyone who can tell me where I can find Kim Soon Ja."

Several of the girls looked interested, but the mama-san hustled over and spewed out a quick burst of Korean. All the girls started shaking their heads from side to side. Hunter's anger boiled up. He turned, grabbed the older woman by her arm, and pulled her close.

"I want to know where she is and I want to know right now."

"*Ah po!* That hurts," she howled. "Not know. Nobody know. Why you hurt me? She no stay this place."

Seeing the startled look on the faces of the girls and the hurt but stubborn look in the older woman's eyes, he realized that the ugly American act wasn't working. He let go of the woman's arm, scooped up his money and the picture, and left.

He tramped up the narrow street, pausing when he reached the main drag. He forced himself to relax, mentally shifting gears as the life in the village flowed around him. A base taxi screeched to a stop at the narrow street's entrance. Three GIs in stained, dusty fatigues piled out. They were young, full of life and randy energy. Each carried a case of American beer and a case of soft drinks. Hunter knew they were on their way to their hooches. The two cases of drinks which had cost them about four dollars would be sold by their *yobos* for nine dollars, and the profit would almost cover the cost of the evening's entertainment.

As he watched them he wished his life could be that innocent again.

Chapter 16

What next? he wondered. So far he had failed to make much of an impression on Chicol Village. He noticed a girl coming up the alley. She seemed to be checking him out. Hell, everybody seemed to be looking at him these days. Late twenties, attractive in a wholesome way, five-two or -three with a trim figure. She seemed vaguely familiar, but half the Korean women he'd seen seemed vaguely familiar, which was, he decided, wishful thinking. Then he realized she was one of the girls who'd been in the Playboy Club.

She stopped a few paces from him, still looking directly at his face. He trotted out his best friendly smile and said, "You looking for me?"

Slowly she said, *"Na."* Yes. "Maybe. I think I know you. You officer. Used to have *yobo* at Five Spot club?"

That surprised him. The Five Spot was a big club located on the MSR. On Hunter's Green Bean tour it had been the club where he had selected his first Korean girl. On a later visit it was where he had met one of the most sexually athletic and mercenary women he'd ever known.

"That's right, but how did you—"

"No talk here," she said quickly. "Too many people see. You come with me, *na?"*

"Why not?" After all, she didn't look too dangerous. She turned and took off at a brisk clip up the hill. When they were halfway back to the gate, she turned into a narrow path between two buildings that led to an area of residences. Most were the traditional *L*-shaped brick buildings behind concrete walls.

After a few twists and turns she stopped in front of one and used a key to open the gate. She motioned for him to follow and stepped in. It was a better-than-average compound, fairly new construction, concrete that was clean and uncracked. The wooden porch that skirted the front of the building even had some paint on it. There were five individual rooms in the building.

Three small children played in the courtyard with a miniature soccer ball. When he entered they stopped playing and stared at him. He smiled and waved. The two older ones just continued to look, but the youngest quickly put up a hand to cover a grin.

He followed the girl to the room on the end. That was a positive sign, since it was usually the largest room and cost a bit more. She used another key on a large, American-made padlock that secured the door. She pulled back the sliding door and pushed aside a pink curtain that hung just inside and served as a screen. She looked at him. "Come."

He slipped off his shoes, placed them on the porch next to hers, and went in. He was impressed. A quick way of determining the success or failure of a girl in the village was by her room. Sometimes there was only cracked linoleum, a sagging bed and battered cabinet. This was not one of those rooms. It was clean and neat with lots of pink and frills, new wallpaper, and shiny linoleum.

At the far end of the room was a large, comfortable-looking double bed with a bright nylon comforter on top. Next to the bed were two large, ornate wardrobes with combination locks built into the mother-of-pearl decorated doors. At the near end of the room there was a comfortable Korean-made sofa and the inevitable AM-FM stereo console. He was surprised to see that it was not one of those strange Korean brands that never worked right. This was a new Panasonic. He was even more surprised by the Toshiba portable television set and the small Sanyo refrigerator. A TV, especially a Japanese brand, was a luxury, but he had never been in a hooch before that had a refrigerator, even a small one.

He saw two picture frames on the wall behind the sofa. He walked over and looked at the collection of snapshots they contained. She was in most of them, some with other girls, but in a few there was a self-conscious American with a receding hairline who appeared to be in his mid- to late thirties. In a few of the photos he wore the uniform of a tech sergeant.

The woman came over and pointed to the man. "My old *yobo*. He nice man."

"Did he give you all this?"

"*Na*. He really good to me."

"I guess. But how did he do all this on five stripes?"

"Have good job. He fly on airplane all the time."

Hunter understood. The only thing that kept the black market in Korea even halfway under control was the stringent rationing on Japanese- and U.S.-made goods. It did not stop it, just limited the action. One big hole in this system was the air traffic between Korea and Japan. Most GIs stationed in Korea were lucky if they got one trip to Japan during their tour, and most bought things to take back to the world with them when they rotated. Unless of course one had a job as a crew member on the airplanes flying back and forth between the two countries.

On one of his early trips from Kadena to Korea he had started talking to a young load master assigned to the aircraft on which he was flying. He knew the aircraft, a C-51, an old four-engine transport, made several trips a month to Korea.

"Doesn't all that traveling get to be a drag?" he had asked.

The young sergeant had smiled and explained that a nineteen-inch black-and-white TV purchased in an electronic store just outside of Yokota Air Base in Japan for $91 could be sold in Chicol Village for $275. When the aircraft landed, Hunter had noticed the crew off-loading about a dozen boxes which did not have military markings on them, boxes which were just the right size to hold a nineteen-inch television.

The woman said, "He leave two months ago. We stay almost one year. We love together too much, but he have wife and kids back in States. He love them too, so he go back." She turned away from the pictures. "You want *mech ju?*" Beer.

"That would be nice."

She got some Korean bills from her purse, went to the door, and called out to one of the children, who came and took the *won.* She came back and sat down on the sofa and patted the cushion next to her. Hunter went over and sat down.

"What's your name?" he asked.

"Pak Sumi," she said, saying it the Korean way with the family name first.

"So, Sumi, how do you know me?"

"Before, maybe two years, you Okinawa GI." He nodded. "You have Five Spot *yobo,* Miss Pak."

He smiled. "Ah yes." He remembered her well, the beautiful but avaricious Five Spot Pak. "She wasn't really my *yobo.* We were just, ah, friends for a couple of weeks once upon a time. The next time I came back to see her, she said she was going with a young lieutenant—a weather officer, as I remember—who wanted to marry her."

"Yes, he too much crazy for her."

"Did they get married?"

"No. She marry major."

"Major? What major?"

"Major was lieutenant's boss. When lieutenant leave, he send letters to major to give to Miss Pak. Boss like Miss Pak too much. He di-borse wife in States. They marry."

Hunter couldn't help laughing. "Another victory for true love—village style."

Even Sumi grinned a little at the joke.

"Now you're working at the Playboy Club?" She nodded. "Do you know the girl in the picture, the one I'm looking for?"

"*Anniyo.*" No. "I'm only stay Playboy since my *yobo* leave; when he stay, I no work club."

"You didn't know her?" Hunter asked. She shook her head, no. "So why did you . . . ?"

"Playboy mama-san tell everyone no talk to you. She say you bad man, you make *manee* trouble." Much trouble. "But I'm remember you when you come Five Spot. You always nice guy. I no like Playboy mama-san, so I think I talk to you, maybe can help."

"That's nice." Hunter was getting a good feeling about this woman. She could be hustling him, but he didn't think so. She projected a basic honesty and sincerity. He told her what he remembered from Crandell's stories about Kim's friend who worked at the Playboy.

Sumi nodded thoughtfully, then said, "I know one girl, she stay village long time working Playboy Club. She know everybody. I think she know if I show her picture."

"Great. Can we go to her hooch?"

"I not know where she live." He knew the disappointment showed on his face. She quickly said, "But tonight, maybe she come club, no have *yobo* now."

"Well, okay . . ." He was a bit put off by that. More frustration. Then he realized that a headache had started, deep down, working its way up. He rubbed his neck, hoping to ease the tension.

"*Yobosayo,*" called out a young voice from outside the door. The all-purpose Korean word for "hi," or "hey, you," similar to *aloha* in Hawaiian. Sumi went to the door and returned with two large bottles of Crown Beer, Korea's other brand. Hunter thought it was slightly inferior to OB, although the difference was minimal at best, like that between okay and not bad.

Sumi put the bottles on a wood tray with an opener and two plastic glasses. Then she brought them over, knelt down and put the tray on the table in front of the couch. Using both hands, she opened one bottle and poured beer into the glass nearest Hunter.

Before she could pour for herself, he leaned forward, took the bottle and, also using two hands, poured beer into her glass. The gesture delighted her, and she smiled and clapped her hands in appreciation.

"You number one man."

He could live with that. The beer looked good and he decided one beer wouldn't hurt. He took a long swallow. It was cold and tasted great.

Sumi went over to the shelf of records beside the stereo and leafed through the albums, finally selecting one and putting it on. He expected Korean music, but was surprised to hear Johnny Mathis singing "The Twelfth of Never." It was a song which no matter where he heard it, always took him back to his high school days and making out while parked in his old '52 Dodge, a car he had purchased with his father's help after he turned sixteen and got his driver's license.

He took a long pull on the beer and looked around the room again. Kansas City was never like this.

Chapter 17

Sumi returned and sat next to him, curling her feet under her. He felt his tension drain away as they sat drinking beer and listening to Mathis' liquid, romantic sounds. Almost casually Sumi rested one hand on his shoulder. It surprised him. Until that moment, he realized, he had been so intent on his search for Crandell's elusive fiancée that he had not thought about this woman in a sexual way. He was surprised partly because he was thinking it now, and partly because he hadn't thought about it before. Like most men, he was hardly ever in the presence of an even moderately attractive woman for more than a minute before he considered her potential as a bed partner. And this one was more than just moderately attractive.

He turned and looked at her. Their faces were only inches apart. Slowly that distance decreased. It was an experimental kiss, testing the emotional water to see if it was warm enough. He discovered it was warmer than he'd imagined and getting hotter by the moment. He felt a fever flash of desire.

They shifted about. She slid into his arms and pressed against him. The kissing led to touching, buttons unbuttoned, zippers unzipped, hooks unhooked, all the while hands and lips exploring. After a long while Sumi pulled back and placed her hands against his bare shoulders to hold him back while she took a long, deep breath.

Her blouse was opened, bra unhooked and hanging loose, exposing breasts that were small but tipped with swollen, invitingly saucy brown nipples. Her slacks were on the floor at their feet. Her yellow panties were still on but pulled down around her thighs. Hunter's shirt had disappeared somewhere along the way and his jeans were unzipped.

She smiled. "Go bed, I think."

"Bed." He pretended shock, then shrugged. "Well, if you insist."

With a rueful smile she said, "You too much play-boy."

He stood, kicked off his jeans, and went to the bed, removing his shorts and socks before slipping under the light nylon blanket. He lay on his back and propped his head up on a pillow to watch Sumi. Unself-consciously she removed her blouse and bra, and wearing only her yellow bikini panties, she carefully folded her clothes and hung them in one of the ward-robes.

Then she picked up his things, folded them, and placed them in a neat pile on the couch. Her body was sexy-cute, full without being too fleshy and nicely rounded in the right places. Finished with the clothes, she got a Panasonic electric fan from one corner and walked to the foot of the bed. She leaned forward to adjust it, and the position caused her breasts to hang forward just a bit, creating a most erotic view. She turned the fan on low so air circulated about the bed. It was not hot now, but he knew that soon the fan would be welcome.

When it was adjusted to her liking, she straightened up and walked around the bed. Seeing him watching her, she grinned and gave her hips a saucy roll, then giggled and shrugged out of the panties and quickly slipped in next to him.

She kissed him lightly, but when he reached for her, she gently pushed him back, sitting up beside him with her knees tucked under her chin.

Mixed signals.

He was not sure what to do next, so he leaned back, telling himself to be cool. He asked, "Did I miss something here?"

She smiled provocatively, her eyes were wide, gaz-ing directly into his. The steady, unnerving look charged the room with sexual energy. She pulled the blanket down until only his thighs were covered. In a languid motion she reached forward, her hand palm up, and lightly raked her carefully manicured fingernails down his chest and stomach, stopping just under his belly button. His head jerked back and erotic shivers danced in his central nervous system.

She stopped, looking as if she was uncertain, and said, "I think you have many girls in your life." Before he could muster a protest, she added, "I think you know about sex more than I do."

"Well, ah, I've been around, and . . ."

"Is true. You know more about sex."

It was an allegation an experienced man could hardly deny. He started to make a condescending reply when she did that thing with her fingernails on his chest again—only this time she did not stop at his navel. And again she purred, "I think you know more about sex than I do."

His only response was a smile: he knew when he was being conned. But he also had the feeling he was going to like the payoff. The cover was gone now. He lay there waiting, at full mast.

She moved so that she was poised over him, her feet flat on the bed on either side of him. Then, smiling deviously, she slowly lowered herself until he just barely penetrated her slippery warmth. She paused, tossed her head back, causing her shiny black hair to swirl about her face, and looked into his eyes again. Her voice, husky now, again repeated the taunting phrase, "You know more about sex than I do."

At the same moment she slid herself down. Her firm bottom slapped against him as she took all of him deep inside of her. A shock wave of physical pleasure surged through him. Sumi was in total control now. In a slow, deliberate movement she rose up until they were almost separated, then came grinding down, at the same time repeating the taunt, "You know more about sex than I do."

Overwhelmed, his hands clutched at wads of sheet; he could only hang on as she rode him, repeating the phrase in her low, purring voice, over and over, until he reached a nerve-jangling, body-twitching, shuddering orgasm.

While he came, she held him deep inside her until he was finished. Then she drove herself again, pumping up and down, their wet bodies slapping together, until suddenly she tightened her legs and arms around him, and she achieved her own climax.

They lay that way, Sumi on top of him, for a long time. Neither had to ask if it had been good for the other. When he felt he was finally capable of speech, he cleared his throat. "Look, ah . . ." He stopped—the words had come out in a high squeak. He swallowed and carefully started again. "Look, Sumi, any time you want another lesson, feel free to call on me."

He let out a yell as she took a layer of flesh on his side between her fingers and pinched hard.

Sometime later he lay on his back contemplating the ceiling. Another hooch, another girl, another pleasant but meaningless sexual episode.

So what do you expect, to hear bells ring? his voice asked.

Maybe. He just wasn't sure. But he knew something was missing. Once upon a time the act had been enough, but now it wasn't, and he didn't understand why. Feeling Sumi's naked warmth beside him, he was saddened by the realization. Earlier she had said, "You too much playboy." Maybe it was true. Maybe he had been in so many beds that no one bed could satisfy him. The thought was unsettling.

Sumi stretched, then slipped from the bed. Crossing the room she squatted down, feet flat, legs doubled, her cute bare bottom almost touching the floor, the position GIs called the *kimchee* squat. She poured water from a brass kettle into a shallow pan and cleaned herself. When she was finished, she emptied the pan, filled it with clean water, and came to the bed. Using a small hand towel she washed him. As she was finishing she looked at him and asked, "What you thinking?"

"Nothing. Nothing important." He paused, aware

of the inadequacy of his answer. "Just wrestling my conscience."

She looked at him thoughtfully as she finished the wash. She disposed of the pan and towels, and came back and sat next to him, running her hand through the thick, dark hair on his chest. *"Manee* hair," she said. "Korean man no have hair."

"Have you made love to a Korean man?"

"Why you ask?" There was defensiveness in her voice. He shrugged and smiled, to show her it was not a serious question. She loosened up. "Humm, little bit." He waited, sensing that there was more. "First time when I stay my home. I'm high school girl. My brother's friend like me. Long time he try, but I'm not do. Then he have to go Army." She shrugged. "I lose my cherry for him. He stay Pusan, find another girl. When I'm find out I leave my home, come Osan."

"Was he the only one?"

"No. After I stay this place about one year, KNP man like me." Korean National Police. "He have wife, but he want me. All girls tell me stay with him, that way no trouble for club. I try for three months but no good. Korean man not good to businesswoman. All time jealous about GIs. Sometimes he tell me he love me, then he hit me. So I go see his boss, ask him to make him leave me alone."

"Did he help you?"

"Oh yes," she said, looking disgusted, "He help, after I give him present for money. And for my body." She looked at him to gauge his reaction. He tried to look reassuring. "After that," she said with finality, "I no take Korean man."

The hand which had been playing with the hair on his chest was a lot lower now. Her fingertips lightly brushed his skin in slow, revolving strokes. She looked down and pretended to be surprised by his body's response. With an innocent expression she said, *"Chagie* no sleep?"

He looked down to where her hand was. "Doesn't seem like it."

She leaned forward and kissed him. It was a slow,

deliberate, tongue-licking, lip-sucking kiss that went on for a long time. When it ended she smiled and said, "Now I do for you."

"Do for me?"

For just a second he wondered what sort of wild position she had in mind to top the last performance, but her intention had nothing to do with positions. She started by kissing his lips, his nose, his eyes, his ears. Then she began moving down his neck, kissing and softly sucking his flesh. When she reached his chest she brushed her lips and tongue across his skin. In turn, at each of his small nipples she first licked and then took them between her lips, sucking softly and lightly biting them to increase his pleasure. In the beginning he had been only mildly aroused, but as she continued down, he felt himself getting stronger.

Who says sex is all in your head? his inner voice said with a snicker.

After softly licking and sucking his navel, she stopped and looked up at him, seeing that he was watching her. "You like?"

He figured it was a rhetorical question. The answer was right in front of her. Not trusting his voice, he bobbed his head back and forth. Her smile said that she really knew it all along. "My old *yobo* teach me. I no do unless I really like man."

He knew it was her way of telling him that she thought he was special. Moments later he lost track of time. She seemed to know that getting there was half the fun. But only half. After a long time his back arched, his teeth clenched, and she took him all the way.

Chapter 18

A pleasant aura of good sex filled the room. Lying languorously in bed, he watched Sumi across the room, again in the *kimchee* squat, wearing only the yellow panties and brushing her teeth. Like most of the Koreans he had known she took teeth brushing very seriously. She'd been at it for more than five minutes, vigorously driving the brush back and forth, digging into every crevasse and cranny; foam covered her mouth, most of her hand, and ran down her chin.

Koreans were known for their excellent teeth, and after seeing them brush he knew why. He had done his best to modify his own dental habits, but try as he might, after about two minutes he just couldn't find anything to clean that had not already been scoured three or four times. Still, when he gave up, he always felt guilty.

The headache which had threatened earlier had vanished completely. He considered that he'd discovered a new cure for migraines, but doubted the doctor would give it to him as a prescription. The thought made him grin. For the first time since leaving San Antonio he felt totally at peace with himself. Maybe he ought to forget the Crandell quest, just lay back and enjoy. He wasn't sure now that anything in the village had changed. Maybe the place was just a little older, a little more sophisticated. Possibly he was using Crandell's death as an excuse—maybe it was just yellow fever.

Finished with her teeth, Sumi pulled on an old pair of slacks and a shapeless pullover man's shirt that Hunter guessed had once belonged to her old *yobo*.

Then she started cleaning, first emptying the pan outside, then wiping the floor with a rag, finally putting everything back in its place. He had noticed before that most Korean women were fanatical housecleaners: always wiping, washing, and mopping everything in sight.

The Mathis album had been replaced with the Supremes, who were advising everyone to "stop in the name of love." Too late for that, he thought, knowing it was a smartass remark.

After everything was tidied up, Sumi came back and sat next to him. She gave him a long, appraising look. "You very different."

"What makes you think so?"

"Face not really handsome, but strong. Body good too. Most Air Force GIs too soft."

"Thanks, I guess." The remark made him realize that it had been four days since he had last gone jogging. His "good body" was not going to last long if he didn't get back at it.

"You stay?"

"Well, ah, I don't know, I . . ."

"I know you look for another girl. I see picture. She very young, very beautiful." She paused and brushed an imaginary spot on the sheet. "She your *yobo* before?"

If you want out, now's your chance, Captain Playboy, his inner voice advised.

He considered it, but decided on the truth. "No, actually, I've never met her." Sumi looked surprised. He told her about Crandell's death and why he had come back to Osan, a short version. "So I want to find her to see if she knows anything about what happened to my friend."

When he stopped talking, Sumi continued to gaze at him for several long moments, then she said, "Humm. I'm sorry for your friend. I'm not know. That time my old *yobo* stay, he don't like Playboy Club so we don't go there." Hunter was congratulating himself on being truthful when she added, "But I think maybe your friend is not the only reason you look for her."

He tried to look surprised; whatever could she mean? She nodded knowingly. "Anyway, I help you. Tonight we go club, find girl who stay Playboy long time. She will know."

Considering what had happened between them, this was more than he could have hoped for. He reached over and took her hands in his and held them. Looking directly into her eyes, he said, "Miss Pak Sumi, I want you to know that I think you are a very special woman. Thank you."

She stared back at him for a long time, then suddenly got up and went over and began cleaning again. As he watched her, he became aware of the odor of meat being barbecued coming from somewhere outside. He looked at his watch: ten after six. Not only was he hungry, but he also felt like another beer. He heard voices through the thin walls.

"Hey, *yobo,* bring me another beer." The voice was American.

A few seconds later a Korean female voice said, "You be careful, *yobo,* no burn chicken."

The man answered, *"Yaba, yaba, yaba,* you talk too much."

There was something familiar about the man's voice. Hunter rolled out of bed, found his shorts, and got up. Sumi watched as he put on his jeans and shirt. He went to the door, slid it to the side, and stuck his head out.

Sure enough, it was Ron Shaw. Wearing cutoff fatigue pants and a white T-shirt that was having trouble containing his stomach, he was tending a small metal barbecue grill covered with chicken.

Shaw realized someone was watching him and looked up. When he saw who it was, he grinned widely. "Well, I guess I don't have to worry about you being a funny-guy anymore. Glad to see you made it to the vill."

Hunter said, "What are you doing here?"

"I live here," Shaw said, motioning toward the hooch door behind him. "What's your excuse?"

"Ah, well, I was looking for Miss Kim and . . ."

Shaw laughed. "I don't think you're gonna find her in Sumi's hooch."

"Yeah . . . ah, I mean no, she . . . ah, Sumi is an old friend of a girl I used to know, and we ran into each other and . . . ah, hell, forget it."

"Hey, Mike, I understand." Shaw lowered his voice. "I think Sumi is a fantastic lady. The only thing that keeps me from taking a shot at her is that if my *yobo* found out she'd cut my balls off."

Hunter nodded. "As reasons go, that's a good one."

They both laughed, then Shaw said, "Ah, I don't know, even if it happened, the Air Force would still let me work."

"What do you mean?"

"Whoever heard of an information officer with balls?"

"Too true," Hunter answered, and they both laughed again.

"*Yobo*," called a female voice from inside the hooch, "who you talk to?" The curtain over the doorway was pulled aside and a girl stepped out. Not just a girl, but a very girl-girl. A lovely pixie not quite five feet tall, she had lustrous black hair in a China doll cut. Shaw had said she was good-looking, which was true, but he had not mentioned that she was also young. Very young.

Shaw looked embarrassed. "*Yobo*, this is Mike, my new *chingo*." Friend. "He's the guy I told you I met on the airplane coming back from Japan. Mike, this is my *yobo*. Her name is Kim too. Kim Minh Ah."

Another Kim. Korea seemed to have only about fifteen family names, six of which were Kim. Hunter gave a slight bow of his head. "*Anya hasha meka*, Miss Kim. It's very nice to meet you."

The young girl had an odd look on her face. "*Oh mo*." After her expression of surprise, she whispered loudly, "You say he look for girl. Why he stay Miss Pak?"

Rolling his eyes heavenward, Shaw quickly said, "It's a long story, *yobo*. I'll tell you later."

She nodded, but the look on her face said she wasn't

sure what was going on and furthermore she didn't approve. She started to go back inside, then paused, and said, "I think new *chingo* is number one playboy."

After she went inside, Hunter said, "Cute little thing. By the way, when's her birthday?"

Shaw looked confused. "Why do you want to know?"

"When she turns seventeen I want to buy her a present. Is that going to be this year?"

"Hey, she's not that young . . . not quite." Looking mortified, he added, "At least she's not working in one of the clubs."

Hunter nodded, "That's true. Gee, Ron, I hadn't realized you were such a humanitarian."

"Okay, I'm a nasty GI. So what're you doing with Sumi?"

"Funny you should ask. She's working at the Playboy Club, where Kim's friend used to work." He told Shaw how they had met and about her offer to help. As he was finishing, Sumi came out of her room. She was surprised the two knew each other.

When that was straightened out, Shaw said, "Look, you two hungry?" Hunter said yes. "Why don't you join us? We got plenty of chicken, rice and a ton of *kimchee*."

Hunter looked at Sumi, who nodded yes. "Okay, thanks, I'll buy the beer."

Sumi went in to help Shaw's *yobo* with the rice and *kimchee*. Shaw called one of the hooch mama-san's kids over, and Hunter gave him money to go get more beer.

"Nice place you got here," Hunter commented. "All the comforts of home."

Shaw cocked his head. "You trying to be a smart-ass?"

As they both laughed, the door of the hooch on the other side of Shaw's opened. A tall, good-looking black man in his middle twenties stepped out. He was wearing a fancy dress shirt and slacks that had obviously been made by one of the village tailor shops which specialized in the bolder fashion statement in civilian clothing favored by black Americans. He had a precisely trimmed mustache, hair cut in a moderate Afro that exceeded Air Force standards only modestly. He was almost as tall as Hunter but leaner. He nodded at the two men, showing a friendly smile.

"Hey, Winston," Shaw said, waving.

"Anya hasha motor pool," Winston answered, using a GI corruption of the Korean greeting.

"Mike, this is Hank Winston. He's a broadcast type for the AFKN radio station here at Osan. We work together some. Hank, Mike's new, a pilot. He's going to be working for flight safety."

Hunter was mildly surprised to see a black GI living in this end of the village. Before, black troops had congregated in the section of the vill known as Papa Joe's, named after the Korean who owned a bar that catered to blacks.

Don't be such a prejudiced pig, his inner voice chided. *He can live anywhere he wants to.*

"Nice to meet you," Winston said, sticking out his hand. They shook the conventional way, rather than the new lengthy series of slaps, taps, and waves that symbolized the black power movement which was sweeping through the military.

As their hands parted, a Korean woman came out of the same hooch. She was tall, five-six or -seven, middle to late twenties, attractive; but what struck Hunter most was the reserved look on her face. It was in contrast to both her hairstyle and clothing, which reflected black styles.

She spoke to Winston in Korean and he answered back, also in Korean. Hunter had observed that more black than white GIs made an effort to learn the language of the locals in overseas locations. Another manifestation of the not-so-invisible line that separated uniformed Americans from each other.

After a short exchange with the woman, Winston said, "Got to flee. I promised to take Song to bingo at the NCO club. Nice meeting you, sir."

Hunter nodded. He knew the "sir" was Winston's

way of letting him know that while the "Ron, Mike, and Hank" talk was okay for down here, if they met on base correct military courtesy would be observed.

"Nice meeting you too," Hunter said.

Chapter 19

After Winston and his girlfriend left, Hunter observed, "Seems like a nice guy."

"Yeah, he's keeps it all together, which isn't easy with all the problems we've been having. You know sometimes I even forget he's black." After he realized how that sounded, Shaw quickly added, "Not that I'm saying blacks are, ah, not good guys, just that Winston doesn't act like, ah . . . which doesn't mean I am, ah . . ." He stopped, looking helplessly confused.

Hunter laughed. "I think that about sums up the white liberal position."

"Fuck me to tears," Shaw said irritably. "Let's talk about something else. You think Sumi's friend can help you find the missing *yobo?*"

"I don't know," Hunter said. "Sometimes I think the whole idea is a little crazy."

Shaw's face took on a pensive look. "That's what I thought when you first told me about it. But a funny thing happened this afternoon. I got a call from the OSI. That guy Troxler, the one who talked to Reyes, he called and asked about you."

Hunter thought about that for several moments. Was someone out there keeping track of him? First the cops on base, then the OSI. It occurred to him that the OSI's interest could have resulted from his conversation with Colonel Davies. Maybe the base commander was leery about having an officer drop in out of nowhere and start poking around in what he considered a closed subject. That did not make Davies guilty of anything. It could be just that old CYA—*cover your ass*—syndrome. Hunter asked, "What did he want?"

"He wanted to know about you. What're you doing
. . . like that."

"So?"

"Yeah, well, Troxler leaned on me . . . and I guess
I talked." Hunter gave him a sharp look. "Maybe
more than I should have, but fuck, the OSI scares me."

"What did you tell him?"

"Oh, just about everything I knew, like how you
were interested in finding out more details on how your
friend died because you didn't believe he got drunk.
Stuff like that."

"Well, that isn't too bad—"

"And that you wanted to find his former fiancée."

Silence filled the void between the two men. Hunter
stared out to the west, where the sun was dropping in
a glorious golden splash on the horizon. Finally he
looked at his new friend with helpless frustration. "It's
a good thing you didn't get taken prisoner by the North
Vietnamese. You probably would've ended up editing
the base newspaper at the Hanoi Hilton."

"Hey, I got a very low tolerance for pain."

"Over the fucking telephone?"

"That's as close as I wanna get to the OSI. You
gotta understand, I got a wife and two kids back in the
States and I'm taking care of Kim here, and I've cut a
few corners, and—"

"I'm sorry, Ron. You're right. You've got to protect
yourself. Besides, if he'd come to me I'd probably have
told him the same thing." He didn't add, "Maybe not
as quickly," but he knew it wasn't right to let his problems threaten his friend's world.

"What do you know about this Troxler?"

"He's new, transferred in about a month ago. He
seems to be in charge, but in the OSI, who knows?"

OSI agents didn't wear uniforms and weren't required to reveal their rank. The theory was that if no one
knew their rank, they could not be intimidated during
an investigation by someone with a higher rank. When
dealing with an OSI agent you never knew for sure if
you were talking to a major or a tech sergeant.

Shaw went on, "Actually, I was glad to see a new

man come in. The guy that ran the office before Troxler was an asshole buddy with Colonel Davies and his number one hatchet man, Lieutenant Colonel Donley, the cop squadron commander.''

"Sounds like a chummy little group."

"Yeah, a triumvirate of pricks. They were always doing their best to nail some poor fucking GI's ass for peddling a few cartons of cigarettes on the black market.''

"Very sympathetic types."

"Yeah, especially Davies. He's such a hypocritical sonofabitch. He'll cut the balls off any officer who gets known for spending too much time in the vill."

"That doesn't seem to bother you."

"They've dropped a few hints my way, but I keep a low profile. I never take Kim to the officers' club and we don't run the vill much. If we want to party, we go to Seoul. Outta sight, outta mind works pretty well.''

"A brave position."

"I know, I know. But my boss is the kind of supervisor who writes officers' effectiveness reports exactly the way he thinks Colonel Davies wants them. I'm coming up for captain and I don't want to blow it.''

"Got to play the game," Hunter said reflectively. "But I'm beginning to wonder if it's worth it."

Shaw grinned. "Like they say, the game may be fixed, but it's the only game in town." In a serious tone he added, "The worst part is that Davies is the last one who should be pointing the finger. I happen to know for a fact that he's screwing his secretary on the sly. He thinks nobody knows about that."

Hunter remembered his guess about the secretary and chalked one up for his side.

"The only good thing about it," Shaw added, "is that she's a lousy lay."

"How do you know that?"

"There was this good-looking young airman who worked in the command section. He was getting some of that on the side when Davies wasn't around. He said she was terrible, but he kept punching her every chance he got. He figured he was fucking the old man at the same time.''

''Fate works in strange and wondrous ways.''

''Yeah. I tried to talk him into going to the vill and catching the clap and passing it along to the secretary so she would give it to Davies, but he was afraid to do it.''

''You can't win 'em all.'' Hunter laughed and took a swig of beer. ''What about the general, is he screwing around too?''

''No, he hates Koreans. All the bastard can think about is making his second star. He'd sell our asses to the Russians if it'd get him promoted. He's done some shitty things in the past.''

''How so?''

''I wasn't here, but I heard about when he first took over. He decided the way to win the hearts in the Pentagon was to clean up the vill.''

''I know the type,'' Hunter said. ''Sanctimonious bastards who think they can scare the men into keeping their pants zipped. In Thailand we had a commander who wrote letters home to wives and parents of men who caught VD. After one suicide and a second attempt the Air Force finally got that idiot out of there.''

Shaw nodded and said, ''Our general tried something like that. He started a big campaign to discourage the troops from going to town. He established this rating system for bars, number of fights, number of cases of VD, like that. Any bar that exceeded a certain limit would be shut down.''

''What happened?''

''As the luck would have it, the first club to hit the magic number was Papa Joe's.''

''Did he close it?''

''Sure enough.''

''And?''

''The blacks threatened to burn the whole fuckin' village down. Just like Watts. And there were some hints that the base would be next.''

''How'd he handle that?''

"Just to show he wasn't prejudiced, the asshole ordered the two white clubs with the highest numbers closed."

"Did that make the blacks happy?"

"No, but it sure pissed off the white guys. Also the Koreans. Things got very tight around here. Then the word came down from the Blue House in Seoul, knock that shit off." The Blue House was Korea's White House, and Park Chung Hee didn't have the bothersome problem of the democratic process.

Shaw said, "Seems our general hadn't realized that the money generated in this town goes a lot farther than Chicol Village."

"Did he give in?"

"Oh yeah. But he also developed a permanent hard-on for the Koreans. He really hates 'em. Which does wonders for our community-relations programs." Shaw shook his head sadly. "It was about that time the general brought Colonel Donley in to be the top cop. They're old buddies from 'Nam. Donley is tough and strict as hell. He really makes life miserable for the troops."

"Maybe I should have gone back to Thailand. The war is beginning to sound a lot simpler."

Shaw looked troubled. "Yeah, but then I get to thinking about what is going on here and I wonder if maybe they're right. Maybe we oughta pack up and get the hell out of here."

Surprised, Hunter asked why.

"Look at what goes on here, it's just crazy."

Hunter sighed. "What you're trying to say is that if Osan didn't exist, you and a lot of other good ol' American boys wouldn't be faced with a temptation you can't pass up."

Shaw looked uncomfortable. "Something like that."

"Well, in a way, Ron, you are right. Except you're forgetting that what happens here doesn't happen just because this is Korea. The same thing is going on back in the good old U.S. of A. Men with wives and children have affairs and mistresses in New York and Los Angeles. Even in Des Moines."

Shaw pretended shock. "In heartland America?" They both laughed, then Shaw got serious again. "But what about all the bad crap? What about the guys who get ripped off by the girls?"

"That happens," Hunter said. "I've also heard about a number of girls who have been fucked over by some of our wonderful American lads. People will be people, even in Chicol Village."

"I just don't know for sure what's right."

"Look, if you're worried, don't play the game. Hell, Ron, this is heavy stuff. Sex. Love. That's real life. And as far as I'm concerned, it beats bowling for something to do."

"Aw, Christ, Hunter, you—"

"Hey, it's okay to deplore it. There's a lot to deplore. But if you do, stay on base and deplore it. Go to the hobby shop and take up jewelry making, study brain surgery by correspondence, or get involved in the base chapel program—whatever turns you on. But the village rats don't burn down the church, so if you don't like the vill, leave it the hell alone."

There was a long silence. Then Shaw said, "Jesus, Hunter, if the Officers' Wives Club ever finds out about you, man, they'll put out a contract on your ass."

Sumi and Shaw's *yobo* had finished setting out the food. The younger girl pushed a plate at Hunter and in an irked tone said, "Hey, too much GI bullshit. Eat now."

Shaw waited until his *yobo*'s back was turned and smirked.

During the meal Shaw stuck to chicken and rice. He seemed surprised to see Hunter dig into the various dishes of *kimchee*. "You really are a Korea freak if you can gag down that stuff."

"It's an acquired taste," Hunter said, using his chopsticks to transport a large portion of won bok cabbage glistening with flakes of hot red pepper and garlic to his mouth. He smiled widely and smacked his lips. As with many Americans, when he had been new to Korea, he had a difficult time even being in the same room with *kimchee*. That was due to its unusual and pungent odor. There were those, in fact, who said, "Odor, hell, that shit stinks."

But in time Hunter had learned to appreciate Korean food. Much of it, he found, was seasoned with variations of the same basic ingredients: salt, soy sauce, chopped green onions, sesame seed oil, sugar, *aji-nomoto* (monosodium glutamate), and lots of mashed fresh garlic and hot red pepper. For meats, fish, and poultry it was most often made into a thick basting sauce. The ultimate Korean dish made with these ingredients, however, was *kimchee*. Vegetables such as won bok cabbage and dakon radish were chopped up and soaked in salt for hours, sometimes days, then seasoned. Which made *kimchee* unlike anything American. The result was food that was distinctive both in odor and taste, and which took some getting use to.

Kimchee's historic advantage was that Korean peasants could make and store it in autumn, in large jars, and it would last all through the long, brutal winter. The disadvantage was, when *kimchee* sits, it ferments, getting stronger and more odorous. Even Hunter found winter *kimchee* tough going.

Many GIs, especially those who resisted new ideas, often equated *kimchee* with other smelly substances. But, as Hunger discovered, once you opened your mind to a new taste, it could be addictive. Since living in Korea—and Thailand, where the food was if anything even hotter—he often added hot sauce or red pepper to American dishes such as beef stew and even hamburgers.

Koreans were so addicted to *kimchee* that if they went for a day or two without it they began to experience something akin to withdrawal symptoms. In Vietnam, the Korean military, who were in the war at America's urging, had to start a special airlift just to get *kimchee* to their men to keep them from rioting because all the Americans were providing them to eat were GI rations like steak and potatoes.

It was after eight when they finished the dinner. Hunter told Sumi, "I'm going to see if my friend who has the brass shop is back yet. As soon as I'm done, I'll come back and we'll go to the Playboy Club.''

Sumi nodded, then as Hunter started to leave, she said, "You sure you come back?''

He turned and saw doubt in her face. He smiled his most reassuring smile. "I'll be back.''

Chapter 20

When he got to the shop he was happy to see that Lee was there, looking no older but a lot more prosperous. He was talking to another Korean, a shorter, slim man dressed in a worn gray suit, white shirt, and dark narrow tie. He was vaguely familiar.

When Lee saw Hunter, he said, "My friend, nice to see you again. My wife told me you come back."

"Good to see you, Lee. How's business?"

"So, so," Lee said, putting on a look which tried to suggest that he was barely getting by.

Looking around the big, expensive shop and at the gold Seiko on Lee's wrist, Hunter grinned and said, "Halfway to the poorhouse, right?"

A big smile cracked Lee's face. He shook his head, "You still same." Indicating the second man, he said, "You remember my friend, Mr. Pak?"

The name tickled Hunter's memory. Pak had worked on the base for many years. Come to think of it, Hunter remembered, he worked for the Osan security police squadron. He was a valuable friend to Lee because he kept him informed and out of trouble whenever the base went on one of its periodic black-market crackdowns. Hunter remembered Pak as an anxious, slightly fawning individual. Pak put out his hand and smiled. "Nice to see you again, Captain. I hear you come back."

"You did? From who?"

"Huh?"

He realized he was acting paranoid again. "I just wondered who told you I was back."

"Oh." He pointed at Lee. "He told me."

Of course. Just because Pak worked for the base cops was no reason to get crazy. Pak spoke to Lee in Korean, then added in English, "I have to go now. Good to see you again, Captain."

"See you around, Pak."

After Pak left, Lee got out his most commercial smile. "You come back to Korea again. Maybe you need more brass."

"Lee, I got enough brass to last me two lifetimes. I think I got at least one of everything in this store."

"Better buy two, maybe you lose one."

"Thanks, but no thanks."

"Humm," Lee rubbed his chin reflectively, "You don't come back for brass, maybe you must come back for . . ." he smiled knowingly, "something else."

"As a matter of fact . . ." Hunter pulled out the pictures of Kim Soon Ja as Lee nodded his head in triumph. "Actually, I'm looking for one particular girl."

He handed the picture to Lee, who looked at it. His eyes widened in surprise. "This is a very beautiful girl, but I don't remember you stay with her before."

"I didn't. I don't know her. But I'm trying to find her. Do you know who she is?"

"No, I would remember this one. But there are so many girls this place. I don't look too much or my wife gets *dingee, dingee.*" Crazy. "Too much trouble. *Meon homnida.*"

"Yeah, sorry about that." He told Lee a little about the girl. "I was hoping you could help me find the man who worked on her marriage paperwork. I figured he might have some idea where she is now."

"Sure, I will check, see what I can find."

Hunter thanked him and after they talked about old friends and old times for a few minutes he headed back to pick up Sumi.

Out on the street, things were really humming. It was the bewitching hour. It seemed as if everybody was on their way to or from somewhere. The gray Ford Falcons from the base taxi fleet jostled with the yellow and green Korean-assembled Toyotas and Datsuns local taxis. Groups of GIs were going up and down the hill, from club to club, drink to drink, girl to girl. Women selling flowers were pushing their faded blossoms at passing GIs while kids charged back and forth bugging them for coins.

Beggars were begging, hustlers were hustling, pimps were pimping. *Just another fun night in the vill.*

Chapter 21

He picked up Sumi and they walked to the club. Along the way Hunter noticed several GIs in the street go out of their way to get a better look at her. She had changed: some artfully applied makeup, hair brushed to a glistening luster, a tight-fitting miniskirt which emphasized her good legs and a lightweight sweater that swelled high and sassy. When she was glamorized for the evening, he realized that even though she wasn't as beautiful as Crandell's Kim, she was still a pretty nifty number.

"Manee epuda," he had told her when she had stepped out.

"Komop sumnida," thank you, she said, smiling.

Before the Playboy Club was in sight the music reached out and grabbed them. He recognized Led Zeppelin's "Whole Lotta Love." There were several young GIs hanging around the entrance. Several had large bottles of beer and a glazed, disinterested look in their eyes. Apparently the base wasn't stressing drug and alcohol control at the moment.

He and Sumi attempted to weave through the crowd gracefully, but he accidentally brushed against one skinny, scruffy kid about five-eight who was clutching a liter bottle of OB. Staggering back, the youth snarled, "Hey, man, watch where the fuck yer goin'."

Hunter briefly considered taking the half-full bottle of beer away from the little shit and using it to pound his skinny behind into the ground, but decided it wasn't worth the effort.

Inside the club, he couldn't see anything at first. That was another reason he disliked the Playboy. As one of the darkest clubs in town it was hard to see what the girls inside looked like.

He followed Sumi through the crowd. Led Zeppelin had given way to the Rolling Stones, who couldn't get no satisfaction. They passed the music booth tended by a young Korean kid about sixteen years old who was playing records. Despite his youth he already had the sharklike look of an experienced hustler. After Hunter's eyes adjusted to the gloom he noticed that while the place was quite crowded, he seemed to be one of the few males over twenty. On the dance floor a flock of people were undulating to the loud music. At the next table three young GIs sat drinking beer, smoking cigarettes, and eyeing the girls.

Sumi went and got two beers, then told him to wait while she tried to find the woman she thought might know something about Crandell's Kim. He worked his way through the beer and was checking out the dancers when he noticed a commotion near the entrance. Two black GIs had entered the club, joining what until then had been a lily-white crowd of GIs. They stopped just inside the entrance, faces ominously deadpan. Hunter had the feeling they hadn't come to listen to the music.

Because of the zonked-out condition of most of the customers, it took several moments before the presence of the blacks became general knowledge. The music, now Credence Clearwater, continued to play, but a sense of awareness slowly filtered around the room. The group on the dance floor thinned and tight knots of people formed, creating an emotional space around the newcomers.

Suddenly three more blacks pushed into the room, moving past the two standing on either side of the entrance. They all wore fatigues but were hardly in uniform. Shirt tails hung out, sleeves were rolled up, and they were carrying liter bottles of beer. The one in the middle, a large, barrel-chested man with long arms and a huge head set on a short, thick neck, seemed to be the leader. Hunter was surprised to see a security police badge pinned to his open fatigue jacket.

At the next table one of the young GIs spoke in loud whisper, "Hey, what're those guys doing in here? This is a white club."

One of his friends, a light-haired overweight young man, said, "Why don't you go tell 'em that, Frank? I'm sure they'll leave."

The third man at the table said, "Hey, man, you know who that is? It's that fuckin' SP Masterson. He's one mean motherfucker. A couple of weeks ago he kicked the shit outa two white guys outside the NCO club."

The music died suddenly and the room lights were turned up, leaving the few couples left on the dance floor looking confused. The large black GI the man at the table had called Masterson stepped onto the dance floor and squared off in front of one of the couples that was still there. He glared at the man, a slender white GI with a protruding Adam's apple who had been dancing with a short, slightly stocky Korean girl with large breasts.

"Hey, bitch," Masterson snarled in a loud voice that bounced around the room, "what're you doing in this muthafuckin' place?"

The GI started to protest. "Hey, fella, you shouldn't oughta talk like that to the lady. She—"

"Don't fuck with me," Masterson warned, "That's my woman."

"No, no," the Korean girl screamed shrilly. "I no your *yobo*. I only stay you one time. I already tell you no more."

The look that came over the GI's face said he was a man who wished he was somewhere else. Still he tried to maintain some dignity. "Look, man, maybe you better leave—"

Before he could finish, Masterson roared, "Muthafucka, I'm tired a' your shit." He put one hand on the GI's chest and shoved, sending him stumbling backward. An angry murmur ran through the crowd.

At the next table Frank was still making suggestions: "Hey, somebody oughta do something."

His portly friend said, "Okay, you go first, Frank.

Johnson'll back you up. I'll stay here and guard the beer."

As the crowd of white GIs attempted to gather their collective nerve to face the five menacing black men, Hunter sighed and stood up. Time to exercise the power of authority granted him by Congress. He walked onto the dance floor and in his best command voice, said, "Okay, hold it. Everybody calm down."

Masterson, who had hold of the Korean girl's arm, turned to Hunter. He was only an inch or so shorter, but his wide chest more than made up for that. He looked very unimpressed as he said, "Wha' the fuck you want, Chuck?"

Hunter pulled out his wallet, removed his ID card, and held it up so the man could read the rank. "I'm an officer and I want you to cool it."

That's really telling him, Captain Gung-Ho, Hunter's inner voice sneered.

He added, "That's an order. Now just break it up and—"

"Fuck you, muthafucka!"

What did he say? Hunter looked at Masterson with disbelief. Fuck you, motherfucker? Hunter's mind echoed his incredulity. He can't say that. It was a rule. Hunter was an officer and enlisted men had to obey the orders of officers. They taught him that in officers' school.

Then he was really seeing the man's face for the first time, and he realized he was standing eyeball to eyeball staring at the rawest hate he had encountered since the blazing guns of Hanoi. Got to take command of the situation, he told himself, like a good officer should.

Why don't you tell him he's out of uniform? his voice said sarcastically.

"Now look, fella, calm down and take it easy."

"You think you can make me take it easy, muthafucka?" Masterson spoke in a harsh growl as he stepped forward so his face was only inches from Hunter's.

His voice screamed, *Get serious. This guy is crazy and that officer shit ain't getting it.*

Masterson's hand shot out and thumped Hunter in the middle of his chest. It didn't really hurt, but it knocked him back two steps.

All the bullshit drained away and the warrior instinct in Hunter took control. The endless hours of exercise and training combined with an adrenaline rush honed in mortal combat, his body tightened. He shook off the punch and stepped forward. His eyes narrowed. In a low voice he said, "Let's dance, asshole."

Somewhere deep inside his head Masterson seemed to recognize that a change had taken place. For just an instant an emotion other than outraged fury showed in his eyes. He realized Hunter wasn't intimidated. But he couldn't stop now. He had too much reputation at stake, too much pride. His right hand rocketed forward, aimed at the officer's stomach.

Hunter's stomach was no longer there. He had pivoted and the blow glanced off his side. As part of the same movement he planted his left foot and brought his right leg up in a swift tae kwon do side kick. His foot slammed into Masterson's stomach. The black man lurched backward, air exploding from his lungs. An angry look mixed with surprise and pain came over his face as he staggered to maintain his balance.

But with an angry gesture Masterson shook it off and charged back. He aimed a vicious left jab at the officer's body. Hunter was able to avoid the full force of the punch, but it still banged his ribs hard enough to send a shock of pain through him. The black man was stronger, but Hunter moved quicker. Slashing with his left, he aimed the hard ridge of flesh along the bottom of his palm at Masterson's head—not his hard jawbone but in the center of his opponent's thick neck, just under the Adam's apple.

The big man's eyes bulged, his mouth opened, and he gagged for air. Hunter stepped forward and drove his fists solidly into the man's midsection just below his breastbone. Whack, whack. Each move was precisely designed to do maximum damage. The combination of punches and the kick were not just to hurt the big man, but had the primary objective of denying him the breath anyone engaged in heavy physical activity dearly needed.

Masterson was reeling now, but to Hunter's amazement he didn't fall. The man had an amazing capacity for damage. Hunter stepped back to give himself room for a move he had practiced over and over. He planted his right foot and executed a perfect roundhouse thrust kick. The move combined the force from the rotation of the body with the snapping movement of the kicking knee. His foot slammed into the big man's head. Flesh ripped and blood spurted. Masterson reeled backward.

Done correctly, this move would finish a fight. Hunter was so sure of the move that he stepped back to give the man room to fall down. But he'd underestimated Masterson's strength. The black man gagged a few times, swayed, then seemed to suddenly gather himself and charge at Hunter, both big, long arms swinging. Off guard, Hunter took a solid punch in the stomach and a glancing blow on the side of his head as he backpedaled, attempting to block the fusillade of blows. Barely avoiding a roundhouse punch, he bumped against a table and chairs.

Enough of this shit, he decided. He reached behind his back, took hold of the top of a metal chair, jerked it around, and caught it in both hands. With the legs pointing forward, he rammed it at Masterson and caught him with two of the legs—one in the stomach and the other in the chest. That punched the man back. Before Masterson could recover, Hunter raised the chair high, and with all the strength he could muster, brought it crashing down on Masterson's head and shoulders.

The lightweight metal chair was a twisted wreck. But then so was Masterson. He went down on his hands and knees. Blood gushed from several openings in his head, flowed down, soaked his clothing, and dripped onto the concrete floor.

Hunter stepped back, quickly looking around. Masterson had come in with friends. He saw two of the other black men, looking surprised, then angry—starting to advance on him. At the same time a group of white GIs, taking strength in their numbers, started to push forward.

A shrill whistle blast cut through the superheated atmosphere, and the room filled with uniformed security policemen. Hunter realized moments later there were only four of them, but with one carrying a large shotgun and two others with drawn .38s they seemed like a crowd.

The three armed men were young, but the fourth man was older. The sleeve of his severely starched fatigue uniform, ironed to a knife-edge crease, had seven stripes. That made him a senior master sergeant. He was a hard-looking, muscular man with short blond hair in a precise military cut above eyes that were icy blue chips. He wasn't carrying a gun, only a nightstick, which he held loosely pointing down. Despite that, he looked like the most dangerous man in the room. The name tag above his right shirt pocket read "BULLIS."

He walked with deliberation into the middle of the club and stood looking around. It was then that Hunter realized he was one of the two men who had been in the security police jeep near the BX earlier that day. After looking around the room, the sergeant's eyes fastened on Hunter and he slowly walked over and stood inches from him.

Before Hunter could think of anything to say, the NCO raised his nightstick and pushed the end up against the officer's chest. "I think we have us a troublemaker," he said.

He was big, as tall as Hunter, and he had the lean waist and heavy shoulders of a man who worked out to keep himself in shape. Slowly Hunter reached into his shirt pocket and took out his ID card for the second time. He held it up for Bullis to see.

The man's cold eyes flickered across it. "Is that supposed to impress me?"

That wasn't the right answer. Hunter looked at him

thoughtfully. In carefully measured words he said, "What you mean is, is that suppose to impress me, sir. Or Captain. Your choice, but you'd best start using one or the other. And the answer is, yes, it is supposed to impress you, Sergeant."

He leaned hard on the "sergeant" to make sure the NCO got the message. "Also, I suggest you move that stick—unless you want to eat it."

"Don't try pulling rank on me," Bullis retorted, unimpressed by Hunter's threat. "Not even officers can get away with coming to the vill and starting a riot."

Hunter was just about to take the man on, damn the consequences, when another voice cut in.

"Hey, wait a minute, Sarge." It was the white GI who had been in the original confrontation. "Look, the captain here, he didn't start nothing. Your boy, ah, the guy over there, he came in here and started it."

He pointed to Masterson, who was being helped to his feet by two of his friends under the scrutiny of one of the SPs. There was blood on his face and the front of his uniform, but he looked as if he wanted to fight again. The men helping him held tight and talked rapidly to him in low tones.

The young GI continued, "Him and them other guys came pushing in here, just trying to cause trouble."

Now others were talking. "Yeah, it wasn't the captain's fault."

"He tried to stop the fight."

"He told everybody to cool it."

"The nig—the black guy, he swung first. The captain was just defending himself."

In the face of the overwhelming testimonials, Bullis stepped back two paces and lowered the nightstick, but the uncompromising look on his face didn't change. He held up a hand, which stopped the talking.

"Okay, everyone settle down. Give your names to Airman Ucko there." He indicated another cop who'd come after the initial tussle. He was tall and lean, with burnt-out eyes and a face that was way too old for a man with no stripes on his arm. Bullis added, "After you've done that, go back to whatever you were do-ing.''

Turning to the cop watching over Masterson, he said, ''Take him out.''

The crowd melted away, leaving Bullis and Hunter standing alone in the middle of the dance floor. Hunter was expecting an apology, but when Bullis spoke, the words were hardly repentant. ''You were lucky this time. Maybe you shouldn't push it.''

By the time the remark registered, Bullis had wheeled and was following his men out of the club.

Chapter 22

The music was back on and the lights were down, although not as low as before. A few couples drifted back to the dance floor as Steven Stills sang the unofficial anthem for American GIs in Korea: *"Love the one you're with."*

Hunter went back to his table. His ribs hurt where he had taken one of Masterson's best hits, and the solid shot to his head had set off an ache which was getting worse every minute. No pills, so he tried a swallow of beer from the cup still on his table. It was warm and flat. He grimaced.

"Hey, man . . . ah, Captain, that was good going." It was Frank, the outspoken young man at the next table.

"Oh, thanks . . . I guess."

"You sure showed that nigger."

Several seconds passed. Hunter suppressed a flash of indignation at the use of that word. Instead he chose words that were meant to remind these young men that it was time to give up old racial stereotypes. "Nigger? I thought that was an out-word this year?"

"Well, yes, but look, Captain," said Johnson, the third man at the table, "you were the one kicking ass."

Another moment passed. Tiredly Hunter answered, "Yeah, no one can accuse me of not carrying my share of the white man's burden." He turned his back to the group, not wanting to continue the conversation.

"What did he say?" asked Frank. "What did he mean?"

The pudgy one answered in a loud whisper, "Who

knows? Hell, he's an officer. They ain't like real people."

Ignoring his pain, Hunter took a sip of beer and tried to ignore the conversation behind him.

Sumi came back, her face showing concern. "How you feel?"

"I'm okay," he said, grimacing as a band of pain tightened around his head. "Well, sort of."

She complimented him on his fighting skill, then asked, "How you do?"

"Being able to move quickly is something I can't take credit for. I was born with it. I studied tae kwon do and learned a few good moves. The rest is just practice." He took another sip of beer. "Let's talk about something else. Did you find the girl you were looking for."

"She no come tonight. Her friend tell me she have date. She go NCO club, play bingo."

Everyone was playing bingo at the NCO club. Hunter wished he too had gone there. Shaking his head with frustration, he said, "Beautiful, just fu—ah, just great."

"No worry, GI," Sumi said, grinning. "Friend tell me where she stay. Tomorrow we find."

"*Cho sumnida.*" The Korean expression close to "wonderful." Hunter felt better. Just being with this cute, resourceful lady also helped. Except the pain in his head didn't seem to be getting any better. He rubbed the back of his neck and looked at his watch. It was almost eleven, close to curfew.

He knew that in Korea nothing moved between midnight to 5:00 A.M. because of a strictly enforced curfew. City streets were empty except for police. In the countryside the military threw up armed checkpoints on all major and minor roads. Curfew violators were not treated lightly. The U.S. military backed up the Korean law with its full weight, and GIs caught off base and outside quickly learned that curfew violation was no laughing matter. Hunter suspected that much of the U.S. backing of the curfew policy was because it got the troops out of the bars and into bed for a full night's sleep.

He looked at Sumi. "Well, it's almost curfew. I guess I'd better head back to the base."

She looked at him for several seconds. It was the kind of look a patient parent would give a child who obviously did not know what was good for it. "Why you go base? Head *apo*. You stay my room. I give you number one massage. You feel better."

It was a tempting offer. Still, he didn't want her to mistake his friendly feelings toward her for something more. She seemed to read his mind. "No worry, I know you look for . . . somebody else."

The first time he woke up it was just after six. Flat gray light was coming in the window. Somewhere nearby a rooster crowed. He had been dreaming, chasing after the familiar figure. He'd come closer this time. So close he started to reach out, to touch . . . then he woke. He looked over and saw Sumi, naked, next to him in the bed. Looking at the soft curve of her back, the amber glow of her skin, he felt lonely.

Carefully, trying not to disturb her, he slid closer. When their bodies touched, Sumi snuggled against him without waking, fitting herself against his body. He put an arm around her, his hand resting on her breast, and he drifted back to sleep.

The next time he woke he was alone. More light came through the small window, but it was still gray and overcast. He looked at his watch: half past eight. Outside he heard the clanging of the gate, voices speaking, the yip of a dog. Without warning he was seized with an anxiety attack. Had Sumi gone to tell them about him? Were they coming to get him?

He bolted straight up in bed, propelled by an urge to jump up, grab his clothes and run from the room. Then, as quickly as it came, the anxiety faded. He was left, heart thumping in his chest and wet with sweat, as he realized the paranoia had almost got him. He looked around, spied his shorts lying twisted on the floor beside the bed. He retrieved them and as he pulled them on, he heard footsteps outside. The door slid open.

Sumi stepped in carrying a large brass tea kettle which had steam rising from the spout. "You not sleep?" He said no. "How you feel?"

"I'm okay."

"You like coffee?"

"I'd love coffee."

She set the kettle on a table, went to a cabinet, and pulled out two jars of instant coffee. "You like real coffee or this one?" She held up a jar of green label decaf.

"The real thing." Hunter always figured drinking coffee without caffeine was like making love without a partner.

She made two cups and brought it over on a small tray—special service. The coffee was strong, hot, and good. While they drank it, she told him that she had been to see the woman she had been looking for the night before. She had taken the picture of Kim from Hunter's pocket and shown it to her.

"At first she no want to tell me. She hear about what mama-san say yesterday. But I tell her if she help, you will give her five thousand won. Is okay?"

"Sure, sure." Five thousand won was almost fifteen dollars at the current rate. Not much for Hunter, but pretty good by village standards for just talking. "Were you able to find out where she lives?"

"She say she see you Miss Kim before, but she not really know her," Sumi said. "She think she no stay village now." He experienced a rush of disappointment, and it showed on his face. When he saw a sly smile working at the corners of Sumi's mouth, he knew she had set him up. Casually she added, "But she know room where Miss Kim stay before. With captain *yobo.*" Now the smile was all the way out. "I can show you."

"That's wonderful, Sumi. Thank you very much."

As he said it, he remembered one late night in Thailand, after one of the bad missions. He had started it, telling stories about his first pre-*Pueblo* trip to Korea.

Then Crandell started talking, about Kim as usual. This time his story was about the place where they had lived together in the vill.

"I was surprised when she took me there the first time. It was way back in the village, but it wasn't like the standard hooch. This was a Western-style house, with rooms, indoor plumbing—although it didn't work very well because of the terrible water pressure in the vill."

Crandell said the house was owned by a Korean woman who was the widow of a retired U.S. Air Force master sergeant. "Her name was Mrs. George T. Walker, but she went by Lena." Lena and the sergeant had come back to Korea to live after he retired. Unfortunately, a couple of years after that, he drank himself to death. He left his GI insurance to her, and with that and the money she had saved over the years, she discovered that she was a rich widow. "She built the house with some of that money."

She rented two rooms to Crandell and Miss Kim. He said Mrs. Walker kept her house in mint condition, unlike many Korean buildings, which were nice when they were first built but which deteriorated quickly from lack of maintenance. Her place was painted once a year. Hunter remembered Crandell's description, white on the outside with a striking shade of blue on the roof tiles. She told Crandell that shade of blue had been her husband's favorite color.

Crandell discovered he liked living in the village "as long as I could get back to the base when I wanted a hamburger or a hot shower." He obviously liked Lena Walker. He talked at length about her, saying she was "one heck of a fine woman." He said that in the beginning she spotted his sanctimonious attitude right off, and at first she didn't give him a break. "I thought she was picking on me, but pretty soon I realized she was just trying to get me to be less judgmental, to accept cultural differences as not necessarily something bad."

She had been to the States and enjoyed reading American magazines. "So I started buying them and bringing them home. Soon we were friends. In fact, whenever Kim and I would get into it, Lena would be there, not taking sides, just mediating until we both realized how dumb we were acting. She helped a lot.''

Hunter finished his coffee. A house, not a hooch, painted white with blue roof tiles, owned by Mrs. George T. Walker. And Sumi knew where she lived. He felt he was finally getting close to Kim Soon Ja. As he dressed quickly, he saw the dispirited look on Sumi's face, and he felt a moment of guilt. When he was finished, he pulled out his money clip and peeled off a ten and a five and put it on the table.

"That is for the girl who told you about the house," he said. Then he added three twenties. "That's for you. For your help, and for"—he shrugged slightly—". . . for everything."

Unsmiling, Sumi looked at the money and nodded. He hoped the sixty dollars would help her. It was hardly small change. The current monthly steady-*yobo* rate, according to Ron Shaw, was going around twenty-five to thirty dollars. But the look on her face said she knew money was cheaper than feelings.

Good old Michael Hunter, patron saint of the business girl, his inner voice snickered. *You better hope the GI Central Enforcement Committee doesn't find out about the way you're throwing money around. They'll put out a contract on your ass for contributing to outrageous inflation.*

He shook his head, trying to rid himself of the voice. Damn, he thought, between the headaches and my sarcastic conscience, I'm gonna end up a raving loony in the old soldiers' home. After leaving her home, Sumi led him twisting and turning though the back side of the village. It was a cool, gray, unfriendly morning. Heavy slate-colored clouds hung low and threatening in the sky. They rounded a corner and there, sandwiched between two drab, standard, concrete Korean hooch buildings, was a white house with a blue tile roof.

Sumi stopped and looked down. "I think better I go now. You no need me."

"Sumi, thank you. You've really helped me and I appreciate it." He paused. "If things were different, maybe—"

She reached up and put her hand against his mouth. "No say." She turned and was gone.

Chapter 23

Hunter stepped up and knocked on a large iron gate set in a concrete fence. A dog inside started yapping loudly. After a few moments a woman's voice spoke sharply to the dog, but it did not seem to mind and went right on barking. The gate opened about a foot. For some reason he expected to see a mama-san, but the woman standing there looking at him was hardly that. She was tall and slender. He judged her somewhere in her thirties. Still, despite being dressed in a pair of faded blue jeans and an old sweater, she was attractive enough to make him aware of it.

"Mrs. Walker?"

She looked at him for a long time, her face impassive. Finally she said, "Yes."

"My name is Mike Hunter. Paul Crandell was my friend."

Her face remained solemn. She looked at him for a long time before saying, "You stay Thailand before?"

"Yes."

"In his letters Crandell talk about you." She stopped, looked back at the compound behind her. He had the feeling she was trying to look back into the past, when Paul Crandell had lived there with the girl he loved. She turned back to Hunter. "He is dead."

"I know. I heard about it when I was in the States. In the hospital."

"What you want?"

"I want to know how Paul died. I'm looking for Kim Soon Ja."

Another long pause. "She doesn't stay this place anymore."

"Do you know where she is staying now?" More silence. Her eyes became dark, melancholy. "Mrs. Walker, Paul once told me that he considered you to be his friend. I don't think the full truth has been told about his death. I want to know that truth. I think the person who can help me is Kim Soon Ja. If you really were Paul Crandell's friend, you will help me find her."

"What you do if you find?"

He was sure this woman knew something. He was also sure that if he was not careful she would close the gate and her mouth, and he would have a hell of a time getting either open again.

"I want to talk to her. I want to help her if she needs it. Paul Crandell loved her—not just GI love, but the real thing. I'm not here to hurt her."

She studied his face carefully before answering. She seemed to find whatever it was she was looking for. "Crandell was good man."

"Yes. He saved my life. In Vietnam."

She made her decision and opened the gate. "Come in. We talk."

He followed her into the compound. The house was as clean and well kept as Crandell had said. It had a roofed porch area in the center with two large easy chairs facing outward with a table between them. Half a dozen Korean and U.S. magazines were on the table. On either side of that area were sliding doors which opened into the house itself. Lena Walker sat in one chair and motioned for him to take the other.

"You like coffee?"

"Yes, please."

She leaned over, pushed open the nearby sliding door, and called out something in Korean. Then said, "House girl get."

They sat for a couple of minutes, appraising each other, and neither spoke. The house girl, a youngster of about fourteen, came with a tray. There were two cups, a pot of hot water, a large jar of Maxwell House instant coffee, a box of sugar cubes, and a jar of

CoffeeMate. As the widow of an American military man, Mrs. Walker had BX privileges.

After she spooned out the coffee and added water, she asked, "How you like?"

"Cream and half a spoon of sugar."

She fixed it as he instructed, saying, "My husband always say he like coffee like he like woman, hot and black."

Hunter smiled. "It's an old joke, but not very popular anymore."

"I know. Black and white too many problems now. My husband not really bad man, he just talk a lot. In the mornings we drink coffee, but the rest of the day he drink OB."

"How long ago did he die?"

"Umm, almost two years."

Looking at this woman, he could hardly believe that she had been married to a retired sergeant who had died two years ago. "How long were you married?"

"He come Korea first time 1956. We meet 1957. We steady for six months. After he go back to States, he keep writing to me. Then, 1959, he come back to Korea. We get married."

"You must have been very young when you met him."

She smiled, giving Hunter a look which said she knew he was sweet-talking her. "Not so young. When we marry he is thirty-seven, me twenty-six."

"Have you been to the States?"

"Oh, we go. First time, Warner-Robbins, then Altus."

Warner-Robbins Air Force Base in Georgia was just okay, but Altus was a bleak, godforsaken place in the middle of nowhere in Oklahoma. "Those are not such great places."

"Yes, I don't think so. I don't like too much. My husband he not like either. So we come back to Korea. We stay Kunsan for two years, then Air Force say go Biet-nam." She pronounced it in the Korean way, substituting the letter *b* for *v*. "He tell Air Force no fucking way; then he retire."

As with many people who speak a second language, she spoke the curse words without the emotional impact they had for the native speakers. She took a sip of coffee and said, "But I'm think retirement not so good for him. He no work, drink too much, then he die."

Doing a quick calculation, he realized that at age thirty-six, Lena Walker was an attractive, moderately wealthy widow. With those things going for her, he decided that if she slept alone, it was strictly by choice. He also figured that that was enough small talk. "Do you know how Paul Crandell died?"

The abrupt transition brought the dark look back to her face. "Everybody say accident."

"What did Kim Soon Ja say?"

There was a long pause. "After, I don't see Soon Ja anymore."

"Wasn't she living here?" She was silent. "Did she leave before or after Paul died?"

The answer was a long time in coming. "Before."

It was not the answer he had wanted to hear. He felt a sense of disappointment mixed with regret. "How long before?"

"Almost two month."

He looked out at the dull gray morning sky. The clouds were thick and low in the sky. He felt like it looked. He picked up his cup and took a long, slow drink. Putting the cup down, he said, "I want to do what is best for Paul. And for the woman he loved. Why don't you just tell me what you know?"

She was looking away, avoiding his eyes. Without facing him, she said, "I'm afraid for Soon Ja. Not her fault. She is very . . . special woman. She is too pretty. The mans, ah, men, they like her too much."

The last words were said with vehemence. She turned and looked directly into Hunter's eyes. He could see pain and desperation. "You must understand, she is too young. She does not know about life!"

"Did she have something to do with Paul's death?"

She reached over and took hold of his arm. Her fingers dug into his skin. "I'm think he die because of Soon Ja. But I'm not believe it is her fault."

Hunter sat looking into her eyes, which were cloudy with emotion. After several seconds she released his arm, leaned back in her chair, and started talking, her voice low, controlled.

"When Crandell leave Korea, Soon Ja try very hard to be good girl. She no go place where GIs stay, stay home, only go see lawyer or go base try to finish papers for marry. She even go U.S. Embassy in Seoul couple times. But many problems. Korean government people want money to finish papers."

Hunter nodded as if he expected that. Lena did not like that. "Even your embassy, some civilian work there, he try to get Soon Ja to go bed with him to finish papers more fast."

Hunter rearranged his face. He did not doubt what she said. He'd seen it before, those with power who had no respect for the people that power was supposed to be used to serve. It was a flaw common to politicians and bureaucrats.

Lena continued, "One day after she came from base she tell me she meet number one honcho. He very important. He will help her with papers. He tell her come back. She go couple times."

She paused, and her face showed the pain again. "Then one day he say she have to go Seoul. New friend will take her. And she go." She stopped talking. He could see her teeth biting at her lower lip, and lines showed on her forehead. She looked in the direction of the base and there was resentment in her eyes. "She no come back for three days."

"What happened?"

"I'm really worry," Lena said. Her face showed the old concern. "I'm not know what to do. Then, three days, she come. She very tired, look very sad. She don't talk, just pack clothes, all her things, in bags. She say she have to leave. She say sorry. Before she go, she say keep Crandell's letters, she will come here to get them."

Hunter hadn't known what he expected to hear, but it was not anything like this. "Did she want to go?"

"No!" The word came out like a shot, full of fury. "She won't talk, but I can tell she not want to."

"Do you know who the man from the base was?"

"Soon Ja never tell me, but I see one time."

"When?"

"After she pack her clothes. Then jeep come. Security police jeep."

That fucking tears it, Hunter thought.

As much as he had hoped it would be different, he knew the answer would involve the base cops. "Do you know who it was?"

She shook her head from side to side. "I'm not know names. Two men in jeep, one young man, few stripes, I'm think he is just driver. Other man, I'm think he is the one."

"Who is he?"

"Security police sergeant-honcho. He have eight stripes." She paused, then added, "Black man."

"Black?" Hunter's surprise was obvious. Lena nodded yes. He remembered the day before, the jeep in front of the exchange, with two NCOs who seemed to be watching him. One was Bullis. The other, the chief master sergeant, was black. His mind raced. Thoughts were competing, getting all mashed together, jangled up. That the man was black was a shock. That it was such a shock was, he knew, prejudice. It wasn't supposed to matter. He was one of those who always advocated such thinking. What was really important here was that someone—black, white or, Air Force blue—had misused Kim's trust, had made her do something which her friend said she didn't want to do.

Lena said, "Soon Ja no tell me, I see with my eyes. I'm surprised. Before Soon Ja afraid of black man."

That confused things even more. The pieces just did not seem to fit in any logical way. Still, it wasn't the first time he had seen life become twisted beyond what seemed to be known reality. Anything was possible.

"Did you see her after that?"

"She come see me a few times, to get letters Crandell send. She doesn't talk much. She say too much talk make trouble. I know she stay Osan first, but later new man too nervous. He tell her she have to go live in Suwon.''

"Suwon?"

That was a surprise. Suwon was a large city about twenty miles north of Osan on the MSR to Seoul. It was a historic Korean city with a large Korean Air Force base located on its southern boundary. Although the base was Korean, there was a small U.S. Air Force detachment of approximately five hundred people assigned there. He was familiar with the place because once he had been diverted there when weather prevented landing at Osan.

"Why did he make her go there?"

"He don't want anyone to know he keep Soon Ja, so he tell her to move. Have house near small GI village at Suwon base.''

That was even more unusual. Possibly he was worried about his boss, the lieutenant colonel Shaw had talked about, finding out he was keeping a girl in the vill.

"What else did she tell you about this . . . man?'' He almost said "new *yobo*," but he wasn't about to use those words.

"She say she not want to, but cannot stop, she is afraid.''

"Afraid of what?'' The words came out in a harsh rush, betraying his anger. Slower, he said, ''I don't understand that. How could someone make her to do something she didn't want to do?''

Now it was Lena's turn to get angry. "How long you stay Korea, Captain? You think Korean girl just like GI? Soon Ja is not business girl, but she live in this GI place. She have captain *yobo*. Many people think she is business girl. She no have rights like American. You think she can make trouble for big shot security police GI?''

He considered his answer carefully. "Yes, I think she could if she was careful. And smart. I think *you* could.''

Lena smiled in spite of herself. "Maybe. But I'm not young girl. Soon Ja never have to be strong before. She always have family or nice man to take care of her. She never learn to handle bad man."

"Okay," he sighed. "I guess it can happen. Do you know where she's staying in Suwon?"

"I only know is close to place where Suwon have GI bars. She don't want me to know. She is ashamed."

"So, Paul figured out from her letters that something was wrong and then he decided to come back."

Lena nodded.

"What happened when she found out he was coming?"

"She come here for letters. I read to her. When Crandell say he is coming, Soon Ja crazy. She not know what to do. Worry so much."

"Then what?"

"Last time I see her is when she come to meet Crandell. She tell me she have to talk to him, to make him understand problem. But she is afraid, not know what security police man will do."

Hunter had a pretty good idea what the answer to that one was. He asked Lena what had happened after that.

"I'm not know for sure. I never see her again. She never come back to Osan. But later, somebody tell me they see her at terminal with Crandell. Then two more days, I hear that Crandell is dead."

"And you don't know what happened to Miss Kim?"

She was silent again, looking at him with that same penetrating look she had given him earlier. Finally she said, "I think she still stay Suwon. My friend, she go Suwon base couple of weeks ago to see Suwon GI *yobo*. She say she see Soon Ja in store. Soon Ja see her but no speak. Old mama-san with Soon Ja, watch her too much."

Chapter 24

After leaving Lena Walker, Hunter wearily trudged back to the main street. The dreary morning seemed to be taking its toll on village businesses. Only a few people were out buying fish, rice, and packages of food from the small Korean shops. The overcast was thicker, covering the vill in a cool gray shroud. By the time he reached the street he felt chilled.

The lousy weather increased the demand for base taxis. Usually they were not busy at this hour, having completed the morning roundup of village rats, shuttling them back to barracks for a quick shower and change into a uniform before they went to work. He shared a taxi with two young enlisted men who were late getting to work. On the way, one started talking excitedly to the other.

"Did you hear what happened last night?"

"Man, I didn't hear nothing," his companion answered. "Mimi was half loaded when I got home. She was drinking and playing cards with her girlfriends, lost more 'en thirty bucks. I got so pissed off I coulda shit. I wanted to beat the crap outa her, but I got shit-faced instead."

"You didn't hear about the trouble?"

"What trouble?"

"The fucking niggers went crazy!"

"So what else is new?" his friend said with a yawn.

"No, man, it's serious this time. The girls were all talking about it this morning. They hit a bunch of the white clubs last night. Gangs looking for trouble."

"Anybody get hurt?"

"The Stereo was the worst. They really got into it

there. I heard one white guy got knifed. And someone said there was a fight in the Playboy, but I don't think it was too serious.''

Hunter almost asked, How serious did you want it? But he chose to stay silent.

The second GI said, "Man, I'm glad I'm getting short. This place is really turning to shit. Hell, they got their own clubs, their own girls—some are even as good-looking as the ones in the white clubs. What do they want?''

"Yeah, I know," his friend commiserated. "They're just crazy. But you can bet there's gonna be some shit now. We can't let 'em get away with this.''

Hunter wanted to say something. To lecture. He wanted to tell the two young men that the black man just wanted to be a man. The kind of man who could go anywhere he felt like, not just to his clubs; to be able to choose any girl, not just the ones who went with people of his color. He felt like saying many things, but he remembered the way he had felt when Lena Walker said that the man Kim had gone with was black. So he kept silent.

When the taxi reached Hunter's BOQ the meter showed thirty-five cents. He gave one of the two GIs a buck and told them to pay for the taxi when they got to where they were going. They looked surprised. As Hunter walked off, he heard the first one say, "Hey, that guy must be an officer.''

As the taxi started to pull away, he heard the other one answer, "I guess they get horny too, just like us enlisted swine.''

He smiled. Some do.

The low clouds seemed to have inhibited normal activity on the base as well. Few people were out and about as he walked to his building. Inside, he took off his clothes, wrapped a towel around his waist, grabbed his shaving kit, and headed for the latrine. He was the only one in the shower, which could accommodate four people. He took a long, leisurely scrub and soak. Washing away the village, he hoped he had not encountered anything that soap could not wash away.

Back in his room he changed into clean civilian clothes. Then he called Ron Shaw.

"Coffee-break time."

"Where the hell have you been?"

"Chasing ghosts. Meet me at the club and I'll tell you all about it."

When Shaw arrived, Hunter was in the dining room finishing a plate of his favorite military breakfast, creamed chipped beef on toast, better known to generations of GIs as SOS—shit on a shingle. It was the special and cost fifty cents. Noting Hunter's civilian clothes, Shaw said, "You still loafing?"

Hunter smiled. "Actually, I meant to tell you how nice you look. I've always admired a man in uniform."

"Some of us have to work," Shaw said, his voice heavy with martyrdom. "We can't all be fighter pilots."

"Never fear, America," Hunter proclaimed in his best radio announcer voice, "Lieutenant Ron Shaw, United States Air Force, is alive and well on Freedom's Frontier in the Land of the Morning Calm, protecting motherhood, apple pie, and the American Way from the godless communist hordes."

Sitting down, Shaw said, "Did you hear about what happened in the vill last night?"

"Better than that."

Shaw looked at him sharply. "I'm almost afraid to ask what that means."

"I was part of it." He gave his friend a short account of the events of the previous evening in the Playboy Club.

"Oh, fuck me to tears," Shaw moaned. He looked around in a way that suggested he would be happier if no one he knew saw them together. Then he giggled embarrassedly. "It didn't take you long to get into the spirit of things."

Then the younger officer recounted details of events the night before which had been discussed at the base commander's morning staff meeting. Four of the bigger clubs had been raided by groups of black GIs. The stabbing at the Stereo was the worst incident. Fortunately, the victim had not been badly hurt and was recovering. There was also a big fight at the A-Frame, which resulted in three men—two black and one white—going to the base dispensary.

Shaw added, "The worst thing is that I'm afraid our dumbshit general will use this as an excuse to put the vill off-limits."

"What would that accomplish?"

"It might keep the fighting and killing on base."

"You think it'll get that bad?"

"I told you, this place is ready to blow. I think it's started."

As they both sat considering that unhappy prospect, Fred Reyes walked up to their table. He had a pompous, good-little-bureaucrat expression on his face. "Captain Hunter, for your information, Mr. Troxler from the OSI called me again yesterday afternoon."

The accusatory tone in his voice made it clear that the statement was meant to be disturbing. Hunter looked up at him. "Have you been selling cigarettes on the black market again?"

"Very funny," Reyes responded curtly. "He called to talk about you. He wanted to know if you had contacted me about Crandell's death."

"And?"

"Well, naturally, I told him about our conversation."

"Naturally."

"He is the OSI."

"So I've been told," he said. "What did you talk about?"

"Everything we discussed."

"Including the pictures?"

"Well . . . yes."

"What did he say?"

"Nothing, he just thanked me for the information."

"Okay." Hunter broke eye contact with Reyes and picked up his coffee cup. "Thanks for the information." As he took a sip of coffee Reyes turned and marched away. When Hunter looked back at Shaw he saw him smiling.

"You know, somehow I get the impression that you and good ol' Fred are never gonna be what you could call really tight."

Putting the cup down, Hunter sighed. "It's not Reyes. Hell, he doesn't count. What bugs me is that every time I turn around some law-type is looking over my shoulder."

"They tend to get involved in things like death and riots."

"Yes, but their concern seems a little late in coming, especially the OSI."

"Maybe your friend was into something illegal."

"No way. Paul Crandell was the straightest of straight arrows."

"He shacked up with a *yobo*. A lot of guys get into strange shit because of that."

"Hey, he was going to marry her."

"So why are the OSI and the base cops involved?"

"As soon as I locate Miss Kim, maybe I'll find out."

"I think I may be able to help you out there."

Hunter's surprise showed. "How's that?"

"You remember the guy you met at my place last night?"

Slowly Hunter said, "The black guy, ah, Winston?"

"Careful." Shaw grinned. "Your prejudice is showing."

"Yes, I suppose."

"Anyway, like I told you, Winston is really straight. I've known him ever since I got here. He isn't the typical, ah . . ."

"Now who's prejudiced?" Hunter asked.

Shaw looked embarrassed. "Aw, goddamn it. I wish everyone was the same color. Then I could hate whomever I wanted, purely for personal reasons, and not have to worry about this racial shit."

"It wouldn't help. If people didn't have something obvious such as skin color to discriminate against, they'd find some other reason. Like maybe people who are left-handed.''

"Hey, I'm left-handed."

"Yeah, I know. That's why I won't marry your sister.''

Shaw nodded. "That's probably best, since the only sister I got is a brother.''

The waitress came by and refilled their coffee cups. After adding sugar and white stuff, Shaw went on, "As I was saying, after Winston came back from the NCO club he stopped by to talk to me. He thinks he may know something about your Miss Kim. He wasn't sure, so he didn't want to say anything when he first saw the picture. But after I explained why you were looking for her, he said he would check into it and let me know.''

"But he didn't say what?'' Hunter asked. Shaw shook his head. "That sort of fits.''

He told Shaw about his conversation with Lena Walker.

"Are you sure the black guy was a chief master sergeant in the SPs?''

"That's what Lena Walker said. She's been around the Air Force long enough to know the difference. Why, do you know who he is?''

"There's only one black chief in the base cop squadron. But hell, I like the guy. He's always been straight with our office. He's a picture-perfect Air Force senior NCO.''

"Who is he?''

"Chief Master Sergeant Willis Washington. He's NCOIC of the cops. Bullis, the senior master you ran into at the Playboy Club, is the number two NCO.''

"That puts it right up there,'' Hunter commented dryly.

The expression on Shaw's face had gone from pensive to forlorn to downright wretchedly miserable. "I really wish you hadn't said the security police were involved. I already told you that their boss, Colonel Donley, is the meanest motherfucker in Korea.'' He paused, thinking, then added, "Maybe in the whole

Pacific. And that includes Ho Chi Minh and Kim Il Sung.''

"Maybe he should check out his own house," Hunter said.

"You best be careful. I know two guys who got on the general's shitlist because of the vill. He sicced Donley on them and pretty soon he had them both wrapped up in nice, neat little packages. One was a master sergeant. He wasn't a bad guy, he just liked to live well, so he was doing a little black marketing on the side. He got busted to buck sergeant and shipped to Greenland. The other was a captain, a hell of a good procurement type who was set up by some smart Koreans who didn't like him. He's a civilian now."

"I'm not into the black market, and so far the Koreans are not the people who worry me."

"Still, watch out, buddy. Maybe you ought to hang it up. Shit, you already tangled with one of Donley's men, and you can bet our wonderful general's already gotten a full report on last night with your name prominently mentioned."

"Hey, I'm clean. What can he do?"

"You're not listening!" Shaw was almost shouting now. "You're asking what can an Air Force general do to a captain who's annoying him?" The younger man was waving his arms dramatically, which caused officers at other tables to notice. "I'll tell you what he can do, buddy. If he likes, he can have *them* give you a brain transplant! And they'll probably use the brain of an ass-kissing, alcoholic lieutenant colonel." Noticing the looks he was drawing, he paused, took a deep breath, and in a lower voice he added, "They got a lot of those."

Hunter smiled. "As long as it isn't anything serious."

"I'm not kidding, Mike. What about orders? He could have your ass shipped out of Korea quicker'n you can say *kimchee.*"

"Yeah," Hunter agreed, "he could do that."

"Bet your ass he could. And I wouldn't like that. You're the first flying type I ever been tight with."

"You're just a sucker for a pair of silver wings."
Hunter took another sip of coffee, then said, "Tell me
about Donley. You make him sound like a real terror."

"He scares me," Shaw said with sincerity. "He's
one of those quiet types, always looks serious, comes
on like your favorite uncle, acts as if he's concerned
about your welfare. But watch out. If you get on his
bad side he's the kind that stays up nights thinking of
ways to shaft people he doesn't like."

"Sounds like a real sweetheart."

"Yeah. He was in 'Nam before he came here. That's
where he got to know our wonderful general. I heard
he got in some trouble there, but the general pulled
his nuts out of the fire."

"What kind of trouble?"

"I don't know; being a prick, I guess."

"That usually doesn't get you in trouble in the senior ranks."

"Sorry, I lost my head," Shaw said sarcastically.

"Part of what bothers me is that things are just too
fucked up around here. Something is going on and I'm
convinced that somehow Paul's death is part of it."

"I don't want to believe that," Shaw said in a desperate tone. "How can this be happening? We're the
good guys—at least that's what I thought when I joined
up."

"Most of us are *still* the good guys," Hunter said.
"But the war, and this life—some get seduced by the
sheer magnitude of their power. They forget that with
the power there is supposed to be responsibility.
They're supposed to use it to accomplish the mission,
not for personal goals."

"But what happens when they are using it for themselves? After all, Donley, Davies, the general—they're
running this turkey ranch."

"Yes, but the power's not absolute. The system may
do its best to play the blind man, but abuse of power
is still not officially condoned. If there's something
wrong, you can bring it down by exposing it. Christ,
you're the journalist; you are the guys who are supposed to be the watchdogs of democracy."

"Out there." Shaw's voice had climbed to a high-pitched squeak. "That's the civilian media you're talking about. In here, I'm just another running dog for the system." He leaned back and rubbed the back of his neck. "I really don't know what the fuck is going on. At first I thought all this stuff about your friend's death was just so much blue smoke and mirrors. I figured at worst it was just CYA. Maybe someone screwed up and just didn't want to admit it. Hell, I know people who will hedge if you ask them for the time of day. Now I'm not so sure. Maybe there really is something serious going on. And that scares me shitless."

"There's got to be someone in the power structure around here who's straight," Hunter said.

"The real problem is the general. He's so star happy he makes it easy for guys like Davies and Donley to screw the troops. Hell, any officer with balls is automatically eliminated." He thought a minute, then said, "There must be somebody you can talk to—they can't all be . . ."

Hunter considered the suggestion. "If I knew who to trust I would, but right now I don't think I'm willing to be candid with anyone, especially the local law."

"Jesus H. Fucking Christ, I sure hope you're wrong. If the cops are into this thing . . . well, I don't even like to think about it. Shit, they got the guns."

"Yeah, that's my problem."

Chapter 25

After Shaw went back to his office, Hunter reconsidered everything that had happened since arriving at Osan. He concluded he had nothing but theories until he talked to Kim Soon Ja, who, according to Lena Walker, was no longer in Chicol, but was possibly living in the small GI village near Suwon Air Base. The next logical move, he decided, was to head for Suwon for a little reconnoitering. He considered going back to his room and getting a weapon for backup, but Lena said Kim was being watched by an old woman. He figured he should be able to handle her without a gun. In addition to the fact that carrying a personal weapon around in Korea could buy a lot of grief.

He paid his check, decided to be a big spender, and tossed a buck on the table. As he walked out of the club, a captain in a flight suit was on his way in.

"Hey, Mike Hunter, right?" he asked. Hunter didn't recognize the man, who quickly added, "I'm Matt Zhalan, met you yesterday at the safety office."

"Oh, yeah. Hi." They shook hands. "Did you ever get your phone call through to Kimpo?"

"No way. I finally sent them a message," Zhalan said. "By the way, we got a call from the base commander's office this morning. They're looking for you. Colvin told them you were processing and they acted pissed because he didn't know where you were. Maybe you ought to check in with them."

"Sure, I'll do that," he said. "Thanks." So, good old Colonel Davies wanted to see him. Probably about last night's little fracas in the Playboy Club. Well, screw him.

He saw a taxi coming back from the vill. He yelled. The taxi darted over, lurched to a stop, and he piled into the broken-down backseat. Most of the base taxis had backseats that sagged like a bed in a short-time hotel—too many heavy loads of black-market goodies, he supposed.

"Thataway," he told the Korean driver, pointing toward the vill. The Korean wheeled the vehicle around and headed back up the hill to the gate. The sun was trying to pick a few holes in the clouds, but it looked like a losing battle. Once they were through the gate Hunter asked, "You know how to get to Suwon?"

The driver glanced over his shoulder. The look on his face suggested that not only was that a dumb question, but that all smartass GIs ought to be boiled in soy sauce. Nodding, he muttered, *"Na."*

The silent ride took twenty-three minutes. The road wound north through fields of rice, cabbage, and red peppers. About halfway there they went up the highest hill on the drive. Looking to the left, Hunter saw a crude sign over the worn steps that led back to a memorial to Task Force Smith. It commemorated the point where, in 1950, the U.S. Army first encountered the North Korean invasion force. A small group of soldiers whose heaviest weapons had been machine guns had set up here to stop the communist invaders who had slammed across the 38th Parallel, smashed through Seoul, and were heading for Pusan to consolidate the invasion. Since the North Korean force was spearheaded by a tank column, the battle had not been much of a contest. The men in Task Force Smith fought courageously and were able to slow down the far superior force, but in the end they'd gotten their asses whipped. Hunter knew from reading about that war that the time they bought helped the rest of the U.S. Army get its act together and set up a perimeter around Pusan which held until Douglas MacArthur executed his bold landing behind the North Koreans at Inchon. His U.S. Army and Marine units, fresh from bases in Japan and Okinawa, cut the invasion force's supply line, trapped them, and in very short order beat them so badly that the North Korean forces ceased to exist.

It was just after noon when Hunter's taxi skidded to a stop in front of a cluster of shops across the street from the entrance to Suwon Air Base. Hunter remembered the time he had been diverted here because of bad weather and then, due to a maintenance problem, had ended up staying overnight. Suwon was a main ROK Air Force base, with new F-5 Freedom Fighters and older Korean War-vintage F-86 Saber Jets. Prior to the capture of the USS *Pueblo*, the only U.S. troops stationed here had been a small detachment of Air Force advisers who helped the Koreans maintain and fly their U.S.-built aircraft.

During the buildup that followed the capture of the U.S. Navy spy ship, Suwon became home to a detachment of more than five hundred U.S. Air Force people supporting five aging F-102 Interceptor aircraft. The "duces" were there to counter North Korean MiGs and Soviet Bear Bombers that regularly tested the air defenses of the south.

When Hunter learned the U.S. Air Force felt it needed five hundred GIs to support five TDY aircraft, he burst out laughing. Later, he realized, it was sort of reassuring. It was comforting to know the Air Force did not expect its people to exist in a semi-combat zone without basic creature comforts to make life tolerable; things like a movie theater, BX, library, hobby shops—and most important, an NCO and officers' clubs.

The officers' club, where Hunter had spent the first part of that evening long ago, had been a real kick, especially after he discovered there were only twenty-five officers assigned to the base. For such a small place, however, they had an interesting array of bar games which keep the club smoking from happy hour into the wee hours. Later in the evening, two Suwon officers, the chief of administration and the public-affairs officer, took Hunter on a grand tour of their little vill, Seryu Dong. Directly across the MSR from the main gate of the base, the tiny vill was just completing a building boom. The small vill had a handful of shops, but the main attraction was three bars and two hundred girls. Just about right, Hunter figured, for five hundred GIs.

After paying off the taxi, he looked around and discovered that the place looked pretty much the same since his visit here more than a year before. The collection of shops catering to the GIs was still there: tailor, shoemaker, a couple of dress shops, brass dealer, and a small store. The shops flanked a short alley which led back to the bars. He walked down the dirt strip past a small restaurant with two tables sitting out front which served, according to its sign, American fried chicken. He had eaten there. The only thing American about the chicken was the money he paid for it.

At the end of the alley was a sign proclaiming: "UN TOWN." That was a holdover from the days when the U.S. military had tried to sustain the myth that the United Nations, representing its member countries, controlled the foreign military forces stationed in Korea. Instead of passing under the aging sign, which led back to rows of hooches, he made a right turn and was in the center of the action in Seryu Dong.

It wasn't much. A open dirt area with a couple of shops and the three bars, more or less in a circle. Now, just after noon on a duty day, it was dead except for several kids playing with a broken wagon. Charley Pride music was coming from one of the bars. The others, even though their doors hung open, were silent.

Since it was the only place showing signs of life, even if it was country and western, he decided to try the club with the music. The faded sign over the entrance said "ROSE CLUB." Inside, rough concrete walls had been splashed haphazardly with dark paint. There were tables and chairs that looked as if they might have been there to greet MacArthur. In the light of day the place reeked with shabby indifference. Of course, he knew, after dark, with colored lights, loud music, and fancy ladies, it would look a lot better.

Hell, there wasn't a bar in the world that didn't look better after the sun went down.

The only person in the place was a girl behind the bar reading a Korean comic book. Using the Pacific Air Force scale of ten, she was a weak four, way below what Hunter considered as the PACAF cut-off. She looked up as he crossed the room and sat on an aging, not too steady barstool.

"Do you serve beer in here?" he asked, and even as he said it he wondered why he was being such a smartass today.

"What you say?" She knew it too—there was instant hostility in her voice.

"I said I'd like an OB, please." He switched to sincere.

The girl—or, now that he was up close and could see the wear and tear on her face, woman—wasn't easily appeased. "Maybe you some kind of wiseguy GI."

He tried for complete innocence. "Never happen, baby."

Shaking her head with irritation, she said, "I think so."

She pulled a bottle of OB from a large ice chest, opened it, and put it in front of him. To improve relations, Hunter tossed down a five hundred won note for the two hundred won beer and said, "Keep the change."

Her hand quickly forked in the bill and the look on her face improved considerably. "I no see you this place before."

"I don't come downtown too often." That was true enough, at least for this vill.

"You have *yobo?*" A wiseguy GI was one thing, but business was another.

"Funny you should ask," he said, digging out the picture. He put it on the bar. "I'm looking for a girl. I heard she was living around here. Her name is Kim Soon Ja."

The girl picked up the picture and studied it. Her face showed just enough of a reaction to make him believe she recognized the face in the picture. "Why you want to find?"

He trotted out the story about money from an old boyfriend. Hunter had faith in cash. After all, they did not call themselves business girls just because it was a euphemism. She looked at the picture again. To sweeten the pot he said it was two hundred dollars. That was the kind of money one would not want to see another member of the club miss out on. He could almost hear her eyes spinning, and when she looked back up at him, jackpot melons were showing.

"Okay, you wait, my friend go tell her."

"Ah, wait a minute," he quickly protested. "She's an old friend. I really want to surprise her. That's why I told my friend I would bring the money."

He tried to make it sound as if he was hoping for a freebie for the favor of delivering the money. It was a reason she could understand.

The girl looked unsure. "She stay home. Have mama-san stay all time. Don't like GI to come."

That confirmed what Lena Walker had told him. It certainly sounded as if she was being guarded. It did not mean she was blameless as far as Paul's death, but it put some points on her side of the scoreboard.

"Look, I'm not going to make problems." He reached into his pocket, pulled out his money clip, and got a five-dollar bill—the going short-time rate—and put it on the bar. "That's for showing me where she lives."

The fiver took the day. Quickly she said, "I have to work, but I can find boy to take you. Okay?"

"Okay."

Her hand moved even faster than before as she claimed the bill. She went to the front door and called out a few words of Korean. After a moment two boys who had been playing came over. She spoke to them, then turned to Hunter. "They take you." He thanked her. She added, "You give boys tip for service, okay?"

Help keep Korea green—bring money.

He followed the two boys, who appeared to be about seven and eight, down the alley to the MSR, past the

stores and the walled compound where many Korean
Air Force officers lived. Passing a field of cabbage, he
estimated they had walked less than a hundred yards,
the Koreans packed a lot of living into a small area,
when the two boys turning up a narrow dirt path that
led to a cluster of new brick Western-style houses. All
of the people he had seen so far were Koreans.

Hunter was surprised when he saw the new single-
family houses. Small and boxlike by American standards, they were large and luxurious compared to
others in the area. He guessed the residents were not
poor farmers. Each unit was separate from the others
and each had its own high, brick wall. The boys passed
several, then stopped in front of one with a heavy, iron
gate. He dug out a couple of hundred-won bills and
handed them to the boys. As the boys scampered off
down the hill, Hunter observed that despite the attempt
at creating a modern Western look, the surrounding
walls still had chunks of broken glass set in concrete
along the tops.

Tradition dies hard.

Chapter 26

He stood for a moment, wondering what was the best approach. Finally he decided to go with military traditional: *damn the torpedoes, full speed ahead.*

He stepped up to the gate and tried the handle. Surprisingly, it was not locked. He gave the gate a hard push and it swung open. He stepped in. Instantly a large black shape uncoiled itself from one corner and leaped at him, in a barking, snarling frenzy. He jumped backward, then realized the dog was on a chain and that the chain was about five feet short of where he was standing.

Too bad, doggie.

He glanced from the dog to the house and found himself staring into the eyes of a lean, hatchet-faced Korean woman who looked as if she had been down some mean streets. Her eyes were black pinpoints behind narrow slits. Tightly compressed lips made her mouth an almost nonexistent line. She had to be over fifty, but instead of mellowing, the years had sharpened her. She walked halfway across the small compound toward him, shaking her head back and forth and motioning for him to leave. When he did not move, she stopped, blocking his way to the house.

And a very plush house it was, although it was apparently still being constructed. To his left he saw building materials, sand, and a pile of bricks. Looking back at the woman, he decided to play it like a good ol' country boy, lost and bewildered. Maybe a little Korean would warm her up. He put on his best ingenuous smile. *"Anya hasha meeka."* He almost added *"y'all."*

Nothing. Not a twitch. If she wanted to play it hard, that was okay too. He checked her out—maybe ninety pounds. He figured he could handle her. He took a step forward. Then another person came out of the house. This one was a man. Actually, to be perfectly accurate, he was more like a tank on legs. The palace guard had been reinforced.

Dressed only in a pair of cutoff GI fatigue pants, the Korean wasn't as tall as Hunter, but with those wide shoulders and muscular chest it hardly mattered. Then there was his stomach. It was hard and flat, and it had never seen a baked potato with butter and sour cream. Sturdy arms hung loose at his sides. His face was impassive, but his eyes were steady, alert. He might as well have been wearing a big neon sign that flashed on and off: "Black Belt! Black Belt!"

Hunter figured if he couldn't dazzle them with brilliance, maybe he could baffle them with bullshit. "I was just on my way to San Diego and I got lost. Could you tell me how to get back on the interstate?"

Something happened in the black belt's eyes. The corners of his lips bent up in a pernicious smile. His face did not offer Hunter comfort—because on it was a look of recognition. It indicated the Korean had been waiting for him.

The man took a step forward. His moves carried the same implication as a marksman loading his rifle. Hunter figured he could retreat, beat it through the gate, and run like a stripe-assed monkey being chased by a pack of hungry lions. But then he would never know. Not for sure. And running wasn't what he had come for.

He took a quick step toward the Korean woman, who was about four feet in front of Black Belt. As part of the same movement he grabbed her by both arms and pushed her backward. Surprised, she went reeling into the advancing man. She screamed as she sailed back and bounced harmlessly off his broad chest, falling directly in front of him.

It had the desired effect: surprise and confusion. The man stopped, and in that time Hunter darted sideways to the pile of construction materials. By the time Black Belt got around the woman, Hunter was holding a heavy brick in each hand. The Korean's reaction was to smile wider. Hell, he probably went out each morning and broke a dozen of the bricks with his head just to work up an appetite for breakfast.

But Hunter liked that. The man's smile was a perfect example of what karate did for a person, creating a supreme confidence. The bricks were as much diversion as anything. Hunter did not want Black Belt to suspect that he was facing a man who had some training in his own art.

The Korean tightened up, going into a low stance, bent forward, arms out, legs stiff, as he slowly advanced. Hunter stayed tall and awkward-looking. Knowing tae kwon do made maximum use of the legs to deliver deadly kicks, he was sure of the Korean's first move. After all, even black belts go for the cheap shot when they think it will play.

He wasn't disappointed. With blinding speed the Korean faked a chop, then straightening up, pivoted, and unleashed his left leg, sending his foot flashing through the air. Right where Hunter's chest should have been.

Only it wasn't. He was able to sidestep only because he was able to anticipate the move. And, unfortunately, not as quickly as he intended, because Black Belt's foot still made contact. Pain shot through his left arm and he dropped the brick in that hand. But the Korean had put too much faith in the kick and had not bothered to prepare a backup move. Hunter was able to jump in close and slam the brick in his right hand against the side of the Korean's head, mashing his left ear.

That had to hurt.

Blood blossomed from the mangled flesh. It also ruined Black Belt's concentration and kept the hand he slashed at the side of Hunter's face from taking his head off. Still, the hit was good enough to set off an explosion in Hunter's head. Ignoring the pain, he leaned in and smashed the brick again in the same place, then jumped back to get out of the range of a deadly foot that flew past only inches from his chest.

They stood for a moment, blood rushing, eyeing each other. There was a new look in Black Belt's eyes. Some of the confidence was gone. As was most of his left ear, which was now a bloody glop. A stream of red ran down the side of his head, onto his shoulder, trickling over his smooth, hairless skin and down his chest. Reacting to the pain, he blinked his eyes and shook his head back and forth every few moments.

On one of those blinks, Hunter launched the brick as hard as he could throw it. His aim was good: it slammed against the Korean's forehead at the brow line. At the same time Hunter charged in and used a kick of his own. Only this one owed more to the Mafia than the martial arts.

Right to the groin. Black Belt went down on his knees, head forward, twisting in pain. From the way the man was carrying on, Hunter did not expect him to get up anytime soon. However, better safe than sorry. He picked up one of the loose bricks, went around behind the man, and hit him again, this time in his right temple.

That rang his chime. But he was still conscious, so Hunter used the brick again, slamming it against the back of his head, at the base of his skull. Black Belt twitched, then went limp, and tumbled forward.

Mama-san gawked. She could not believe it. This fucking GI had whipped Black Belt's ass. He smiled at her. "Don't take it so hard, I cheated."

She whirled and darted in the direction of the dog, which was barking frantically and trying to rip the post to which it was chained out of the ground. Hunter leaped after her, caught a handful of long skirt before she got on the dog's side of the chain, and jerked back sharply. That caused her to stumble and fall to the ground.

He stood for a moment, breathing deeply, surveying the scene. Back Belt was bleeding and twitching. Mama-san was moaning and whining. And the damn dog was going crazy, jerking on his chain and barking and snarling with frustrated rage. As for Hunter, he was breathing so hard his chest burned. There was a big blood smear on his shirt, his arm vibrated with pain, and his head was throbbing.

What a mess.

Then she appeared.

Emerging from the dim interior of the house. Her face was pale. With no makeup her face seemed paler. And there was something else, something that dulled that bright inner light in her eyes that Crandell had captured so well in his photographs. But the high cheekbones and well-defined lips were the same. As was the long black hair and slender figure. It was definitely Kim Soon Ja.

"Kim," he said loudly. "I've come to get you. To take you away. Hurry."

She just stood there, blinking in the cloudy-bright light. His words did not seem to register. Neither happiness nor fear showed on her face, just an empty, uncomprehending stare.

"I'm Paul Crandell's friend. I'm here to help you." His name seemed to cause a small ripple of reaction in her face, but it died quickly. She was, he realized, totally space city. Zonked, loaded, high, cruising somewhere in a different world.

Mama-san was up again, screaming in Korean. He grabbed a handful of skirt again to keep her immobile. Black Belt was groaning. The damn dog was roaring. Hunter experienced a sudden panic attack, unable to think what to do next. The old woman made a savage jerk and almost got free.

Enough was e-fucking-nuff.

He jolted forward, caught mama-san, and hauled her back. He pressed his thumbs into the sides of her scrawny neck and squeezed. It worked just like the demonstration in karate class. The pressure cut off the flow of blood to her brain, and those narrow eyes actually popped open for a moment, then rolled up in her head as she went limp. If he held it a few more seconds she would die. But he decided that no matter how badly she had pissed him off, that might be a bit much. He released the pressure and lowered her to the ground. She'd be out for a while.

He went to Kim. She was dressed in a pair of wrinkled white slacks and a pale yellow blouse. When he took her hand, for a moment she held back. "Come with me," he told her. "I'll help you."

The resistance faded. He led her across the courtyard and out of the compound.

"*Waygaray* . . ." She looked confused. "Where—"

"*Bali-wa!*" he told her, Korean for "Come, hurry." That helped.

They rushed past a group of Koreans who, apparently attracted by the noise, stood watching as the big American led the Korean girl away from the house, down the dirt street, and toward the highway. No one did or said anything. That figured. The locals undoubtedly knew Kim was living with an American, and they'd learned over the years that it didn't pay to get involved in the affairs of crazy GIs.

They reached the MSR and crossed it just as a Korean taxi came cruising by. Hunter flagged it down, pushed the girl in, and piled in behind her. He told the driver, "Chicol Village."

Chapter 27

Once the taxi was moving and he was sure they were not being followed, he started to relax.

"*Oh mo.*" Suddenly Kim had come alive. She shook her head while rubbing her eyes, trying to make sense of what was happening. She mumbled something more that Hunter didn't understand.

The taxi driver was looking in the rearview mirror now. Quickly Hunter took her hand, started rubbing it, and said, "You're okay. *Cho sumnida.*" That's good, the only phrase he knew which came close to covering the situation. Thankfully, it seemed to work. The girl—no, woman—slumped in a corner across from him. Her faced turned and she stared out the window at the passing rice fields with unseeing eyes.

Looking at her, Hunter realized she was thinner than in her pictures. The skin around her eyes was puffy and darker than it should have been. But even without that exciting, vital quality captured in Crandell's photographs, she was still one of the most beautiful women he had ever seen.

He was still holding her hand. "Miss Kim, can you talk to me?"

Her head moved slowly. She looked at him. He thought for a moment that she was going to speak, but she went back to staring out the window. He reached over and took her slim jaw in his large hand and gently turned her face toward him.

"Miss Kim, my name is Mike Hunter. I was Paul Crandell's friend." As before, Paul's name made something deep in those dark, glazed eyes move. "Do you understand?"

Within moments the light went out.

"Beautiful," he mumbled exasperatedly. Out of frustration he shook her head. "Aw, come on, lady, what are you on?"

It didn't help. She was drugged, but with what he had no idea. His knowledge of chemicals was limited to pot and the painkillers given him in the hospital. He guessed Kim was tranked to the eyeballs with some type of downers. He made a few more attempts to talk to her, but finally gave up.

He had problems of his own. His arm hurt and his head was vibrating with pain. At one point he experienced vertigo, and the taxi seemed to slip and slide beneath him. Thankfully, it only lasted a second or so, but even after things settled down, he was still shaky. Kim mumbled again in Korean, something he didn't understand. He wondered if this was a permanent condition. Did her cop boyfriend keep her doped all the time? Probably not. She wouldn't be much fun like that.

Hunter figured his appearance on the scene must have motivated her boyfriend to sedate her, just in case. If so, that was another point in her favor. Then he realized he was kidding himself. Point in her favor, hell. Having come this far, unless someone could come up with pictures of her pushing Paul's body into the cold, dark water he was going to have a hard time believing that Crandell's death had really been the fault of this exquisite woman child.

Captain Romantic, always a sucker for a pretty face.

Whatever she had been given, it had to wear off sooner or later. His next problem was what to do with her until she could talk. Even if he could get her through the gate, he didn't think it was a good idea to take her on base. He still didn't know for sure what was going on, or who was involved, so the fewer people who saw them the better. The best bet would be to stash her somewhere until she was coherent. But where?

Come to think of it, going back to Chicol probably was not the smartest move. However, he couldn't think of an alternative. Anyway, Korean girls, even a knock-out like this one, were not particularly conspicuous in the vill. He considered a large, Western-style hotel a few miles from Chicol, but decided once the cops discovered she was missing, that would be too obvious. There was his friend, Lee, but he remembered Lee's pal, Mr. Pak, who worked for the cops, who was still an unknown factor. There was Shaw's hooch, but if they knew anything at all about Hunter they probably knew about that friendship.

If he was going to keep her in the vill, the best place would be one with which he had no previous association, at least since his arrival this time. Thinking back, he remembered Five Spot Yim. When he had come back to see her the last time, she had been staying with the lieutenant and couldn't take him to her room. They'd ended up in a small hotel tucked in an alley just off the MSR. Its advantage was that most of the customers were Korean.

When they hit the outskirts of the village, Hunter directed the driver to the hotel. As he hustled the girl inside, he did not see anyone who seemed overly interested in their arrival. An old mama-san took his money, five hundred won for one night, and led them to a room on the second floor. If she thought anything about Kim's spaced-out condition and the blood smears on his shirt, she didn't let on.

The room was small, and hot, just large enough for one double bed and a small table. The cracked linoleum on the floor nicely complemented the dirty, faded wallpaper and the single low-wattage bulb that hung from a frayed cord in the middle of the ceiling. A small window overlooked a narrow alley and an old building across the way which seemed to be a furniture factory. He opened the window and fresh, albeit slightly dusty, air oozed into the room.

Always nice to go first class, his voice said sarcastically.

For another five hundred won, mama-san agreed to bring him a bottle of OB, ice, and some peanuts. Kim had immediately crawled onto the bed, pulled the thin nylon spread around her, and closed her eyes. After the old woman left, he kicked off his shoes and sat down on the bed, nudging the girl over until there was enough room for him to stretch out. From all indications he was in for a long wait. He forced himself to breathe deeply and slowly, attempting to disassociate himself from the ache in his head. It helped—a little.

The old woman came back with the beer and had even thought to include two glasses, which looked as if they might have been washed as recently as two days before. He filled one glass with melting ice cubes, added beer, and quickly drank the whole thing. Looking at the girl lying there oblivious to the world, he wished he had something stronger than beer for the pain that was skateboarding around inside his head. He thought longingly of the bottle of pills back in his BOQ room.

Thinking about drugs, he remembered the only heroin user he had ever been acquainted with: a likable young flight-line mechanic in Thailand who got caught by the SPs in Korat City with a spike in his arm. Before he had been shipped off to detox, he admitted to Hunter that he had been using the stuff for more than six months. He started by smoking heroin-laced joints—he called them nails—and graduated to using a needle. Thinking back, Hunter remembered how the young man's performance had deteriorated. Basically, he seemed like a good kid, but the worst thing was the young man had admitted that given the opportunity, he would go right back to using heroin.

That memory made Hunter wonder about the girl. If the cop had her on heroin . . . well, he was not sure what he would do, but somehow he would see to it that the bastard's life was unpleasant—and as short as possible. He checked her arms and legs, but did not find anything that looked like needle marks. He didn't think heroin came in pill form, so he felt better. Still, he knew many drugs that were sold only by prescription in the States could be bought over-the-counter in Korean drugstores. That was why all drugstores were off limits to GIs—but not to their girlfriends. Another nearsighted rule.

He sipped the beer. Kim slept on. He was bored. The pain in his head throbbed relentlessly. Soon the beer was gone. His head still ached. So did his arm. Finally, a little after four, he checked the girl for the hundredth time. Still in the twilight zone and it didn't appear as if she was going to be returning to Planet Earth anytime in the near future.

He decided to make a quick trip to the base for his pills, a shower, and a change of clothes. He also wanted to see Shaw. He needed to tell someone about what had happened.

He left the room, located the mama-san and gave her a thousand won to keep an eye on the girl and make sure she did not leave until he got back. He said she was sick and needed rest. He also promised her another thousand if she carried out his instructions. The old woman's eager nod indicated that she thought that was a good deal.

Outside, he took a path he remembered that led to the main street going to the gate. Just as he got there, a base taxi came cruising along. He hailed it and got in. Maybe his luck was improving.

Besides not wanting to walk, he figured his chances of getting past the gate guards wearing the bloody shirt would be better in a vehicle. Traffic at the gate seemed to be a little slow, but he did not anticipate a problem as he pulled out his green ID card and pressed it against the taxi window so the guard could see it. Normally, they just gave ID cards in the hands of Americans a quick glance and then passed them through.

Not this time, however. The guard, a young two-striper, actually leaned over and appeared to be reading it.

Damn.

Sure enough, the guard motioned for Hunter to roll down the window. As he complied, he felt a river of cold shit pumping into his heart. The young airman asked, "Are you Captain Michael Hunter?"

The answer that jumped into his head was an old cartoon gag line: "General Mills, this is Captain Kangaroo, I'll meet you at the officers' club." The second thought was that maybe he could run for it. They wouldn't shoot him—or would they? The young cop just stood there looking both polite and official as hell.

"Yes, that's me."

"Sir, would you step out of the vehicle?" He stepped back, his hands tightening on his M-16.

"Why?" Blind obedience was not Hunter's long suit.

"Sir, I have orders, if you come through the gate we are to take you to Lieutenant Colonel Donley, the security police commander."

"Why?"

That's telling him, his inner voice sniggered.

"Sir, those are my orders. No one told me why, sir. Now please get out of the vehicle." The tone in the kid's voice indicated that he was getting irritated by this smartass officer who was fucking with him and that he would not mind in the least using the butt end of his M-16 on the sonofabitch if he did not start getting with the program.

Hunter knew that arguing with the guard was useless. He was just following orders. "Okay," he said, getting out of the taxi. He paid the driver the fare, twenty-five cents. "Let's go see the man."

Chapter 28

With the young cop following six steps behind, Hunter walked across the road. He used the time to compose himself. On the surface he was icy cool, but underneath, his warning sensors were lit up like the emergency panels on a Thud which had just come out on the losing end of a tangle with a SAM. He wondered who was really waiting inside. Was it Colonel Donley, or was it actually Chief Master Sergeant Washington?

The cop shop was one of the old buildings, just inside the base fence. Immediately beyond the front door was a high desk with several NCOs on duty. Two were talking football while a third just looked bored. The young cop announced, "This is Captain Hunter."

That got their attention. The sergeant who was making a point about the prowess of the Dallas Cowboys stopped in mid-sentence. The one who had looked as if he was going to fall asleep was suddenly on his feet. He was looking at Hunter as if he were a North Korean with fifty pounds of high explosives strapped to his back. Hunter felt like blowing him a kiss.

"Hey, Bullis," he roared, "we got that captain you said the colonel was wanting to see."

Hunter looked in the direction the man was shouting. Several of the men in the next room were black, but none of them had eight stripes on their sleeve. The one person he did recognize was tall and blond, his old buddy from the Playboy Club, Senior Master Sergeant Bullis.

A spiteful smile that reeked brutal intent covered the NCO's lips as he walked into the outer office. He didn't stop until he was only inches from Hunter. In a low, malevolent tone he said, "I believe I told you not to push."

Hunter decided to play it official, at least as long as he had rank on his side. "Sergeant," he said, leaning hard on the word, just to keep things in perspective, "why am I being detained?"

"Detained?" Bullis rolled the word around as if he was examining it. "I don't know if you are being detained. What I do know is that Colonel Donley, who is the chief of security police on this base, gave orders to find you and bring you in so he could talk to you. Do you have some objection to that?"

Bullis threw the colonel's name at him just to make sure Hunter understood the pecking order in this building.

"Where is he?" Hunter asked.

"In his office," Bullis said, indicating the back of the building with a nod.

Hunter put on his hardest look. "Get out of my way, Sergeant." That was to let Bullis know that the pecking order was still a one-way street—down. He stepped forward, forcing Bullis to move back several steps or be bumped. As he retreated, the man's expression changed from surprise to anger. At the doorway he stopped, blocking Hunter.

The place got very quiet as everyone watched the two big men. Bullis' eyes narrowed and for a moment Hunter thought he might actually do something stupid such as striking out. But Bullis caught himself in time. His anger was replaced by a noncommittal expression. He stepped back and with overly excessive courtesy, said, "Of course, *sir.*"

He put as much contempt as possible in the last word, and Hunter had to admit he did it very well. He went past Bullis to the back of the building. He wasn't sure what was going on, but the hostility in the room was thick enough to cut with a bayonet. He also had the feeling that being nice to Bullis, or anyone else in this place, would only be interpreted as a sign of weakness. He was convinced now more than ever that Paul Crandell's death was intertwined with some of the people in this place. He vowed silently to find out who it was and make them pay.

Wonderful, Captain Heroic, but they have the guns and they may just decide to shoot off your balls.

He knew he must be quicker and smarter, or that was a realistic possibility. And he doubted they would stop there. He walked to the back, passed a desk where Mr. Park, Lee's friend, stood talking to a couple of NCOs. The Korean glanced at him but gave no sign of recognition. A few others who had not heard the exchange in the outer office seemed unaware that anything out of the ordinary was happening. If indeed there was a conspiracy, Hunter did not think it involved all the security policemen. But which ones were involved, and who was directing it?

The back of the building was partitioned for a private office. An older Korean secretary sat next to a door marked "COMMANDER, SECURITY POLICE." Hunter thought he detected a slight smile pass across her face as he pushed through the office door without knocking and walked in.

The man seated behind the large wooden desk at the end of the air-conditioned room was dressed in a Class A summer blue uniform. There were silver oak leaves on his shoulders, half a dozen rows of ribbons on his chest, and, to Hunter's surprise, navigator wings. He'd once been an air crew member. Despite his reputation as a hardass, Hunter entertained the possibility that the man might be straight.

Bullis charged in right behind him. "I'm sorry, sir. The bast—ah, he wouldn't wait."

The lieutenant colonel put down some papers he was studying and looked at Hunter. He was somewhere in his early forties. His iron gray hair was cut in a precise flattop, a style that was only beginning to disappear from the career ranks of the military. His face was arresting, actually handsome in a way. He reminded Hunter of Spencer Tracy—but without the actor's sense of humor. The eyes were different. No twinkle. These eyes were deep, intense, and totally lacking compassion.

The office, like the man, was carefully arranged. Dark paneled walls complemented thick, deep blue carpeting on the floor. The room's adornments did their best to project the impression of a place inhabited by a man of importance. The area behind the colonel's chair was a display of certificates and plaques proclaiming that the man behind the desk had received recognition and awards during a distinguished career. Framed photographs showed him in a variety of uniforms and settings: as a stiff lieutenant standing near a B-47 bomber, a captain in mess dress at some formal occasion, as major in security police in Germany, and as a lieutenant colonel in jungle fatigues in a setting that was obviously Vietnam.

To the side of his desk was a table with a collection of manufacturer's models of past and current aircraft in the Air Force inventory. The B-47 was there and, Hunter noticed with a certain resentment, the Thud. That model had been promised to him on a number of occasions but never delivered.

Before the colonel answered Bullis, Hunter said, "What's going on? Why was I stopped at the gate?" It was the good-offense-is-the-best-defense ploy.

Unfortunately, Donley seemed to know that one. He continued to stare at Hunter, letting those eyes work for a while. Then he said coldly, "Captain Hunter, I will overlook the fact that you came barging into my office. But from this moment on, you will observe proper military courtesy, which includes standing at attention and saying sir."

With admirable precision Donley had quickly established his dominant position of authority. Hunter, assuming a stance close to that of attention, was not totally cowed. "Yes, sir. But I still want to know why I was stopped and hauled in here."

"And you will answer questions, not ask them." The colonel's voice lashed back almost before he finished. Donley was, Hunter had to admit, very good at this. Much better than the base commander, who relied too much on his charm and those sincere blue eyes. From the corner of his eye Hunter saw Bullis smirking.

With icy dispassion Donley said, "Hunter, I think you are a troublemaker."

"Why is that, sir?"

He looked at the dried blood on Hunter's shirt. "Apparently you have been in another barroom brawl. After the trouble you caused last night I would have thought you knew better."

"Just a minute, sir. I didn't cause the trouble last night, I was trying to stop it. There are a bunch of witnesses who will support that."

"Do you have the names of those witnesses?" Donley smiled for the first time. "Because I have signed statements by witnesses who say you were responsible for the trouble."

Remember, dummy, Bullis and his boys were the ones who took the statements.

After considering that statement, Hunter relaxed. Donley had just committed a major fuckup. Hunter's Rule Number 13: Accept military authority in any of its forms from autocratically benign to bureaucratically stupid—as long as everyone plays by the rules. Donley's remark made it obvious someone was pissing in the punch.

"So, from now on, Captain, I am going to make it my personal business to see that you don't have the opportunity to cause any more trouble."

Hunter considered walking around Donley's desk to the table holding the model airplanes, picking up the model of the F-105, and shoving it up the man's ass. Instead he said, "I see you have the model of the Thud in your little toy collection."

It wasn't what Donley had expected. "What?" He half turned to look, then caught himself and turned back. "Those are not toys. They are models of aircraft which I have been associated with either as a navigator or in the security police. The F-105 is one of the aircraft stationed here in Korea. Now to get back—"

"Yes, well, I too have an association with the Thud. I flew in Vietnam. In combat." He leaned heavily on the last two words. The photos on Donley's wall indicated a long Air Force career. As both a pilot and a Vietnam veteran, the man had not spent all his time in cushy assignments. Hunter was trying to remind him that between pilots, men who had been in war, there was supposed to be a bond.

"That doesn't cut any shit around here, mister." The cold tone of Donley's voice told Hunter that the only bond the colonel was interested in was the one he intended to wrap around Hunter's gonads. "This isn't Vietnam and you are just another man who can't keep out of trouble."

"My biggest trouble is that I can't forget that another man who flew the F-105 in Vietnam was one of my best friends. Captain Paul Crandell. He saved my life when we were shot down. Then later, when I was in the hospital, he turned up dead. Right here at Osan." Hunter paused for a moment, then as Donley started to speak, he quickly added, "And I really resent that."

The look on Donley's face turned remote, slightly puzzled. "Crandell? The name is familiar, but I don't remember—"

"An accident here at Osan, he—"

"Oh, yes. The officer from Korat. He got drunk downtown, fell into a ditch, and—"

"You guys got this written down somewhere?" Hunter asked. "Or did you get together in the base commander's hooch and memorize it?"

It was a wild card—throw a little shit in the game just to see what happens. And Donley almost lost. "Why, you insolent bast—" As he stopped and took a breath, Hunter could see the years of experience at work. "I have no idea what you are talking about, Captain." He smiled that cold, hard smile.

It was apparent to Hunter that this man was no fool. He was obviously a bastard, one of those officers who relishes his power and uses it with a scornful vengeance. The problem was, Hunter still didn't know if Donley was involved in Crandell's death or whether he was being manipulated by Washington and Bullis.

"Sergeant Bullis," Donley said, "I want you to—"

He stopped when Hunter cut in. Making his voice loud enough to be heard by everyone in the next room, he said, "Colonel, I want it on the record that I don't trust you or Bullis. And I don't intend to go anywhere with either of you unless there are other people present."

Holy Mother Air Force, you got brain damage from eating kimchee. Do you expect to get away with this shit?

He wasn't sure. Technically all the rules and regulations, as well as pure physical force, were on the other side. But Hunter was betting on the system. That great, clumsy, bungling, blind bureaucracy. In a dark alley these two could shoot him full of lead, chop his body into dog meat, and piss on the remains. But here, in this military office with everybody watching, the system also worked for him. As long as he didn't make a mistake.

Donley and Bullis knew it too. He saw it in their faces. Donley leaned back, weighing his options. Bullis was enraged, barely able to control himself. In a cold voice Donley said, "The base commander is waiting for you. He told me to provide you with an escort and make sure you get to his office."

Hunter said, "That sounds reasonable. Always glad to cooperate. But I'm not riding alone with either one of you."

Donley's face was dark with smoldering rage. The intensity made Hunter wonder if he'd made a big mistake. Involved or not, Donley was obviously a dangerous man to have for an enemy. After several seconds Donley said, "Sergeant Bullis, please arrange for a jeep to take the captain to the base commander's office."

As Bullis wheeled and marched out of the office, there was an undisguised look of loathing on his face. Hunter wasn't sure if it was for him or Donley—or both of them.

Chapter 29

A young three-striper drove Hunter to the headquarters complex in an SP jeep. He was armed, but only with the standard .38 pistol. Donley had said that Hunter wasn't under arrest, but he wasn't exactly free either. It was quarter to five, fifteen minutes past the end of the duty day, and the headquarters complex already felt empty. The sound of the young cop's boots and Hunter's shoes clopping on the plywood floor echoed off the walls as they marched down the long, dim, deserted hall. When Hunter veered off into the open doorway of the Information Office, the young sergeant started to protest. Holding up his hand, Hunter said, "I want to talk to a friend of mine. It will only take a minute. I promise."

The young cop looked unsure, but followed Hunter into the office. Ron Shaw was at his desk, reviewing news stories written by his enlisted staff for the next issue of the weekly base newspaper.

"Hi, I was waiting for you to call—" Seeing Hunter's escort, Shaw's eyes widened. "Jesus, Mike, what's—"

"I'm on my way to have a little chat with Colonel Davies. I was wondering if you'd come along."

"Ah, well . . ." He wanted to tell his reluctant-looking friend about Kim, but not in front of one of Donley's people. The expression on Shaw's face reminded Hunter of a fly tangled in a web who sees the spider closing in. Shaw played with the papers in front of him for several moments, then with a deep sigh, started shuffling them into different baskets on his desk marked IN, OUT, and HOLD. Hunter noticed the HOLD basket got the lion's share of the action. Running out of papers, Shaw stood up, smoothed the front of his tan uniform shirt over his ample stomach, and asked, "Uh, Mike, what's going on?"

"I have the feeling this session with Davies might get a bit thick. I'd like a witness. Right now you're the only person on this base I trust."

"Lucky me," Shaw said, gulping.

Hunter smiled. "What the hell, Ron, it's only a career."

"Yeah, I know." He sighed nervously. "But like they say about the war, it's the only one I got."

"Ron, you gotta ask yourself, what's more important, making captain or being on the side of truth and justice?"

"Hey, I already donated. I'm not supposed to give again for three months."

Hunter nodded toward the door. "Let's do it."

When the three men entered the base commander's office, Hunter saw that the Korean secretary was gone, but the master sergeant was still on the job. The triumphant look on his face when he saw Hunter followed by the cop said: "See, God really does answer prayers."

"I believe the colonel is expecting me?" Hunter said.

"You bet yer as—ah, yes, he is." Then, looking at Shaw, the sergeant asked, "What are you doing here, Lieutenant?"

Hunter answered. "I asked him to come."

The NCO's face turned dark. "Just a minute, I better ask Colonel Davies about that."

"Sure, we'll wait."

In less than a minute both the sergeant and Colonel Davies came back to the outer office. The colonel's face was the perfect picture of the stern yet fair senior officer. "Lieutenant Shaw, I don't understand why you are here. What I have to say is official business between Captain Hunter and myself."

"Well, ah, I—"

Before Shaw could backpedal himself out of the office. Hunter spoke up. "Colonel, I just went through a rather insulting session with your director of security police. From now on, I want someone I trust around when I am being interrogated by any officials. If you don't think Lieutenant Shaw is suitable, I'll be glad to wait for a representative from the JAG."

The JAG was the Judge Advocate's General, the Air Force's legal people. It was a bluff. He didn't trust any member of the JAG's office he did not know any more than Davies. But it worked. "Ah, actually, Captain, this isn't a court-martial. I don't believe it's necessary at this point to bring in the JAG. If the lieutenant's agreeable, so am I."

Hunter started to relax, then Davies added, "Lieutenant Shaw, I hope you have fully considered what your association with this man might mean to you, ah, later on."

It was a threat, and not a subtle one. But it had an unexpected effect on the younger officer. Sucking in his paunch, Shaw said, "Yes, sir. I've thought about that. But I know Captain Hunter pretty well. I know that he is a former combat pilot with a distinguished war record. He is also my friend. Until someone can prove that he has done something wrong, I'll give him my help if he wants it."

Right on, Lieutenant Stoutheart.

Davies looked miffed. "Well, then, why don't you both come in? Oh, and by the way, you too, Sergeant." Apparently Davies wanted a witness too. He told the young security policeman, "That will be all, son. Thanks for your help." The young man beamed. He didn't often get a pat on the head from Steve Canyon.

The sergeant picked up a file folder with several papers inside and fell in behind Hunter and Shaw, who followed Davies into the office. As they entered, Hunter whispered to his friend, "Just give me a few good men and we'll take that hill."

Shaw, halting next to the sergeant by the door, looked pained as Hunter took the required position at attention in front of the base commander's desk. Davies, sitting down, looked at Hunter sharply. "What did you say, Captain?"

Quickly shifting gears, Hunter said, "Sir, I want to know why I've been hauled in here, practically in irons."

Surprised by the sudden assault, Davies fumbled for a moment. His sincere blue eyes blinked in confusion as he attempted to take control of the interview. "Well, ah, you have been causing a lot of trouble." He pointed at the blood on Hunter's shirt. "Just look at you, apparently you have been fighting again, and—"

"Don't jump to conclusions, Colonel," he said. "You can't nail me for a torn shirt with a little blood on it."

Davies' mouth tightened and his eyes lost most of their sincerity. "No, not for a shirt. However, there is some question about your conduct off base in one of the clubs in the village. You were involved in a fight in a bar, I believe."

That was neat, Hunter thought. He had not accused Hunter of starting a fight, just being in a fight, which was true. "I tried to stop some trouble in that club. It happened when I gave an off-duty security policeman an order to stop pushing people around. Instead of obeying the order he started a fight with me. I had no alternative but to defend myself."

"That's your version. I've been told there are others."

"So I've been told, but if you can't come up with witnesses who will tell the truth, then I'll get them myself."

Quickly Davies said, "I didn't say you were not telling the truth. I only said that there are conflicting stories that need to be investigated. After all, what took place there has created very serious racial tension on this base."

Shaw, who had been silent up to now, blurted out, "Wait a minute, Colonel. You can't blame the racial problems at Osan on Mike. That's bullsh—I mean that just isn't so. Everyone knows those problems have been brewing for months."

"I'm not blaming the entire problem on Captain Hunter," Davies said irritably. "I am suggesting that until last night we had it under control. And that if he had not severely aggravated them by his assault on a Negro NCO, then the other events of the evening might not have happened."

"Colonel Davies, I read the report on last night's incidents. It said there was some evidence that indicated much of what happened was planned in advance." The disgust in Shaw's voice was obvious. "You can't charge the captain with—"

"Nobody is charging anyone with anything, Lieutenant Shaw. At least not yet. I said it needs to be investigated."

That seemed like as good a point as any to get back in the conversation. Hunter said, "As long as I'm not charged with anything, I guess we'll be—"

"Not quite so fast," Davies said. Then Hunter saw it, the smug look of victory on the older officer's face. "Until I am thoroughly satisfied that you are not responsible for what happened last night, I'm restricting you to the confines of this base." Hunter's eyes narrowed as Donley smiled smugly. "And that is a legal order which the JAG has already approved."

Wonderful, wonderful!

It was done very well too. Nothing specific, just the possibility of guilt. No serious action, only temporary restriction until after an investigation. Nothing to which Hunter could officially object. Except for the fact that it shut him off completely from Soon Ja.

The sergeant handed the papers he was holding to Davies, who said, "Just so there won't be a misunderstanding, here is a letter with my signature informing you of this action. The consequences of violating restriction are detailed. You would be well advised to take note of that." He handed two sheets of paper to Hunter. "Sign the original. The other is for you."

Hunter had to work hard to control the impulse to smash the man's specious face. Instead he concentrated on reading the letter. It was all there. ". . . restriction until such time as . . . violation could result in court-martial action . . ." He took a pen from the out-stretched hand of the sergeant and signed the top copy. When he finished, he left the pen on the desk instead of handing it back to the sergeant, knowing as he did it that it was a petty act.

Davies picked up the letter and checked the signature. Then he looked up, smiled, and said, "Now, you are dismissed."

In the outside hall, Shaw said, "I think he gotcha."

"Yeah," Hunter said, his voice heavy with resignation, as they walked back to Shaw's empty office. "It's too bad, but he's not as dumb as he acts."

"Well, hell," Shaw said in a hail-fellow tone, "it's not so bad. What's a few days' restriction?"

After closing the hall door, Hunter told Shaw about finding Kim, and that he had her stashed in a hotel down in the village.

"Oh, fuck me to tears."

"You took the words right out of my mouth."

"What're you gonna do?"

"I don't know. This restriction could've been cooked up just to keep me out of the way while they look for her."

"Aw, Mike, I don't like Davies, but do you really think someone in his position would be involved in . . ." He let the sentence hang.

"Boggles the mind, doesn't it?"

"What gets me," Shaw said, "is why Davies would even have time to fuck with you. This base has problems a hell of a lot more important than someone getting in a fight downtown."

"What do you mean?"

"This morning after I talked to you, we had a mini-riot. About fifty blacks got together and marched up to the general's office. They demanded to talk to him, to air their grievances."

"What happened?"

"The shitbrain called Donley and his boys to run 'em off. But at least Donley is a little smarter than the general. He sent Washington to talk to them. After Washington did some fancy footwork they gave it up.

But for a while there I thought we were gonna have Watts right here at Osan.''

"I was wondering where Washington was. I didn't see him when Donley and Bullis were leaning on me.''

"Right now Washington is a very popular man with the command section—if you catch my drift.''

"The establishment's man in Papa Joe's Alley.''

"Something like that,'' Shaw said.

"Beautiful, just fucking beautiful.''

"Yeah, except that I don't think that even Washington's gonna be able to keep the lid on much longer. The general and most of his ass-kissing colonels still think they can order the problems away. But I was listening to what the blacks were saying. A lot of their grievances are legit, and they're tired of being shit on.''

"You may be right, but who knows when, and if, anything will happen? The main thing is to make sure Soon Ja is safe.''

"How you gonna do that? You can't leave the base.''

"That's right. But you can.''

Shaw's eyes got large. "Aw, Mike, I don't—''

"Ron, I know this is asking a lot. I wouldn't do it if I could think of any other way. I'm sure Miss Kim is the key to this whole thing. Also, there's got to be a reason why the cops are so interested in keeping track of me. To find out the truth, I have to keep her safe until she can tell me what she knows.''

"Well, I suppose maybe—there's this one Korean who works for the mayor down there, he owes me a favor. The command section tried to jerk his base pass, something about black marketing, but I fixed it so he could keep it.''

"Can you trust him?''

"I think so. He hates Donley and most of the command section because they always take a condescending attitude toward Koreans, but he likes me.''

"Sounds like the right man to ask for help.'' Shaw nodded but did not move. Hunter said, "You need taxi money?''

"Well . . .''

Hunter took out his money clip, slipped out a five-dollar MPC note, and handed it to Shaw. The glum-looking younger man accepted it but still didn't move.

After several moments Hunter added, "So, I guess you'd better be going."

Flinching, Shaw said, "I know, I know."

Chapter 30

When Shaw was underway, Hunter went back to his BOQ room, dug out his pills, and took two for the pain in his head, which was hammering a dull beat. He removed his dirty clothes and went to the showers. As he washed away the dirt and turmoil he considered his situation.

You're really humming, his inner voice chided, *restricted to the base like some dumbshit airman who caught VD.*

It was ludicrous. An Air Force officer had died in a way that was beginning to look like murder, and the only person who cared was being restrained by the military system with rules meant to punish wayward enlisted men. And the worst thing was, once put into operation, the system functioned most effectively. If he were caught disobeying a lawful order from a superior officer, he could be court-martialed. Which could ruin his whole day, not to mention his career. He could even end up in jail. While he didn't think that was too likely, he didn't care for the other options either. One thing he was sure of, if he was caught off base Davies would indeed push it, and Hunter had a good idea what area he would choose to put it.

This just wasn't supposed to happen. He was an officer, one of those who administered the rules. Sure, he had done his share of griping about the petty annoyances connected with military life, but he knew he was protected by the buffer of rules and regulations, something unique to the United States military, which limited the power of those in authority to disregard the constitutional rights of any individual, right down to the lowest-ranking enlisted man.

As a rated officer, Hunter was a member of the elite. All officers were supposed to be equal, but everyone knew pilots were more equal than others. Members of a special fraternity, where senior officers administered the rules as would a benevolent father to a spirited son. A chumminess prevailed, from the most hardheaded colonel to the shiniest new lieutenant. In this club, pilot's wings were the membership card.

Even at that level there were problems. Not the least of which was the system-bred company man—bureaucrats in uniform who substituted following rules for doing what was right. Those who emphasized regulations instead of people. It was a structure which too often created authority gods, purveyors of inane and sometimes insane decisions made in the name of maintaining the status quo. However, when such individuals created a mess which became insufferable, the system usually neutralized them. If you were one of the clever ones, you learned to sidestep that sort of person, making sure he did not get you before the system got him.

Hunter had always prided himself on being one of the clever ones. He had skated to the edge often enough, but instinctively knew when it was time to make a sharp right turn and shoot back to center. Now he was on a new course which was taking him beyond the world he had always known. Suddenly he was on the outside looking in, completely at odds with his old world and becoming more isolated with each passing moment.

It wasn't a comforting realization.

He put on clean jeans and a shirt that had been tailor-made in Bangkok. Thinking of that, he experienced a wave of nostalgia for Southeast Asia. At least there the only danger came from the enemy. That was beginning to seem like the good old days.

Finished dressing, he went to the club to wait for Shaw. Just as he was about to enter the lounge, a voice came from down the hall: "Hey, Hunter, you ever see the base commander?"

It was Matt Zhalan, who had told him earlier that Davies was looking for him. "Oh, yeah, I saw him."

"You get everything straightened out?"

"You could say that."

"You don't remember me, do you?" Zhalan asked.

Hunter took a closer look at Zhalan. He appeared to be a bit younger than Hunter, about the same height, trim build, medium brown hair and a war-zone mustache that was becoming popular with a lot of men in the military, especially fighter pilots, worn as long as the Air Force regulation on hair length could be stretched. All in all, the typical media image of the gung-ho fighter jock. But not one who was familiar to Hunter.

"No, I can't really—"

"We met once. I was new in Thuds at Tahkli when you were doing your second tour at Korat. You were one of the legends, the Hunter, for all us FNGs."

"The SAM put a little tarnish on that legend."

"Not really. You lived to tell about it."

Hunter smiled. Now, if he could survive Colonel Davies he'd really have something to talk about. To Zhalan he said, "So, other than the telephones, how do you like Korea?"

"Korea's fine, but I don't like the Safety Office. Your coming in may be a good thing for me."

"How's that?"

"I been trying to get a job with the Army, coordinating close air-support training up on the DMZ area."

"Better watch out. You get up there with the Army and you'll end up flying helicopters."

"Yeah, low and slow, a fate worse than death."

Hunter invited Zhalan to join him for a drink, but he said he had to leave. In the cocktail lounge, Hunter selected one of the low captain's chairs and ordered a beer. The chair on either side was empty, but the rest of the room hummed with happy-hour activity. He sat watching the familiar scene, pondering how such trouble could be happening to such a nice guy like himself.

Everyone else in the room seemed to be having a wonderful time. Across the bar a major and a lieutenant colonel, both in blues, were flirting with a cute young lieutenant-type nurse dressed in starched hospital whites. A few feet from them a bunch of fighter jocks, in flight suits with zippers pulled down to indecent levels, were talking and flying with their hands, telling tales of past missions and the thrills of the wild blue. Jeanne was joking with a group of senior officers as she served their drinks. Down the bar a young first lieutenant in summer khakis was in deep conversation with an attractive Korean lady.

At another time he would have been part of it. In the middle of the group of fighter pilots. Or more likely, across the bar trying to talk the nurse away from the two older officers and back to his BOQ room. Now he felt like the guy who all the other members knew was delinquent on his dues and about to have his club card cancelled. Strangely, the further this new, lonesome track carried him from the center of that familiar world, the less meaning it seemed to have.

He had another beer and marveled at how all these people could be in here, spinning their lives away, blissfully ignorant of the fact that one of their own had been stuffed into a dirty stream until the foul, dark water filled his lungs and took the life from his body. He felt a sudden urge to jump up and scream, *Wake up, you shit-brained scumbags. The assholes are devouring the world while you fat slugs sit here playing with yourselves.*

Then, as quickly as it had come, the frenzy passed. Damn, those pills again. The sudden flashes of paranoia and burst of anger were, he was fairly certain, a result of the painkillers. At least he hoped it was the pills.

Got to watch myself. After all, many things were permitted in officers' clubs: lying, conniving, or trying to seduce a best friend's wife. However, screaming "Wake up!" was definitely not the right stuff.

As the bartender set another beer in front of him, a deep, resonant voice intoned, "Captain Hunter?"

Surprised, he turned quickly and looked up toward the sound. He saw a belt buckle. Sure, the chair he was sitting in was low, but this was absurd. There should have been a neck or at least a chest at that height. He pushed back and looked higher. Way up. Whoever it was, he was really tall. His head was lost somewhere in the upper darkness of the room.

A new wave of anxiety swept through him. They'd called out the death squad. He had to get out of his chair. He couldn't fight stuck down here—

"My name is Troxler," the giant said. "Mind if I join you?"

What? Oh, the pills again. As he struggled to keep the quaver in his voice from being obvious, he said, "I don't mind."

As the man sat down in the next chair, Hunter realized that he wasn't really a giant, just extra-large. Say about six four or five, maybe two hundred and thirty-plus solid-looking pounds. Somewhere in his forties. Hunter took a deep breath to calm down. Who did this guy say he was? Oh yeah, Troxler. The OSI.

Wonderful, wonderful.

Now he had met all the Osan law types. He wondered if this meeting was going to be as many laughs as previous ones. He would also like to know what rank this guy was in real life. He knew most OSI agents were NCOs. This guy was probably a tech sergeant, maybe even a drinking buddy of Bullis and Washington. Law types had their special fraternity too.

The bartender came over and Troxler ordered a scotch and water, then looked at Hunter and said, "I understand you've been restricted to the base."

What was he doing, rubbing it in? Smiling wolfishly, Hunter said, "My what big ears you have, Grandma."

The big man ignored the sarcasm. "Want to tell me about it?"

"What's to tell? I started a rice riot in peaceful Chicol Village, and now the base commander is protecting the community from my bad influence.''

"Not what I meant. Tell me about your friend.''

The realization that Troxler was talking about Crandell's death shocked Hunter. What did he want? Was this some sort of trap? "From what I've heard, you've got the reports, and you've been talking to everyone I've talked to. I guess you know as much about him as I do.''

Troxler had a large head with thinning, wavy gray hair and bushy eyebrows sitting on top of intelligent-looking, dark brown eyes. For just a moment his face reflected a deep weariness. That was quickly replaced with a professional look. It was not a mean, I'm-gonna-tear-your-arm-off look such as the one Bullis favored. Nor an I-shouldn't-be-wasting-my-time-on-this-piece-of-crud look like Donley's. Not even the I'm-the-big-daddy-rabbit-around-here, so-you-must-tell-me look that Davies usually tried to affect. Troxler's face expressed a friendly concern that generated trust.

Answering Hunter, he said, "I understand you think there's been an—an injustice.''

"Injustice!'' He experienced an angry flash. "You mean because they're calling Crandell's murder an accident?''

Whoops, he hadn't meant to say that. The damn pills were still rattling around in his brain. *Be cool, fool.*

"Why do you call it murder?''

"The same reason I gave Colonel Davies,'' he said defensively. "The report said he was drunk and fell in that ditch. Crandell didn't drink, and he wasn't the sort of person who fell into ditches.''

"He was the kind of person who was going to marry a—'' The look that swept over Hunter's face caused Troxler to pause. ''. . . to marry a girl who lives in the village. And, as you know, most of those women are business girls.''

"Fuck you!''

It came out louder than he expected. So loud that

several faces nearby turned and looked in their direction. Hunter carefully arranged his face in a pleasant smile until the faces turned away. Then, looking at Troxler and keeping his voice low and calm, he said, "What I meant to say was, fuck you."

The man still didn't look annoyed. And that annoyed Hunter. Troxler said, "Okay, he was an officer who was involved with a girl from the village. Of whom we know very little. Which means that since we know nothing, anything is possible."

He paused. Hunter did not comment. He went on, "Curiously enough, that lady seems to have disappeared."

Yeah, Hunter thought smugly, from you, and Washington, and all the rest of the cops—and I ain't talking.

"You know anything about her?"

Casually, Hunter said, "I know I'd like to talk to her. I'd like to know what she has to say about Paul's death."

Troxler leaned forward, his eyes digging into Hunter's. "Why is it I don't think you're not telling me everything?"

"That's easy," Hunter said, sliding his chair backward to increase the distance between them, "because you're not wearing a hat." Troxler looked puzzled. "You see, I been wondering about your hat. Is it white? Or is it black?"

He could tell from Troxler's reaction that he understood. The big man reached for his drink, and in one long pull he emptied the glass. After he set it down he stared at the water rings the glass made on the polished black bar top. "I been reading your record, Hunter. You're a hell of a combat pilot."

In spite of himself, Hunter smiled at the compliment, but before Troxler got any mileage out of it, he added, "But you got a maverick streak—and that's just a euphemism for being a smartass. Despite that, so far you done good. But if you keep going the way you are, sooner or later you're going to get in trouble." He waited a moment, then, his voice heavy with authority, he said, "And it may just be sooner."

"Flattery will get you everywhere," Hunter sassed, trying to live up to Troxler's characterization.

"You work at it too hard, and it ain't that cute to start with."

"You mean I don't get good marks for ass kissing and boot licking? That's too bad. Maybe it's because I just spent six months in a hospital for doing a job that very few others in this Air Force are qualified to do. And that was my second time around."

He stopped long enough for a swallow of beer, then as Troxler started to say something he quickly added, "So what, right? Do I think someone owes me something because of that? Not really. Do I think I paid my dues in this chummy little club of ours? Bet your ass I do."

"Hunter, I'm getting tired of trying to be nice to you. You're still in the military and—"

"Don't lay that duty, loyalty, honor trip on me," Hunter flared. "I've been there. So was Crandell. Flying and fighting while being screwed to the wall by impossible rules and restrictions made for political considerations. They sent us after the same targets day after day until the enemy could set their watches by the sounds of our engines. We got beat to death by guns that were protected because they were in civilian areas. But we did it anyway. I did it, and so did Crandell. All I want is for the Air Force to say he was a good officer, not some pathetic fool who got drunk and fell into a ditch and drowned."

Hunter stopped. It had been a long speech and Troxler actually looked embarrassed. "If it wasn't an accident, what was it?"

You've gone too far, dummy. Shut up.

He had to be more careful. There was something about this big oak tree of a man that inspired confidence. But he needed more than just a gut reaction before he was willing to trust him. Lamely he said, "Who knows? Remember, you're talking to a maverick, an irresponsible officer who starts race riots."

The expectant look on the big man's face wilted, replaced by weary disgust. Unable to face Troxler's penetrating eyes, Hunter looked away, at the crowd across the bar. The group of pilots had broken up, and several had moved in on the two senior officers, attempting to filch the good-looking nurse.

When he looked back, Troxler said, "Hunter, you're involved in a potentially dangerous situation. I hope you are as capable as you think."

Was that a threat? Actually, it sounded more like a warning. Who the hell was this guy? What side was he on? The only thing Hunter could think to say was "I hope so too."

Troxler dug out his wallet, removed a business card, and handed it to him. "Here's my number. When you are ready to stop acting childishly, call me. I can help. Until then, try not to do anything stupid."

He stood up and lumbered out of the room.

Hunter was left wondering if maybe Troxler really was one of the good guys. Well, maybe, but maybe just was not enough. He still wanted to know what color hat the man wore.

As he sat mulling that, Jeanne, the waitress, came over and slipped into the empty chair. "You find girl you look for?"

His suspicion circuits lit up momentarily, but no, not Jeanne. He had known her too long. He just couldn't believe she was one of the bad guys. But why was everyone asking him about Kim? Affecting casualness, he said, "No, I'm still looking."

She leaned closer, lowering her voice. "I ask, but nobody want to talk about her. One thing I know, you better take it easy. Now too much trouble this place."

Another person warning him off. Or was it a threat? "Jeanne, if you know something—"

"No." Her face went blank. "I'm Korean. Good Korean girl work hard, don't talk too much, don't make trouble for GIs. That's rule for Korean people who work in GI places."

"But, Jeanne," he protested, "there's already trouble—"

"GI trouble. Not Korean trouble."

She knew. At least some of it. Maybe all the Koreans knew, but didn't want to get involved. GIs came and went, but the Koreans had to live here. She said, "Your friend, I'm sorry for him, but he is dead. No matter what happens, you cannot change."

She stood up and went back to work. From the jukebox, Janis Joplin was singing about how she would like to have a Mercedes-Benz. But she wouldn't need it now. She was dead too.

Then Ron Shaw entered the bar. As soon as Hunter saw his friend's face, he knew Kim was gone.

Chapter 31

"They got her," Shaw said as he sat down.

"How?"

"I went to see the guy I told you about. He wasn't wildly enthusiastic, but he said he would help."

"Okay."

Shaw explained that he had gone to the hotel, but when he checked the room it was empty. He found the mama-san but at first she told him she didn't know anything about Soon Ja. Shaw said he told her he was going to call the KNP. "I dropped the names of a couple of the top Korean cops, everyone knows who they are, just to let her know I was serious." Then the mama-san loosened up. She told Shaw that after Hunter had left, three GI SPs had come in. They knew Miss Kim was there, and told the mama-san that the big GI and the girl were into drugs. Naturally the old woman didn't object when they got Soon Ja and took her away. She told Shaw that the girl was still acting *dingee, dingee* when the SPs took her away.

Shaw paused and looked at Hunter, who was staring at the glass in front of him. He said, "They told her not to say anything if you came back, so I guess . . ."

His voice trailed off as he saw the look that came over his friend's face. Hunter's eyes stayed fixed on the half-empty glass in his hand. Amber liquid sloshed softly from side to side as his fingers tightened around it. His outward calm belied the scream of anger that raged in his head. As he stared at the glass, it became fuzzy and indistinct. He blinked his eyes a couple of times, but the hazy image did not clear. He was aware that the hammering inside his head was back.

"Mike, I'm sorry, I—"

"It's not your fault. It's . . . ah . . ." He couldn't find words that were right, his mind was dulled. Somewhere in there, in some remote recess, beyond the ache, his voice was calmly explaining, *It's the emotional tension. Just calm down and you'll feel better.* That voice was, however, in competition with the beast. And the beast wanted him to break something. Throw the glass, send it flying across the room, smashing against the pillar next to where the two senior officers were now standing by themselves, having just watched one of the pilots waltz off with the nurse. The beast wanted him to pound sense into this collection of maggots, to make them realize evil was winning.

Slowly, by concentrating his attention on his fingers, he made them relax. He carefully placed the glass on the bar. It took extreme effort.

"What should we do now?"

Hunter had momentarily forgotten his friend. Surprised by the voice, he turned, then letting the beast loose a bit, said, "I don't know about you, but I think I'm gonna kill somebody."

"Damn, Mike, take it easy."

"I don't know how much good it will do, but I can promise you, some sonofabitch is going to die."

"Mike," Shaw hissed, looking around, "that's not helping. You—"

"Yeah, I know," he said, sighing. The rush of pain was receding.

"Do you know who—"

"Mama-san said two of them were young guys, but she said the one in charge was a big sergeant honcho. And black."

"Washington," Hunter said. "Now I know why he wasn't around the cop shop when I was having my little meeting with his boss."

"I guess those people in Suwon must've called down here to let Washington know what had happened as soon as you took off. They were probably waiting somewhere on the MSR for you when you came back.

They must have followed you, and then all they had to do was wait until you left.''

"I suppose."

"Something else that really blew my mind," Shaw said. "My Korean friend, when I told him about the girl, he acted like he knew something about it."

"What do you mean?"

"When I asked for his help, he started asking questions. So I told him I needed to hide a girl so the base cops couldn't find her. He said something about how the security police were very bad now, how he understood. Then I mentioned that her boyfriend was an officer who drowned in an accident that maybe wasn't an accident, and he knew Crandell's name."

Hunter nodded. "Yeah, I'm beginning to think that a lot of the local Koreans are aware of what is going on." He told Shaw about his conversation with Jeanne.

"That's amazing," Shaw said, then added, "By the way, did I tell you that Jeanne owns the hooch where I live?"

"What?"

"Yeah. I found out one time after I saw her visiting the mama-san. Later, I was drinking with her husband, and he told me his wife is just the manager, that Jeanne owns that building and a bunch of others. I kidded her about it one time. She wasn't too happy about that. She said that since we're friends, she doesn't mind my knowing, but she doesn't want everyone to know."

Hunter nodded. He had only been half listening to his friend while he tried to think what to do next. One thing for sure, he had to get off the base now. He told Shaw.

"Damn, Mike, breaking restriction could get you in a lot of trouble."

"Ron, breaking restriction is rather minor compared to what is happening here."

"Damn, I don't know what to think anymore," Shaw said. "It's not gonna be easy. Security at the gate has been beefed up and they're checking everyone's ID real close."

Hunter rubbed his head, feeling tired. "You got any ideas?"

"Who, me?" Shaw looked surprised. "Well, I suppose . . . ah, how well did you say you know Jeanne?"

"I already told you she's been trying to help. Why?"

"One thing I know for sure. If the Koreans want to get something off the base—it's gone."

Although Shaw might be overstating the case a bit, Hunter knew what he meant. He remembered the B-diamond goats. It had happened way back in the dark ages before the *Pueblo* when Osan was a forgotten housekeeping operation with only the nuke-alert birds. Those aircraft and their bombs were kept in B-diamond, guarded behind a high double fence. The nuclear-storage bunkers were covered with several feet of earth with grass growing on top. Since the aircraft were always on alert and hardly ever flew, it was easy duty for the troops stationed there.

Too easy. A zealous new wing commander from Japan decided during an inspection visit that the place wasn't military because of the high grass growing around the bunkers. Most grass at Osan was cut by Korean grounds workers, but they were not allowed into B-diamond because of the nukes. So the enlisted maintenance troops ended up being tasked to mow it. After a few turns with an old push mower, one desperate young GI had a brilliant idea. Buy a few goats and let them graze. The officer in charge, hoping to keep his men content, approved. And everyone was happy.

For a while.

Then one day one of the goats was missing. They were still trying to figure out what had happened when a second goat disappeared. It became painfully obvious that hungry Koreans were getting the goats. From inside a top-security, nuclear-storage area. The idea that U.S. Air Force security was only as good as the Koreans' desire to circumvent it was bad. The knowledge that they couldn't figure out how to stop them was terrible. But the thing that really scared them shitless was knowing what would happen to their careers when the Air Force found out.

In the best military tradition, everyone involved covered it up. The remaining goats were quickly removed. Everyone who knew about the incident was sworn to secrecy. The enlisted men, who had less to fear, extracted one concession for their silence. Thereafter the officers took turns cutting the grass.

"Yes," Hunter answered Shaw, "if the Koreans want it, they can get it."

"That's right," Shaw said, grinning. "So sit tight, I'm gonna talk to Jeanne."

Since Hunter didn't have a better idea, he nodded. Having someone to whom he could confide made a difference. The ache in his head subsided and his vision was crisp and clear again. He switched from beer to coffee. He finished one cup and was working on a second when Shaw returned.

Smiling deviously as his eyes darted from side to side, his friend said, "Okay, I think you're set."

"Did she ask you why?"

"Nope."

Hunter wondered about that, then remembered the knowing look in her eyes earlier. Fifteen minutes passed, then Jeanne came by and nodded. Shaw followed her from the lounge. In a few minutes he returned. In a loud voice he said. "Hey, Mike, come on in the back. There's a guy in the stag bar I want you to meet."

Hunter knew about the stag bar in back, but since one of the things he liked best about bars was meeting ladies, he did not frequent the place that much. As he followed Shaw he wondered why his friend wanted to go there. Before they reached it, however, Shaw turned and led him out a back door into the dark night. It took several moments for Hunter's eyes to adjust to the darkness. Then he saw a large black van parked near the building. Painted on the door of the van was "OF-FICERS' CLUB."

"Your transportation awaits, buddy," Shaw said, indicating the open back door of the truck. "Jeanne fixed it. It's supposed to look like a trash run, but the Koreans on the gate will figure there are black-market goodies inside, and they'll pass you through, expecting a cut later.''

''I hope you're right.''

''Trust me. Have I ever let you down?''

''Let me count the ways.''

''Nice talk, GI,'' Shaw said, grinning. ''After you get downtown, go to my place and wait till I get there. I'm gonna hang around a few minutes to make sure no one is checking.''

The ride went off without a flaw. Hunter hid under a pile of cardboard, sweating as they approached the gate. But they hardly slowed down as the guards quickly waved them by. The driver went down the hill until he came to the alley nearest Shaw's hooch. He turned in, pulled well off the main street, and stopped the truck. Lifting the cardboard, he motioned for Hunter to come out.

In all the time the driver had not spoken, and Hunter had supposed he did not speak English. As he slid forward into the passenger's seat, he said, *''Komop sumnida,''* Thank you.

The man nodded. ''Take it easy, Captain.''

The night was cool and the smell of rain was strong, but it was not deterring action in the vill. GIs and Koreans flowed around the parked vehicle, and Hunter knew it was best not to linger. He got out and quickly walked down the alley, keeping his head down, shoulders hunched, doing his best to look like a tired airman hurrying home to his *yobo*.

He reached Shaw's compound, opened the gate, and stepped in. No sirens or shouts, just the usual sounds of people living came from inside the rooms. As he walked across the concrete, the mama-san's door slid open a couple of inches, a pair of eyes checked him out, then the door closed. Sumi's room was dark and locked. Light showed through rice paper panels of Shaw's hooch door, and inside the Beatles were singing, ''Can't Buy Me Love.''

He stepped up and knocked on the door's wood

frame. After a moment it slid open and Shaw's Miss Kim looked out. The eyes in her pixie face were bright, but there was no recognition there.

"Hi. Remember me?" Nothing. "Mike Hunter?" Like talking to the wall. "The other day when you cooked chicken . . ." Still nothing. "I stayed with Sumi, and—"

"Oh mo." Korean for "Son of a gun, what a surprise." A big smile lit up her face. *"Ada sumnida,* you butterfly captain."

"Well, yes, I guess that's me."

She slid the door open wider, but did not invite him in. *"Yobo* no stay."

"I know, he'll be here as soon—"

"I not know where he stay." Her face clouded as she spoke. He saw a fire flash of anger in her eyes. He started to explain, but she cut him off. "I think maybe he go butterfly too."

"Oh no. He's helping—"

"Really piss me off."

There weren't many girls who could say that and still look cute as a frisky kitten, but she accomplished it with ease. He said, "Really, he'll be here in—"

"Maybe I go club." She wasn't listening to him. "I can catch GI easy." She held up her hand and snapped her fingers. Cutely.

"I am sure you can," he said, trying to sound sincere, "but you don't need to do that because—"

"I think I better go."

Before he could say anything the gate swung open and Shaw stepped in, saying, "Hi, *yobo,* sorry I'm late. Hi, Mike, good to see you made it."

"You don't know how glad I am to see you." The conversation with Shaw's *yobo* had not helped his aching head.

Chapter 32

Since neither Shaw nor Hunter had eaten, they had food delivered from a Chinese restaurant. While they talked they ate *yakimondo,* Korean spring rolls, *yaki-meshee,* fried rice, and *kalbee,* highly seasoned, barbecued beef short ribs. There was also rice and half a dozen varieties of *kimchee* in small dishes. The food, a few more pills, and avoiding beer considerably improved Hunter's physical and mental well-being.

By the time they were finished, he had decided on his next move. Information about the security police was crucial, and he hoped to get that through his friend, Lee, the brass dealer. Knowing it was best not to chance being seen in the vill, he again asked Shaw for help. "Talk to Lee, tell him I need to see him. Ask him to come as soon as possible."

After Shaw left, Minh Ah, who had been quietly listening to the conversation, said, "You have much trouble."

"Yes," Hunter answered slowly, "but it's not just my trouble. It has been here for a long time. I've just stirred it up a bit."

"I hope you no make trouble for my *yobo.*"

"I'm trying not to get him into anything serious. He's my friend."

"I'm like him very much." The girl was serious, obviously worried by the things she had heard. "He very good to me. I'm no want him to have hard time."

He wanted to explain that he didn't intend to create problems for his friend, but that at this point he had to rely on the few people he knew he could trust. He wasn't sure this child-woman would understand—hell, he wasn't sure he understood. He was saved from trying by a knock on the door.

His first thought was that Shaw had returned, then he realized that Shaw would not knock. He jumped up, quickly moved out of the sight of anyone outside the door, and motioned for Minh Ah to answer it.

His tension was transmitted to the girl, who, eyes large with anxiety, slowly pulled back the door.

"Is your old man home?" The voice had a soft black lilt. Hunter tensed.

"He no stay," the girl answered quickly. Hunter started to relax. She added, "But his friend, captain, he stay."

Oh hell. Hunter prepared to come out fighting as the girl pulled the door aside. Then he saw it was the man from the next hooch—what's his name—Winston.

" 'Lo, Captain," Winston said, not missing Hunter's rigid stance. "Actually, I guess it's you I should talk to."

"Oh." Shaw had said Winston was a good guy, still . . .

Looking Hunter square in the eye, he said, "I guess you know that there are a few brothers looking for you. Some of them are po-lice." He pronounced the word the black way, with a heavy accent on the first syllable. Otherwise, Hunter noticed, he adjusted his speech patterns so that there was no trace of an accent. "You aren't real popular in some parts of the vill."

"So I've heard."

"Just so you understand, Ron told me about your friend who died, and why you're looking for that girl in the picture. He also says you're righteous."

Hunter dropped his hands, but his reflexes were still in the combat mode. "I suppose that depends a lot on where you're at."

"Yeah." Winston nodded, suddenly showing a rueful smile. "Like being a black man in a white man's world. Hard to be sure about that." He paused, then added, "But I know one thing for a fact, this place got jacked outa shape a long time before you showed up.'' He paused, then smiled. ''Okay if we sit down, man?''

Hunter relaxed. ''Good idea.''

They sat on opposite ends of a couch. Minh Ah went over and sat on the bed and pretended to be busy. Winston leaned back and sighed. ''You know, I really like Korea. This is my second tour, and I'm on an extension. The first time I was here, before I reenlisted, I had to live down in Papa Joe's Alley. Not that it was bad, it was just the place where the niggers lived.'' He said the word without any special emphasis, but Hunter sensed the control that took.

''Now things are different. I can live almost any place I want. Oh, some people don't like it too much, but still I can do it. That was one reason I thought things were really changing, really getting better. Then suddenly everything started getting . . . confused. Part of it's what's happened back in the world. Part of it's 'Nam. And part is . . . damn, I'm not sure what to call it.''

He paused, looked down, thinking. His head came up, his eyes steady. ''But I don't figure it's all your fault.''

''Maybe I could use you for a character witness. The base commander seems to think I'm a one-man race riot looking for a place to happen.''

''That pitiful asshole. If that man had a brain he'd get arrested for smuggling shit.''

They both laughed, even though it was an old joke. The last of the tension was gone now. Winston said, ''Anyway, when Ron first told me about why you were looking for that girl, it reminded me of some stories I heard from some brothers, security police brothers. Then something happened earlier today that I think is part of it.''

''What's that?''

''My friend, he's on the cops, but he isn't too happy with the way things happen in that squadron. He came over to see me earlier and told me about a deal he was in today. I think it involves the girl you're looking for.''

"What is it?"

"Late in the afternoon, just before he was supposed to get off, he got picked for a special detail by their NCOIC."

"Chief Washington?"

"You know about him, huh? Well, Washington took my friend and another cop downtown to a hotel to pick up a Korean girl. He said she was the most beautiful thing he'd ever seen. But he also said that she seemed like she was totally stoned. The thing that bothered him was that from the way Washington was talking, he seemed to know her pretty well. Washington said something to her like 'If you hadn't got your captain boyfriend killed, none a this shit woulda happened.' "

Winston paused, then added, "I thought about your friend."

"Do you know where the girl is now?"

"Yeah, I know, but you ain't gonna like it."

"Where?"

"Seoul."

Oh, Sweet Jesus, Hunter thought. Seoul was two or three million people going on five or six million.

Winston went on, "My friend said that after they picked her up, they took her to a hooch in the black section. They kept her there for a while, then a Korean showed up. He's a bad-ass black belt who works for the cops, but according to my friend, he was in bad shape. Someone had really kicked his ass."

Hunter figured he knew who that was. Winston said, "Washington and the Korean did some talking, but they kept it private. After they finished, they got a taxi, and the Korean and the girl got in. He heard Washington tell the Korean to stay in Seoul until Washington told him different."

"You got any idea where in Seoul?"

"Naw. My friend ain't that tight with Washington 'cause he don't play games. But he said it must be serious 'cause Washington was sweating bullets."

Hunter nodded. His mind raced with the new information. He asked Winston a few more questions, but didn't learn anything more of value. He said, "Look, thanks. I want you to know that I really appreciate it."

"Sure, that's okay." Suddenly, without either of them willing it, there was an uneasiness between them. The black-white wall loomed up. Standing, they looked at each other for a moment. Winston moved to the door, starting to leave, then he stopped. "One more thing. The other night, in the Playboy Club, you were in a fight with a brother."

Hunter nodded, wary again.

"The guy who told me about what happened today, his best friend is the dude you punched out." He paused, then said, "I just thought you ought to know."

Then he was gone.

Hunter sat silently, reflecting on the estrangement of differences—that despite a similar cultural upbringing, people of different races would have to work so hard to find common ground. A few minutes later, Shaw returned with Lee. The brass dealer was wearing a nervous grin. "Hunter, you in some kind of shit, huh?"

"Up to my chin. I need some help." Lee shrugged. He didn't like it, but he didn't run either. Hunter went through the story quickly, outlining what had happened and what he had learned, including what Winston had just told him. The Korean's face reverted to a deadpan look, but his gleaming eyes darted back and forth, betraying his anxiety.

"I know already. Some things. I don't think you can do anything, but"—he grinned nervously—"you don't stop."

"Not until it's finished."

"Or someone finish you," Lee blurted. Hunter smiled, hoping the smile looked more confident than he felt. Lee said, "Okay, okay, I'll help you if I can."

"Good. The Korean who took the girl to Seoul works for the security police. So does your friend, Pak. Do you think he will help us find out where they have taken her?"

Lee grinned. "Pak works for the SPs second, works for me first."

"I sort of figured that."

"His house is not far from here. I go find him."

As Lee stood up, Hunter said, "Thanks, my friend."

"Friend, sure," Lee said, flashing his best merchant smile, "but when this shit is over, you have to buy a lot of brass."

After he left, Shaw offered Hunter an OB. He declined. He wanted a clear head. Shaw, however, looked like he badly needed the one he was opening.

Chapter 33

It was just after ten when Lee returned with his friend. Pak was wearing the same wrinkled gray suit as the day before. *"Anya hassayo,* Captain."

"Hello, Mr. Pak." Ignoring the chairs, they all sat down on the floor cushions. Hunter said, "Lee told you what this is about?"

"Yes, he told me."

"I need your help. Some members of the security police are involved in the disappearance of a girl I'm looking for. You work there, maybe you owe somebody, so if—"

The little man sat up, fiddling with his dark tie for a moment. Then he said, "Captain, I got a job. Work is important. Many people in Korea don't have such a good job. But I do my work and I do not owe anybody. Right now many things happen I do not like, I would like to see change."

"Okay, Pak, I understand." Hunter told him the story about finding, then losing Soon Ja. "Can you help me?"

The look on his face went from serious to downright solemn. After a silence he said, "The Korean man is Mr. Kim. He is special assistant to Sergeant Washington and Sergeant Bullis. He is very tough man." Pak paused, looking intently at Hunter. "I do not understand how you were able to beat him."

"I cheated."

"Umm." Pak looked as if he still didn't believe it. "Mr. Kim is not really bad man, just not so smart. Bullis show him much money."

Hunter nodded. The poor selling out to the rich was

hardly unique. He hoped Americans would never have to find out how easy it is to sell themselves to a richer or more powerful nation. He asked, "Do you know a place in Seoul he would take someone he wanted to keep out of sight?"

Pak's head shook from side to side, and Hunter felt a sudden letdown. *Wonderful, just . . .* "But I have heard about such a place, and I think I know how we can find."

Pak said that there was another SP, a man who had been a member of the Washington-Bullis rat pack, but who several months earlier had gotten caught in Seoul by U.S. Army CID agents in the act of peddling a load of black-market television sets. According to Pak, Bullis had been pissed because he warned the man he was being watched by the CID and the guy had gone ahead anyway. Because of that Bullis had done nothing to help, and the man had his nuts crunched but good.

As a result, Pak said, he lost the TVs, got busted from a staff sergeant down to Airman basic, restricted to base for three months, and was fined two thousand dollars. The fine came out of his pay each payday leaving him with zero income. As a result his *yobo* packed up everything that was left and split. Then the hooch mama-san gave him the heave-ho.

"Funny story," Hunter said, "but how—"

"He has been to Seoul house."

"Ah."

Pak smiled. "I know where he stay. He is not on restriction anymore. But no money, so no *yobo*, no go GI bar, only place he go is *makalee* house."

Hunter knew of such places. *Makalee* was a cheap alcoholic home brew made from fermented rice dregs. It looked like gray skim milk and the only time he'd tried it, it tasted much worse than it looked. It was, however, the drink of the poor and the alcoholic, and was dispensed in hole-in-the-wall joints called *makalee* houses.

With Pak leading the way, the three men avoided the main streets where Hunter might be seen. The night had a raw, threatening air as they trekked through a series of dark, winding back alleys. They crossed the main drag once, the MSR once, and ended in front of an iron door in a somber brick building down yet another dark back alley. As best Hunter could figure, they were somewhere on the southeast side of the vill beyond the black section. He did know he had never been this deep in the Korean part of Chicol before.

Pak pushed the door open and led the way down a short flight of steps with only a flickering light coming from somewhere at the bottom. They went through a doorway and entered a room where the only light came from a few candles. The first thing Hunter noticed was the dank smell. The second was that the place had a dirt floor. Even for an old Far East pub rat, that was a first.

"How you like?" Lee was grinning.

"Unique ambience."

"He stay this place because old *yobo* like to come here before," Pak said. "But she know he come, so she don't stay anymore." Hunter saw Pak look around the half-dozen tightly grouped tables. Wait a minute, he realized. Those weren't tables, they were old wooden Air Force communications cable spools turned on their sides.

Nice touch.

"Over there," Pak said, pointing to a table in a dark corner.

As his eyes adjusted, Hunter saw the man, the only Anglo face in the place, lean and bitter-looking. He was sitting alone, still dressed in a fatigue uniform, morosely staring at the drink in front of him. There was something familiar about that face.

Pak motioned for them to follow him and walked to the table. The man looked up. The face and the name over his pocket clicked. Ucko, the older-looking airman he had noticed with Bullis the night before in the Playboy Club.

"Oh, shit." Ucko was looking at Hunter as the three pulled up chairs and sat down. "Pak, what the fuck you bring him—"

"Kenchana," Pak said, smiling. "He want to talk to you."

Ucko finished the liquid in the glass in front of him. "I don't fuckin' want talk to him. He—"

Hunter had already decided the best tactic to take with this man. He reached into his pocket and pulled out his money clip, freshly loaded with twenties at the officers' club. The wad got Ucko's attention.

Thumbing one bill so it peeled away from the rest, Hunter said, "Understand you've had some bad luck recently."

Ucko's eyes were fastened to the money. They didn't move when the mama-san from behind the bar came over and said something in Korean. Lee ordered a round and she left.

Hunter thumbed another bill. "Understand you use to be real close to Washington and Bullis?"

Reluctantly, his eyes still on the money, he said, "Yeah . . ."

Hunter hit another twenty. "But Bullis screwed you over."

Ucko just sat there staring at the money. A moment later the waitress returned with four pint mason jars, three quarters full of whitish fluid. Ucko grabbed the one set before him and took a long drink.

Grimacing, Hunter hit another twenty. "I understand Bullis and Washington have a little retreat in Seoul."

"I, ah, it ain't a good idea to talk about Bullis. He—"

Hunter pulled the four twenties from his money clip, dropped them on the table. Then he slowly pulled out a fifth bill and dropped it on the pile. Smiling, he said, "One hundred. More than the average airman no-stripes takes home in a couple of paydays, especially one who's paying off a big fine." Ucko looked like he'd been stung. "Man with that kind of cash could probably find himself a new sweetie."

Ucko licked his lips, and his eyeballs were doing everything but reaching out and grabbing the pile of

MPC. Hunter said, "Now where in Seoul did you say this place is located?"

"Ah, Nam Song Hill."

Nam Song was a mountain range that cut through Seoul. The highest point was Nam Song Hill. On top was a public park and on the winding roads were homes of the affluent.

"Can you take me there?"

"Forget it!"

Hunter reached for the money, but before he could pull it back Ucko grabbed his hand. "Wait, wait a minute." Hunter paused. "I got the address. One time I had to meet Bullis and Mr. Kim there, and Kim wrote it down in Korean so I could show it to a taxi driver. I kept it."

Ucko reluctantly released Hunter's hand, then quickly pulled out his wallet and started digging around. As he dug among bits of folded paper, old match covers, ticket stubs, and receipts, Hunter saw that it didn't contain any cash. Finally Ucko extracted a soiled business card. He handed it to Hunter. There was Korean on one side, English on the other. It belonged to Black Belt. On the Korean side something was written in ballpoint pen.

Hunter handed it to Pak, who read it, and nodded. "It is Nam Song address."

Hunter took the card and put it in his own wallet. Watching, Ucko asked, "You won't say where you found out?"

Hunter shook his head. He was seized with the urge to get moving. He needed his gun and . . . he looked at his watch. Oh, Sweet Jesus, it was already eleven-ten. Almost the bewitching hour—midnight curfew. Even if he took off right now, there was no way in hell of getting to Seoul this late.

Lee seemed to read his thoughts. He put his hand on Hunter's arm. "Too late. Tomorrow."

Without thinking, Hunter picked up the jar and took a swig. "Oh, Lord," he said, shivering. *Makalee* was just as bad as he remembered. However, the warm feeling in his stomach wasn't all that unpleasant. What the hell. He took another swallow. That made his friends smile.

Pak called for another round. The *makalee* seemed to loosen Ucko up. Hunter started asking questions to find out what else he knew. Not much, it seemed. Crandell's death had happened after Ucko flunked out of the group. He'd heard gossip but didn't really know anything except there was a beautiful Korean girl involved.

"How the hell have Washington and Bullis got such a firm grip on things down there?" Hunter asked. "I thought Colonel Donley ran things."

"He does," Ucko said emphatically. "And he's one mean motherfucker. But Bullis has his number. One time we were drinking and he told how tight he was with the colonel. They was in 'Nam together, but it was before then that counted."

Ucko took another drink. "Ya see, Donley, the perfect officer, ain't so perfect. Way back, him and Bullis were stationed together at Langley in Virginia. That's where Bullis helped Donley get rid of his wife."

Hunter was astonished. "Get rid of his wife?"

"Yeah, Bullis told me. Donley was married to an alcoholic. She was a real pain, always calling him on the telephone, raising hell with the staff, coming on base bombed, causing trouble, like that. Of course, I don't blame her. Being married to that evil bastard would make a Mormon drink. Bullis said everyone knew about her and it was really crimping Donley's career. She also had this disease, like diabetes, only the reverse."

"Hypoglycemia." Hunter had known of a similar case. It was caused by low blood sugar, a complication of alcoholism—too much booze and not enough food.

Ucko nodded. "Bullis told me she kept passing out, going into a coma and having to be hauled to a hospital or die. He said he helped Donley take her a couple of times. Then one time when Bullis took Donley home after work and they found her passed out again, Donley blew up and started crying how she was killing his career. Bullis suggested maybe they should just leave her and go back to the squadron and work late. Donley went for it. Then, when he was sure it was long enough, Donley went home. Of course, he called for an ambulance, but by then she was dead meat.''

Ucko took another drink, then said, '' 'Course I can't prove none a that, but since then Donley has taken real good care of Bullis.''

Hunter looked at Pak and Lee. The two Koreans seemed just as amazed as he was. "No wonder Bullis is able to do whatever he likes. What about Washington?''

"Wash was straight when he got here. But he was already having money problems—too many kids back in the States and he's got a taste for the ladies, the young ones, so you know . . .''

"Yeah," Hunter said, "I guess I do.''

They left Ucko sucking up another jar of *makalee*. Pak said he had to get home. The night was thick and threatening, heavy with the smell of impending rain. Lee went with Hunter back to Shaw's hooch. Standing outside the gate, Lee said, "You go to Seoul tomorrow?''

Hunter nodded.

"Okay, but you take it easy. I want you to come back. Still have to buy brass.''

Chapter 34

After listening to Hunter, Shaw said, "You going to Seoul?"

"I'd be gone now except for curfew, but I'll get going in the morning."

"Look, ah, maybe I should go with you."

The offer, totally out of the blue, surprised Hunter. He looked at his earnest, overweight friend sitting across from him clutching OB, and he felt a surge of real affection. From the time of their crazy meeting in the Yokota BOQ, Shaw—often nervous, yet unhesitating—had offered his assistance. Without it, Hunter knew, he would never have gotten this far. But for what he had to do now, he knew he could not involve his friend further.

"Thanks, Ron, but I don't think so. This thing has already burned up one friend. I don't want it to happen to another."

Shaw's face showed a curious mixture of protest and relief. Fishing out his key ring, Hunter added, "But I do need your help for one last thing. Here are the keys to my BOQ room. This key is for the door, and this one fits the bottom drawer in the locker. I need the boots with the side zippers from the closet. Then, in the locked drawer there's an AWOL bag. Bring that too."

"What is it?"

"You'll be happier if you don't know. And maybe you should take a taxi through the gate. Also, it wouldn't hurt if you sort of kept the bag out of sight. Pretend it's full of cosmetics."

When Shaw left, Hunter checked the time: close to

eleven-thirty. Shaw would have to hustle to get back before the cops closed the gate.

Minh Ah, who had been in and out several times since his arrival, looked at him. "You no go base. Where you stay tonight?"

"I, ah, I really don't know."

"Miss Pak, she home now. She say white and black GIs fighting too much in club."

Sumi. He experienced a flash of guilt. He had been so busy he had forgotten about her. He was sorry about that. However, now that he had actually found Kim one time, had been with her, even in her condition, he knew everything was different.

"I don't think I should—"

"Igoo!" Oh my! "Where you going to go?" Angry impatience was obvious in her tone. "Everybody got to stay someplace."

It was two minutes past midnight when Shaw returned. "Jeez, it's scary out there."

"Why's that?"

"There's a mean, nasty smell in the air. I saw two fights. One on the base and one at the gate, where four cops were getting it on with half a dozen black guys. They didn't even have time to worry about me."

"At least it was good for you."

"You're telling me." Shaw held out Hunter's bag as though it was full of rattlesnakes. "I peeked, and I'm sorry. You know, you can get into real trouble with that stuff."

"You keep saying that."

"Don't remind me."

He went through the bag, in addition to the weapons. Shaw had gotten a light jacket and his pills. While Hunter checked the guns, he said, "I don't think Washington and Bullis and whoever else is in this have the vill sewed up as tight as they think."

"What do you mean?"

"Apparently there's a lot of unhappy people around here, both on and off base. They know something's going on, something they don't like, but so far they just haven't had any idea what to do about it. Given the chance, it's my opinion, they'll gladly put the screws to the evil bastards.''

Shaw took a long pull on his beer. "Hope to hell you're right.''

He thanked Shaw once again before leaving. He went to Sumi's door and knocked. She was expecting him. She was wearing a shortie nightgown that nicely complimented her trim figure, and reminded him of the pleasurable passion they had shared together.

"I'm happy to see you again.''

"I'm happy too,'' he said, at the same time realizing what a curious dilemma he had gotten himself into. He really liked this woman. He wanted to show her friendship, affection even. But to do so would be violating the feelings he finally admitted he felt for Kim Soon Ja.

"You tired?'' she asked.

"Yes. It's been a long day.''

"We go bed, you can rest.''

"Look, ah, I—''

"Ada soy yo.'' I know. Minh Ah obviously had talked to her. He gave in, undressed, and got in bed. When she came to him she was holding the bottle of baby oil, "You still like massage?''

"Oh yes.''

"I'm think so,'' she said, smiling. He turned on his stomach and she began doing her magic to his sore, tired muscles. He was almost asleep when she asked, "You find Miss Kim Soon Ja?''

Several moments passed before he answered. "Yes, I found her. But someone took her away from me. In the morning I'm going to get her back.''

For a long time she did not say anything as she continued to work her fingers in the hard flesh of his back. Then, softly, she said, *"Ada sumnida.''* I understand.

He did not remember falling asleep. Or when the dreams started. Apparently the combined effects of stress, anxiety, and the painkillers. His dreams were stronger, longer, more vivid. The burning Thud. Trapped and helpless. Plunging endlessly, screaming as death came closer and closer. Then, when he didn't think he could stand it any longer, he was no longer in the airplane, but on the streets of the Asian city. Only it was different this time. He knew he was in Korea, that the people around him were Koreans. The figure he was chasing seemed closer. He sped up, rushing faster, running, not caring what others thought. Getting closer. Closer. He reached out and caught the shoulder of the person. He thought it was going to be Paul Crandell. He started to speak to his friend. The person turned around. It was not Paul at all. It was Kim Soon Ja.

He awakened, groggy, unsure of where he was. He lay in the darkness remembering the dream. Now it all made sense. He had just never been able to admit to himself that all along he had really been chasing her.

Slowly weariness and the drugs made him sleep again.

At five-thirty the alarm clock went off. Groggy, not sure where he was, he groped for it. Finally he got it shut off. He looked at the sleeping woman next to him, the dreams still in his mind. As he slipped from the bed he remembered there had been another dream after he had gone back to sleep. This one had started out as a repeat performance: falling out of the sky, screaming in terror. Then he was not in the burning aircraft, but in Kim Soon Ja's arms, being comforted and caressed. The comfort turned to passion, rising and exploding in a fury of frenzied lovemaking.

Fully awake now, he looked down at Sumi. He suspected it had not been a dream, and that the woman he had made love to in the night had not been Kim Soon Ja.

So much for good intentions.

Chapter 35

It was still dark when he left Sumi's hooch. Thick, damp fog shrouded the village, giving everything a mystical quality. It was not raining, but he was willing to bet it would be before long. He pulled his jacket tightly around him, attempting to keep the wet chill from seeping into his bones. He hoped the weather was better in Seoul.

Making his way to the main street, he passed a few other lone figures floating by at this early hour. There were no taxis cruising. Cautiously he started back toward the base gate. The main street was silent and empty. He was glad of that. Two Korean taxis were parked near the gate. The drivers sat together in the first vehicle, sharing a cigarette. He knocked on the window next to the driver. When it lowered a few inches he asked, "Anybody want to go to Seoul?"

They both shrugged. It was early, they had not finished the cigarette. After a moment the driver pointed to the backseat. Hunter sighed and got in. He settled back and waited as the cigarette was passed back and forth a few more times. He was impatient, but decided a few more minutes would not matter.

When the cigarette was finished, the second man got out and went back to his own vehicle. Hunter's driver fired up his engine, popped the clutch, and sent the machine screeching into the middle of the empty, wet street. Barreling downhill in first, he slam-shifted into second and just managed to miss a large container of trash on the wrong side of the dark, foggy road. By the time they got on the MSR beyond the village, the driver had settled down. In fourth gear, not distracted by shifting, he did a fair job of aiming.

Although Hunter had had less than five hours' sleep he felt rejuvenated. His headache was gone, his vision sharp and clear. He was experiencing the same tingling anticipation he had always felt after takeoff on a combat mission. Death was out there, waiting. Survival depended on professional skill, speed, and the impersonal whims of the faceless bastard god that ruled a warrior's fate.

He was ready, as ready as it was possible to be. He pulled the small bag closer. The big Browning with an extra clip of bullets was inside. The smaller .25 auto was in his right boot. One thing he had learned flying combat, there is no such thing as too many weapons. The night before, Shaw had watched him as he checked each gun. "Jesus, Mike, if the KNP catch you with that stuff, they'll lock your ass up forever."

"No sweat, Ron," he said. "I know a Korean general who's tight with Park Chung Hee. We used to fly together. For a thousand dollars he can fix anything."

"A thousand?" Shaw looked stunned. "In Chicol you can fix anything for a couple of hundred."

"Yeah, well, this guy is a two-star in Seoul. Prices are higher in the big city."

Light was spreading through the eastern sky as the driver sent the taxi into a bone-pounding, rock-slinging slide, and turned off the MSR onto the access road leading to the recently opened express highway. They raced toward the toll booth, careening around and in front of a large U.S. military truck to get there first. Of course, while the driver paid the toll, the Army truck vehicle sailed past in the free lane. U.S. military-aid money had paid a major share of the cost for the road, and official U.S. vehicles were exempt from the toll.

The taxi was an older-model, Korean-made, bastardized copy of the Japanese Toyota. He had heard that, using the learned technology, the Koreans were soon going to start producing a car that was entirely a homemade product. He wondered if they would end up selling them in the States. If so, that would certainly give the Japanese a bad case of heartburn.

The taxi purred along the new highway. He remembered watching construction of the road from the air when he had been flying during the time of the *Pueblo*. Although he could hardly see it on this foggy morning, he knew it was the latest type of divided four-lane expressway. The highway ran the full length of the country, from Seoul to the southern port city of Pusan. It was an extraordinary accomplishment when one considered that prior to that, the only road north and south had been the old, crumbling two-lane MSR.

To justify the use of U.S. military-aid dollars to pay for it, the highway had been designated as an emergency military route. In addition, there were several extra-wide stretches incorporated into its length that could be used as emergency airfields in the event that the shooting war started again. As a pilot Hunter was not totally convinced of the feasibility of that plan, but for the present it made for one hell of a nice highway.

At quarter to seven the taxi rolled across the wide Han River bridge, the southern boundary of the capital city. A leaden light permeated the wispy, clinging fog that swirled around the highway as his driver challenged the limited visibility with almost total abandon. He was glad few other vehicles were on the road at this hour.

They left the highway and rolled down into the streets as the big city was waking up and stretching. The early morning overcast did a kindness to the place, which was, after all, a huge, crowded, bustling industrial giant. Although he had heard Seoul was improving, in years past he had always considered it to be the drabbest of capital cities in Asia.

Glancing out the window, he saw a horse-drawn cart vying for space with large buses, lumbering trucks, and a variety of vehicles. The Koreans were still using the old, Japanese-built, small three-wheel trucks. In an early compromise during their recovery from World War II, the Japanese had married the front of a motorcycle with the back of a pickup. The result was an inexpensive little machine that did a heavy job. There was one problem: it was erratically unstable and often tried to kill its driver when it made a turn. With progress, the Japanese had outlawed the dangerous machines. Then, in their usual endearing way, they proceeded to export them all over Asia. Most, it appeared, to Korea.

About three miles into the city, having jostled successfully with the early morning traffic, the driver pulled to a halt across the street from a large dirt field that served as one of the city's main transportation hubs. Long lines of buses were filling with crowds of people in a general melee of controlled confusion that was made even more frantic because of the bad weather. In Korea the masses moved by bus; only a few people had reached the privileged ranks of private-vehicle ownership.

But Hunter did not want a bus. He told the driver, "Nam Song Hill."

"No can do." The driver turned around, wagging his hand from side to side, palm out, in the negative gesture common throughout Asia.

"Why not?"

"Osan taxi can only come this place. No can drive Seoul."

"Why?"

"Maybe Seoul taxi driver catch me, beat shit out of me."

Hunter wasn't happy with the answer, but it was a valid reason—from the driver's point of view. He pulled out his money clip, braced for the battle he knew would come, and asked, "How much?"

"Six thousand won."

Six thousand was, ah, how much? Let's see, four hundred was more than a dollar, so four thousand was over ten, and six was, ah, more than fifteen. He remembered paying five dollars for the same trip when he had been here before. Even considering inflation that was a bit steep. He said, "Too much."

The driver, a pro at this game, immediately screamed like a gored ox, "No too muchee. All time, go Seoul, six thousand! Why all time cheap, fucking GI say too muchee?''

"Bullshit," Hunter growled, using the most common GI expression in Korea after "how much?" He said it with a maximum of sneering contempt. It was part of the game.

"No bullcheet!" the driver yelled. "All time six thousand."

"Two thousand."

The driver looked as if he was about to have a heart attack. "No two thousand. Everybody pay six."

"All time I pay two thousand," Hunter said. Then, twisting the knife, "Sometimes only one thousand five hundred."

"Four thousand." The driver spat out the concession with supreme contempt.

The argument continued until they both agreed on three thousand, three hundred. As Hunter handed over the money, he knew it was twice what a Korean would pay. Of course, he also knew the Korean's answer was that GIs made at least ten times as much as the average Korean. The American would then say that when he was spending his money in Korea, he was willing to pay a fair price and no more. In the end no answer was acceptable to all, so the Koreans charged as much as the traffic would bear, the GIs paid as little as possible, and the arguments went on forever.

He was not completely out of the Osan taxi before three Seoul drivers were after him. They pestered him so violently that he got irritated, hissed a phrase that suggested their mothers had mated with monkeys, and stalked off. Once away from the bus stop, all the taxis on the now crowded streets were occupied. Finally he saw one pulling to a stop a half block away. He broke into a gallop and just managed to beat out a mother and her two children.

As he wedged in and pulled the door shut in the face of the miffed woman, his inner voice commented, *Doing your bit for international relations*.

This driver was one of those flat-faced Koreans with eyes that looked like ancient evenings. He did not understand English or Hunter's bad Korean. The American handed him the paper on which Mr. Park had written directions. The man took it, looked at it for several moments, then turned it sideways and continued to stare at it.

Hunter reached over and jerked it from the man's hands. Putting on his most winning smile, he rolled down the window and motioned to the Korean woman who was still standing just outside the vehicle looking indignant. When she leaned over, he handed her the paper and pointed to the driver. She read the paper, then told the driver where to go.

A wide smile split the man's face. "Nam Song?"

"That's what I said," Hunter howled desperately. He accepted the paper back from the Korean woman, bowed slightly and said, *"Komop sumnida."*

The man drove like he read: full speed and no skill. The small car lurched and jerked through heavy morning traffic made all the worse by wet streets and the slowly dissipating fog. The man was one of those drivers who always made the wrong move at the wrong time, avoiding collisions by mere millimeters. Hunter tried not to look. Once before, exasperated by a Seoul driver's ineptness, he had offered the man double the normal fare if he would let Hunter drive. The driver made it obvious that he thought the American was crazy. After that experience Hunter had decided that when traveling in an Asian taxi, the best bet was to hang on and hope fate was in a generous mood.

Once they reached the road going up into the hills, the traffic lessened. In some ways this crowded city, with the mountains running around its northern edge, then cutting down through the middle, reminded Hunter of San Francisco. The southern edge of the mountains were near the large U.S. Army base, Yong Song, headquarters for the Eighth Army, the senior U.S. command in Korea. The highest point in the south was Nam Song Hill. There were two ways to get there, by vehicle or on a skilift-style trolley which was mostly for tourists. As the taxi jerked along, Hunter almost wished he had taken the trolley.

When they got up above the first layer of dirty air, it was cleaner but still cool and gray. Patches of fog from low-hanging clouds whispered along the sides of the hills like reluctant ghosts. It was days such as this which had earned Korea its nickname, Land of the Morning Calm.

The skyline drive was quite a change from the over-crowded city below. The hills were green with trees, although none were very tall. During World War II, in the final phase of their fifty-some year occupation of Korea, the Japanese had savagely raped Korea's forests. Only through strict conservation efforts in the past few years had the hills and mountains in the country once again become green.

The mountains were also home for the country's affluent, which included many expatriate Americans as well as Korea's emerging upper-class government, military, and business leaders. There were also the ever present military fortifications and checkpoints. His driver slowed as they approached one. When the Korean soldier saw Hunter's Anglo face, he waved the vehicle on.

An Air Force cop Hunter knew had explained the realities of the security system. "Both U.S. and Koreans use the round-eye, slant-eye system. Round eyes mean you are automatically okay, slant eyes have to be checked." Hunter opined that seemed a bit discriminatory. The major said, "The South Koreans have been catching North Korean infiltrators for more than twenty years, but so far they ain't yet caught one with round eyes."

Hunter was jerked back to the present as the taxi began to slow down. They were nearing a new, large villa situated behind a strong, high wall. Motioning for the driver to keep moving, he hissed, "Don't stop here."

The driver just gave him a blank look and kept pointing at the villa, nodding his head back and forth while Hunter kept waving frantically and hissing threats at the man. All to no avail. The taxi stopped and he realized he was making more noise trying to get the driver to move on than if he just got out.

He pulled out a wad of won and handed it to the driver—no arguments this time. He started to tell the man to wait, but, clutching the won and smiling at his good fortune, the Korean did not intend to give the American a chance to change his mind. He gunned the vehicle and took off with a screech of rubber.

So much for the stealthy approach.

Hunter stood silently after the taxi disappeared. Waiting, listening. In the next few minutes a couple of vehicles passed. Besides that there were only the birds. The villa remained silent. Maybe it wasn't the right place? There was something written in Korean on the gate, but it did not look anything like what was on the paper.

Standing there wasn't going to get it done. Time to arm the bombs, set the switches for release, and roll in. Checking to see that the road was clear as far as he could see through the fog, he took the Browning from the bag, thumbed back the hammer on the already chambered fourteenth round, and walked up to the gate. Holding the gun down by his side, he carefully tried the gate's handle.

Locked. If this was the right place, they had learned a lesson from Suwon. Using his left fist, he knocked on the iron panel. The noise echoed loudly in the early morning stillness. Otherwise, he didn't hear anything. He waited for what seemed like hours, then banged on the panel again.

Without warning, the gate jerked open about a foot and Hunter was looking at the surprised, battered face of Black Belt.

It was the right place.

Chapter 36

The Korean's eyes blinked. Hunter figured that meant he was surprised. It took Mr. Kim a moment to really believe it. Fingering the gauze bandage that covered his ear, he smiled. It was a I'm-gonna-tear-your-arm-off-and-beat-you-to-death-with-the-bloody-stump smile. He had made a mistake underestimating this American the first time, and the smile said he wasn't going to do that again.

Hunter believed him. He lifted his right hand and pointed the 9mm automatic at Black Belt's flat, hard belly. "Up against the wall, motherfucker!"

While it would have been awkward for the Korean to actually follow the instruction literally, he got the message and raised his hands. Koreans understand force—everyone over the age of twenty had vivid memories of the vicious war that had raged back and forth across their country. In the first month the communists had almost pushed the South Koreans and their new American allies right off the end of the peninsula. After the Inchon landing the North Koreans were run back north. During those intense, deadly first six months of the war, Seoul changed hands several times before the lines were stabilized more or less where they had been before it started. It took two and a half more years of hacking away at each other before the cease-fire was signed.

That stopped most of the shooting, but an actual peace treaty was never signed. Technically, the war was still on. Since then Koreans have lived with the possibility of resumed combat, nasty border clashes, and infiltration of spies and saboteurs. That threat was the reason, or excuse, why Hunter and approximately fifty thousand other Americans were stationed in the country every year. And Koreans lived, as they had for as long as most could remember, with a loaded gun pointed at their heads.

This situation created a tangible respect for loaded guns. The blank expression that came over Black Belt's flat face was the ageless face of Korea—aware that a wrong move might be the last move.

The Korean was not the only one caught up in conflicting realities. Until this moment Mike Hunter had never faced the possibility of killing another human being outside the arena of combat. In the war he had killed. The enemy—and others. Even though combat pilots talked about bombing targets—buildings, bridges, and vehicles—they knew that people were part of those targets, often the most important part. As a pilot Hunter had always done his best to be on target.

He had also engaged in personal aerial combat with enemy pilots on several occasions, and in one of them he had destroyed his adversary's aircraft. Because there had been no parachute he knew he had also killed the pilot. In combat he always carried a side arm: first the Air Force-issue .38, later the Browning and the smaller automatic he purchased in Hawaii. For most pilots a handgun was akin to the fancy patches sewed on their flight suits or the long mustaches they all wore—more a psychological decoration than a practical item of equipment. Unlike most, Hunter had actually used his gun to kill a North Vietnamese soldier when he was on the ground waiting to be rescued.

Yet until this moment, he had never stood five feet from a man who wasn't a soldier with his life depending on whether he could pull the trigger. Those thoughts flashed through his head in the time it took for Black Belt's eyes to blink. Then Hunter smiled, because he knew that if this human version of a junkyard dog twitched, he would happily blast his spleen into the next fucking dimension.

"Back up," he ordered. The Korean, seeing the deadly intent in Hunter's eyes, did as instructed. An

Air Force security police station wagon was parked just inside the gate. These guys did not hesitate to use an official vehicle whenever they felt like it. The house was Western in style, almost European. Hunter backed Black Belt up to the main entrance.

"Open it and go in. Slowly," he told him.

The room they entered was ornately decorated. Thick rugs on the floor looked Persian, and the heavy, hand-rubbed teak furniture was similar to what he had seen in the more expensive shops in Hong Kong. Casually enhancing the room were numerous art objects from Japan, Thailand, and Taiwan. Not the run-of-the-mill GI bargain stuff; these things had cost someone a bundle.

Distracted by the room, he did not notice the movement behind him until there was a sudden scream, immediately after which his head exploded from a heavy blow from behind. He pitched forward onto the floor. The automatic went one way, the bag the other. A grinding wave of pain slammed through his head. He didn't lose consciousness entirely, but reality was a slippery customer. He knew he was down on his hands and knees, he could feel the thick carpet under his fingers, but he could not see anything clearly because his eyes refused to focus.

A few more shots like that and you'll be able to rent your head out for a sponge.

He felt awful. When he raised his head, a large shape was looming over him. Slowly his eyes cleared and the blurry figure of Chief Master Sergeant Washington was visible. He was pointing an Air Force-issue .38 at Hunter.

Damn. He should have realized there was someone in the house. The young cop had told Winston that Black Belt had taken Kim to Seoul in a taxi. Which meant someone else had come in the staff car.

Very good, his voice congratulated, *but just a tad slow.*

He saw someone to the right and behind Washington. It was Black Belt, who looked like he wanted to rush over and stomp Hunter into the expensive rug.

Then he heard a sharp sigh. Standing on the other side of Washington was Kim Soon Ja. She was staring down at him, one hand to her mouth, her eyes wide with frightened surprise.

But there was life in those fantastic eyes now. Apparently they had stopped giving her whatever it was that had put her in la-la land. Even in this situation he could not help noticing how beautiful she was.

"You just don't give up, do you, Captain?"

Washington's words were strained and tense. The man was wound very tight.

Big deal. You'd be tense too if some slippery dick kept stomping on your foreskin.

"You just gotta keep it up," Washington snarled angrily. "Keep pushing until you get yourself killed— just like your friend."

That cleared up any nagging doubts about Crandell's death. He wondered if the man was aware he had just admitted to murder. Then again, why should he care? He had a gun.

Hunter asked, "Are you going to shove me in a *benjo* ditch like Crandell?" A sharp intake of breath hissed between the big NCO's lips. Hunter added, "Considering everyone knows I have been asking questions about Crandell, don't you think that'd look pretty suspicious?"

Washington's head bobbed in short, sharp jerks as he considered the question. "Yes. Very suspicious. And in the long run I don't know if it will help. But I know one thing for sure: if you're around, there isn't a chance in hell of getting outa this shit."

You have got to quit asking dumb questions.

Hunter's vision was clear, but pain still pounded in his head. He looked at Kim. Her face, now free of the effect of the drugs, was animated with confusion. Those wide eyes, disheveled hair, and long, slim legs beneath a short, dark skirt made him think of a frightened fawn suddenly caught in onrushing headlights on a dark night. Although she was obviously fearful of Washington, when she spoke there was spirit in her firm voice. "Who is he?"

"Why, Miss Kim, this here is Captain Mike Hunter," the chief said with undisguised disdain. "He's been tearing up the whole damn country to get to you."

The beautiful young woman looked down at him, and now there was anger mixed with the confusion in her eyes. "Why you do?"

Pulling himself up in a crouch, Hunter looked at her. "Don't you know who I am? Paul was my friend. We flew together in Thailand."

"I know." Her eyes glistened as tears welled up. "I know you his friend. But why you come now? Too late. Paul die. Is my fault. I am bad person. Now God punish me."

"No, that's not true." He reacted to the anguish in her voice; it was so strong he could almost touch it. He recognized the streak of religious-based fatalism in her comment, that God was punishing her because she had not been able to live up to some self-imposed standard. A theme common to many who have been force-fed more religion—whatever brand—than they can digest.

Vehemently opposed to such sophistry, Hunter wanted to reassure her that it was not her fault. He yearned to reach out and protect her from the pain, to hold her—oh yes, he wanted to hold her, to take her in his arms. Suddenly he was facing it squarely; he had always wanted her. Sure, go ahead and admit it, he told himself. From the first moment he had seen Crandell's photographs that face had scorched itself into the inner recesses of his soul. Whatever else this was about, a lot of it was to find out if any real woman could live up to the fantasy he had built around the image in those pictures.

With that revelation came a flash of high-energy anger. In one sudden movement he was standing. Washington recoiled backward several steps and jerked his gun threateningly. He shouted, "Watch it, you bastard, or you're dead."

Hunter's adrenaline was pumping, that same mad rush of potency which had kept him alive in the skies over Hanoi when a thousand guns were trying to blast him into oblivion. This time, however, the threat to his survival was a single man. One highly trained individual who was not going to make the mistake of underestimating him again.

Black Belt came in low, arms in the classic offensive position. Infused with the rush of vitality, Hunter squared off with the man, feinted with his right arm, and kicked out savagely with his left foot. And ended up on his back on the floor gasping for breath, trying to recover from the foot the Korean had planted in his chest after easily avoiding the American's kick.

So much for one-on-one.

"Hold it, Kim," Washington said. The Korean did not like that, but he stopped.

Hunter looked up at the big NCO who had caused all this pain and death. But instead of an onerous manipulator he was looking at a man who seemed barely able to maintain his self-control. Washington's eyes were wide with dread, beads of panic sweat stood out on his large head; dark, damp circles of perspiration soaked his uniform shirt under his arms and across his belly.

Hunter pulled his legs up and shifted to a squatting position with his right leg out of view of the two men. Washington warned, "Just stay where you are. I don't want to kill you."

"What's one more murder to you?"

"Goddamn you, I never murdered anyone."

Hunter looked at him as he slipped his hand down the side of his trousers. He challenged, "What about Crandell? You pushed his head under the water and held it there."

"That wasn't me," Washington protested, his voice ringing loudly in the room. "I didn't touch him. Bullis did it. I didn't like it but—"

Hunter's hand was under his trouser cuff and into the top of his boot. "So you had Bullis do it for you so you could have Crandell's woman."

"Me?" Washington's voice came out in a high-pitched shriek. "You think I'm the one? Oh, you stupid motherfuckin' bastard. It's not me."

"What're you talking about?" For a second Hunter almost forgot about the small gun which was now in his fingers.

"You dumb prick, it's Donley. He's the one who's crazy about her. He's responsible for all this shit!"

Chapter 37

Hunter was dumbstruck. The wretched look on Washington's face was proof of his words. In a grotesque way it made sense. Of course, Donley was the man who had let his wife die. It was only one more step to murder. He looked at Kim: her eyes were downcast. Sure, she would have trusted a senior officer, a man who was a combination authority and father figure. The knowledge overwhelmed him. It also made his anger all the more intense. Donley, a senior officer, one of the system's gatekeepers, was the chief conspirator. The betrayal of trust was even greater.

"Sergeant, what is he doing?" Mr. Kim was paying more attention than Washington. He had seen Hunter's hand dig in his boot.

"Hey, what are you—"

Even as the NCO spoke, Kim leaped into motion, hurling himself across the space that separated him from Hunter. He was fast, as fast as any human being Hunter had ever seen, but unlike Superman, he was not faster than a speeding bullet. Or two.

Hunter got off the shots just as the Korean slammed into him. At first he didn't know if he had hit him because they both went cartwheeling backward. Their tangled bodies crashed into an elegant, hand-carved, four-panel screen, turning it into so many toothpicks. Hunter fought frantically to free himself, only slowly coming to realize that the Korean was dead weight. As he pulled himself away from the body, he saw one bullet had hit the man in the chest, the other in his throat.

Kim Soon Ja screamed. At any moment Hunter expected to hear the crack of Washington's .38, feel a bullet rip into his body. As he struggled to get up, Washington rushed over. He slashed at Hunter's hand with the barrel end of his pistol. The blow sent the .25 automatic spinning out of Hunter's hand. Washington scooped it up and jumped back, still keeping his gun pointed at Hunter.

The sergeant's eyes went to the Korean. Kim lay twitching, blood pumping from his wounds each time his heart beat. The big NCO's eyes were like chalk pools. He shook his head, sending large drops of sweat flying. In a horrified croak he said, "Look what you done."

Hunter gazed at the Korean. Kim appeared to be dying. He felt a vague sense of regret, not guilt for shooting the Korean but because he was only an instrument for others. Kim's biggest crime was that he'd sold himself to the wrong person.

"Meon homnida." Sorry about that.

"How can this be happening?" Washington moaned, shaking his head as if he were caught up in something he didn't understand.

Hunter smiled. "It's called payback."

"Listen, Hunter, I never wanted any part of this," the big sergeant protested, his voice betraying his indecision. "I tried to stay out of it, but the colonel and Bullis, they just kept getting me in deeper and deeper."

Hunter stood. "You were there. You're just as dirty."

"I never touched your friend. Bullis did it all."

From the edge of his vision he saw Kim, behind Washington, edging across the room toward where Hunter's big automatic had come to rest when he had been knocked down the first time. He worked hard at keeping his eyes focused on the chief's face.

Keep his attention, his inner voice shrilled.

Hunter said, "I don't buy it. You're a professional lawman, but you participated in a murder. It's the same as if you pushed Crandell's head under the water yourself."

The words were more for Kim's benefit than for Washington. He didn't want her to lack for motivation.

"Goddamn it, Hunter, you keep talking and I'm gonna have to kill you." Despite the desperation in the man's face, Hunter had already arrived at the same conclusion. In the long run, no matter how much Washington protested that he did not like it, he was going to have to deal with the threat Hunter's existence posed to his own survival.

"That goddamn big shit Donley," Washington protested. "It was his fault. He drags you down. I was a good cop before I got to this fucking place. But Donley had it all figured out. 'Sergeant, you don't want to end up poor.' He said we could make enough from here so when we went back to the world we wouldn't have to end up eating shit on our miserable retirement pay."

"So he forced you?"

Still mimicking Donley's ponderous voice, Washington said, " 'Be smart and you'll end up a rich man.' It was little stuff at first. Bend a regulation. Falsify a report. Look the other way when the BX was getting ripped off by the truckload."

Hunter took a step forward, just to keep him occupied. The gun in his hand jumped up, and he yelled, "Don't try it, Hunter."

Hunter had to concentrate intently not to let his eyes follow Kim sliding along the wall behind Washington. She was almost to the Browning. He summoned up his nastiest smile. "So you couldn't help yourself, you just went along."

"Yeah, I went along. Take care of the blacks." Washington's voice nearly cracked. "That was my main job. Take care of the niggers. Keep things cool, make sure there was no trouble for Donley and his pals. 'Don't worry, we'll take care of you, Chief.' " He paused, and Hunter saw deep pain on the man's wide face. "Yeah, they took care of me—they made me into this."

"Why did you get involved in Crandell's murder?"

"It wasn't supposed to be murder. It's that cunt's

fault. She makes men crazy. You and that other captain—even Donley. You all just won't leave her alone. I could understand Crandell. At least he was engaged to her. But Donley, good Christ, he was always such a coldhearted bastard. I never thought he cared that much about women. A little action when his horns got up, but otherwise it was like he couldn't care less, especially for slants. Then he met her and he was like a kid with his first hard-on.''

"So he set her up?"

"Sure, he tricked her. Used every maneuver he could to hold onto her. The worst thing is, she hates him. She wouldn't never cooperate. But he just wouldn't let her go. Then he found out her boyfriend was coming back. He went bug fuck.'' Washington paused, remembering. "Bullis found out Crandell was a real straight arrow, so Donley figured if he knew his hammer was shacking up with someone else, he'd take off. But oh no, the young captain, he was righteous. He still wanted her. He was gonna blow the whistle. He went to see Colonel Davies.''

Washington stopped and laughed, but it was a forced croak, without humor. "What a joke. Davies is Donley's buddy. And of course he called him right away.''

Paul *had* been to see Davies. "You mean the base commander was in on Crandell's murder?''

"No, not directly. He told Donley because he didn't know what else to do. I think he figured Donley would handle it politely, like maybe getting outa the picture. The sonofabitch didn't realize how flipped out Donley was about her. Then he told me and Bullis to take care of it. I didn't know what Bullis was going to do until . . .'' He stopped talking, his eyes begging for understanding.

The enormity of it was staggering. And he seemed to expect some sort of sympathy. Was everyone at Osan tainted? "What about Troxler? Is he another good old buddy of Donley's?''

"The OSI agent?'' Washington looked surprised. "Christ, no. In fact, Donley's real worried about him.

He's got the feeling that Troxler is out to hang his ass.''

So the big man's hat was white. Behind Washington, Kim was kneeling down, reaching for the big automatic. Quickly Hunter said, ''I saw you and Bullis watching me near the BX the second day I was at Osan. How'd you pick up on me so quick?''

Washington grinned, a dark, pernicious smile. ''That letter you wrote to Colonel Davies, asking about how Crandell died. One of Bullis' black-market buddies works in officers' records. He knew about the letter and flagged your name when the base got notification of your assignment here. Donley figured you were trouble. He told Bullis and me to keep an eye on you. You fooled us by getting here early, but we had you as soon as you dropped off your hand-carried records.''

Kim had the gun now. The large 9mm automatic was a real handful. She stood, pointed it at Washington's back. Hunter tried not to look at her as the barrel wavered erratically. Would she be strong enough to pull the trigger?

When it went off, the explosion was thunderous in the small room. The noise surprised Hunter almost as much as Washington. Of course, she didn't hit anything. She had shoved forward as she yanked the trigger, causing the muzzle of the gun to point down and to one side. The bullet shattered a tall, exquisitely painted Chinese vase resting on a low table a few feet to the left of Washington. Kim, also surprised, dropped the gun just as Washington, his eyes dancing crazily, spun around to see what was happening.

For a moment he must have thought he was shot. It took him too long to realize that he was okay. Hunter covered the space between them in one bound. He caught the barrel of the .38 in his left hand as Washington started to turn back. He twisted it up, barrel pointing away.

The chief was heavier than Hunter, but he had not been in an intense physical-conditioning program for the past few months. Still, with all that beef backing him up, he was no slouch. He pumped a heavy left hand into Hunter's stomach, which was powerful enough to rattle the younger man's teeth.

It was also, Hunter decided quickly, time to end this before it got out of hand. Bending his right hand back, palm out, he rammed it straight upward, driving the heel of his palm into Washington's face right under his nose. Done correctly it was a killing blow.

This one was a little off, but still effective enough to crunch most of the bones. Blood gushed. Washington uttered a strangled gasp of pain, and his grip on the pistol weakened. Hunter wrenched it from his hand, pivoted back, and then rocketed his tightly clenched fist straight at Washington's head.

Not at the sergeant's large, heavy jaw. Hunter had learned years before that hitting someone in the jaw was a good way to mangle one's hand without doing a lot of damage to the other guy. This blow was a few inches lower, slamming into the NCO's thick neck just to the side of his Adam's apple.

The chief, already having trouble breathing through his mashed nose and the blood streaming down into his mouth, gasped for air and gagged. His knees sagged, he staggered backward, clutched at his throat with one hand, and held the other up in a mute plea for mercy.

Remembering Crandell, Hunter felt no remorse or charity for the man. And he did not want him in any condition to cause more problems. He pivoted, swung his leg up, and drove it straight back into Washington's stomach. The force of the kick drove the NCO backward; he crashed against the wall, hung for a moment, then slid down, still and unmoving.

Hunter stood poised, waiting. Adrenaline charged excitedly through his system as he surveyed the damage. But the chief was down for the long count. Looking at the .38 he'd taken away from Washington, he considered putting a couple of bullets into him. Just for good measure.

But that might be considered overkill. He turned to Kim. She was standing there wide-eyed, looking shocked. Like someone at the racetrack who bet on the favorite, then watched as the sure winner faded at the finish and was run over by the long shot.

"It's all right, Soon Ja," he said, putting on his most reassuring look, "you're safe now."

"Safe?" She looked at him. He could see she did not fully understand what was happening.

He picked up his AWOL bag, put the .38 inside, then collected the Browning. As he added it to the bag's contents, he looked at her and smiled. "Thanks for the help, lady."

Her eyes blinked. "I did not hit him."

"No, but you scared him. That gave me the chance I needed. Otherwise, well . . ."

She nodded. And looked pleased. He took the Beretta from the chief's pocket, replaced the expended shells, and put it back in his boot. Then he went back to Washington's unconscious body and dug through his pockets until he found the keys for the station wagon. The man was breathing in labored gasps, but he didn't appear to be dying. Hunter wasn't as sure about Mr. Kim.

He considered what to do. It would be nice if he could go to the nearest U.S. authorities for help. Unfortunately, he had no way of knowing how far Donley's influence extended. He didn't want to end up talking to some other crooked law type who was in league with the Air Force colonel. At the moment the only person he knew he could trust was Troxler. And he was at Osan.

Looking around, Hunter saw a telephone. It would have been nice if he could have picked it up, called Troxler, and had him come and wrap everything up. But it didn't work that way. The U.S. military phone system in Korea was one of the most antiquated in the Pacific. And the Korean civilian telephone system, a hodgepodge of prewar Japanese and pilfered U.S. equipment, was even more unreliable. And, as he'd learned at the Osan flight safety office, they were still not connected.

"Come on," he said, "we're leaving."

She nodded eagerly. He could feel the end drawing

near, but it wasn't over yet. He had managed to over-come Black Belt and Washington, but they were the easy ones. They were only the stooges for the real thugs, Donley and Bullis.

Outside, the weather had worsened. Thick fog had closed in, cutting visibility to about ten feet. As he opened the passenger door for Kim, she looked at him and said, "Why you do?"

He didn't answer her immediately. The easy answer was that he had done it to right the injustice done to his friend. Yet he knew that was only half the answer. "I did it for Paul," he said. A beat later he added, "And I did it for you."

"For me?" She looked puzzled. "Why for me?"

They stood there beside the station wagon looking at each other. He searched for the right words, but when he couldn't decide on anything he liked, he fell back on an easy answer, one that every GI in Korea has in his book of Ten Easy Phrases for All Occasions. *"Moola."* I don't know.

She pondered that for a moment, then gave up and got in the car. He walked around to the other side, opened the door, and slipped behind the wheel. Why for her? Because she was different. Because she was something special. Because she was the stuff of dreams—a unique combination of beauty, vitality, and sex appeal. It was a quality randomly bestowed by fate, one that could be neither learned nor earned. While Kim undoubtedly knew she had it, he could tell it still amazed her almost as much as it did the men who came in contact with her. It was a captivating force that could drive a man such as Donley, who had not seemed to need women, to places in his mind where he had never gone before. Now that he had met her, Hunter understood why Donley had acted as he had. In a way Hunter pitied him, but he could never forgive him for wantonly destroying a better man's life.

Now it was Donley's turn for payback.

Chapter 38

"Where we go now?" Kim asked as the station wagon rolled slowly down the fog-shrouded road.

Hunter didn't think she was going to be crazy about the answer. "We've got to get away from here; then I'm going to take you to a man named Troxler. He is OSI. I want you to tell him everything you know about Paul, Colonel Donley, and the others."

"He stay Seoul?"

"No. He's at Osan."

The expression on her face turned almost as cloudy as the weather outside. "Maybe better I stay Seoul. I can go my auntie's house. She—"

"Miss Kim," he said using the formal manner of address, "I know you don't want to go back, but if you really loved Paul, you will do it. That is the only way we can make sure that Colonel Donley will go to jail."

"Colonel is police. He will not go to jail."

"If you do as I ask, I promise you he will go to jail."

He saw her perfect white teeth biting her full lower lip, and could see fearful hesitation on her face. He understood her reluctance. It was possible that with what he knew already, he would be able to get Troxler to act without talking to the girl. But Hunter saw this as an opportunity for self-redemption. He wanted her to stand up and be counted, so that later she would have something that would help her through times of guilt over Crandell's murder.

"Without your help Paul's death may go unpunished."

"I'm . . ." She was still afraid. He could feel her stare at him, probing, questioning. After a long moment she seemed to gather courage. "All right, I do. I do for Paul."

"Cho sumnida." Very good.

After a few seconds she smiled hesitantly. "Sure, good. Easy to say."

Hunter realized she was making a joke. He liked that.

The station wagon, like so many U.S. military vehicles in Korea, wasn't that old, but it was already a wreck. The body creaked and rattled, the engine whined asthmatically, and the wheels began a gentle shimmy at thirty-five miles per hour. Still, because of its huge size—the English called them Yank Tanks—and the raw power put out by the V-8 engine, it was an intimidating machine among the smaller Korean vehicles on the crowded city streets.

Once off Nam Song they were under the clouds and fog. After they got through the heavy Seoul traffic and across the Han River bridge, a light rain started falling. Despite the weather, just beyond the highway he could see farmers working in the green rice paddies, gathering the last crop of the growing season. They were bent over, hands moving with the methodical rhythm of generations, oblivious to the new concrete expressway that hummed with the sounds of the modern world.

He looked at his watch: 10:17. With luck he figured they would be back at Osan before noon and have the whole thing wrapped up in time for happy hour. The thought made him smile. He was once again thinking like a regular Air Force officer.

He glanced at Kim. Tension was still visibly etched on her face. Putting on his most confident smile, he reached over and patted her hand. "Don't worry, Soon Ja, everything will be okay."

She looked at him, then at his hand on hers, and backed away. He saw her face change: awareness. She began to comprehend what was happening here. She said, "I remember. In his letters Paul told me about his friend, the crazy pilot. That is you, *cra?*"

"Crazy pilot? Well, yes, I guess that's me."

"Now I'm know. He like you very much. He tell me someday he want me to meet you."

He nodded. "Paul was like that."

"So you come back for him?"

"To find out what happened."

"My fault he die. I'm bad person."

There it was again. But he did not buy it. "Did you tell the colonel about Paul?"

"Never!" The word exploded from her mouth. "He have man follow me when I go to meet Paul. He already know his name. When he find out who I meet, colonel knew why he come back."

"So it wasn't your fault. It was something you couldn't do anything about." There was still doubt on her face. "Paul loved you. There was nothing wrong with that. His love for you was good for him. When I knew him he was a happy man because of you."

"But he come back Korea for me. If I don't write to him—"

"You didn't know what would happen. No one could have known." It was, Hunter knew, Crandell's fate to face a man his life had never prepared him for. The Colonel Donleys of the world were the exception, not the rule. Crandell came from a way of life which isolated him from men like that. Except for his bad luck to graduate from college at a time when there was a war going on, he would never have been in the military. He just wanted to do his duty, then return to the civilized world he knew, a life where the Donleys didn't have guns.

"Don't blame yourself for something you could not change. Just make sure that the person who really is responsible pays."

"I'm not mean for it to happen," Kim explained, pleading for understanding. "When Paul leave I'm not bad girl. I see lawyer for marriage paperwork. But always more papers. Police check. Health check. Parents must sign. When I go Seoul, American man works at embassy give me hard time. First he say I must have more papers. Then he tell me he can fix—if I go for date with him. I tell him no way.''

He wasn't surprised. Misuse of power was not limited to just Americans who were in uniform.

"When I go back to base, SP sergeant also make trouble. I can tell he want to catch me. I'm act like I no understand. Colonel is watching. He ask me if I have problem. He is older, an officer, so I think okay. I tell him about my problem. He tell me he can help.''

She was speaking in a low voice, almost reciting the words as if she had memorized them. Hunter had the feeling she had told the story over and over in her mind, trying to understand what had gone wrong.

"I go see him two times. He say he can fix everything. Next time I go see him he say I have to go embassy in Seoul.''

She paused, looked down, then sniffed. "He tell me he is going to Seoul, he can give me ride. Almost I say no, but he always respect me, never show his heart, so I believe him.''

He saw her shaking her head slowly from side to side as she remembered. "So I think okay. I go. When we get to Seoul he say have to go to friend's house who will help with papers. We go, but friend no stay. He say we wait. Then he order food, something to drink. He have Johnnie Walker, always he drink Johnnie Walker. I drink little bit OB. We wait, drink more. I'm feel little bit drunk. I want to leave. He say no.''

Her voice failed for a second. She stopped. She took a breath. "Then he try to kiss me. I tell him no can do, I'm going to marry. But he no stop. He keep pushing me, want me to go bed with him.''

She stopped again. She was staring straight ahead out of the rain-covered windshield. She looked at him. He saw her trying to gauge his reaction to the story. If this had been his first trip to Asia, he might have been shocked by this tale. But long ago he had come to understand the ways of GIs and the golden butterflies of the Orient.

"When colonel start forcing me I try to stop him,

but he is man. Pretty soon I know I cannot make him stop.''

Another pause. Hunter added one more item to his long list of reasons of why Donley deserved to be crucified. The vill was not anarchic. There were rules. One of the most basic was that all relationships, whether for love, lust, or money, were formed by mutual consent. While no formal enforcement procedure existed, it usually wasn't necessary because of the unusual balance of power—the GIs had the money, but it was the Koreans' country. Most people had neither the inclination nor the influence to break the rules.

Unfortunately, Donley had both. But Hunter meant to see that he did not get away with it.

''After, I think I can get away from him. I am ashamed, but I'm not hurt. But he won't let me go. He keep me in house for three days. Then I'm fight him hard. He get tired. When he go away, he sent Korean man to watch me. One day when Korean man is not watching, I run away. I go to my parents' house.''

''Good for you.''

''Not good. Colonel have my marriage papers. He know where my parents stay. He sent KNP man to get me. Colonel tell me if I don't follow his words he will make big trouble for my family. I see even Korean policeman help him. What I'm going to do?''

''So you stayed?''

''*Na.* At first I am frightened. Colonel find house in Osan, but he no like because I have friends there. Then he makes me go house in Suwon. He don't know my friend get letters from Paul, keep them for me.''

''Lena Walker,'' he said.

That surprised her. ''How you know?''

''Paul told me about her. I found her house. She told me some of what happened.'' The surprised look on Kim's face turned thoughtful as he continued, ''But she didn't know about the colonel. She thought the man you went with was Sergeant Washington.''

''I'm ashamed, so I don't tell her. But I write to Paul, I tell him I need help. He already know something is wrong, he come right away.'' She continued, telling him that she had run away from Donley and gone to Osan to meet Paul. They went to a hotel. At first she would not tell him about the colonel. ''I just say I'm have *manee* trouble, we must leave Chicol Village.''

But Paul kept asking questions, and finally she told him what was happening. He was shocked, and mad. He told her he was going to the base to report what had happened. She tried to stop him, but he believed in the system. He didn't come back.

''I wait for long time. Then Sergeant Bullis come. He say he take me back to Suwon house. I'm crazy. I try to fight, I scratch him, bite him, but I'm not strong enough.''

Bullis again. Hunter's malice toward the man increased.

Kim had been there two days with the mama-san watching her. Then Donley had come and told her that Paul had been in an accident and was dead. ''At first I'm no want to live, I want to kill myself. Colonel bring doctor, give me shot, many pills. I sleep too much. All time mama-san talk to me, tell me nothing I can do, have to stay for colonel now.''

''So you quit trying to leave?''

''No. I'm no more care what happen to me. Many times I leave, but always he find me.'' She ran away several times. Once, afraid to go home, she went to stay with a girl she had known in school who was living in Tong Doo Chon, the large village next to one of the biggest U.S. Army bases in the north near the DMZ.

''Still he find me, I'm not know how. After I stay two weeks, again KNP and Sergeant Washington come, make me go back.''

That made Hunter feel better about leaving the black NCO lying there in a bloody heap.

''One thing I'm know, colonel is very smart man.'' She looked at Hunter with a thoughtful expression as she said it. After a moment of hesitation she asked, ''Are you more smart than colonel?''

Yeah, dummy, his voice echoed, *are you smarter than the colonel?*

He examined the question carefully, then, almost as much to himself as to the girl, he said, "I don't know if I am smarter, but Donley has made mistakes. He's done things which at the time may not have seemed to count for much. But I've added them up. And I don't think I'm the only one who's counting. With what I've found out and what you have to tell, we'll get him."

"Maybe you can do. You are good fighting. I no think anybody can beat Mr. Kim."

"I was lucky."

She thought about that. "Maybe lucky is better."

Chapter 39

They left the expressway at the Osan turnoff, drove down the access road to the MSR, and immediately encountered a long line of vehicles of every type, jammed up and barely moving. They were still more than two miles from the base.

"Must be an accident up ahead," Hunter said, guessing. A bad wreck on the two-lane MSR could quickly choke off the heavy traffic using the road. Trucks, buses, taxis, and horse-pulled carts were bumper to bumper, each trying to outjostle the other to gain a few feet of forward motion. It was worse than the L.A. freeways at rush hour. The rain was down to a drizzle for the moment, but the heavy gray overcast hung low in the sky, threatening that there was more to come.

It took more than an hour to creep, crawl, slam, jam, and generally bulldoze the lumbering station wagon through, over, around, and down approximately a mile of crowded road. Now and then a vehicle going north would pass, apparently getting by whatever was causing the mess. At one point when they were stopped window-to-window with a northbound taxi, Hunter told Kim to ask the driver what was causing the problem.

After several quick exchanges, she said, "He say big trouble in Sukogay."

The driver had used the old Korean nickname for the village, which someone had once told Hunter meant "place of mud." "What kind of trouble?"

"He say all GIs go crazy. Black man fighting white man. Too much trouble, many people hurt."

Apparently Shaw's predicted riot had happened. In a way Hunter was glad: that would shake things up. But the timing was terrible. "Can we get to the base?"

She spoke to the taxi driver again. "He say no can go. KNP make everybody go around."

"Go around? There's no way around Chicol."

She spoke to the driver again. "Say can do. Police make everyone go through rice fields by Paradise Lake."

Now, that was something he wanted to see. Paradise Lake was the ironic name bestowed by some long-forgotten GI with a twisted sense of humor to the man-made watershed east of the village behind a high hill. The lake's original purpose had been to provide irrigation for the surrounding rice fields, but an enterprising Korean had turned it into a recreation area of sorts.

The last time Hunter had visited, there had been a rickety wooden building housing a couple of ancient Ping-Pong tables and a small shop which sold beer, soft drinks, nuts, and dried fish. The recreation czar also had a "fleet" of five old, leaky rowboats for rent to those who wanted to take a shot at catching the two fish he stocked in the lake. On long, hot summer weekends when the charms of Chicol became less than overwhelming, the place did a brisk business from bored GIs and their *yobos*.

He remembered a narrow, rutted path that even the Korean taxis hesitated to use that led into the place from the south, but north of the lake was solid rice paddies. He was sure there was no road that way.

After another thirty minutes they arrived at a traffic-control point manned by a uniformed KNP. Sure enough, he was diverting traffic from the MSR and sending all the vehicles out along the top of a dirt dike that wound through individual paddies. Hunter tried to talk his way through, but the Korean cop was not impressed. Hunter wished he had also lifted Washington's badge.

"No can do," the man said with finality. "You go

same like everybody. Next checkpoint you GI SPs stay. They take you base.''

After a short argument, during which time a large truck and a small bus driven by Koreans squeezed past him, he gave up and started moving.

Next checkpoint his SPs, huh? Actually, they weren't his, they were Colonel Donley's, and he was in no hurry to meet them. The vehicles crept along the top of the narrow dike. The rain and heavy traffic had made its surface slick with glassy mud, and as the American GIs who fought the Korean War discovered to their dismay, there is no thicker, slipperier, nastier mud in the world than Korean mud.

It took all his concentration to keep the big station wagon's large wheelbase centered on the narrow path. A gasp escaped from Kim when they passed a large, overloaded truck that had slipped off and was lying on its side in a paddy. His feet flew between the clutch, brake, and accelerator to make sure they did not join it.

Remarkably they, and most of the other vehicles, navigated the treacherous route to the lake where the actual road began. Half a dozen vehicles were pulled over to the side, and the old man who ran the Paradise Lake operation was doing a booming business providing refreshment to drivers celebrating making it that far.

Hunter would have been relieved too, but he knew somewhere not far ahead were the base cops. Before they reached the top of the hill, he saw the old Paradise Club. Years before, when the area just outside the base had been off limits, the Paradise Club had been a big operation. But its time had long since passed, and now the old building was deserted and surrounded by high brush. He made a quick decision, turned the station wagon out of the stream of traffic, went around behind, and pulled in close to the old building to make the vehicle as inconspicuous as possible.

He shut off the engine. ''We'll walk from here.''

Kim gave him a disdainful look. ''Walk?''

"Well, it's either that or we'll be meeting Colonel Donley's boys."

"*Igoo.*"

"Make that *manee igoo.*"

Kim sat for a moment looking out at the mist. Then she smiled weakly and said, "Umm, nice for a walk, I think."

He got out, went around, opened the door, and held out his hand to her. She took it and stepped out. Afterward, she made no attempt to pull her hand away from his. Holding his bag of guns in one hand and Kim's hand in the other, they darted across the two lanes of traffic and into the trees. Walking steadily, they headed for the lowest part on the hill line up ahead. By the time they reached the top, his shoes were caked with mud. Kim had removed hers and was walking barefoot. The mist, getting heavier, had completely soaked their clothes, causing them to cling to their bodies. Despite the cold and wetness, the visual effect on Kim was stunningly sexual.

Catching him looking, she said, "No look, you make me embarrass."

Downhill was easier, and soon they neared the village from the back side. Kim led, pointing to a path that went between some walled homes. "This way, close by A-Frame."

The A-Frame club had been named after the traditional wooden frame Korean farmers used to haul heavy loads of just about anything on their backs. The club was one of the big, older places at the bottom of the hill across the MSR and down an alley a short way.

They were close now. He looked at his watch: it was almost three. Not much chance of making happy hour now. Still, he decided to maintain a cheerful outlook. "See, Soon Ja, no problem. Pretty soon we'll be—" They rounded a bend in the alley by the A-Frame and were face-to-face with five black GIs lounging around the entrance to the building. Dressed in various combinations of fatigue uniforms and civilian clothes, they were drinking from large bottles of Korean beer and American whiskey. "Oops."

The men, all young, were obviously half shitfaced, and quite surprised to see Hunter and the girl.

"Hey, muthafucka, look at this." The man who spoke was a rail-thin, light youngster who did not look a day over sixteen. He was wearing a fatigue uniform, unbuttoned jacket hanging out, and no hat.

"Ain't this some shit," growled one of his buddies, a dark, hulking man a few years older. He had on fatigue trousers, tennis shoes, and a net T-shirt.

A third member, big beer belly hanging over the belt on his cutoff jeans, said, "Hey, I thought we run all these honky bastards back onto the base."

Kim shrank back behind Hunter, and her hands clutched his arms. Heaving an inward sigh, he cranked up his best good ol' boy smile. "You are absolutely right. Except that we just came from Seoul. We didn't get the word. You know, there's always ten percent that don't know what's going on. Right? But we're going straight to the base. You'll still have a perfect record."

That took several seconds to register. The young, light-complected one who had spoken first stepped forward and pointed his beer bottle at Kim. "Maybe we can let him go, but we sure as shit gonna keep that hammer. She's fine."

"Hey, *yobo*," called out an individual who hadn't spoken before, "I ain't never seen you in Papa Joe's. You think you too good for a black man?"

Kim pressed closer to Hunter's back. Still working the smile, he said, "Look, guys, nobody's looking for trouble, so why don't we all just—"

"Ain't nobody got trouble," announced the thick-waisted man. "Nobody but you, muthafucka!" He punctuated his pronouncement by smashing the bottom of his large bottle of beer against the side of the building. He held up the jagged remains for Hunter to see.

The youngest one now had an ugly grin and an open knife with a long blade. That made him look a lot older. Holding it jive-ass style, he stepped out in front of his friends. "You see how it is, muthafucka: two brothers are dead. Now we gonna make up for that."

Wonderful, wonderful.

Moving quickly, Hunter unzipped the AWOL bag, reached in, and pulled out the Browning. He held it up and thumbed back the hammer. It was remarkable how loud that click sounded in the now silent alley.

"Awww, shee-yit," whined the young man, stopping suddenly. "He got a gun."

"Yeah," Hunter said, "and it's a big one."

Casually he lowered his arm so the gun barrel was pointing at the young man's crotch. "This one won't kill you, but you'll have a lot of years to sit around and wish it had."

One of the men howled, "Muthafuck that muthafuckin' muthafucka!"

Amazing. That was the first time Hunter had ever heard that word used as a noun, adjective, and verb to form a completed sentence. Regardless, the comment seemed to sum the situation up as succinctly as possible.

Hunter ordered, "Everybody drop what's in your hands."

"I think he's bluffing," ventured one of the men still in the doorway who hadn't spoken before. Hunter looked at him and knew he was the leader. He had the cold, deadly eyes of a natural stone killer. From the looks on the faces of the others Hunter could tell they were considering the possibility that the leader was right.

He swiveled slightly, aimed, and squeezed the trigger. The bullet exploded into a concrete block two feet from the leader's head, leaving a large, jagged hole. All the men jerked, eyes widening. The loud crack, which echoed off the buildings in the narrow alley, was a definite attention-getter.

"Playtime's over," Hunter said. He meant it.

They got the message, quickly dropping what they were holding. In the alley in front of the club was a concrete structure that was a public rest room. It was there to keep drunk GIs from peeing in the alley. However, because the local plumbing was terrible, there was always a strong odor of urine inside, and only Koreans used it. Drunk GIs still pissed in the alley.

Hunter motioned to the facility. "Everyone inside."

"Hey, man," one protested, "that place stinks." Hunter's eyes narrowed. "Okay, man, we going."

As they reluctantly filed in, Hunter said, "Don't let me see anyone coming out."

As soon as the last man disappeared from sight, he and Kim took off at a brisk pace, past the small building and down the alley toward the road. From behind, one of the men shouted, "We'll get you, muthafucka. Someday we'll get you for this."

"Yeah, maybe," he answered softly as he put the gun back in the bag, "but not today."

He had expected the gunshot to attract some attention, but strangely the alley remained empty until they were around the last bend, which took them out to the intersection of the MSR and the street to the base. Here they encountered a small crowd of angry Koreans. Obviously the troubles were affecting business.

He took Kim's hand in his and they started across the street. Abruptly a horn beeped loudly, scattering the Koreans. A security police jeep roared up and screeched to a halt just in front of them. There were three men in the jeep, but the one that got Hunter's attention was the man sitting in front on the passenger's side. Hunter's only consolation was the equally surprised look on Senior Master Sergeant Bullis' face.

The look quickly turned deadly. The blond NCO started to stand up in the seat while reaching for his holstered gun.

Run, you goofy bastard, screamed Hunter's voice.

That seemed like as good an idea as any. Still holding Kim's hand, he bolted around the jeep and across the street. Loud shouts trailed behind them, mostly Bullis' bellowing voice, but he didn't pause or look back. They plunged ahead as he desperately tried to convince himself that Bullis would not dare shoot them in the back, not with a crowd around.

Apparently he was right. There were no shots. Hunter did hear the roar of the jeep's engine and a screech of tires as the driver gave pursuit. On the other side of the intersection, Hunter dragged Kim through a narrow opening between two buildings. Too small for a vehicle, it was barely wide enough for a large person to move through without turning sideways. He remembered the path, a shortcut that wound up through a jumble of buildings and came out beside the railroad tracks which cut through the village about two thirds of the way down the main street from the base.

Running desperately, he was surprised to see Kim staying right behind him without stumbling or protesting. It was amazing what proper motivation could do for a person. Once they were through the buildings and out beside the railroad tracks, they slowed down, hoping to attract as little attention as possible. His eyes searched the nearby area for Bullis and his boys, but the only people he saw were more angry Koreans.

He did not like using the main street, but it was the shortest route to the gate. Even though he was sure to run into more security police there, he figured he could cause enough of a ruckus to make sure he got an opportunity to talk to Troxler. They covered about fifty yards when he glanced back and saw Bullis' jeep pushing up the street through the crowd. Kim's eyes followed his. When she saw the GI cops, she looked at him with frightened desperation.

They were almost to a side street that led back around to an area of the village where many Koreans lived. Taking her hand, he said, "Sorry, we're gonna have to run again."

She nodded numbly as they took off, full tilt, drawing some harsh looks from the already disturbed Koreans they passed. At the end of the alley was the Carnegie Club. He considered turning in there.

This is no time for a drink.

He also decided it wasn't much of a place to hide either. Club owners and cops were too well acquainted. He remembered that behind the club was the large village market. No tourist place this, it was where village Koreans did their shopping. Slowing to a quick walk, they entered the crowded market. He was happy to see it had not changed. It was a vast place, honey-combed with hundreds of small, crowded stalls with counters piled high with various kinds of food, clothing, pots and pans, books, toys, and a thousand other items. It was the Korean equivalent of a K-Mart.

The market was not inside a real building, just poles supporting a roof of tin and sheets of plastic. The light was natural, coming from a few openings and plastic panels in the roof. Usually crowded—and this day was no exception—it was an easy place to get lost in. Just what Hunter had in mind.

They slowed, threading through narrow aisles. He whispered, "Try not to attract too much attention."

Oh sure. One large, desperate-looking GI dragging a young, beautiful, frightened Korean girl behind him—not much chance anyone will notice.

They hurried on. He had never been this deep into the market before and had no idea where he was going, except that it was away from Bullis. After several twists and turns they abruptly were out of the market, into a narrow, open area surrounded by walls and rooftops. These were the homes of the Koreans who lived and worked on the base and in the village. There were three narrow alleys leading off in different directions.

He looked at Kim. She looked back and shrugged. Apparently she wasn't familiar with this part of the vill either. Hunter picked one leading right, deciding it was the best chance to get back to the street and the base. As they walked, the narrow alley widened and appeared to be going in the right direction. They rounded a bend and he recognized the shops at the end. It wasn't the path that exited just in front of the gate, but one that came out about half a block down. *Close enough for government work.*

Chapter 40

They emerged from the alley onto the main street and jerked to a stop. A crowd of more than a hundred angry black troops were milling around the entrance to the base. The chain-link gates were closed, and Hunter could see a dozen or so security police with M-16s on the other side facing the mob. He grabbed Soon Ja's hand and dragged her into the nearest doorway, a Korean tailor shop that was locked up tight.

"Maybe not so good," Kim said.

"Maybe terrible," Hunter answered.

As he considered what to do next, he saw three jeeps race over the hill from the base, roar down, and pull to a screeching stop just inside the gate. A man dressed in the fashion of the moment—full combat getup, helmet, and bulletproof vest—stood up in the lead jeep and lifted a battery-powered bullhorn.

"You men calm down." Hunter recognized the voice: Colonel Donley. *Oh, wonderful.* "We're going to open the gate. You men will come through one at a time and not make any trouble—"

"We want the general," someone screamed. Immediately the words were seized on and the mob started chanting. *"We want the general! We want the general!"*

Mixed in were lesser chants: "Fuck you, whitey!" "Burn the mothafucka down!" "Kill the honky bastards!" "Kiss my black ass!"

Donley kept trying, but the bullhorn was smothered by the chanting. A young black airman dressed in civvies who had come up the street to join in noticed Hunter and Kim in the doorway and looked surprised.

He edged over, looking them over, then grinned. "Wild shit, huh?"

"Oh yeah."

"Ah, look, man, ya know this ain't a real cool place for white dudes right now." He looked around, checking to see if anyone was watching him. "If I was you, I'd disappear."

"Thanks," Hunter said, "but we got to get to the base."

"Yeah, well . . ." He shrugged. "Good luck."

The volume of the chants diminished as the crowd seemed to tire of it. Now the bullhorn voice could be heard again: "The gate is being opened. You men line up and enter single file."

"I got your file, Jack," someone yelled, "in my ass."

"Come on," Hunter told Kim. He had decided to try it. Once inside he figured he could raise such a ruckus there was no way Donley could keep him from Troxler. With the bag in one hand and Kim's hand in the other they moved out of the doorway.

"I don't think . . ." Kim didn't like it, but she let him lead her into the crowd. The first few blacks they encountered looked surprised, but not threatening.

"Excuse me. Pardon me," Hunter said as they weaved through the gathering. "Excuse me. Please let us through. Pardon me." It was working. The throng was giving way with only a few resentful looks. The gate was opened now and three armed cops from the other side came through. Just keep moving, Hunter told himself, only a few more yards to go. This wasn't so hard, "Excuse me," just look respectfully determined and—

As the three SPs pushed into the crowd, someone yelled, "Hey, watch it, mothafucka!" A howl of angry voices erupted, followed by pushing and shoving up front.

Suddenly the whole assemblage was in motion, flailing about, voices shouting, arms swinging, legs kicking. Kim screamed. Hunter grabbed her, hugged her close. Sudden pain erupted from the side of his head when someone hit him from behind.

"Kill the mothafuckers!" was the mob's new chant. The roar was suddenly split by a burst of automatic-weapons fire. Hunter hoped the shots were in the air. Whatever, it didn't seem to deter the horde which continued to press forward.

Looking for a way out, Hunter saw a furious black face staring directly at him. "Get that honky fucker too!"

This ain't working, Captain Dorkface. Holding Kim tightly, he whirled, put one shoulder down, and charged. *Like the Marine said, you ain't retreating, you're just attacking in a different direction.*

The surprised men at the back of the pack fell back enough to let them slip through. However, sensing panic, the angry young man yelled, "Don't let that white bastard get away."

Hunter saw that the alley they had come from seemed to be clear. He dodged toward it, but some newcomers, seeing what he intended, cut them off. He took the only option left, the open doorway where they had been earlier. The tailor shop's door was still locked. He considered kicking it in, but it was too late.

"Look like you fucked, whitey."

"Whatcha gonna do now, asshole?"

He pushed Kim behind him and turned to face the sullen group of hotheads ringing the doorway.

"Now, look, men, we don't want any trouble. We—"

"Fuck you."

Fuck me? Well, fuck you too. No, wait, that probably wasn't the best way to handle things. He started to unzip the bag, "Men, don't make this any worse . . ."

The roar of an engine cut through the voices, followed by the crack of a pistol shot. The faces in front of them swiveled. A voice bellowed, "Get outa the way or you dead motherfuckers."

The men backed off, then turned and ran.

Thank the Lord. Hunter took Kim's hand and

stepped out of the doorway. And was looking at Sergeant Bullis pointing a .38 at his heart. "Don't move, you bastard."

Oh shit, oh dear.

At that moment Hunter realized it was raining again. He wasn't sure when the drizzle had started. The water was cool, sobering. A drop formed on his forehead, trickled down into his left eyebrow, then dropped into his eye. He had to blink and shake his head to see, wondering as he did: would Bullis shoot him for that movement?

"Get 'em in here, quick," the big sergeant instructed the two cops riding in back. They jumped out, swung the barrels of their M-16s in the direction of some blacks standing across the road watching, and moved toward Hunter and Kim.

Hunter considered going for one of the guns in his bag. But looking into the large, round opening of Bullis' .38, he knew he'd never make it.

The elder of the two SPs, maybe twenty-one, was a buck sergeant. He covered Hunter while the other, a pale young man who was trying without much success to get a mustache going on his upper lip, pushed Soon Ja toward the jeep. Bullis switched to the backseat, then grabbed her arm, pulled her in, and shoved his pistol into her side. She squirmed and Hunter could see that she was close to tears.

"Get that bag," Bullis said.

One of them grabbed it from Hunter and tossed it to Bullis. Then the two took Hunter's arms and manhandled him into the front of the jeep. When they started to climb in, Bullis told them, "You two stay here. You help the colonel."

Judging from the screaming around the gate, the colonel could use any help he could get. The two men looked surprised, then apprehensive. The older one said, "Sarge, I don't think—"

"Irwin," Bullis snarled, "no one asked you to think. Just do what the fuck you're told."

"We're going," said the other cop, a young dark-haired Latino whose name tag read "FERNANDEZ."

"Whatever you say, Sarge."

Bullis nodded, then told the driver, "Get us outa here, Ledford. My place."

As the driver gunned the engine and hauled the steering wheel around, the jeep squealed about and shot down the street. Hunter felt the sting of the light rain coming over the windshield of the open vehicle, covering his face. Slowly he started to move his hand toward his boot.

"Hunter," Bullis said, causing him to look around and see that the sergeant still had his gun still pressed against Kim's side. "I know you're a crazy motherfucker, but if you try anything, prettyface is gonna get it first."

Bullis was too ready, too tight. Hunter's hand stopped. Better to wait until the man was less on guard. Besides, his headache was getting worse.

The driver said, "Sarge, are you sure this is the best way? I think—"

"Ledford," Bullis said, cutting him off, "if I was you I be thinking about all those black-market goodies you and your *yobo* been running. So do me a favor: keep your fucking opinions to yourself. Just do what I tell you."

Stomping on the driver seemed to increase Bullis' sense of being in control. Smiling, he said, "How'd you find prettyface?"

Hoping to jar the NCO's self-confidence, Hunter said, "One of your people told me that after Washington picked her up at the hotel, your Black Belt took her to Seoul."

He turned so he could look at Bullis. "Then from a couple more of your cops I got the location of the Nam Song house. When I caught up with Washington and Mr. Kim, they decided it was best to cooperate."

Bullis' face lost its satisfied look. "I think you're shitting me."

"Easy to find out."

Not sounding nearly as confident, he said, "You

want to tell me who gave you all that wonderful information?''

"Not hardly."

Bullis sighed, "It doesn't matter. Everything is totally fucked. Last night, late, we found out you got off base. But with the girl stashed in Seoul we figured it was no sweat, that we could bag you in the morning. Then Donley got worried, with good reason, I guess, and sent Washington off to Seoul to baby-sit her. Less than two hours after he left, the whole place went bat fucking crazy."

"What happened?" Hunter wasn't really that interested; he just wanted to keep Bullis talking—rather than thinking.

"There was another bad fight at the Stereo Club last night. Some of the niggers went in and started pushing people around. But a gang of white troops were laying for them, and about fifty of 'em came charging in with clubs, bottles, whatever, and jumped the niggers. There was a lot of fighting. Five people got hurt. One nigger was cut bad. He died a couple of hours later."

The jeep reached the bottom of the hill. The driver turned south on the MSR and headed up the hill past the Five Spot and beyond, to the edge of the black section. Hunter was surprised that this man who threw the word "nigger" around so freely would have a hooch there.

Bullis continued, "That all happened just before curfew. We got it quieted down and it looked like we might get away clean. Unfortunately, the blacks who shack up downtown were up all night, drinking, talking, and generally getting all fired up. When they started coming back to the base there were some fights. When they got on base they started talking to their brothers. Suddenly most of the niggers walked off their jobs and headed downtown. They hit the gate in a group and pushed through before there were enough guards to stop 'em."

The jeep turned into a narrow alley in the twilight zone between the white and black sections of the town.

Bullis' voice suddenly sounded tired. "Since then it

been crazy time. At first they were just yelling and carrying on. Then they broke into small groups and started attacking any whites they could find. Busting up hooches. Hell, they even set fire to the Playboy Club. With Washington gone, we didn't have a nigger with enough horsepower to talk to them. I went and tried. Damn near got my ass in a sling.''

That didn't surprise Hunter.

The jeep pulled up and stopped in front of a walled Korean house. Bullis told Ledford, ''Go see if Yi's there.''

Hunter asked, ''Was that the end of it?''

''Hardly.'' Bullis grinned. ''Of course, that really pissed off the Koreans, and suddenly we had gangs of *kimchee*-snappers beating the piss outa both black and white GIs, anyone who gave them a hard time. One of my patrols had to save six niggers from getting their asses whacked by a gang of slopes.''

''Who needs the North Koreans when we got each other?''

''Yeah. So we finally got the base sealed up to keep any more GIs from getting out and joining in, but later we discovered some slippery dick had cut a hole in the back fence. I been out here since mid-morning chasing my own ass rounding up GIs and getting 'em back on the base.''

He paused, looked impatiently at the compound, then continued, ''Then, after you and prettyface got away, I got a radio call from Donley telling me he was going to the gate. He ordered me to get up there. As we were coming up, I saw you two get chased into that doorway.''

''What with a riot and all, surprised you had time for us.''

''I always got time for her.'' Bullis turned a murderous glare on Soon Ja. ''You just don't have any idea how much trouble this cunt has caused me. You just can't begin to—''

He was interrupted by Ledford, who returned, followed by a dumpy Korean woman who took off down the alley at a quick lope. Ledford said, "Yi's not here. His wife's gonna find him."

Bullis got out of the jeep and stood for a moment thinking, all the while holding his gun loosely at his side. Hunter considered going for his boot gun, but he had a feeling that Bullis was one of the good ones when it came to guns and had a willingness to use them. He didn't detect any of the reluctance he had sensed earlier in Washington.

Finally Bullis said, "Out, we'll wait inside." After they were standing, Hunter saw a quizzical expression on the NCO's face. He hefted Hunter's bag, shaking it. Hearing the guns rattle, he opened it and looked inside. "Well, well, look what we got here." He seemed to consider that for a moment, then a wicked glint came into his eyes. "Two in here. You got any more?"

"What do you mean?" Hunter tried to look like the newest-born baby lamb, but Bullis had that sixth sense a professional cop develops after years of dealing with liars, thieves, and malefactors of all persuasions.

He ordered, "Against the jeep and spread 'em."

Slowly Hunter did as instructed. Bullis patted Hunter down. When he got to the boots, he grunted, then tugged the Beretta from the clamshell pocket. He stood up, holding the small gun by its barrel, and smiled. "Close, but no cigar."

Chapter 41

There was a deceptive calmness about the place. The same *L*-shaped building, the same gray concrete walls, the row of hooch doors, the unpainted wooden porch and concrete courtyard with large pottery jars used to store *kimchee* during the winter. It was so like other compounds Hunter had been in before that for a moment he was tranquilized by a seductive urge to relax.

Reality returned with a jerk when Kim screamed. After telling the driver to wait outside, Bullis had ordered Hunter to enter first. Then, apparently out of sheer spite, he pushed Soon Ja roughly through the gate. After her yelp of surprise as she almost fell, she quickly regaining her balance, whirled around, and slapped Bullis. Seeing it happen, Hunter leaped out, caught her, and pulled her back from the blond NCO, who had his gun up and looked as if he was going to pistol-whip her.

"Pyong-shin banco sikeya!" Hunter didn't recognize the words she spat at Bullis, but it was obvious she wasn't complimenting him on his savoir faire. Hunter couldn't help smiling as he restrained the incensed young woman. Despite her fear, there was an obvious limit as to how much she would tolerate.

Bullis also held back, despite looking as if he wanted to come over and beat her. Harshly he snarled, "You don't know how much I hate that fucking bitch. I swear to Christ she's the cause of all our problems."

In a deprecating tone Hunter said, "The fact that you and Donley are thieves and murderers has nothing to do with it."

"It's her fault. We had a nice little operation going.

Black marketing, money changing, taking a cut whenever we caught someone into something good. Making good money. We looked the other way for officers involved in piddly little shit, but made sure they knew they owed us. Things we learned in 'Nam.''

As he paused, his eyes fastened on Kim, showing the naked hate festering in his head. ''That was until Donley met prettyface and went crazier than a strip-assed ape. From then on we spent half our time chasing after her every time she ran off. Then her old *yobo* showed up—Captain Super Straight. Donley was insane because he knew she loved him. He wanted him dead. I guess he figured if Crandell was permanently removed she'd change. What a sick joke. The crazy bastard actually wanted love.''

''So you killed Crandell.''

Bullis hesitated, then seemed to decide there was no reason to lie. ''Yeah, I took care of your ol' flying buddy and that's the pure and simple truth. I did it to protect everything we had going.''

''Isn't murder a step up from black marketing and the rest of what you were into? Even for you guys?''

''You been to 'Nam.'' The way Bullis said it, it was an answer, not a question. As if after that experience, everything subsequent was a given.

''Yeah, I've been there.'' Hunter's contempt was obvious.

''I forgot,'' Bullis sneered. ''Sure you were there. One of those shit-hot fighter-pilot heroes. Flying out of Thailand, bombing from a couple of miles up, coming home to hot showers, good food, and plenty of sweet Thai pussy. Well, I put my time in the Delta guarding bases. We spent the days taking rockets and all night fighting off sappers. That was a different war, asshole. I earned mine.''

''I won't swap war stories with you about who had it rougher. But however bad you had it, there were thousands of Army and Marine grunts who had it worse than you ever dreamed of.'' Bullis started to reply, but Hunter cut him off. ''And no matter how bad it was for you, you're free and alive. A lot of those fighter pilots you think were living in luxury are either dead or rotting in the Hanoi Hilton. So don't tell me that you got a free ticket coming just because you were in Vietnam.''

''Shut up, Hunter, I—''

But Hunter wasn't ready to shut up. ''You also got an armful of stripes, which I doubt you had before Vietnam. You're a career man. Nobody drafted you against your will.''

''But 'Nam was so fucked up,'' Bullis said quickly. ''That place just dragged you down.''

Shut up! Hunter's inner voice screamed. But he was angry and, ignoring his better judgment, he said, ''What really honks me off is every crooked sonofabitch running around whining and blaming all his nasty habits on the war.''

He was about to say more—the words had already formed in his mind: ''The war may have sharpened your knife, Bullis, but I'd be willing to bet you were always a corrupt bastard.'' *Oh, yeah, good one, he'll probably shot your dick off for that.* Hunter bit off the words and kept silent.

The compound gate opened. A Korean man, followed by the woman who had been there earlier, entered. The woman hurried quickly into the cooking room at the end of the building.

The man looked at Bullis, then at Hunter and Soon Ja. His face was all harsh angles: jutting cheekbones, thin slits for eyes, narrow chin, prominent Adam's apple, and thick black hair chopped short on the sides. His age could have been anywhere from middle twenties to early forties. His body was all muscle and sinew, without an ounce of fat. He was wearing an old, dirt-stained, strap T-shirt, a shapeless pair of well-worn, cutoff trousers, and battered, rubber-sole slippers. When he saw the gun in Bullis' hand he looked unhappy. ''What is happening here, Sergeant? Why you bring these people to my house?''

''Don't give me any shit, Yi,'' Bullis challenged. ''I can have your ass busted anytime I feel like it.''

The Korean's face got a bit grimmer. "Sergeant, you cannot use my place like this. I won't let—"

Bullis was in a mean mood. He interrupted, "Hunter, meet Mr. Yi. One of the leading citizens of Chicol Village. The hardworking Korean some like to hold up as a good example." The NCO smiled viciously. "See the clothes he's wearing? Looks poor, doesn't he? He used to be poor, but in the last two years he's become a rich man. That's because we made him one of the biggest black-market drops in the vill."

Yi's face had gone completely blank, as if Bullis was talking in a language he did not understand. But Hunter had experienced the Korean temper enough to know that inside, the man was seething. He said, "Sergeant, I ask why you bring these people my house?"

"Because, Yi," Bullis snarled, "I have to have some place safe to keep them until it gets dark enough so I can kill them. And I own you."

Tension and anger were making the American careless. Keeping face was extremely important to Koreans, and Bullis had just stomped all over Yi's. While everything Bullis said was probably true, it violated Korean custom to put it that way. Business was business, and for this moment living off the Americans was the biggest business going. To the Koreans it was the overpaid, oversexed, and over-here GIs who created the demand. If Yi didn't cater to it, someone else would, so why shouldn't he and his family be the ones who profited? However, having the nastier realities of it thrown in his face was a humiliation.

Bullis pointed to the room at the end of the building. "You two, that's my hooch. Get inside."

Hunter took Kim's hand. He could see she was working hard to keep from crying, yet in those eyes he saw more than fear. He saw anger at the helplessness of their situation.

"Toeshima shipsheo," he said softly. Take it easy. "I'll think of something."

Her answer surprised him. "I'm not sorry for myself. I'm sorry for Paul—and you."

Inside, the room reflected a personality quite different from its occupant. It was neat, well furnished, and projected a woman's touch. It was actually two standard rooms with the wall removed. The first room was a living room with Western furniture, including a fifteen-inch Sony color TV, quite an extravagance since there were no color broadcast stations in Korea. There was also a large, Japanese-made stereo system and a full-sized G.E. refrigerator. The second room, separated by pink curtains made from a sheer synthetic material, was the bedroom. In there Hunter could see more pink and frills. It certainly appeared to have been done by a female, unless Bullis was a closet queen.

"You live alone?" Hunter asked.

"I do now." The answer was curt, making it clear he didn't want to talk about it.

"But you didn't before?" Hunter was not sure why he was pulling the man's chain. Maybe because it was there.

Bullis' expression changed from mean-ugly to mean-thoughtful. "I use to have a *yobo*. Just as good-looking as prettyface. But she was a real woman, not a skinny kid." He paused, remembering; his face went back to mean-ugly. "Caught her fucking around on me, so I whipped her ass and kicked her out."

"I suppose you were completely straight?"

"That's different. I'm a man." The same old song. "I was paying her, I did what I felt like."

"Sure." Hunter grinned at him. "Except I guess she didn't see it that way."

Bullis' face flushed with anger, and he moved closer. *Come on, just a little more.* Hunter was set, his muscles ratcheted tight. But Bullis caught himself in time and backed up. "Sit down on the goddamn floor. And shut the fuck up. I'm tired of listening to you."

Chapter 42

An hour later they were still sitting on the floor, against the back wall. Hunter's legs were stiff and the pain in his head was doing its best to scramble his brain. Kim was sitting next to him, her arms hugging knees which were pulled tight under her chin. The sound of rain beating on the thin roof drummed monotonously. Damp, cool air entered the room from the partly open paper-covered wood frame door. Mother Nature was still playing the coquette—a little drizzle, a little dry. Bullis stood in the doorway monitoring his hand-held radio while looking out at the dreary, silent compound.

He had sent Yi somewhere and dispatched the jeep driver back to the base. Ledford was instructed to tell Colonel Donley that Bullis had gone into the black section to attempt negotiations.

A few minutes later, after a burst of activity on the radio, Bullis said, "Maybe you were telling the truth about Washington. The word just went out that Donley's been relieved. That OSI agent, Troxler, he's in command."

"Troxler?" That was a surprise. The tech sergeant running things? That didn't sound like any tech sergeant Hunter knew. Perceiving an advantage, he said, "So, you might as well be smart and give it up—"

"I got a better idea." Bullis was smiling his mean-ugly smile. Somehow Hunter knew that whatever idea Bullis had, he wasn't going to like it. "You and pretty-face are gonna become riot victims. You made yourself real unpopular with our black community when you kicked ass in the Playboy Club. That young stud you took out was one of their leading bad asses, and you made him look stupid. When they find your bodies it'll seem possible, especially after I spread the word that prettyface was shacking with a nigger and you tried to take her away from him.''

"Won't Donley object?" Hunter was looking for some way to discredit what was actually a fairly viable plan.

Bullis' face distorted with savage contempt. "I don't figure Colonel High-and-Mighty is gonna be in the position to object to anything now."

A chilling breeze swirled through the room. Hunter felt Kim shiver. The waiting was getting to her. He sensed she was very tense. He shifted his position, groaning loudly—louder than was actually necessary. He'd shifted several times before, each time making a big production out of the effort to relieve discomfort. The first couple of times Bullis had quickly glanced at him, but now he hardly took notice.

Exactly what Hunter had in mind. He had maneuvered himself so he was hunched up, his back braced against the wall, his legs drawn up. He took several slow, deep breaths, each time cranking himself just a little tighter. Then, he casually reached over with one hand, took a large portion of flesh on Kim's side between his thumb and first finger, and gave it a hard, twisting squeeze.

Kim, already teetering on an emotional tightwire, let out a long, high scream that could only be described as bloodcurdling. Hunter did his best to look innocently surprised. Bullis whirled around and rushed over to see what was going on.

That was a mistake.

He stepped inside the range of Hunter's legs. Hunter slammed both of them forward like a catapult on an aircraft carrier. He aimed for the man's groin. At the last instant Bullis sensed the trap and twisted away. Not far enough. Hunter's feet slammed into his right hip, sending him reeling to the side and backward. The blond sergeant slammed into the end of the nearby couch and staggered, off balance.

Hunter sprang to his feet. But Bullis was far quicker than Hunter had expected. He righted himself and turned to face Hunter as he charged across the room. Going full tilt, he slammed into Bullis. The momentum carried both men forward, crashing through the flimsy wood-and-paper door. Their tangled bodies sailed across the small porch and out into the rain-soaked concrete courtyard.

When they hit the hard, slick surface, Hunter was on top. His primary concern was Bullis' gun. He wrapped his left hand around the sergeant's wrist and slammed it against the concrete. Bullis lost his grip and the gun skittered away.

By concentrating on the gun, however, he left himself open to the NCO's left hand, still clutching the radio. That oversight was rewarded with a jarring blow to his head. His vision blurred for an instant, then clicked back to normal as he rolled away and leaped to his feet.

But Bullis was up too. For a split second they stood glaring at each other. In that moment Hunter became aware that it was raining again. Even before that thought was fully realized, Bullis dodged after the loose revolver. Hunter jumped too, and got there first, kicking the gun away. It went skipping across the wet surface of the courtyard and bounced against the front wall. The NCO bellowed in rage and kicked savagely at Hunter's outstretched left leg. The kick connected, sending shock waves of pain reverberating up from his knee. Hunter wobbled as he backed up.

Bullis went into a boxer's stance. He waded in and threw a hard right fist that caught Hunter in the side, making him hunch forward in pain. The sergeant followed with a left aimed at his face. Seeing it coming, Hunter ducked and rotated his upper body to the right, then snapped back, driving his elbow into Bullis' exposed rib cage.

Bullis groaned and lurched backward, favoring his left side. He looked dazed. Hunter moved to take advantage of the situation, setting himself up for a kick at Bullis' head. Just as he started to swing his leg, without any warning his world went out of focus and his equilibrium took a crazy, sideways skid. Struggling to maintain his balance, Hunter shuffled backward.

Bullis, still favoring his side, wasted no time taking advantage of the opening. He moved in and slammed a savage combination right and left, stomach and head. Hunter, reeling, staggered back. Bullis, who to Hunter's eyes had become two bleary, hazy figures shimmering in the fading light and rain, probably didn't realize, or care, why his opponent was lurching about. He moved in for the kill. He hammered Hunter in the stomach, then hit him in the head again.

Hunter felt himself helplessly falling backward. He heard a loud, high scream behind him. He knew it was Kim. He also knew his old war wound had manifested itself at the worst possible moment. As he went down his voice consoled, *It's not your fault. You ought to get to play that one over.*

He could feel the cold, wet concrete beneath him. He put his hands on the slick, wet surface, attempting to get up. Bullis loomed over him, rage in his voice. "What's a matter, *sir,* too much for you?"

He punctuated the sentence by stomping savagely on Hunter's outstretched left hand. A burning flash of pain rocketed through Hunter's arm, exploding in his brain. As he lost his support and fell forward on his shoulder, he knew some of his fingers were broken.

"You think you can fuck with me?" he heard Bullis scream, still in rage. He tried to slide away as he saw Bullis swing his booted foot back, then send it slashing forward. The agonizing blow actually lifted Hunter off the ground. He thought he was going to be sick.

After an unmeasurable eternity of wretchedness and misery, he heard Bullis' voice close to him. "I'm gonna blow your motherfucking head off, you cocksucking bastard."

His balance stabilized, his vision cleared. *Too late, just too damn late.* He lifted his head. Bullis was standing over him. He had recovered his heavy revolver, and he thrust it forward into Hunter's face.

He wanted to tell Bullis he didn't care, to go ahead

and do it. But suddenly, cutting through the agonizing aches, he felt fear. A cold chill racked his body. And he knew he did care. But despite the involuntary fear, stronger than anything he had ever experienced in combat, he was damned if he would show it to this maggot of a man.

The sound of the shot was loud. He was surprised he heard it. They always said you never hear the one that gets you. And despite the fact that he was already battered and beaten, it didn't add to his pain as he had thought it would.

What the hell's going on?

In an uncoordinated jerk he thrust himself up on his feet. And almost fell over again. He looked around wildly. Bullis was down on one knee, his other leg canted crazily to the side. Blood was coming from between fingers which were gripping his upper thigh. But he still had his gun, and he was scooting himself around to face the opened compound gate.

"Drop it, Bullis!"

A large figure was hunched down in the opening. Hunter could see a big automatic in a heavy fist. Bullis swung his revolver up. The automatic fired—two quick shots so close together they sounded like one. Bullis' body jerked around as the bullets hit him in the chest. The force knocked him backward onto the wet concrete.

Troxler stepped into the compound. Keeping his eyes on Bullis, he said, "Hunter, I thought I told you to come see me before you did anything stupid."

Hunter's anxiety drained away, leaving him almost too weak to stand. As the big man ambled over, he held out his arms in a gesture of helplessness. "I been trying. Damn, I been trying."

Chapter 43

Hunter sat on the low porch, watching the activity in the courtyard. Kim had found a blanket and put it around him. Using a wet cloth she cleaned the cuts on his face while whispering nice things in his ear about how brave he had been. Seeing the look of concern on that beautiful face greatly improved his condition. Despite that, his head still hurt.

He asked one of the SPs standing around to retrieve his AWOL bag and give him the bottle of pills. When the young cop opened it, his eyes opened wide with surprise. "Holy shit, look at this."

Hunter had forgotten about the guns. "Come on, just gimme the pills."

Troxler walked over. Dressed in a light tan correspondent's suit that was popular with the newsmen in Vietnam, he was the only other person not in an Air Force uniform of some sort. He took the bag from the SP, inspected the contents, reached in for the pill bottle, and tossed it to Hunter. Keeping the bag, he went back to directing the removal of Bullis' body.

Hunter started wrestling with the childproof cap while Kim found a stainless steel bowl, went to the courtyard pump, and filled it with water. By the time she came back, he had managed to rip the top off the bottle and fumble out a couple of pills. He popped them into his mouth and lifted the bowl to take a swallow of water to wash them down.

"Hey, don't drink that," the young cop said loudly.

Hunter paused, feeling the pills melting on his tongue. "Why not?"

"There's a base regulation against drinking water in the vill."

"Oh." He downed a large gulp.

Kim, leaping to the defense of her country, snapped, "Why you say? Water not bad."

The young cop looked abashed. Hunter mumbled, "Give him hell, honey."

His attention returned to the people who were removing Bullis' body. Troxler was giving orders, everyone else was taking them. Without questions. After a while Hunter asked the young cop, "What's Troxler's position here?"

The look on the youngster's face said that was a dumb question. "He's in charge."

"In charge of what?" Hunter persisted. "This detail? The security police? What?"

"Hell, Captain, he's in charge of everything."

"Everything?"

"Yeah, everything. My NCOIC told me Mr. Troxler has been giving orders to everyone, including the base commander."

Hunter digested the news. One thing was certain, Troxler wasn't a tech sergeant.

A medic came and put a few yards of tape on the two smaller fingers of Hunter's left hand, and advised him to came to the hospital in the morning for X rays. Sometime after that, when all the pictures had been taken and Bullis' body removed, Troxler ambled over. "Feel like going to the base?"

"That depends."

Troxler looked flabbergasted. "That was a rhetorical question." Hunter didn't move. The big man shook his head with resignation. "Okay, depends on what?"

"Her," he said, looking at Kim.

"Well, hell, Hunter, I'm not going to leave her here." He smiled graciously, looking at the beautiful girl. "Miss Kim Soon Ja, I presume." She nodded. "The fiancée of Captain Paul Crandell?"

She looked questioningly at Hunter. He said, "Right."

"Miss Kim, I've been looking for you for several

weeks—even before Captain Hunter arrived. Will you talk to me?'' She looked at the younger officer again. ''I want you to tell me everything you know about Colonel Donley, his men, and what happened to Captain Crandell.''

Doubt showed in her large, lustrous eyes. Hunter understood her hesitation about trusting Americans in positions of authority. He nodded encouragingly.

''*Na,* I will,'' she said slowly. Then looking at Hunter again, she quickly added, ''He will come too?''

Troxler looked satisfied. ''He wants you. You want him. I think we got a deal.'' To Hunter he said, ''How about we fix Miss Kim up in the VIP quarters while she is talking to us? Will that suit you?''

Hunter smiled. ''Sounds fair to me.''

''Big of you,'' Troxler said, extending one large hand to assist Hunter up.

The pills were working their usual magic. The pain in his head was almost gone, as was most of the feeling in his farthest extremities. Kim clutched one arm and Troxler supported the other. They walked across the courtyard and through the gate. He got in the back of a blue staff car with Kim.

Going around to the driver's side, Troxler told the ranking NCO, ''I'll drive these two. You follow us.''

The car, with the jeep full of heavily armed security police following, wound slowly down the rutted alley, out on the MSR, and toward the base. The rain had stopped for the moment, but the air was still heavy. The blacktop street was blanketed with dark mud. As they rolled down the hill and turned onto the main street, Hunter noticed that the crowds were gone except for a few Korean national policemen on the empty sidewalks.

He asked, ''What happened to the riot?''

''We got most of the Americans back on base with orders to stay in their quarters. The KNP's done the same for the village. If we get through tonight, which I think we will, we should be in pretty good shape.''

Hunter nodded, then asked, ''How'd you happen along?''

"Hardly by accident. I've been trying to locate you ever since shortly after Bullis grabbed you and the lady."

"You knew he got us?"

"You're not the only one who's aware of what's happening around here. I've been aware of the situation in the security police squadron for some time. To get the information I needed to move, I have developed resources there who keep me informed as to what's going down. One was with Bullis when you got caught. As soon as he returned to the base he came and told me."

"Who's that?"

"The cop? Fernandez. Why?"

"I figured. He tried to stand up to Bullis."

"The problem was, he didn't know where Bullis took you. I didn't learn that bit of information until the driver, Ledford, showed up. Once I got my hands on that young man, it didn't take long to convince him that if he didn't talk to me, his fanny was dog meat and I was the main hound." He paused, then said, "We got there as soon as we could."

"There's just one more thing I'd like to know." Troxler's eyes flicked up to the mirror, so they were looking directly at each other. "Who the hell are you?"

He saw the big man smile. "Right now I'm OSI. The rank is colonel."

"Oh yeah, right now, huh. But who the hell are you really?"

At first Troxler did not answer, but after a few moments the deep voice rumbled back across the seat. "I'm someone who cleans up messes for the Air Force."

"Oh." Hunter wasn't sure what that meant, but he decided he was glad somebody was doing that job.

It was quiet for several moments, then Troxler said, "The other day in the club, you asked what color hat I wore." He paused, then with pride he said, "I like to think it's white—and still fairly clean after all these years."

Chapter 44

When they arrived at the cop shop, Hunter, with Kim holding his hand tightly, followed Troxler into the building. Once inside, the big man stopped to confer with a cadre of officers and senior NCOs who gathered around. Hunter and Soon Ja got a lot of sidelong glances while they waited for Troxler to receive reports and give orders.

"Fuck me to tears," Loudly from across the room. "You're all right."

Hunter turned and saw Ron Shaw hurrying from the back of the building. He wondered if Troxler had hauled his friend in on a co-conspiracy charge or some such thing. He asked, "You in trouble?"

"No, no," Shaw said quickly, his eyes frantically signaling that Hunter shouldn't say anything else. He pointed at Troxler. "After he took over, he called me in to handle community relations with the Koreans." Shaw seemed to stand a little taller as he said it. "I think he likes me."

"What's not to like?"

"My feelings exactly."

Troxler broke away from the coterie and came over. "Lieutenant Shaw here has been helping with the locals," he said. "Seems he's one of the few officers on the base the Koreans actually get along with."

"That's good, Ron's, ah, the lieutenant is a good—"

"Of course, I also kept him around because I know he's been living in your back pocket ever since you got here, and I figured he might lead me to you." Troxler smiled his Papa Bear smile. "But I didn't tell him that."

Hunter wasn't sure if the look on Shaw's face would best be described as agog or agape.

"After you two finish catching up, come on back to my office and we can see about getting things tidied up."

The big man went into the office formerly occupied by Donley. Shaw said, "I thought he really liked me."

"We've all been there at one time or another."

Shaw sighed again, then Hunter saw him taking a long, covert look at Soon Ja. Looking back, he realized he'd been caught. "Just checking." He took another look, even longer. So long Soon Ja started to get nervous. Finally, "Jeez, Mike, she really is some kind of fantastic."

Kim, blushing, looked a bit peeved. "He your friend?" Hunter, struggling to keep from laughing, nodded. Soon Ja added, "I think too much *dingee-dingee* GI."

Before Shaw could say anything, Troxler's voice boomed out of the office. "Captain Hunter, if you and Miss Kim would be so kind."

Shaw twitched nervously. "I think he's ready for you."

In the office Troxler had cups of hot coffee waiting. Pak was along to translate anything Kim didn't understand. They spent more than an hour giving their stories, and a tape recorder was running the whole time. When it was over, Hunter realized that the big man with a fatherly expression on his face had conducted the questioning with extreme courtesy and sensitivity.

Troxler sent the tape out to be transcribed. He said, "Hunter, you should've come to me when you discovered where they were holding the girl."

"At that point I still didn't know the good guys from the bad guys."

Troxler nodded. "Just for your information, I've been working for more than two months to build a solid case against Donley and crew. Word of his activities had gotten around. That's why I was sent here. I about had it all, including conclusive proof, which is required in this business, before you stumbled into the middle of things. I even had most of the story about your friend Crandell, except that I didn't know Donley still had Miss Kim here.''

"So what were you waiting for?"

"The general. He was too close and was holding me off. I was working that one when you showed up and started kicking the slats out of Donley's crib."

"You planning to hold that against me?"

Troxler looked at Hunter a few moments before answering. "No. Actually the fire you built, along with the riot, got the headquarters weenies in Japan off their fannies and forced them to let me move."

"So you relieved Donley and took over. By the way, where is the evil bastard?"

"He's under arrest. I'm shipping him to Japan tomorrow. For a while there I was afraid that the best I could nail him for was black marketing. However, with Miss Kim's testimony, I think I can get him for murder."

"Fat chance the military will allow a senior officer to be put on public trial for murder."

Troxler was not ruffled. "Regardless of who likes it, I promise you he'll pay for that deed."

"I'll believe that when I see it. What about his high-ranking pals?"

"As soon as we realized we had a full-blown riot going, I got on the phone to Japan and convinced them the general wasn't exactly on top of things. The regional commander there called him and told him to report immediately. He's already gone. His deputy is officially in charge, but he's coordinating with me—very closely."

"What about Davies?"

"Mostly he's guilty of stupidity. He's finished here and he'll probably end up retiring in lieu of a court-martial."

"Doesn't seem like enough."

"No, I suppose not. But you've gotten more than one pound of flesh today. Eighth Army found the house on Nam Song. The Korean was dead. Washington was still there. He's in the hospital and he's going to be there for a while. Then he'll also be facing a court-martial."

"So the good guys win."

Troxler ignored the sour note in Hunter's voice. "Yes, I'd like to think so. The system's not perfect. The military is a big organization and there'll always be some who take advantage of that for their own ends. But I like to think that most of us are doing it because we mean to do the right thing."

"So everything goes back to square one. Which means the officers go back to the club, Air Force Korea sends out a new one star who's looking for number two, and some new base commander and top cop come in and go back to making life as miserable as possible for the lowly GIs."

The big man smiled. "Not exactly. The riot's changed that. The people back at headquarters Pacific Air Force in Hawaii and the Pentagon have finally realized how explosive the situation is here. The new general they've picked was carefully selected for the job. I knew him in Vietnam, he's a good man. Very people-oriented. I think even a maverick like you will approve."

Troxler returned the young officer's steady gaze, and after several moments he said, "Anything else?"

Hunter looked at Soon Ja quietly sipping coffee as she watched and listened, then back to Troxler. "No, I guess not."

"In that case, I've made arrangements for the VIP quarters. My driver will take Miss Kim there." He stopped and smiled. "Would you like to go along to help her get settled?"

Hunter couldn't help smiling back. "Yeah—ah, yes sir, I'd like that."

So it was over. He stood up and stretched. He was feeling no pain thanks to the pills and the cups of coffee, which had perked him up. He looked at Kim. "*Yobosayo?*"

She jumped up, rushed over, and took hold of his arm, "We go now?"

He put his hand on hers. "Yes, we go now."

Chapter 45

Troxler had bent the regulations more than a little. The suite of rooms he had arranged were one of two sets on the base usually reserved for visiting generals and high-ranking civilians. The large living room had thick rugs, a plush, American-made couch and easy chair, a large RCA color TV, a new Sony AM-FM stereo radio, and other little niceties. Hunter—battered, bruised, and drained—flopped on the couch while wide-eyed Soon Ja explored. From the living room she went into a large kitchen complete with a full-sized G.E. refrigerator, electric range, and cabinet stocked with glassware and dishes.

After the kitchen she discovered a door into a spacious bedroom with a double bed and a second TV set, also color, although it was only a fifteen-incher. The big bathroom was equipped with a large shower and thick towels. She returned and looked at Hunter. "All for me?"

"Yes," he said, grinning, "at least for the moment."

"Your friend, OSI, he is nice man."

"He's a real peach."

"You stay too?" The expression on her face could not have been more innocent, yet he was pretty sure the question added up to more than the sum total of the words.

"For a while," he said, dancing around the direct implication of her words. "I have a room in the BOQ."

She came over, curled up next to him on the couch, and gazed into his eyes, probing. The look triggered a large burst of adrenaline. He wasn't nearly as tired as he thought. But he was, he realized, apprehensive, afraid of rejection.

She smiled. It was a warm, knowing smile—and the world was suddenly a better place. Looking at him from head to toe, she said, "You know, you very dirty."

He had used the small, cramped rest room at the cop shop to wash his hands and face, but was still a long way from clean. "Yeah, maybe I better go back to—"

"Use bathroom," she said. The tone in her voice was firm; she wasn't asking. "Many towels, no problem."

"Ah, okay."

As he went to the bathroom, Kim went to the television and started twisting knobs. Hunter heard voices speaking in Korean as the door closed behind him: she had found a local station.

Taking off his dirty shirt, he realized he had never been in a military BOQ so generous with linen. He stripped off the rest of his clothes, turned on the water, and stepped in. Doing his best to keep his bandaged fingers dry, he let the hot, clean water do its magic. After a generous soak and a lot of soap, he felt better. As he stood toweling off, looking at his muddy, wrinkled clothes, the idea of getting back into them revolted him. As he considered this, there was a knock on the bathroom door. He opened it enough to look out. Kim was standing there, smiling brightly and holding two large white terry cloth robes.

"Look what I find." She thrust one at him. "You put on. Give me clothes. I wash in kitchen."

Taking the robe, he asked, "You know how to do it?"

"What you think, Korean girl not know how to wash clothes?"

"Sorry." He gathered up his things and handed them to her.

After using one of the toothbrushes and paste thoughtfully supplied by the Q, he left the bathroom wrapped in the thick robe and went in search of Soon Ja. She was in the kitchen. She had changed into the other robe and was washing her dress and underthings along with his clothes in the sink. As she finished with each, she put them on hangers to dry. Looking over at him, she said, "Not like house girl, but not so bad."

"No," he said, "not so bad at all."

She finished and they went back to the living room. Somehow she made the robe, which was a large man's size, appear sexy and seductive. She turned, holding out her arms, and asked, "How I'm look?"

"*Manee epuda.* Very pretty."

She grinned. "This very nice place. I think I like to live here."

"Yeah. Me too."

She was alive with the excitement of a new adventure. Looking so young and fresh, she made him think of a teenager getting her first grown-up dress. She said, "Now I take shower."

After she was inside, he noted that she'd left the door slightly ajar. Hunter sat listening to the sound of running water and looked longingly at the beckoning portal.

Maybe you ought to join her, his inner voice said leeringly.

For a long moment he considered it. Then, giving himself a mental kick in the behind, he went to the TV. The Korean program was some sort of audience-participation game. The point seemed to be for contestants to run around and make themselves look silly in order to win prizes. Just like real life. He switched to the Armed Forces Network. They were up to their usual high standards, an old half-hour episode of *Gunsmoke.*

He turned down the sound and switched on the radio. It was tuned to the AFKN station that originated at Osan. Marvin Gaye was trying to find out "What's Goin' On?" Hunter felt it was an appropriate question, considering the situation, and adjusted the volume to background level. Then he dropped onto the couch and stretched out.

Well, Captain Terrific, you did it. You knocked down all the windmills, slew all the dragons, and rescued the beautiful damsel in distress. And you didn't get your pecker shot off.

He had been lucky. Being trained and being angry helped, but the impish demon, fate, seemed to still be on his side—and who was he to question fate?

Which left the future. Nothing too important, just the rest of his real life. He thought about that. He would have to get back in the real Air Force. Which meant the flight-safety job. Paperwork, reports, staff studies, analyses ad nauseam. Ugh. Well, what had to be had to be. The main thing was to concentrate on getting back to the cockpit. Flying. And getting good report cards so his career would advance. That was the real Air Force.

And where does Miss Kim Soon Ja fit into all that? Good question.

And it was not just how he felt that counted. The lady had a say in this too. He knew he wanted her, but how did she feel? Gratitude, sure. But it took more than that for a relationship. Even assuming she felt the same as he did, would it last? He had a bad track record in that department.

Also there would be prejudice, both racial and social, to be faced. He thought he could handle that. He wasn't the sort who let others' xenophobic notions of right or morality run his life. How would it affect Soon Ja? Well, if what he had seen today was any indication, he had the notion she could hold her own in any situation.

Those thoughts were forever scattered when the bathroom door opened and Kim came out. She had traded the robe for a couple of large, fluffy towels. One on her head was carefully twisted around, Cleopatra style, covering her long hair. It made her appear taller and provided a unique frame for her flawless oval face with its high cheekbones, full, smiling mouth, and those unbelievable shining eyes. Every time he saw her again he was amazed to find that she seemed even more beautiful than he remembered from the time before.

The second towel was a definite improvement on the overlarge robe. Wrapped around her from the tops of her well-shaped breasts to just short of indecency, it was sexier than any miniskirt he had ever seen. He sat up, aware that he was staring, a lewd, teeth-clenched grin on his face.

Straighten up, dummy.

She saw the look and smiled innocently. "Soon Ja okay?"

"Ha!" He knew when his leg was being pulled.

"You not think too ugly girl?"

He took a long, deep breath, exhaled, and smiled. She was in a playful mood. He joined the game. "No, not ugly. Too skinny maybe."

"You think skinny!" Mock anger flashed in her volatile eyes. "Okay, then I go."

"No, you better stay. If I don't take care of you, what are you going to do?"

The little-girl look was back. "You take care of me?" He nodded, responsibly. "You buy rice so poor Soon Ja not starve?"

He nodded again. Effortlessly she seemed to glide across the room. "Then I think I stay."

At the couch she kneeled down so that her eyes were on the same level as his, just inches away. She put one hand on his chest, softly. The blood pounded in his head as he experienced a synapse-sizzling shot of high-voltage excitement.

He covered her hand with his, tenderly. She leaned forward, slowly, until their lips touched. Hesitatingly at first, exploring. Was this real? The answer came quickly. Their lips pressed harder, mouths opened, communicating a burst of shared passion. He felt as if he was whirling on a merry-go-round of pleasure, faster and faster, higher and higher. He could tell from the way she responded that she shared his feelings. It was a kiss full of fire. It was a kiss of promise. It was the kiss for which kissing had been invented.

When their lips parted, he saw a flustered look of

surprise in her eyes. She hesitated for a moment, restraining him as she looked deep into his eyes. To makes sure. Then, almost jumping forward, she was in his arms, pressing to him, all resistance, all restraint gone. The thrill was intense. This woman who had possessed him from the impersonal depths of a photograph, who had haunted the hallways of his mind, was now his.

The towels and robe no longer separated them. Her flesh was firm and warm, almost feverish to his touch. He could feel strength under her golden hide. They slipped from the couch, pressing even closer. Their mouths trading love kisses. Hands seeking, exploring. His mouth slid down her neck. He trembled slightly as he covered her firm, round, budlike nipple with his lips. Her back arched slightly. Then he felt her lips on his ear, her teeth biting softly. He experienced a flash fire of passion that was matched by her response. He continued to explore, his hand moving down, caressing, probing, eliciting tremors and soft moans. His fingers became slick and wet as she pressed her sex to them. They maneuvered into positions of accommodation. As he entered her, she gasped sharply and her eyes snapped open. Then she shut them tightly and thrust forward, meeting him, her arms tightening around him.

For a moment he seemed to soar above their two bodies, objectively observing the absolute exquisiteness of their lovemaking. Time and space were separate realities, experiencing and observing. Finally sexual fury shattered the detachment, totally engulfed him in the sensual rhythm of the flesh, bodies slapping together, driving harder, grinding to a mutual high-intensity orgasm.

And this time, in his mind, bells rang loudly.

They basked in the warm, fuzzy afterglow that comes only when sex has meaning beyond the physical act. Holding, kissing, touching, rejoicing, he had a sappy grin on his face. Pure male chauvinism because it had been so good. And they both knew it.

She looked into his eyes, questioning. With a hesitant tone in her voice, she said, "You my *yobo* now?"

Hunter smiled. "Looks like it."

She nodded. Suddenly, charged up like a baby tiger, eyes flashing, teeth snapping, she burrowed about him, emitting deep, sensual purring sounds and depositing velvety butterfly kisses. She bit his lips gingerly and purred, "Again."

And like a true hero, he rose to the occasion.

It was slower this time, more deliberate, with the supreme confidence that it would be good. She lay back with her legs wrapped around him, looking into his eyes with a steady, penetrating gaze. As she received each long, slow thrust she closed her eyes and gasped with pleasure. Then she flexed, held him for a moment, and released. Each moment of this union was equal parts of giving and receiving. When he peaked, no longer able to hold back, she moved in ways which increased and heightened his moment. Then, with perfect timing, she propelled herself up to his level, giving in to recurring bursts of explosive fulfillment.

He was not aware of time passing as they lay, arms and legs entwined. He realized that for the first time in his memory, he was totally satisfied. He reached over and lifted her chin so he could see her eyes. "This may sound a little strange, but I think I love you." He saw a shadow pass behind her eyes. Her sharp white upper teeth bit down on her full lower lip. "Does that make you nervous?"

"Maybe love me is not good."

He held back the quick answer, thinking. Then he said, "I don't believe that."

"Paul loved me. Now he is—"

He put one finger on her lips. "That wasn't your fault. You were caught in a trap. You didn't have the power to resist. But it's over now."

"I was bad, I—"

"Miss Kim, this may come as a surprise to you, but my life has not been perfect. I have done things that I am not proud of. But that was yesterday. I think what is important is what we do today. And tomorrow."

Looking into his eyes, she took hold of his hand and kissed his fingers. Cautiously she said, "Past is past?"

Hugging her tightly, he nodded. "Yes."

Later, he saw that she was asleep. He was not aware of when it happened. Time had passed without notice, without concern. The only light came from a single low-watt table lamp and the flickering eye of the television. The music on the radio had changed. Gary Puckett was telling a young girl to get out of his mind. Some guys just don't have any luck, Hunter reflected.

Sometime after that, there was a knock on the door. Oh damn, he sighed, what now? Probably Troxler or one of his peons. Great timing.

He eased out from the entwined position, carefully covering Kim with a loose towel, and hotfooted it into the kitchen. After grabbing his still damp jeans, he struggled to get his legs into them as he danced his way back to the door.

There was a second, demanding knock.

"Just a second," he called, half tripping as one foot stuck halfway down. At the door, hitching up his belt with one hand, he reached for the knob and opened the door—and was looking into a large tunnel of darkness. It was the barrel of a .45 automatic pistol in the hand of Lieutenant Colonel Donley.

Chapter 46

Hunter blinked and tried to slam the door. Donley put his shoulder forward, holding it back. He said, "I'll kill you."

The fire of barely controlled hatred burned in his eyes, convincing Hunter the man was so far gone he really would. Donley ordered, "Inside."

Hunter considered jumping him right there. But the man was too primed. Hunter figured the odds at better than even that he would die if he tried it. He backed up.

Do something! his voice screamed.

But he couldn't. Donley was in control. His once handsome face was strained and gaunt from the malice boiling in his gut. He followed Hunter into the room, kicking the door shut.

It took Donley's eyes a moment to adjust to the dimly lit room. Then he saw her sleeping on the floor in front of the couch, long golden legs poking from beneath the fluffy white towel. A flash of inner agony crossed his features. Then, almost as quickly as it had come, it was replaced by malignant rancor. In that moment Hunter had seen utter anguish. He pitied Donley for the uncontrollable emotions that had brought him to this moment in his life. Hunter understood. The colonel had risked everything for this woman, and now she was lost forever, and his world was in shambles.

Even bad guys fall in love.

"Bitch." It came out softly the first time, and small bubbles of saliva accompanied the word to his lips. "Bitch." Louder. "Bitch, bitch, bitch!"

Kim jerked awake. She rose up blinking, clutching

the towel. When the image before her registered, her eyes filled with confusion and opened wide. Then fear. She opened her mouth. Donley saw what was coming. "Don't scream. I'll shoot you both right here."

"Easy," Hunter cautioned.

She closed her mouth. There was no sound.

Hunter put a toe in the water. "I don't think you'll shoot anyone here. It would make too much noise."

"Try me."

Donley was not going to argue. It was up to Hunter, believe him or don't. Looking into those mad, deadly eyes, Hunter was forced to believe him.

"Get your clothes on." Donley said to Kim. The words were slow, flat, evenly spaced, but Hunter sensed each one was a knife in Donley's black heart. Finally, looking back at Hunter, he said, "You too."

Kim rose slowly, holding the towel to cover herself. She pointed to the kitchen. Hunter said, "The clothes are in there. We washed them."

Donley jerked his chin, motioning for them to move. Hunter followed Kim into the kitchen. He got his things, then said, "How about we give her some privacy? Just to keep everything cool."

Donley thought about it for a moment, then nodded and backed up. Just enough so that if she tried to do anything but dress, he could see.

As he pulled on his shirt, Hunter said, "I thought they had you locked up?"

For a moment he didn't think the older man was going to answer. Then a thin, humorless smile showed on his face. "I was confined to quarters. There was a guard—but he went away. There are people on this base who would rather not see me go to trial."

"Beautiful," Hunter muttered, pulling on his boots.

"Soon Ja," Donley said impatiently, "get out here or I'm coming in to get you."

She came through the doorway as if responding to a whiplash: her face strained, eyes bright and glistening from barely controlled tears. Despite her fear she wasn't totally humbled. Giving Donley a look of harsh anger, she said, "You are really crazy man. Why you don't die?"

An icy silence followed. For a second Hunter thought the colonel was going to shoot someone. The moment passed. "There's a staff car outside," he said. "Hunter, you get in front. Soon Ja will be right beside me. If you try anything she gets the first bullet."

Hunter couldn't believe it. It was so similar to the earlier episode with Bullis. These guys just kept coming. He nodded dumbly, at a loss for the moment, and walked to the door.

Outside, it was night and the rain had started again. The steady drizzle made the green lawn and blacktop street glisten darkly. He hoped for a crowd hanging about. But the only person in sight was a lone GI a half block away, head down, hands tucked in his pockets as he hurried in the rain. Probably on the way to the gate, Hunter thought, even though everyone was restricted. He remembered the *Pueblo* time, when the gate had been closed for more than a week. Still, GIs were down at the fence every night, stuffing money through the wire to their *yobos*, to keep their happy homes away from home intact.

The inside of the damp staff car smelled of mildew and broken dreams. The cop radio was shut off. When Hunter was behind the wheel, he adjusted the rearview mirror so he could see into the backseat. Donley was on one side holding the .45. Kim pushed herself back into the corner on the opposite side.

The colonel told him to start driving, giving instructions about which way to turn. The route took them toward the flight line. When Donley told him to turn right, Hunter knew they were skirting D-diamond, heading away from base operations. He was amazed to see that after several twists and turns, Donley had somehow gotten them out onto the flight line heading toward the end of the ramp without passing a security checkpoint. Theoretically that was impossible.

Donley seemed to sense his thoughts. "I always told them the security on this base was lousy, but they'd never give me enough people to do it right."

Hunter couldn't help but marvel at the remark. This murdering bastard who had used his people for black marketing, corruption, and every sort of devious conduct was at heart still the petty bureaucrat, complaining that his job had been made impossible because of restriction from above.

"If your men spent more time on the flight line and less chasing girls in the vill, security might have been a lot tighter."

"Shut up."

Apparently Donley didn't care to engage in a debate. "You sure you can handle this by yourself?" Hunter asked, hoping to rattle the man. "You don't have Bullis along to hold your hand like you did when you murdered your wife."

"How did you—" Donley bit the words off, took a deep breath, and released it slowly. "I must admit, Hunter, you amaze me. You seem to have a unique talent for digging up things which are very bad for your health."

What's your next great idea, Captain Stupid?

For the moment Hunter decided to keep quiet and follow Donley's directions. They were driving down the main aircraft taxiway, toward the east end of the ramp where aircraft had to taxi to in order to turn onto the active runway for takeoff. The headlights of the car illuminated the construction equipment Hunter had noticed when he landed at Osan. Just beyond was the area being widened and lengthened.

"Over there," Donley said, pointing to the construction site. Once they were past the large machines, he told Hunter to stop the car and get out.

Once outside, Hunter was in the steady drizzle, getting wet again. He watched Donley get out and pull Kim along. He asked, "What's this all about?"

A grim smile stiffened the man's features. "You and Soon Ja are about to become part of the permanent facilities here at Osan." He pointed to a dirt area being prepared for concrete. "Without you two, or your bodies, it will be much more difficult for anyone to convict me of anything serious."

Hunter doubted that. Troxler had Kim's statement as well as a mass of evidence about black marketing and other activities. But he didn't think he could sell that to Donley at this point.

The colonel reached into the car and removed the keys. He tossed them to Hunter. "There's a shovel in back. Get it." Once Hunter had the shovel, the older man pointed to a spot in the raw earth. "Dig."

Hunter's inner voice lamented, *Can you believe this? The old dig-your-own-grave routine.*

On the other hand, he reflected as he looked at the shovel, why not? It certainly made more sense than for Donley to kill them first and then have to do the digging himself.

And here he was doing it. Anything to buy time. It was rough going and he was soaked from the rain on the outside and sweat on the inside. He dug inexpertly, what with his aversion to manual labor and the bandaged fingers. Still, however slowly, the damn hole kept getting larger.

Think of something!

He was trying, but a growing sense of dread was taking over. Keeping it under control was a major effort which didn't leave a lot of resources for creative thinking.

As he dug he became aware of the muted roar of aircraft engines. The sounds were coming across the open expanses of the level flight line from near the control tower. He looked down the taxiway and could see faraway lights from a moving aircraft.

"Quit stalling," Donley said. "Dig or I'll kill you right now."

Hunter wanted to say something smartass, but he found his throat was too constricted to cooperate. As he tossed the next shovel full of dirt, he took another look toward operations. Now he recognized the high-pitched whine mixed with a noticeable vibration, the unmistakable sound of the four turbo-prop engines on a C-130, the Air Force's large combat transport aircraft. He moved another shovel of earth, wishing he was on that C-130, going anywhere away from Osan.

After a few more shovels of dirt, the engine sound was louder. He had worried that the aircraft might just be being moved for maintenance, but now he was sure it was rolling out for takeoff. It would have to pass nearby.

He began to hope. When it taxied past, the flight crew could hardly miss seeing them. If they radioed the control tower, maybe someone would come and check. That was possible. Right?

So they see you, so what? his inner voice reasoned. *When they see the Air Force staff car, they'll just figure someone is out doing what he's supposed to be doing.*

Unfortunately, Hunter knew that was the most likely possibility. The next time he looked up, he saw that, if nothing else, the approaching aircraft was making Donley nervous. He had pulled Kim to the car and pushed her inside. Smart move. If the flight crew saw a Korean girl, even they would have a hard time passing it off as business as usual.

Hunter's mind began to explore other possibilities. But Donley was thinking too. He moved away from the car, careful not to get too close to Hunter, and around to a position between the younger man and where the C-130 would pass. From there he could keep his gun handy without it being seen from the cockpit.

The huge bird, painted in combat camouflage dark greens and blacks, engines roaring, was lumbering closer. The colonel's face reflected his apprehension as his head flicked back and forth between the approaching bird and Hunter. Down in the hole Hunter's hands tightened on the handle of the shovel. Donley, focused more and more on the airplane, pulled the gun tight against his stomach, out of sight from the C-130 crew.

This is it, Hunter's voice shrieked, *go for it!*

The next time Donley looked away to check the progress of the aircraft, Hunter bounded up and out of the shallow hole and charged.

Sensing danger, Donley's gaze snapped back to Hunter. Anger mixed with confusion flashed across his features. If he shot Hunter, those in the aircraft were sure to see him. But if he didn't . . . In confusion he took several steps backward, away from the younger man to the edge of the taxiway.

At the same time the C-130, engines screaming in the night, bright taxi lights piercing the blackness, lumbered closer. It was less than fifteen yards away now and closing quickly. Hunter, holding the shovel at high port arms, had gotten to only a few feet from Donley.

Realizing he had no choice, the colonel jerked his hand up, and fired—but a millisecond late.

The bullet whined past Hunter as he cocked his arms and brought the shovel's tip around in a vicious short arc aimed at Donley's head.

Seeing it coming, the older man stumbled backward, onto the concrete taxiway, retreating enough to take only a glancing blow. Still, the force of the hit caused him to back up even further.

Hunter, off balance from the swing, struggled to right himself as the thunderous roar of the four turbo-prop engines blotted out all other sound.

Donley got his footing first. He jerked up the gun and fired a second shot. A jolt of pain seared through Hunter's left thigh. He felt himself twist and stumble.

He was hit.

Donley had won.

A fiery sting ripped through Hunter's system as he fell to his hands and knees. The cold reality was, he knew, that he was a dead man.

He heard a scream and glanced back, Kim was out of the car now, her face twisted with terror, staring at him. Hunter looked back at Donley, expecting another bullet.

And then he saw something incredible. With his back to the moving C-130, Donley had retreated away from Hunter into the path of the aircraft's huge wing, which loomed up behind him. There was a thudding sound. Donley's body jerked violently off the ground in a motion too quick for the eye to see in the near darkness. What Hunter did see was wildly flailing arms as Donley cartwheeled in the air like a child's kite caught in an angry tornado. His body remained airborne for a moment, then, like a battle-stricken Thud, he bored in, then crashed—a shapeless mass on the wet concrete in the Korea blue rain.

The C-130 continued forward for a few feet, then began to brake. The roar of the engines decreased as the pilot throttled them down and brought the big bird to a halt.

Hunter looked down: the pain was coming from his leg. It burned like the fire of hell, and there was a lot of blood. But checking closer, he found a bloody furrow of torn flesh, gruesome but not too serious. He took out his handkerchief and pressed it against the wound, then got carefully to his feet. He was weak and the damaged leg wobbled, but he was able to stand.

He limped toward the crumpled body. He had an inkling of what he would see, but he was drawn by the need to know for sure that this man could no longer inflict pain and suffering on any other innocent person.

Hunter stopped when he could make out the details of the sprawling form that had once been Lieutenant Colonel Donley. He had no head.

Hunter looked up with grim satisfaction at the outboard engine on the wing of the C-130. The crew had cut back the power, reducing the noise level. The shiny, four-blade propeller was whirling slower, but still moving at a deadly speed.

"Yobo!"

He turned. Soon Ja was running to him. Her hair was damp and clinging to her head. Her face wet with rain displayed the last traces of fear mixed with relief.

He held up his hand. "Stay back. Don't—" She stopped.

He looked down at the body one last time. *Say goodbye to the colonel.*

His voice hard, Hunter said, "Good-bye, asshole."

He turned and limped back to where Soon Ja was waiting. Both were soaked through by rain. He took her in his arms and pulled her head against his chest. "It's all over."

As they stood holding each other, they heard shouts cutting through the sound of the idling aircraft engines. Two members of the C-130 crew had come around the back of the bird. They were waving and yelling. He felt Kim's body tense.

He held her tighter. ''Ignore them. It's only the Air Force.''